NORDENHOLT'S MILLION

NORDENHOLT'S MILLION

J. J. Connington

introduction by Matthew Battles

afterword by Evan Hepler-Smith

THE MIT PRESS
CAMBRIDGE, MASSACHUSETTS
LONDON, ENGLAND

This book was set in Arnhem Pro and PF DIN Text Pro by New Best-set Typesetters Ltd. Printed and bound in the United States of America.

Library of Congress Cataloging-in-Publication Data

Names: Connington, J. J., 1880–1947, author. | Battles, Matthew, writer of introduction. | Hepler-Smith, Evan, writer of afterword.
Title: Nordenholt's million / J. J. Connington ; introduction by Matthew Battles ; afterword by Evan Hepler-Smith.
Description: Cambridge, Massachusetts : The MIT Press, [2022] | Series: The Radium age | Previously published, 1923. | Includes bibliographical references.
Identifiers: LCCN 2021049849 | ISBN 9780262544283 (paperback)
Subjects: LCGFT: Apocalyptic fiction. | Science fiction. | Novels.
Classification: LCC PR6037.T4627 N67 2022 | DDC 823/.912—dc23/eng/20211014
LC record available at https://lccn.loc.gov/2021049849

10 9 8 7 6 5 4 3 2 1

CONTENTS

Do we really know science fiction? There were the scientific romance years that stretched from the mid-nineteenth century to circa 1900. And there was the genre's so-called golden age, from circa 1935 through the early 1960s. But between those periods, and overshadowed by them, was an era that has bequeathed us such tropes as the robot (berserk or benevolent), the tyrannical superman, the dystopia, the unfathomable extraterrestrial, the sinister telepath, and the eco-catastrophe. A dozen years ago, writing for the sf blog io9.com at the invitation of Annalee Newitz and Charlie Jane Anders, I became fascinated with the period during which the sf genre as we know it emerged. Inspired by the exactly contemporaneous career of Marie Curie, who shared a Nobel Prize for her discovery of radium in 1903, only to die of radiation-induced leukemia in 1934, I eventually dubbed this three-decade interregnum the "Radium Age."

Curie's development of the theory of radioactivity, which led to the extraordinary, terrifying, awe-inspiring insight that the atom is, at least in part, a state of energy constantly in movement, is an apt metaphor for the twentieth century's first three decades. These years were marked by rising sociocultural strife across various fronts: the founding of the women's suffrage movement, the National Association for the Advancement of Colored People, socialist currents within the labor movement, anticolonial and revolutionary upheaval around the world . . . as well as the associated strengthening of reactionary movements that supported, for example, racial segregation, immigration restriction, eugenics, and sexist policies.

Science—as a system of knowledge, a mode of experimenting, and a method of reasoning—accelerated the pace of change during these years in ways simultaneously liberating and terrifying. As sf author and historian Brian Stableford points out in his 1989 essay "The Plausibility of the Impossible," the universe we discovered by means of the scientific method in the early twentieth century defies common sense: "We are haunted by a sense of the impossibility of ultimately making sense of things." By playing host to certain far-out notions—time travel, faster-than-light travel, and ESP, for example—that we have every reason to judge impossible, science fiction serves as an "instrument of negotiation," Stableford suggests, with which we strive to accomplish "the difficult diplomacy of existence in a scientifically knowable but essentially unimaginable world." This is no less true today than during the Radium Age.

The social, cultural, political, and technological upheavals of the 1900–1935 period are reflected in the proto-sf writings of authors such as Olaf Stapledon, William Hope Hodgson, Muriel Jaeger, Karel Čapek, G. K. Chesterton, Cicely Hamilton, W. E. B. Du Bois, Yevgeny Zamyatin, E. V. Odle, Arthur Conan Doyle, Mikhail

Bulgakov, Pauline Hopkins, Stanisław Ignacy Witkiewicz, Aldous Huxley, Gustave Le Rouge, A. Merritt, Rudyard Kipling, Rose Macaulay, J. D. Beresford, J. J. Connington, S. Fowler Wright, Jack London, Thea von Harbou, and Edgar Rice Burroughs, not to mention the late-period but still incredibly prolific H. G. Wells himself. More cynical than its Victorian precursor yet less hard-boiled than the sf that followed, in the writings of these visionaries we find acerbic social commentary, shock tactics, and also a sense of frustrated idealism—and reactionary cynicism, too—regarding humankind's trajectory.

The MIT Press's Radium Age series represents a much-needed evolution of my own efforts to champion the best proto-sf novels and stories from 1900 to 1935 among scholars already engaged in the fields of utopian and speculative fiction studies, as well as general readers interested in science, technology, history, and thrills and chills. By reissuing literary productions from a time period that hasn't received sufficient attention for its contribution to the emergence of science fiction as a recognizable form—one that exists and has meaning in relation to its own traditions and innovations, as well as within a broader ecosystem of literary genres, each of which, as John Rieder notes in *Science Fiction and the Mass Cultural Genre System* (2017), is itself a product of overlapping "communities of practice"—we hope not only to draw attention to key overlooked works but perhaps also to influence the way scholars and sf fans alike think about this crucial yet neglected and misunderstood moment in the emergence of the sf genre.

John W. Campbell and other Cold War–era sf editors and propagandists dubbed a select group of writers and story types from the pulp era to be the golden age of science fiction. In doing so, they helped fix in the popular imagination a too-narrow understanding of what the sf genre can offer. (In his introduction to the 1974 collection *Before the Golden Age*, for example, Isaac Asimov notes that although it may have possessed a certain exuberance, in general sf from before the mid-1930s moment when Campbell assumed editorship of *Astounding Stories* "seems, to anyone who has experienced the Campbell Revolution, to be clumsy, primitive, naive.") By returning to an international tradition of scientific speculation via fiction from after the Poe–Verne–Wells era and before sf's Golden Age, the Radium Age series will demonstrate—contra Asimov et al.—the breadth, richness, and diversity of the literary works that were responding to a vertiginous historical period, and how they helped innovate a nascent genre (which wouldn't be named until the mid-1920s, by Hugo Gernsback, founder of *Amazing Stories* and namesake of the Hugo Awards) as a mode of speculative imagining.

The MIT Press's Noah J. Springer and I are grateful to the sf writers and scholars who have agreed to serve as this series' advisory board. Aided by their guidance, we'll endeavor to surface a rich variety of texts, along with introductions by a diverse group of sf scholars, sf writers, and others that will situate these remarkable, entertaining, forgotten works within their own social, political, and scientific contexts, while drawing out contemporary parallels.

We hope that reading Radium Age writings, published in times as volatile as our own, will serve to remind us that our own era's seemingly natural, eternal, and inevitable social, economic, and cultural forms and norms are—like Madame Curie's atom—forever in flux.

INTRODUCTION: BENIGNANT FASCISM

Matthew Battles

Have I got a story for you: two decades into the century, with the world increasingly connected by networks and ecosystems under tremendous strain, a pandemic sweeps the planet. This familiar scenario is the situation presented in *Nordenholt's Million*. The era is not our own, however, but the turn of the last century. First published in 1923, authored by the Scottish chemist Alfred Walter Stewart under the pen name of J. J. Connington, *Nordenholt* speaks to the anxieties of its age—and our own as well.

*

Our narrator, Jack Flint, "a very fair representative of the better type of business man," pays a visit to Wotherspoon, a popular-science writer and deliverer of "courses of popular lectures on the work of real investigators," who potters self-importantly about in his gentlemanly laboratory near London's Regent's Park. When Flint arrives, Wotherspoon is waxing enthusiastic about global ecology. "We are all parasites on the plants," he notes; "we cannot live without them." Bacteria play a crucial role in this cycle, Wotherspoon further points out, with certain varieties "fixing" nitrogen, rendering it accessible to plants. Referring to the vast farming operations feeding Europe and

North America, Wotherspoon warns Flint that "we are actually depleting the soil of these nitrogen compounds at a very rapid rate indeed."

Before the microscopic bête noire of *Nordenholt's Million* takes the stage, the book is aware of humankind's capacity to tip balances at global scales. Wotherspoon offers a profound perspective here: a view that seems to prefigure the "Gaian hypothesis" regarding planetary atmospheric homeostasis, which Lynn Margulis and James Lovelock would develop together half a century later. Not bad for a dilettante! The "Nitrogen Catastrophe" of *Nordenholt's Million* also predates the so-called Green Revolution: a transformative break with traditional farming practices made possible largely by the refining of fossil fuels, stealing from millions of years of plant life to produce higher yields in the present. (As Evan Hepler-Smith discusses in his afterword, Alfred Walter Stewart was writing for popular audiences about the nitrogen cycle—like his foil, Wotherspoon—before his publication of *Nordenholt* as J. J. Connington.)

Wotherspoon's concern, however, is not with these nitrogen fixers, but with their opposite, the "denitrifying bacteria," which make nitrogen inaccessible to plants. Their discussion of denitrifying bacteria is interrupted, however, by the apparition of a luminous sphere— probably an outbreak of ball lightning, a favored science-fictional deus ex machina. Thus electrified, the "denitrifying" bacterium Wotherspoon has identified in his amateur lab, *Bacterium diazotans* (*diazotan* being the Polish word for *dinitrate*) begins proliferating, embarking on an inexorable planetary invasion growing outward from London.

The progress of the blight follows the new network of the airlines servicing London. "London lay like a spider at the centre of the web of communications," Flint opines, "the like of which the world had never seen before. . . . For good or ill, humanity was becoming linked together until it formed a single unit." To Flint, these networks were not the harbinger of a brighter future, but the sign of an apex— perhaps even a limit. "It was the Golden Age of humanity," he declares, "yet few of us recognised it. We looked either backward into the past or forward into the future . . . while all about us lay Paradise, and the Earth blossomed like a huge garden which was ours for the taking."

The arachnoid metaphor is telling. What else does the spider of empire parasitize in Flint's paradise of the twentieth century? In the year *Nordenholt* was published, Mahatma Gandhi was serving a ten-year sentence for sedition, having sought to reimagine systems of land tenancy and agriculture through which the British had ruled India for more than a century. At the same time, the seeds of the Dust Bowl were being sown in North America. Like Connington's Nitrogen Catastrophe, it sprang from global forces: the Russian Revolution disrupting harvests in Ukraine and Central Asia, bringing rising wheat prices worldwide, pressing the farmers of the Great Plains for greater yields from Texas to Alberta. Wielding mechanized farm implements and fortified by the belief that "rain follows the plow," farmers left fields bare in the winter and burned the stubble, setting the stage for a vast unsettling of arid topsoil in the region once termed "The Great American Desert."

Agricultural uncertainty long haunted the Empire, even as Britain's extractive land-use policies funneled carbohydrates from Ireland, the Americas, and India. Flint notes that, at the time of the *B. diazotans* outbreak, "almost half of our cereals were homegrown"; he fails to mention what a radical change that represented historically. A century earlier, foreign grain had counted for only 2 percent of English cereal intake; by the 1880s, 45 percent of British grain, and 65 percent of her wheat, came from foreign fields (figures from Robert Ensor, *England 1870–1914* [1936], Oxford History of England). Nitrogen, too, was an elemental factor in the British Empire's global reach. The mid-nineteenth century was an era of "guano mania," when nitrogenous deposits—often on far-flung oceanic islands uninhabited but for seabirds, but within the reach of the Royal Navy—were prized as an ingredient in both fertilizers and gunpowder.

Flint compares the rapid proliferation of *B. diazotans* to the Irish famine of the mid-nineteenth century, noting that "since the potato blight in 1845, no such rapid and extensive destruction of food supplies had been known." Its proximate cause, too, was a microorganism: *Phytophthora infestans*, the fungus responsible for "late blight" in potatoes. The reduction of Ireland to famine was no mere natural disaster, however, but the result of extractive absentee landlordism and market absolutism. If trade and travel composed the web of empire, famine was a crucial fraction in its pacifying venom.

We don't often consider the New Deal or Gandhi's Satyagraha movement as environmental events. The Potato Blight, meanwhile, often understood as primarily environmental, was deeply political in its origins and its ramifications. The environmental and the historical everywhere are inextricably linked. I mention these environmental-historical processes not because they have any bearing on Connington's fiction; they're beyond the scope of *Nordenholt's Million*. But I encourage the reader to bear in mind that the world of Connington/Stewart's time offered alternatives to the Taylorism, distrust of democracy, and benignant fascism practiced by Nordenholt and his minions.

*

The anxieties brewing in *Nordenholt's Million* are those of an empire built on the extraction and appropriation of ephemeral natural resources. We can situate Connington's novel, too, at the intersection of genres that would come to pattern the science-fictional space. The genealogy of the plague apocalypse runs back to Mary Shelley's *The Last Man* (1826), through Jack London's *The Scarlet Plague* (1912), and forward through books like *The Earth Abides* (George R. Stewart, 1949) and Michael Crichton's *The Andromeda Strain* (1968).

A number of post-apocalyptic novels exhibit the pattern of what Brian Aldiss, in his critical omnibus of science fiction, *The Billion-Year Spree* (1973), calls the "cozy catastrophe," in which a small band of survivors manages an idyllic existence in the wake of civilizational demise.

John Wyndham's *The Day of the Triffids* (1951) gets off to a properly apocalyptic start, with blinding meteors and carnivorous plants making quick work of humankind, and ends with a polygamous band of survivors holing up in the Isle of Wight. John Christopher's *The Death of Grass* (1956), like Connington's novel, features an agricultural plague. In later science fiction, the cozy catastrophe becomes notably *ungemütlich*—J. G. Ballard's *The Drowned World* (1962) begins looking out on a flooded London from a balcony at the Ritz Hotel; Ursula K. Le Guin's vast *Always Coming Home* (1985), an ethnography of a post-civilizational neo-indigenous world, is written like a reference work; in David Markson's *Wittgenstein's Mistress* (1988) the last woman in the world treats herself to a tour of empty museums, even living for a time in the Louvre, where she burns artifacts to keep warm.

Unlike these later books, *Nordenholt's Million* presents industrialism not as the downfall of civilization, but as its salvation. In this, no work would seem to bear its influence more than Ayn Rand's *Atlas Shrugged* (1957), with its valley of entrepreneurs "on strike" against a world that refuses to bend to their genius. Like Rand's magnum opus, Connington's fable is architectonic, disclosing the design and construction of a mighty utopia. Nordenholt's refuge may be cozy—it is certainly well supplied with cigars—but it is also the abode of the eponymous million men—and more, with their families, a city of five million, roughly the population of Inner London at the time (according to Great Britain GIS). What Nordenholt builds as a fortified refugium amid catastrophe becomes the thousand-year corporate campus of Jack Flint's Asgard. In this way, perhaps, *Nordenholt's Million* sets a pattern of *Reichbildung* seen in works like Asimov's *Foundation* series (1942–50), as well as B. F. Skinner's *Walden Two* (a behaviorist utopia, with babies raised in incubators and expressions of gratitude forbidden, published—like Orwell's *1984*—in 1948).

*

Not long after the crops begin to fail, Flint is called to a secret meeting of the Prime Minister, his cabinet, and a bevy of industrialists. The meeting has been called by Nordenholt—mysterious financier and master-builder, "the Platinum King, the multi-millionaire, wrecker of two Governments," a Howard Hughes reimagined for Tom Cruise. Nordenholt moves swiftly: at one stroke he blackmails the Prime Minister, brings the Cabinet to heel, and reveals his plan to recruit a million-man labor force for producing nitrogen at industrial scale. These men, with their families and necessary support workers, will be the only group to survive the coming hunger. When the Prime Minister accuses Nordenholt of "proposing to murder a large proportion of the population," the industrialist replies that he is actually trying to "save some millions of them from a certain death. *It just depends upon which way you look at it*" (my emphasis). "We cannot wait for the slow machinery of politics to revolve," Nordenholt declares. "Something must be done at once."

At crucial junctures throughout the novel, Nordenholt concludes that "there's nothing for it." The phrase signals precisely those points at which something else *might* be done: a city not consigned to collapse; a community given the means to provide for itself; a body of workers offered a chance at self-determination. Later in the novel, when Flint's own cry of *there's nothing for it* fails to explain the genocide he has helped Nordenholt to mete out, he falls back on the evil of banality: he was only doing his job, after all.

Women thus far have not factored at all in Nordenholt's plans, for all his motivation to save the species. It falls to Nordenholt's ward, Elsa Huntingtower, to supply the measure of charity and culture his industrial utopia will require. Flint and Elsa grow close, whiling away the hours imagining post-catastrophe cities of milk and honey. Their fantasies will inform the plans Flint implements in the wake of the catastrophe. And when Elsa finally discovers the enormity of her guardian's measures, it is too late for her moral recoil to have any practical effect.

Nordenholt has no time for fantasy, however; his assessments are invariably bleak. "This civilisation . . . is going to starve to death," he tells Flint, "and a starving organism is desperate. So long as it retains its present organised and coherent life, it will be a danger to us; and for our own safety—I mean the safety of the future generations—we must disorganise it as soon as possible." Reading from the other side of Europe's subsequent history, we sense the stirrings of *Lebensraum*, *Blitzkrieg*, and, ultimately, *Endlösung*, in Nordenholt's program of "disorganisation." Ideas very much like Nordenholt's grimly pragmatic political philosophy were already at work in the world when the novel appeared, organizing the rule of Mussolini's National Fascist Party, which took over the government of Italy in 1922.

To prove that his draconian measures have been unavoidable, Nordenholt sends Flint on an undercover field trip to famine-stricken London. At this point, the novel turns from cozy catastrophe to outright apocalypse: skeletons lie in rings round churches and pubs (similar images, seemingly informed by Victorian anxieties, also color Alfred Conan Doyle's 1913 novel *The Poison Belt*); a cannibal mob, led by a wild-eyed African man and his paramour, a fallen socialite called Lady Angela, runs survivors to ground in the ruins. Readers traumatized by racism, patriarchy, and colonialism be forewarned: these passages make hard reading. Casual prejudices overwhelm the narrative here, although there is no mistaking Connington's theme: without proper management, humankind in the face of calamity will fall into bestial orgies of self-destruction. *There's nothing for it*, Nordenholt would say, drawing another cigar from the humidor.

The story of nitrogen's industrial domestication was not so clear-cut as Nordenholt's pitiless vision would have it. The inventor of one of the industrial processes Connington mentions, Fritz Haber, was also a key figure in Germany's chemical warfare program in World War I. Deployed at production scales that Nordenholt would have envied, Haber's process eventually became the basis of both the fertilizer and explosives industries. Despite the destructive powers it unleashed, it won him the 1918 Nobel Prize in Chemistry. In his acceptance speech, he observed that "nitrogen bacteria teach us that Nature, with her sophisticated forms of the chemistry of living matter, still understands and utilizes methods which we do not as yet know how to imitate."

The effects of Haber's invention were ambiguous in ways not immediately visible to his contemporaries—or which they chose not to see. In the same way, the enormity of Nordenholt's benignant fascism would have been convenient for readers in the 1920s to overlook. It's not clear what forces will win out in the midst of our own dark times, either, nor even what such "winning" might mean. We might easily dismiss *Nordenholt's Million* for its racism, its politics, and its imperial presumptions about utopian forms of life. But the novel gives us an uncomfortable, urgent space in which to ask searching questions: What easy assumptions form our responses to the dark times we face? What stories might our descendants wish we had imagined instead?

I GENESIS

I suppose that in the days before the catastrophe I was a very fair representative of the better type of business man. I had been successful in my own line, which was the application of mass-production methods to a better pattern of motor-car than had yet been dealt with upon a large scale; and the Flint car had been a good speculation. I was thinking of bringing out an economical type of gyroscopic two-wheeler just at the time we were overwhelmed. Organisation was my strong point; and much of my commercial success was due to a new system of control which I had introduced into my factories. I mention this point in passing, because it was this capacity of mine which first brought me to the notice of Nordenholt.

Although at the time of which I speak I had become more a director than a designer, I was originally by profession a mechanical engineer; and in my student days I had had a scientific training, some remnants of which still fluttered in tatters in odd corners of my mind. I could check the newspaper accounts of new discoveries in chemistry and physics well enough to know when the reporters blundered grossly; geology I remembered vaguely, though I could barely have distinguished augite from muscovite under a microscope: but the biological group of subjects had never come within my ken. The medical side of science was a closed book as far as I was concerned.

Yet, like many educated men of that time, I took a certain interest in scientific affairs. I read the accounts of the British Association in the newspapers year by year; I bought a copy of *Nature* now and again when a new line of research caught my attention; and occasionally I glanced through some of these popular *réchauffés* of various scientific topics by means of which people like myself were able to persuade themselves that they were keeping in touch with the advance of knowledge.

It was this taste of mine which brought me into contact with Wotherspoon; for, beyond his interest in scientific affairs, he and I had little enough in common. It is over a quarter of a century since I saw him last, for he must have died in the first year of our troubles; but I can still recall him very clearly: a short, stout man—"pudgy" is perhaps the word which best describes him—with a drooping, untidy moustache half-covering but not concealing the slackness of his mouth; fair hair, generally brushed in a lank mass to one side of his forehead; and watery eyes which had a look in them as of one crushed beneath a weight of knowledge and responsibility.

As a matter of fact, I doubt if his knowledge was sufficiently profound or extensive to crush any ordinary person; and as he had a private income and no dependants, I could not understand what responsibilities weighed upon him. He certainly held no official post in the scientific world which might have burdened him; for despite numerous applications on his part, none of the

Universities had seen fit to utilise his services in even the meanest capacity.

To be quite frank, he was a dabbler. He originated nothing, discovered nothing, improved nothing; and yet, by some means, he had succeeded in imposing himself upon the public mind. He delivered courses of popular lectures on the work of real investigators; and I believe that these lectures were well attended. He wrote numerous books dealing with the researches of other men; and the publication of volume after volume kept him in the public eye. Whenever an important discovery was made by some real scientific expert, Wotherspoon would sit down and compile newspaper articles on the subject with great facility; and by these methods he achieved, among inexperienced readers, the reputation of a sort of arbiter in the scientific field. "As Mr. Wotherspoon says in the article which we publish elsewhere" was a phrase which appeared from time to time in the leader columns of the more sensational Press.

Naturally, he was disliked by the men who actually did the scientific work of the world and who had little time to spare for cultivating notoriety. He was a member of a large number of those societies to which admission can be gained by payment of an entrance fee and subscription; and on the bills of his lectures and the title-pages of his books his name was followed by a string of letters which the uninitiated assumed to imply great scientific ability. His application for admission to the Royal Society had, however, been unsuccessful—a failure which he frequently and publicly attributed to jealousy.

It appears strange that such a man as this should have been selected by Fate as the agent of disaster; and it seems characteristic of him that, when the key of the problem was lying beside him, his energy was entirely engrossed in writing newspaper paragraphs on another matter. His mind worked exclusively through the medium of print and paper; so that even the most striking natural phenomenon escaped his observation.

At that time he lived in one of the houses of Cumberland Terrace, overlooking Regent's Park. I cannot recall the number; and the place has long ago disappeared; but I remember that it was near St. Katherine's College and it overlooked the grounds of St. Katherine's House. Wotherspoon carried his scientific aura even into the arrangement of his residence; for what was normally the drawing-room of the house had been turned into a kind of laboratory-reception-room; so that casual visitors might be impressed by his ardour in the pursuit of knowledge. When anyone called upon him, he was always discovered in this room, fingering apparatus, pouring liquids from one tube into another, producing precipitates or doing something else which would strike the unwary as being part of a recondite process. I had a feeling, when I came upon him in the midst of these manoeuvres, that he had sprung up from his chair at the sound of the door bell and had plunged hastily into his operations. I know enough to distinguish real work from make-believe; and Wotherspoon never gave me the impression that he was engaged in anything better than window-dressing. At any rate, nothing ever was made public with regard to the results of these multitudinous experiments; and when, occasionally, I asked him if he proposed to bring out a paper, he merely launched into a diatribe against the jealousy of scientific men.

It was about this time that Henley-Davenport was making his earlier discoveries in the field of induced radioactivity. The results were too technical for the unscientific man to appreciate; but I had become interested, not so much in details as in possibilities; and I determined to go across the Park and pay a visit to Wotherspoon one evening. I knew that, as far as published information went, he would be in possession of the latest news; and it was easier to get it from him than to read it myself.

It was warm weather then. I decided to use my car instead of walking through the Park. I had a slight headache, and I thought that possibly a short spin later, in the cool of the evening, might take it away. As I drove, I noticed how thunder-clouds were banking up on the horizon, and I congratulated myself that even if they broke I should have the shelter of the car and be saved a walk home through the rain.

When I reached Cumberland Terrace, I was, as I expected, shown up into Wotherspoon's sanctum. I found him, as usual, deeply engrossed in work: he had his eye to the tube of a large microscope, down which he was staring intently. I noticed a slight change in the equipment of the room. There seemed to be fewer retorts, flasks and test-tube racks than there usually were; and two large tables at the windows were littered with flat glass dishes containing thin slabs of pinkish material which seemed to be gelatine. Things like incubators took up a good deal of the remaining space. But I doubt if it is worth while describing what I saw: I know very little of such things; and I question whether his apparatus would have passed muster with an expert in any case.

After a certain amount of fumbling with the microscope, which seemed largely a formal matter leading to nothing, he rose from his seat and greeted me with his customary preoccupied air. For a time we smoked and talked of Henley-Davenport's work; but after he had answered my questions it became evident that he had no further interest in the subject; and I was not surprised when, after a pause, he broke entirely new ground in his next remark.

"Do you know, Flint," he said, "I am losing interest in all these investigations of the atomic structure. It seems to me that while unimaginative people like Henley-Davenport are groping into the depths of the material Universe, the real thing is passing them by. After all, what is mere matter in comparison with the problems of life? I have given up atoms and I am going to begin work upon living organisms."

That was so characteristic of Wotherspoon. He was always "losing interest in" something and "going to begin work" upon something else. I nodded without saying anything. After all, it seemed of very little importance what he "worked" at.

"I wonder if you ever reflect, Flint," he continued, "if you ever ponder over our position in this Universe? Here we stand, like Dante, 'midway in this our mortal life'; at the half-way house between the cradle and the grave in time. And in space, too, we represent the middle term between the endless stretches of the Macrocosm and the bottomless deeps of the Microcosm. Look up at the night-sky and your eyes will tingle with the rays from long-dead stars, suns that were blotted out ages ago though the light they sent out before they died still thrills across the ether on its journey to our Earth. Take your microscope, and you find a new world before you; increase the magnification and another, tinier cosmos sweeps into your ken. And so, with ever-growing lens-power, we can peer either upward into stellar space or downward into the regions of the infinitesimal, while between these deeps we ourselves stand for a time on our precarious bridge of Earth."

I began to suspect that he was trying over some phrases for a coming lecture; but it was early yet and I could not decently make an excuse for leaving him. I took a fresh cigar and let him go on without interruption.

"It always seems strange to me how little the man in the street knows of the things around him. The microscopic world has no existence as far as his mind is concerned. A grain of dust is too small for him to notice; it must blow into his eye before he appreciates that it has perceptible size at all. And yet, all about him and within him there lives this wonderful race of beings, passing to and fro in his veins as we do in the streets and avenues of a great city; coming to birth, going about their concerns, falling ill and dying, just as men do in London at this hour. Think of the battles, the victories, and the defeats which take place minute by minute in the tiniest drop of our blood; and the issue of the war may be the life or death of one of us. They talk of the struggle for existence; but the real struggle for existence is going on within us and not in the outer world. Phagocyte against bacterium—that is where the fitness of an organism comes to its ultimate test. A slight hitch in the reinforcements, a minute's delay in bringing numbers to bear, and the keystone is out of the edifice; nothing is left but a ruin.

"It always reminds me of those frontier skirmishes—a mere handful of troops engaged on either side—upon the issue of which the fate of an empire may depend. Get a new set of enemies, some novel type of bacteria with fresh tactics which the phagocytes cannot cope with— and down comes a human being. It strikes wonder into me, that, you know. A human body is so colossal in comparison with these bacteria that they can have no idea even of our existence; and yet they can destroy the whole machinery upon which our life depends. It's almost as if a few shots fired in Africa could crumble the whole Earth into an impalpable dust.

"And it is not only within us that these struggles are going on. When you came in, I was just studying some specimens of organisms which are equally vital to us. Come over here to the microscope, Flint, and have a look at them yourself."

When I had got the focus adjusted to suit my eyes, I must confess that I was astonished by what I saw. Somehow, in the course of my reading, I had picked up the idea that bacteria were rod-like creatures which floated inertly in liquids at the mercy of the currents; but at the first glance I realised how much below the reality my conception had been. In the field of the instrument I saw a score of objects, rod-like in their main structure, it is true, but so mantled with the fringes of their fine, thread-like cilia that their baculite character was almost concealed. Nor were they the inert things which I had supposed them to be; for, as I watched them, now one and again another would dart with prodigious swiftness from point to point in the circle of illumination. I had rarely seen such relative activity in any creature. The speed of their movements was so great that my eye could not follow them in their tracks. They appeared to be at rest one instant and then to vanish, reappearing as suddenly in some fresh spot. I watched them, fascinated, for some minutes, trying to trace the vibrations of the cilia which projected them from place to place at such enormous speeds; but either my eye was untrained or the movements of the thread-like fringes were too rapid to be seen. It was certainly an illuminating glimpse into the life of the under-world.

When I had risen from the microscope table, Wotherspoon took me over to one of the benches before the window and showed me the glass vessels containing the pinkish gelatine. These slabs, he told me, were cultures of bacteria. One placed a few organisms on the gelatine and there they grew and multiplied enormously.

"These specimens here," said Wotherspoon, "are not the same variety as the ones on the microscope slide. They have nothing whatever to do with disease; and yet, as I told you, they have an influence upon animal life. I suppose you never heard of nitrifying and denitrifying bacteria?"

I admitted that the names were unfamiliar to me.

"Just so. Few people seem to take any interest in these vital problems. Now you do know that internally we swarm with all sorts of germs, noxious in some cases, beneficent in others; but I suppose it never struck you that our bodies form only a trifling part of the material world; and that outside these living islets there is space for all sorts of microscopic flora and fauna to grow and multiply? And need these creatures be absolutely isolated from the interests of animals? Not at all.

"Now what is the essential thing, apart from air and water, which we derive from the outside world? Food, isn't it? Did it ever occur to you to inquire where your food comes from, ultimately?"

"Well, of course," I said, "it comes from all over the world. I don't know whether the wheat I eat in my bread comes from Canada or the States or Argentina, or was home-grown. It doesn't seem to me a matter of importance, anyway."

"That isn't what I mean at all," Wotherspoon interrupted, "I want you to look at it in another way. I suppose you had your usual style of dinner to-day. Just think of the items: soup, fish, meat, bread, and so on. Your soup was made from bones and vegetables; your fish course was originally an animal; so was your joint; your sweet was probably purely vegetable; and your dessert certainly was a plant product. Now don't you see what I mean?"

"No, I confess I don't."

"Haven't I just shown you that everything you ate comes from either the animal or vegetable kingdom? You don't bite bits out of the crockery, like the Mad Hatter. Everything you use to keep your physical machine alive is something which has already had life in it. Isn't that so? You never think of having a meal of pure chemicals, do you?"

"It never occurred to me; and I doubt it I shall begin now. It doesn't sound very appetising."

"It would be worse than that; but follow my argument further. Take the case of your joint. Presumably that came from an ox or a sheep. Where did the animal, whatever it was, get *its* food? From the vegetable kingdom, in the form of grass. Isn't it clear that everything you yourself eat comes, either directly or indirectly, from the plants? And aren't all animals on the same footing as yourself—they depend ultimately on the vegetables for their sustenance, don't they? A fox may live on poultry; but the chickens he kills have grown fat by eating grain; and so you come back to the plants again. If you like to look on it in that way, we are all parasites on the plants; we cannot live without them. Our digestive machinery is so specialised that it will assimilate only a certain type of material—protoplasm— and unless it is supplied with that material, we starve. We can convert the protoplasm of other animals or of plants to our own use; but we cannot manufacture protoplasm from its elements. We have to get it ready-made from the vegetables, either directly or indirectly.

"Now the foundation-stone of protoplasm is the element nitrogen. The plants draw on the store of nitrogenous compounds in the soil in order to build up their tissues; and then we eat the plants and thus transfer this material to our own organisms. What happens next? Do we return the nitrogen to the soil? Not we. We throw it into the sea in the form of sewage. So you see the net outcome of the process is that we are gradually using up the stores of nitrogen compounds in the soil, with the result that the plants have less and less nitrogen to live on."

"Well, but surely four-fifths of the atmosphere is nitrogen? That seems to me a big enough reserve to be drawn on."

"So it would be, if the plants could tap it directly; but they can't do that except in the case of some exceptional ones. Most plants simply cannot utilise nitrogen until it has been combined with some other element. They can't touch it in the uncombined state, as it is in the atmosphere; so that as far as the nitrogen in the air goes, it is useless to plants. They can't thrive on pure nitrogen, any more than you can feed yourself on a mixture of charcoal, hydrogen, oxygen and nitrogen; though these elements are all that you need in the way of diet to keep life going.

"No, Flint, we are actually depleting the soil of these nitrogen compounds at a very rapid rate indeed. Why, even in the first decade of the twentieth century South America was exporting no less than 15,000,000 tons of nitrogen compounds which she dug out of the natural deposits in the nitre beds of Chile and Peru; and all that vast quantity was being used as artificial manure to replace the nitrogenous loss in the soil of the agricultural parts of the world. The loss is so great that it even pays to run chemical processes for making nitrogenous materials from the nitrogen of the air—the fixation of nitrogen, they call it.

"Well, that is surely enough to show you how much hangs upon this nitrogen question. If we go on as we are doing, there will eventually be a nitrogen famine; the soil will cease to yield crops; and we shall go short of food. It's no vision I am giving you; the thing has already happened in a modified form in America. There they used up the soil by continual drafts on it, wheat crops year after year in the same places. The result was that the land ceased to be productive; and we had the rush of American farmers into Canada in the early days of the century to utilise the virgin soil across the border instead of their own exhausted fields."

"I suppose you know all about it," I said, "but where do these come in?"

I pointed to the pinkish disks of the cultures.

"These are what are called denitrifying bacteria. Although the plants can't act upon pure nitrogen and convert it into compounds which they can feed upon, some bacteria have the knack. The nitrifying bacteria can link up nitrogen with other elements so as to produce nitrogenous material which the plants can then utilise. So that if we grow these nitrifying bacteria in the soil, we help the plants to get more food. The denitrifying bacteria, on the other hand— these ones here—act in just the opposite way. Wherever they find nitrogenous compounds, they break them down and liberate the nitrogen from them, so that it goes back into the air and is lost to us again.

"So you see that outside our bodies we have bacteria working for or against us. The nitrifying bacteria are helping to pile up further supplies of nitrogen compounds upon which the plants can draw and whereon, indirectly, we ourselves can be supported. The denitrifying bacteria, on the other hand, are continually nibbling at the basic store of our food; decomposing the nitrogen compounds and freeing the nitrogen from them in the form of the pure gas which is useless to us from the point of view of food."

"You mean that a large increase in the numbers of the one set would put us in clover, whereas multiplication of the other lot would mean a shortness of supplies?"

"Exactly. And we have no idea of the forces which govern the reproduction of these creatures. It's quite within the bounds of possibility that some slight change in the external conditions might reinforce one set and decimate the other; and such a change would have almost unpredictable influences on our food problem."

At this moment the thunder-clouds, which had grown heavier as time passed, evidently reached their full tension. A tremendous flash shot across the sky; and on its heel, so close as to be almost simultaneous, there came a shattering peal of thunder. We looked out; but I had been so dazzled by the brilliance of the flash that I could see little. The air was very still; no rain had yet fallen; and my skin tingled with the electrical tension of the atmosphere. Wotherspoon felt it also, he told me. It was evident that we were in the vicinity of some very powerful disturbance.

"Awfully hot to-night, isn't it?" I said. "Suppose we have some more air? It's stifling in here."

Wotherspoon pushed the broad leaves of the French windows apart; but no breeze came to cool us; though in the silence after the thunder-clap I heard the rustle of leaves from the trees below us. We stood, one at either end of the bench with the cultures on it, trying to draw cooler air into our lungs; and all the while I felt as though a multitude of tiny electric sparks were running to and fro upon the surface of my body.

Suddenly, over St. Katherine's House, a sphere of light appeared in the air. It was not like lightning, brilliantly though it shone. It seemed to hover for a few seconds above the roof, almost motionless. Then it began slowly to advance in a wavering flight, approaching us and sinking by degrees in the sky as it came. To me, it appeared to be about a foot in diameter; but Wotherspoon afterwards estimated it at rather less. In any case, it was of no great size; and its rate of approach was not more than five miles an hour.

For some seconds I watched it coming. It had a peculiar vacillating motion, rather like that which one sees in the flight of certain kinds of summer flies. Now it would hover almost motionless, then suddenly it would dart forward for twenty yards or so, only to resume its oscillation about a fixed point.

But to tell the truth, I watched it in such a state of fascination that I doubt if any coherent thoughts passed through my mind; so that my impressions may have been inaccurate. All that I remember clearly is a state of extreme tension. I never feel quite comfortable during a thunder-storm; and the novelty of the phenomenon increased this discomfort, for I did not know what turn it might take next.

Slowly the luminous sphere crossed the edge of the Park, dipping suddenly as though the iron railings had attracted it; and now it was almost opposite our window. For a moment its impetus seemed to carry it onwards, slantingly along the terrace; then, with a dart it swung from its course and entered the window at which we stood.

From its behaviour at the Park rail, I am inclined to think that it was drawn from its line of flight by the attracting power of the metal balustrade which protected the little balcony outside the window; and that its velocity carried it past the iron, so that it came to rest within the room, just over the table between us.

Instinctively, both Wotherspoon and I recoiled from this flaming apparition, shrinking back as far as possible from it on either side. Beyond this movement we seemed unable to go, for neither of us stepped out of the window recess. Between us, the ball of fire hung almost motionless; but before my eyes were dazzled I saw that it was spinning with tremendous velocity on a horizontal axis; and it seemed to me that its substance was a multitude of tiny sparks whirling in orbits about its centre. Its light was like that from a spirit-lamp charged with common salt; for over it I caught a glimpse of Wotherspoon's flinching face, all shadowed and green. As I watched the fire-ball, shading my eyes with my hands, I saw that it was slowly settling, just as a soap-bubble sinks in the air. Lower it descended and lower, still spinning furiously on its axis. Then, after what seemed an interminable period of suspense, it collided with the table.

There came a dull explosion which jerked me from my feet and drove me back against a chair. I saw Wotherspoon collapse and then everything vanished in the darkness which followed the concussion.

It must have been half a minute before I was able to recover from the shock and pull myself together. When I got to my feet again, I found Wotherspoon half-standing, half-leaning against the door, one panel of which had been blown out. The room was strewn with wreckage: broken glass, scattered papers, and shattered furniture. The electric lamps had been smashed by the force of the explosion.

Wotherspoon and I recovered almost simultaneously; and on comparing notes—which was difficult at first owing to our being temporarily deaf—we found that neither of us had suffered any serious injury. A few slight cuts with flying glass were apparently the worst of the damage which we had sustained. There was a sharp tang in the air of the room which made us cough for some time until it cleared away; but whatever the gas may have been, it left no permanent effects on us.

When we had procured lights and pulled ourselves together sufficiently to make a fuller examination of the room, we began to appreciate the extent of the damage and to congratulate ourselves still more upon the escape which we had had. The whole place was littered with fragments of furniture. The incubators had been shattered; and their contents, smashed into countless fragments, lay all over the floor. But it was on the bench at the window that the full force of the fire-ball had spent itself. There was hardly anything recognisable in the heap of debris. The wooden planks had been torn and broken with tremendous force. The little balcony was filled with sticks which had been thrown outward by the explosion; and, as we found afterwards, a good deal of material had been projected half-way across the road. Of the denitrifying bacteria cultures or their cases there was hardly a trace, except a few tiny splinters of glass.

I did not wait much longer with Wotherspoon; for, to tell the truth, my nerves were badly shaken by my experiences. I got him to come downstairs with me and we had a stiff glass of brandy each; and then I telephoned for a taxi to take me home. My own car was standing at the door; but I did not trust my ability to drive it in traffic at that moment. It seemed better to send my man round for it after I got home.

I went back in the taxi, with my nerves on edge.

II THE COMING OF "THE BLIGHT"

Next morning I still felt the effects of the shock; and decided not to go to my office. I stayed indoors all day. When the evening papers came, I found in them brief accounts of the fire-ball; and in one case there was an article by Wotherspoon under the heading: "Well-known Scientist's Strange Experience." One or two reporters called at my house later in the day in search of copy, but I sent them on to Cumberland Terrace. In some of the reports I figured as "a well-known motor manufacturer," whilst in others I was referred to simply as "a friend of Mr. Wotherspoon." I had little difficulty in surmising the authorship of the latter group.

In the ordinary course of events, the fire-ball would have been much less than a nine days' wonder, even in spite of Wotherspoon's industry in compiling accounts of it and digging out parallel cases from the correspondence columns of old volumes of *Nature* and *Knowledge*; actually its career as a news item was made briefer still. An entirely different phenomenon shouldered it out of the limelight almost immediately.

After staying indoors all day, I felt the need of fresh air; and resolved to walk across the Park to Cumberland Terrace to see whether Wotherspoon had quite recovered from the shock. I had not much doubt in my mind upon the point; for the traces of his journalistic activity were plain enough; and showed that he was certainly not incapacitated. However, as I wanted a stroll and as I might as well have an object before me, I decided to go and see him.

Twilight was coming on as I crossed the suspension bridge. Even after the thunder-storm on the previous night there had been no rainfall; and although the temperature had fallen until the air was almost chilly, there was as yet no dew on the ground. I stopped on the bridge to watch the tints of the western sky; for these London after-glow effects always pleased me.

As I leaned on the rail, I heard the low drone of aerial engines; and in a few seconds the broad wings of the Australian Express swept between me and the sky. Even in those days I could never see one of these vast argosies passing overhead without a throb in my veins.

The great air-services had just come to their own; and aeroplanes started from London four and five times daily for America, Asia, Africa, and Australia. In the windows of the air-offices the flight of these vessels could be followed hour by hour on the huge world-maps over which moved tiny models showing the exact positions of the various aeroplanes on the globe. Watching the dots moving across the surface of the charts, one could call up, with very little imagination, the landscapes which were sweeping into the view of travellers on board the real machines as they glided through these far-distant spaces of the air. This one, two days out from London, would be sighting the pagoda roofs of Peking as the night was coming on;

that one, on the Pacific route, had just finished filling up its tanks at Singapore and was starting on the long course to Australia; the passengers on this other would be watching the sun standing high over Victoria Nyanza; while, on the Atlantic, the Western Ocean Express and the South American Mail were racing the daylight into a fourth continent.

I think it was these maps which first brought home to me distinctly how the spaces of the world had shrunk on the "time-scale" with the coming of the giant aeroplanes. The pace had been growing swifter and ever swifter since the middle of the nineteenth century. Up to that day, there had been little advance since the time of the earlier sailing-vessels. Then came the change from sail to steam; and the Atlantic crossing contracted in its duration. The great Trans-continental railways quickened transit once more; again there was a shrinkage in the time-scale. Vladivostok came within ten days of London; from Cairo to the Cape was only five days. But with the coming of the airways the acceleration was greater still; and we reckoned in hours the journeys which, in the nineteenth-century days, had been calculated in weeks and even months. All the outposts of the world were drawing nearer together.

It was not this shrinkage only which the air-maps suggested. In the early twentieth century the telegraphs and submarine cables had spread their network over the world, linking nation to nation and coast to coast; but their ramifications dwindled in perspective when compared with the complex network of the air-ways which now enmeshed the globe. London lay like a spider at the centre of the web of communications, the like of which the world had never seen before; and along each thread the aeroplanes were speeding to and from all the quarters of the earth.

Rapid communication we had had since the days of the extension of the telegraph; but it had been limited to the transmission of thoughts and of news. The coming of the aeroplanes had changed all that. These tracks on the air-maps were not mere wires thrilling with the quiverings of the electric current. Along them material things were passing continually; a constant interchange of passengers and goods was taking place hourly over the multitudinous routes. For good or ill, humanity was becoming linked together until it formed a single unit.

It is curious that all the prophetic writers of the early twentieth century concentrated their attention almost exclusively upon the racial and social reactions which might be expected to follow from this knitting of the world into a connected whole and the resultant increase of traffic between the nations over the now contracted world-spaces. They had seen the interminglings of races which began in the steamship days; and they deduced that the process would be intensified in the new era of air-transit; so that, in the end of their dreams, they saw the possibility of a World Federation stretching its rule over the whole globe and bringing with it the end of wars. None of them, strangely enough, had foreseen the real effects which this intercommunication was to bring forth.

To a certain extent, their foresight had been justified. With the coming of the air-ways, the war-spirit was temporarily exorcised. The vast increase in the size and number of air-craft and the terrors of an aerial war, with all its untested possibilities, served to rein in even the most ardent of military nations. Standing armies still persisted; but their numbers had been diminished to a few thousands; for under the new conditions the old huge and unwieldy terrestrial forces could neither be fed, nor protected from aerial attacks.

Thus as I leaned on the rail of the suspension bridge and looked out over the greenery of the Park it seemed to me a very pleasant world. Those of the younger generation can hardly imagine how fair it was or how inexhaustible it seemed. Thousands of square miles of Africa and South America were still virgin soil, store-houses of untapped resources waiting for humanity to draw upon their abundance. There was food for all the thousand millions of mankind; and, as the population rose, fresh lands could be brought under cultivation for the mere labour of clearing the soil of its surplus vegetation. It was the Golden Age of humanity; yet few of us recognised it. We looked either backward into the past or forward into the future when we sought the Islands of the Blest: while all about us lay Paradise, and the Earth blossomed like a huge garden which was ours for the taking.

I left my visions with a sigh and continued my way across the Park. The prolonged spell of heat was affecting the vegetation. The trees were dusty; and the grass seemed to have lost something of its brilliant green. I remember that after I had crossed the Broad Walk I noticed especially how moribund all the plant-life of the

Park appeared to be. There was an air of decline about it, though no tints of autumn had yet appeared in the leaves.

Wotherspoon was, as usual, in his laboratory. The glass of the windows had been replaced; but otherwise the place was much in its disordered condition. I suspect that he had purposely refrained from getting it cleared up, in order to impress reporters with the actual damage which the explosion had done; and that when the reporters had ceased to call he had left things as they were with the idea of fascinating any visitors who might come.

He was sitting at his writing-desk, surrounded by piles of books from which he was apparently extracting information for the purpose of some fresh article he had in hand; and when I came in he asked me to excuse him for a few minutes until he had got his data completed. In order to amuse me in the meanwhile, he dragged out his microscope and a pile of slides which he thought might interest me.

Before he went back to his work, it struck me that I would like to see the bacteria again; and I picked up from the floor some fragments of glass which evidently had formed part of his cultures, since particles of the pink gelatine adhered to them still. I asked him to fix the microscope for me, so that I could examine these things; and he wetted the stuff with some water and put a drop of it under the lens, leaving me to focus it myself while he went back to his writing-desk. He was soon deep in his article.

As I gazed down at the field of the microscope, I saw again the clumps of bacilli, some floating aimlessly in masses, others darting here and there in the disk of illumination. I studied them for a time without noticing anything peculiar; but at last it struck me that the field was becoming congested with the creatures. I looked more carefully; and now there seemed little doubt of the fact. The numbers of them were increasing almost visibly. I concentrated my attention on a small group in one corner of the slide and was able, in spite of the confusion introduced by their rapid and erratic movements, to feel certain that they were multiplying so fast that I could almost estimate the increase in percentages minute by minute.

"Here, Wotherspoon," I said, "come and have a look through this. These bacteria of yours seem to be spawning or something."

"I wish you wouldn't interrupt, there's a good chap," he said in a peevish tone. "Don't you know that writing takes all one's attention? I can't do two things at once; and this article must be finished on time if it is to be of any use to me or anyone else. Just amuse yourself for half an hour and then I shall be at your disposal if you want me."

It was said so ungraciously that I took offence; and as his original "few minutes" had now apparently extended to "half an hour" I thought it best to leave him to himself. When I said good-night to him, he seemed to regard it as an extra interruption; so I was not sorry to go. I left him still delving into the masses of printed material around him.

And that was how Wotherspoon missed the greatest discovery that ever came his way. It was waiting for him across the table, for I doubt if he could have failed to draw the obvious conclusion had he actually taken the trouble to examine the phenomenon with his own eyes. But his interest was concentrated upon his writing; and his chance passed him by. After Johnston published his views, Wotherspoon made what I can only consider to be a dishonest attempt to secure priority on the ground that he was aware of the facts but had not had time to work out the subject fully before Johnston rushed into print; but he secured no support from any authoritative quarter; and even the newspapers had by that time seen the necessity of consulting experts, so that he was unable to place the numerous articles which he wrote to confute Johnston.

Three days later, Regent's Park again figured in the columns of the newspapers.

The first mention of the matter which I saw was in an evening journal. I had been reading a short account of a locust plague in China which was reported to have destroyed crops upon a large scale and caused a panic emigration of the inhabitants of the devastated district, owing to the failure of supplies. Just below this article, my eye caught a paragraph headed:

STRANGE BLIGHT IN REGENT'S PARK

It appeared that the vegetation in the Park had been attacked by some peculiar disease, the symptoms of which were evidently not very clear to the writer of the paragraph. According to him, the plants were withering away; but there seemed to be no fungus or growth on the leaves which would account for their decrepitude. Trees and flowers equally with the grass were attacked by the blight. While throwing out a hint that the prolonged drought might possibly account for the phenomenon, the reporter indicated that the thing was rather more local than might have been anticipated from this cause; for the worst effects of the blight were to be found in the vegetation of the strip between Gloucester Gate and the Outer Circle in one direction and between the Broad Walk and the Park edge in the other. Beyond this oblong, the damage done was not so readily recognisable.

That evening, as the fine weather still held, I walked through Regent's Park to see for myself what truth there was in the newspaper talk. More people than usual were out; for in addition to the normal crowds of pedestrians, it was evident that others had come, like myself, to examine the blight. The Broad Walk was thronged; for the Londoner of those days was one of the most inquisitive creatures in existence.

It was evident that, considered from the "show" point of view, the state of affairs had been a disappointment to the people. I heard numerous comments as I walked among the crowd; and the tone was one of disparagement. The general feeling seemed to be that the thing was a mare's nest or a newspaper hoax.

"Blight, they calls it?" said one stout old woman as I passed; "I'd like to blight the young feller what wrote all that in the papers about it, I would! Me putting on my best things and walking ever so far on a hot night to see nothing better than a lot of dried grass. I thought it would be fair seething with grasshoppers," and she shook her head till the trimmings of her antique hat trembled with her vehemence. Evidently she had mixed up the Chinese locusts and the Regent's Park affair in her mind.

Other people shared her discontent; and the younger section of the crowd had begun to seek for amusement by means of spasmodic outbursts of horse-play.

What I saw of the phenomenon was certainly not very thrilling. All the grass to the east of the Broad Walk had the appearance of being sun-blasted. The green tint had gone from it and it had turned straw-colour. On the west side of the Walk there were patches of stricken vegetation scattered here and there as far as one could see, but the effect was not so marked towards the Inner Circle.

I stooped down and rooted up a tuft of withered grass in order to examine it more closely; and to my surprise it came away readily in my hand, leaving the roots almost clear of earth. I could see nothing peculiar about the grass itself; even the most careful inspection failed to reveal any adherent fungus or growth of any description which might account for the phenomenon. I began to think that, after all, the whole thing was due to the heat of the past few weeks, and that the local appearance of the effects was a mere chance.

Next day, however, this idea was put out of court by the news that the blight had spread to the other London parks. Hyde Park suffered severely in the corner between the Marble Arch and the Serpentine; the gardens of Buckingham Palace were also affected; and the grass in Battersea Park showed sporadic outbreaks of the disease also.

Victoria Park, however, seemed to have escaped almost intact; though some traces could be detected.

I learned that the Park gardeners had endeavoured to check the extension of the disease—for it spread almost visibly in places—by spraying the vegetation with the usual vermin-killers; but these had been found to have no influence upon the growth of the smitten areas.

By this time, the newspapers had begun to make the matter a main feature. The heading: "THE BLIGHT" occupied the principal column; and correspondence had been opened on the subject in several of the journals. But as yet the matter was not exciting any interest outside London. It was regarded as a purely local manifestation of no particular import; and although some of the writers of London Letters for the provincial Press alluded to it in their articles, it was usually referred to with a sneer at the "silly season attitude" of supposedly weighty newspapers.

This tone underwent a rapid change, however, on the following day. Even the staid dailies of the Provinces became electrified with the news; and over most of the area of southern England the breakfast tables were ahum with conversations on the Blight and its effects; for the morning papers were filled with telegrams announcing the extension of the affected area broadcast over the Home Counties; and the headlines ran:

SPREAD OF THE NEW BLIGHT

ALL HOME COUNTIES AFFECTED

TOTAL FAILURE OF CROPS FEARED

III *B. DIAZOTANS*

At this point, I remember, the long spell of dry weather reached its end. A heavy series of thunderstorms marked its termination; and for three days the country was deluged with rain and swept by intermittent gales. The cracked ground drank up the moisture; but still more showers fell, until there was mud everywhere.

These meteorological changes in themselves were sufficiently grave from the farmer's point of view; but even more serious was the state of things revealed after the rain had ceased. Whether it was due to the weather conditions or whether it was a vagary produced by factors beyond discovery will never be known; but the fact is established that the spread of the Blight became accentuated during the rainy period. Wherever it had secured a hold during the hot weather it became more malignant in its effects; and its extension to fresh fields was so great that hardly a grain-growing area in the country escaped at this time. It penetrated as far north as the Border agricultural districts; and devastated fields were found even in Perthshire.

Since the potato blight in 1845, no such rapid and extensive destruction of food supplies had been known. The standing crops in the affected areas withered; and a total failure of the home-grown cereals seemed to be inevitable. Nor was it only in this section of the food-supply that the attacks of the Blight became evident. Fruit-trees seemed arrested in their productivity; vegetables failed to ripen and began to rot. Everywhere the vegetable kingdom seemed to be falling into a decline. The great market-gardens and nurseries showed the trace of the same mysterious agent. Roses withered on their stems; and even the hot-house plants suffered equally with their open-air fellows. The only crop which appeared to escape the general disaster was hay.

And now it became clear that the Blight, as it was still called, was going to produce effects in the most widely-separated fields of activity. With a total failure of the crops, the financial side of the question came to the front. Throughout the length and breadth of the land, small farmers were beginning to realise that it was to be a year of utter disaster, ending probably in bankruptcy and ruin. The larger land-owners looked forward to the collapse of tenants and the failure of rents. Mortgage-holders began to consider the nature of their security, and when it was agricultural land they were placed in doubt as to their best course; for no one could foresee whether the Blight was a temporary epidemic or a permanent factor which would reappear with the next crops. And all these varying influences had their effects upon the great financial operations of the City; for even in that industrial age the land had maintained its value as a basic security which apparently could not suffer deterioration beyond a definite point.

This, however, was only a minor field of the Blight's reactions. With the probable failure of the home crop looming before him, even the man in the street could not fail to perceive the more obvious results. It meant a greater dependence upon imported food-stuffs and especially imported grain. Argentina, Canada, India and the United States must make up the missing supplies; and since almost half our cereals were home-grown at that period, the price of food was certain to rise by leaps and bounds; so that every family in the land would be affected by the catastrophe.

Then a further factor was brought to light. With the failure of grain and even of grass, it would be impossible to keep alive the cattle which furnished part of the nation's food. The milk supply would be gravely affected also, from the same cause.

It is difficult for us now to look back and catch again the spirit of that time. Never before, even during the war, had the food of Britain been endangered to such a degree. And the steadily rising prices were sufficient to bring home to the most thoughtless the actual imminence of the peril. I can recall, however, that at first there was no panic of any kind. It was assumed by all of us that although we might have to go short of our usual lavish supplies, yet we should always have enough food to carry us through to the next harvest. The whole world was our granary; and if we were prepared to pay the higher prices which we saw to be inevitable, we had no reason to suppose that we should lack imported grain. Our attitude was quite comprehensible under the circumstances, I think. In the past we had always been able to obtain food; and there seemed no doubt that the same would hold good through this shortage.

The newspapers were fairly evenly divided in their expressed opinions. The Government had recently adjourned Parliament, after a session in which their majority had oscillated dangerously more than once, and the Opposition Press seized upon the Blight in order to embarrass the Cabinet, and especially the Prime Minister, as far as possible. They clamoured that the Government should take steps to secure the food supply of the country by making immediate purchases of wheat in the foreign markets. They demanded that a system of rationing should be established forthwith; and that cases of food-hoarding should be stringently punished. Day after day they held up to public obloquy the individual members of the Cabinet, who were then scattered on holiday; the amusements of each of them were described and coupled with sneering hopes that they would succeed better in their games than they had done in the government of the country and the safeguarding of the national interests. Echoes of the Mazanderan Development Syndicate scandal were kept alive in the most ingenious manner.

The Government Press, naturally, professed to see in the inactivity of the Cabinet a proof that they had the matter well in hand. Avoidance of panic, restriction by voluntary effort of all unnecessary consumption of food, and the postponement of inquiries likely to interfere with the wise projects of the Premier: these formed the stock of their leading articles.

The gutter organ of the Opposition retorted by publishing the complete menu of the Premier's dinner on the previous day, which it had obtained from some waiter in the hotel at which he was staying; and it accompanied this item of news by interspersed extracts from the Government organs in which appeals had been made for a less luxurious form of living.

It must be remembered that this stage of the sequence of events occupied only a brief period. If I am not wrong, it was within ten days of the outbreak of the Blight that we got the first American cables announcing the appearance of the epidemic among the great wheat areas of the Middle West. Almost immediately after came similar news from Canada.

The meaning of this was not at first appreciated by the people as a whole. They still clung to the idea that grain would be forthcoming if a sufficiently high price were paid for it; but those of us who had tried to forecast the possibilities of the situation found our worst fears taking concrete form. Soon even the unthinking were forced to understand what the American news implied. If the Blight spread over the wheat-fields of the Western continent, there would be no surplus grain there for export at all. That source of supply would barely suffice for the mouths at home.

Then, following each other like hammer-strokes upon metal, each biting deeper than the last, came the cables from the rest of the world. Egypt reported the outbreak of the Blight in the Nile valley; British East Africa became affected. The news from the Argentine fell like a thunderbolt, for we realised that with it the last great open source of wheat had failed. The Don and Volga basins followed with the same tale. Over India, the Blight raged with almost unheard-of virulence. Then, days after the others, Australia was smitten, and our last hopes vanished.

During all this period, it must be remembered, we had no idea of the origin of our calamities. We referred to the thing always as "The Blight," though it was made clear at quite an early stage that no plant parasite was concerned in the matter at all. The most careful microscopic examination of affected vegetation had been made without revealing anything in the nature of a fungus or noxious growth.

Yet, on looking backward, I cannot help feeling that we, and especially I myself, were strangely blind to the obvious in the matter. I have already mentioned that when I rooted up a clump of grass in Regent's Park it came away from the soil without resistance; and that when I examined the roots I found them almost as free of earthy deposit as if it had been grown in sand. That, coupled with what I already knew, should have put me on the track of the explanation; and yet I failed to draw the simplest deduction from what I observed. To account for this obtuseness, I can only suggest that already the idea of a "Blight" had taken root in my mind; and that I was so obsessed with the idea of a parasite that I never considered the facts from any other point of view. Since others proved to be equally slow in arriving at the truth, I can only conclude that they were misled in their mental processes much as I myself was.

As I have said on a previous page, it was to Johnston, the bacteriologist, that we owe the discovery. It appears that he had been growing some bacteria in cultures; and, whether by accident or design, he had left one of his cultivation media open to the air. On examining the germs some days later, he had discovered in the culture a type of bacterium with which he was unfamiliar. He proceeded to isolate it in the usual way—I believe it is done by dabbing a needle-point into the culture and using the few microorganisms which stick to the needle as the parents of a fresh colony—and he was amazed at its fecundity. There had never been such a case of bacterial fertility in his experience.

A paper in the *Lancet* brought the description of the creature to the notice of the scientific world. Johnston himself had not recognised the nature of the organism, as he had never dealt with this type of bacteria before; but from his description an agricultural bacteriologist named Vincent was able to identify it as being almost identical with one of the denitrifying group, from which it differed only in its immense power of multiplication. It was hurriedly christened *Bacterium diazotans*,[1] on account of its denitrifying qualities. Further examination showed that its capacity for breaking down nitrogenous material far surpassed that of any known denitrifying agent.

With these discoveries, the mystery of the new blight vanished. An examination of the soil of stricken areas showed that it swarmed with colonies of *B. diazotans*—to use the customary medical contraction—and the whole secret of the destruction was revealed.

[1] *Diazotans* is pronounced Di-ay'-zō-tans'.

It was evident that these new and super-active bacteria attacked the soil, disintegrated all the nitrogenous compounds within their range and thus left the plants without nourishment. The death of the plant followed as a natural result; but the matter did not end there. By destroying the nitrogenous compounds in the soil, the bacteria altered the whole texture of the earth in which they grew. All the nitrogenous organic matter which forms so large a part of the binding material of some soils was destroyed utterly; with the consequence that the mineral particles, which previously had been resting in an organic matrix, were now free to move. Only the clays retained their tenacious character: all other soils degenerated into sand.

There has, of course, been a great deal of speculation upon the origin of *B. diazotans*. Hartwell suggested that it came to us from Venus, propelled by light-pressure across the abysses of space. Inshelwood put forward the view that in *B. diazotans* we had an example of bacteria, originally endemic, changing their habits and spreading into fresh regions.

Personally, I believe neither hypothesis. I feel sure that I saw the birth of the first *B. diazotans* on that night in Wotherspoon's laboratory, under the action of the fireball; and the evidence is simple enough.

Every living creature is a wonderfully constructed electrical machine. Each beat of our hearts, each systole of our lungs, each contraction of a muscle in our frame produces a tiny electrical current. Our organism is a mass of colloids and electrolytes which transmit these charges hither and thither throughout our systems; and were we gifted with an electrical sense in addition to those which we already have, we should see each other as complexities of conductors along which currents were playing with every movement of our body.

This complex electrical system is acutely sensible to external electrical conditions. Anyone who has held the handles of an induction coil or who has taken a spark from a Leyden jar knows the physiological effects which these things produce. The influence of high-tension currents upon the growth of plants has been proved beyond dispute.

Now it seems to me that in this effect of an external electric charge upon the internal mechanism of an organism we have a clue to the origin of these new bacteria. I have already told how the fire-ball, in its explosion, shattered the denitrifying cultures in Wotherspoon's room; and it seems clear that at the moment of the concussion there must have been a tremendous play of electrical forces about the spot. We know hardly anything with regard to the nature of the electrical fields existing in such things as these fire-balls; and it is quite possible that they may be different from anything of which we have any knowledge among the more usual displays of electrical energy. I believe, then, that it is in the action of the fire-ball that we must seek for an explanation of the change in habit of Wotherspoon's denitrifying bacteria.

Again, I have mentioned my observation of the rapid multiplication of the denitrifying bacteria which I made with Wotherspoon's microscope on the following day. That also seems to me to have a bearing upon the problem; though I admit quite frankly that my evidence is only that of a layman. It is in every way regrettable that Wotherspoon, having tired of using his room as an exhibit, should have cleared away every trace of the wreckage before any expert examination of it could be made; for in this way the crucial evidence on the point was destroyed.

Further, in support of my views, I would point out that the very first known occurrence of *B. diazotans* was that which had Regent's Park as its site; and that the first place of attack was in the immediate neighbourhood of Wotherspoon's house in Cumberland Terrace. This can hardly be disregarded, when it is considered in connection with the other facts which I have mentioned.

At this time of day there can be no question that London formed the focus from which *B. diazotans* spread throughout the world. I have described the ramifications of the great air-services; and it seems to me obvious that the organisms were carried to and fro upon the surface of the globe by the agency of the aeroplanes. The order of attack at various points indicates this very clearly, in my opinion. First came the American and Egyptian outbreaks; then Uganda and South America; and finally, long after the others, Australia showed traces of the devastation. I have checked the possible dates of arrival in these various places, taking into account the relative swiftnesses of the aeroplanes on the different routes; and the results can hardly be gainsaid. Allowing, as one must, a certain latitude for the time of development of the microbe in various spots, there seems little doubt that the dates of the outbreaks fell into the same succession as the times of arrival of the various London air-services.

IV PANIC

In dealing with the subsequent stage of affairs in this country, I feel myself at a loss. Matters of fact, sequences of events, definite incidents in a chain of affairs: all these can be described without much difficulty and with a certain detachment on the part of the narrator. But when it comes to indicating the transition from one psychological state to another, the task is one which would require for its proper fulfilment a more practised pen than mine; and it is precisely this transitional period which I must now attempt to make clear in retrospect; for without an understanding of it my narrative would lack one of its cornerstones.

Apart from the mere question of narration, however, there is a further difficulty which cannot be evaded. I myself passed through this crisis and underwent day by day these changes in outlook which I shall have to portray; so that the personal factor cannot be eliminated from my account. Yet my own feelings and views must not be allowed to monopolise the field; since they had not the slightest influence upon the main current of popular feeling.

I have used the word "current," and perhaps it is the best one which I could have chosen to express the thing which baffles me. As a man walks by the side of a mountain stream, he sees the volume of the water change as it grows from rill to rivulet and from rivulet to river; yet no single tributary is of any notable size. Gradually, almost imperceptibly, the banks diverge, the sound of the running water grows louder and yet louder: until at last comes a sweep over the rapids and the thunder of the fall below.

It was in this way that events merged into each other between the outbreak and the complete realisation of our fears. The transition from security to panic was not made in one swift step. Rather it came little by little, and at no point could one indicate precisely how the public feeling had changed from that of the previous day. A whole series of tiny impulses, each in itself almost negligible, served to drive us from one mental position to the next; and a complete analysis of the psychology of the time would be an impossible task. I propose, therefore, merely to indicate some of these innumerable factors which played upon our spirits; so that this blank in my narrative may be filled in some way, even if only roughly.

It was not until the Blight had spread far over the Home Counties that the general public became interested in the matter at all; and at this period the mass of people in the country districts were almost the only ones who saw any cause for alarm. The town-dwellers seldom came in direct contact with the sources of their food-supply; in fact it is doubtful if the lower-class Londoner of the old days could have answered a direct question as to the date of harvesting. Food came to them daily in a form which suggested very little with regard to its original nature. Wheat they knew only in the form of bread or flour; meat was divorced almost entirely from the shapes of the animals from which it was derived; tea, coffee and sugar brought with them no visions of tea-gardens on the Indian hills or sugar plantations under the West Indian sun. The furthest traceable point of origin of these things, as far as most of the population was concerned, was to be found in the retail shops. Thus there was a certain sluggishness in apprehension among the main bulk of the people when they read in the newspapers that the crops had failed. To them, it simply meant that we should have to buy in another market; just as they had to go to a fresh grocer when their own dealer ran short of some commodity which they required.

In the country districts, and especially in the great centres of the agricultural portions of the kingdom, the outlook was different, but still restricted in its scope. Failure of the crops to them meant financial loss, hard times, stringency, urgent personal economy and the hope of better luck in the following season. Though closer to the soil, the country folk were unmoved by any outlook wider than that which included the direct effects of the Blight upon their industry. And, indeed, they had little time in which to speculate upon ultimate reactions, for their attention was concentrated almost wholly upon their efforts to remedy the damage already done or to protect from injury any portions of the crop which had not yet been attacked.

Thus at this stage the mental surface of the country as a whole remained unruffled. Here and there, of course, a few of us had grasped what might be entailed if the Blight destroyed the whole of the home supplies; but I doubt if even the most far-sighted had imagined that anything but a local shortage was in prospect.

With the arrival of the American cables, the situation changed slightly. The tone of the newspapers became graver, and they endeavoured to awake their readers to the fact that the possibility of a serious shortage had become a certainty. Edition after edition poured out from the printing-presses and the headlines grew in magnitude from hour to hour. "*The Blight in America*" was the first type of intimation, which attracted but little interest and was placed in the "third-class" column of the papers. Then came appreciation of the importance of the news; the headlines increased in size and moved up nearer the centre of readers' interest: "*Spread of the Blight in the Wheat Districts*." Next came a sudden jump to the first place on the page and heavily leaded type in the headlines: "*Failure of Wheat Crop in America*."

Even at this stage, the readers as a whole failed to connect the news with anything in their daily life. Gradually it was borne in upon their minds that the collapse of the American crops—including the Canadian—meant a very rapid rise in the price of cereal food-stuffs; but further than this they refused to look. At that time the cattle question had not been noticed at all; and the general feeling simply resolved itself into a decision to avoid bread as far as possible and eat meat instead.

With the arrival of reports from the remaining wheat-growing districts, the newspapers increased their efforts to awaken their readers to the gravity of the situation.

"*The World Shortage*" occupied the place of honour in their columns, and was supported by telegrams and cables from all parts of the globe telling the same tale of crop failure with a steady monotony.

As I look back upon these days I can only marvel at the ingrained conservatism of the human mind. It is true that on the whole the public were at last beginning to understand the situation. They had grasped the fact that almost all the known regions of wheat-growing land had been attacked; and that a shortage was inevitable. But, none the less, in their inmost thoughts they still clung to the fixed idea that *somewhere* in the world there was bound to be a store of wheat—or if not wheat, then rice or some other edible grain—which would enable us to pass through the coming winter without undue restriction of our food supplies. It was perhaps a manifestation of that eternal optimism which is necessary if the race is to survive at all; or possibly it represented a trust in the Government's capacity to arrange some means whereby supplies would be forthcoming in due course. Whatever its origin, it was among the most marked features of that strange time.

I remember that one of the side-issues of the disaster created at that stage far deeper impressions than the catastrophe itself. With the failure of the American supplies over a huge area, the Wheat Pit became convulsed with an outbreak of gambling such as had never been seen before. Chicago went crazy; and legitimate business gave place to a fury of speculation which grew ever more intense as the news came in of further extensions of the devastated areas. Before the Blight appeared in America, December wheat had been offered at 233¼; but in the earlier stages of the game of speculation it rushed up to 405: and before the end came it was dealt with at prices which were purely illusory, since they corresponded to nothing tangible in commodities. Thousands of bears were ruined in the preliminary moves; and in the end the whole machinery of the Pit was brought to a standstill owing to there being no sellers.

Of course that series of transactions had no real influence upon the course of events; but the public, both here and in America, failed to see this; and the bitterest feelings found vent concerning "gambling in the food of the people." It is quite possible that the anger uselessly expended on this subject served to keep the public from concentrating their attention upon the real problem of the world shortage. Huge quantities of wheat were dealt with on paper; and the people, being unfamiliar with the methods of Chicago speculation, assumed that these enormous transactions actually represented the transfer of millions of bushels of real grain from seller to buyer. The sharp upward trend of flour and bread prices at home served to confirm their impression that the gambling in the Pit was responsible for their troubles; and Rodman's attempt—which was practically successful—to corner wheat led to violent criticism and even, at one time, to an effort to lynch him.

It was not only in the wheat market that this fever of speculation showed itself. Maize, oats, barley and cotton also became counters in the game and rose to incredible prices. Unknown men appeared in the world of finance and for days maintained their positions as controllers of the markets. Many of the great firms in America ventured their capital rashly and suffered disaster.

In its ultimate effects also, the gamble in food-stuffs exerted a profound influence on the stream of public opinion. The news of the speculations in Chicago, the descriptions of the turbulent scenes in the Wheat Pit, where at one time revolvers were fired by super-excited members, the tales of huge fortunes won and lost in a day, the deep under-current of resentment at this callous trading upon the world's necessities, all tended in the end to bring into view the real state of the wheat question. And now the newspapers were printing the single word FAMINE as a headline; and the people were beginning to ask in ominous tones: "What is the Government doing?"

It was at this time that, to my profound surprise, I received a private letter from the Prime Minister requesting my attendance at a meeting which he had arranged.

V NORDENHOLT

Probably with a view to avoiding the attention of the Press, the meeting was held elsewhere than at No. 10 Downing Street. I found myself in what looked like a Board-meeting room. A fire burned in the grate, for it was a chilly day. Down the centre of the room stretched a long table around which a number of men were sitting, some of whom were familiar as great figures in the industrial world. At the head of the table I recognised the Premier, flanked on either hand by a Cabinet Minister. A chair was vacant half-way up the table, opposite the fireplace; and I took it on a gesture from the Premier.

Almost at once, the Prime Minister rose to his feet. He looked worn and agitated; but even under the evidences of the strain he endeavoured to assume a cheerful and confident air. He was a man I had never trusted; and I now had my first opportunity of examining him at close quarters. In repose, his face fell into the heavy lines of the successful barrister; but when he became animated, a mechanical smile flitted across it which in some way displeased me more than the expression which it veiled. He seemed to me a typical example of the *faux bonhomme*. In politics he had gained a reputation for dilatory conduct combined with a mastery in the art of managing a majority; and his mind was saturated with the idea of

Party advantage. Of real loyalty I suspect he had very little; but when one of his Cabinet blundered heavily, he would step into the limelight with a fine gesture and assume all responsibility. In this way he kept his Government intact and gained a reputation for fidelity without losing anything; for he well knew that no one would call him to account for the responsibility which he had assumed.

"Gentlemen," he said, "you will probably wonder why we have invited you to meet us here to-day. We all know the unhappy state of affairs into which the country has fallen. There is dissatisfaction abroad; and the Government is being held responsible for conditions which were none of its making. I will speak plainly to you, for it is no time for reservations. Something must be done to allay public anxiety, which is growing more intense as time goes on. I am not one of those who take these passing scares seriously; but we cannot afford to ignore the present feeling: and some measures are necessary to satisfy this clamour. It is a time when all of us must come to the aid of the Executive.

"The Cabinet is dispersed at the moment. Many of the members are abroad and are unable to return at present, owing to a disorganisation of transport. But pending their return and the decisions which we shall then be forced to take, I thought it right to call together you gentlemen, large employers of labour, and to enlist your aid in the work we shall have to do. It is essential that the Government should retain public confidence at the present time. I think we are agreed upon that point. Nothing could be more fatal than a General Election forced upon us under the reigning conditions.

"We have taken steps to call Parliament together immediately, in order to lay before it certain measures which we believe will enable us to tide over this crisis. But in the meantime we must try to pacify the working classes, who are being agitated by the dismal forecasts of the newspapers. I have no desire to inquire into the origin of the jeremiads which are being printed daily in a certain group of papers; but I cannot help noticing that they all tend towards a discrediting of myself and my colleagues. There is a cry for action; whereas I think all of you will agree that consideration is required, so that the action, if it should become necessary, may be well-contrived.

"It is in these circumstances that we have called you gentlemen together. We propose to lay before you the main points of our scheme; and when you have heard them, we count upon you, as great employers of labour, to lay the matter before your employés. We shall use the newspapers also to disseminate our proposals; but personal efforts can do more than any printed appeals. I trust that we shall not look in vain for the cordial co-operation which is absolutely requisite at this crisis."

As this speech proceeded, I had become more and more uneasy. Through it all ran the governing thought that something must be done, which was true enough; but the thing which he proposed to do, it appeared to me, was to persuade the country that all was well, whereas I felt that the essential matter was to prepare against a practical calamity.

"We have given a great deal of thought to our proposals, though we have not wasted time in the consideration of details. The broad outlines are all that are required for our present purpose; and we have confined our attention to them. My friend the Home Secretary"—he indicated the colleague who sat on his left—"will be good enough to read to you the heads of our decisions. I may say, however, that these decisions are only of a temporary nature. We may find it necessary to modify some of them in due course; and they must not be regarded as in any way final. Possibly"—he let the mechanical smile play over the company—"possibly some of those present may be able to suggest certain modifications at this meeting. If these modifications are such that we can adopt them, we shall be only too glad to do so."

He sat down; and the Home Secretary rose in his turn. Saxenham had the reputation of being dull but honest. He had no force of character, but he had won his way into the Cabinet mainly because he had never been known to stoop to a false action in the whole course of his career. On this account he represented a mainstay of the Government, which in other ways was not too scrupulous. His brain was one which worked slowly; and his personal admiration for the Prime Minister was such that he followed him blindly without seeing too clearly whither he was being led. He cleared his throat and took up a sheet of paper which contained the Government proposals.

"I think that it will be best if I take the various proposals seriatim and elucidate each of them, as I come to it, by a short commentary.

"*First*, we shall issue a Government statement to the Press with the object of reassuring the public and putting an end to this rising clamour for action in haste. In this statement we shall call attention to the fact that there is at present a twelve-weeks' supply of food in the country, which, with due care, would itself be sufficient to last the population until the next harvest. We shall make it clear that the Government have under earnest consideration the steps which it may be necessary to take in the future; and we shall appeal to the public to pay no heed to alarmist statements from interested quarters.

"*Second*, we shall advise the King to issue a Proclamation on the same lines. We believe that this may have a greater effect in some quarters than an official Government statement.

"*Third*, we shall make arrangements for taking over the food stores in the country, though we hope that it will not be necessary to do so.

"*Fourth*, we shall make arrangements to purchase with the national moneys the surplus food supplies of grain. We shall be able to pay higher prices than private importers; and I have little doubt that we shall thus be able to stock our granaries with food sufficient to carry us through until well beyond the next harvest.

"*Fifth*, we shall prepare a system of rationing, as soon as we have obtained our supplies and know definitely how much food can be allotted per head to the population.

"*Sixth*, since a continuance of the present crisis will undoubtedly lead to widespread distress and unemployment, we propose to take under consideration a system of unemployment relief; so that there may be no centres of disturbance generated among the population by idleness or lack of money.

"*Seventh*, we shall invite the scientific experts on agriculture to devote their attention to the problem of increasing the crops in the next harvest, so that such a state of affairs as this may not again arise."

He paused, with an air of finality, though he did not resume his seat. At the head of the table, the Prime Minister was apparently plunged in thought. Suddenly I was struck by the employment to which the third member of the Cabinet was putting his time. With the sheets of paper in front of him he was constructing a series of toys. A box, a cock-boat, an extraordinarily life-like frog lay before him on the table, and he was busily engaged in the production of something which looked like a bird. I learned afterwards that this was a trick of his, the outcome of his peculiarly nervous temperament. Not wishing to be detected watching him, I turned my eyes away; and as I swept my glance round the table, I suddenly found myself in turn the object of scrutiny.

My first impression was of two steel-blue eyes fixed upon my own with an almost disquieting intensity of gaze. I had the feeling of being examined, not only physically but mentally, as though by some hypnotic power my very thoughts were being brought to light. Usually, in a casual interchange of glances, one or other of two is diverted almost at once; but in this case I felt in some way unable to withdraw my eyes from those before me; while my *vis-à-vis* continued to examine me with a steadfast attention which, strangely enough, suggested no rudeness.

He was a man of more than the average height, over six feet I found later when he rose from his chair. His features suggested no particular race, though there was an elusive resemblance to the Red Indian type which I felt rather than saw; but this was perhaps intensified by the jet-black hair and the clean-shaven face. All these are mere details of little importance. What impressed me most about him was an air of conscious power, which would have singled him out in any gathering. Looking from him to the Prime Minister, it crossed my mind that while the Premier counterfeited power in his appearance, this unknown embodied it; and yet there was no parade, for he appeared to be entirely devoid of self-consciousness. Before he removed his eyes from mine I saw an inscrutable smile curve his lips. I say inscrutable, for I could not read what it meant; but it resembled the expression of a man who has just checked a calculation and found it to be accurate.

It has taken me some time to describe this incident; but actually it can have occupied hardly more than a fraction of a minute; for, as I took my eyes away from his, I heard the Home Secretary continue:

"These, gentlemen, are our proposals; and I think that they cover the necessary ground. We wish especially to draw your attention to the sixth one: for it is that which has chiefly moved us to lay these matters before you ere we make them public. It concerns unemployment, if you remember. We have brought you into our councils because all of you are large employers of labour in different lines of industry; and we would welcome any suggestions from you now with regard to the possible modes of application of this scheme in practice. As Mr. Biles has told you, it is essential at this moment to avoid discontent among the proletariat. Europe is in a very disturbed condition, and a change of Government at this juncture would have disastrous effects. I can say no more upon that point; but I wish you to understand that we urgently require your co-operation at this time."

He sat down; and the Prime Minister rose again.

"I think you will see, gentlemen, from what the Home Secretary has said, that the Government has the situation well in hand. The only matter about which we are at all concerned is the liquor question. It is clear that we can hardly sacrifice grain for the manufacture of alcohol until we are sure that we have in stock a sufficiency of food for the country's needs. A shortage of liquor, however, may lead to industrial unrest; and it is this possible unrest which we desire your help in preventing. We wish if possible to get directly into touch with the workers of the nation; and we have approached you first of all. Later we intend to interview the Trades Union leaders with the same object. But time presses; and I shall be glad to hear any criticisms of our plans if you will be so good as to give your views."

He sank back into his chair and again the smile faded almost at once. For a moment there was a pause. Then the man opposite me rose to his feet.

"Who is that?" I whispered to my neighbour.

"Nordenholt."

Nordenholt! I looked at him with even more attention than before. For two decades that name had rung through the world, and yet, meeting him now face to face, I had not recognised him. Nor was this astonishing; for no portrait of him had ever come to my notice. The daily photo papers, the illustrated weeklies, even *Punch* itself, had never printed so much as a sketch of him. He had leaped into fame simply as a name to which no physical complement had been attached. By some mysterious influence behind the scenes, he had avoided the usual Press illustrator with a success which left him unrecognisable to the man in the street.

So this—I looked at him again—so this was Nordenholt, the Platinum King, the multi-millionaire, wrecker of two Governments. No wonder that I had felt him to be out of the common. I am no hero-worshipper; yet Nordenholt had always exercised an attraction upon my mind, even though he was only a name. In many respects he seemed to be the kind of man I should have liked to be, if I had his character and gifts.

When he rose, I found that his voice matched his appearance; it was deep, grave and harmonious, although he spoke without any rhetorical turn. Had he chosen to force himself to the front in politics, that instrument would have served him to sway masses of men by its mere charm. I thought that I detected a faint sub-tinge of irony in it as he began. He wasted no time upon preliminaries but went straight to the point.

"Are we to understand that this paper in the hands of the Home Secretary contains a full statement of the measures which the Cabinet—or such members of it as are available—have decided upon up to the present?"

The Prime Minister nodded assent. I seemed to detect a certain uneasiness in his pose since Nordenholt had risen.

"May I see the paper? . . . Thank you."

He read it over slowly and then, still retaining it in his hand, continued:

"Perhaps I have not fathomed your purpose in drawing it up; but if I am correct in my interpretation, it seems to me an excellent scheme. I doubt if anything better could be devised."

The nervous frown left the Premier's face and was replaced by a satisfied smile; the Home Secretary, after a pause of mental calculation, also seemed to be relieved; while the Colonial Secretary put down his paper model and looked up at Nordenholt with an expression of mild astonishment. It was evident that they had hardly expected this approval. The hint of irony in the speaker's voice grew more pronounced:

"This scheme of yours, if I am not mistaken, is a piece of window-dressing, pure and simple. You felt that you had to make some show of energy; and to pacify the public you bring forward these proposals. The first two of them achieve nothing practical; and the remaining five concern steps which you propose to take at some future time, but which you have not yet considered fully. Am I correct?"

The Colonial Secretary broke in angrily in reply:

"I object to the word 'window-dressing.' These propos-als give in outline the steps which we shall take in due course. They represent the principles which we shall use as our guides. You surely did not expect us to work out the details for this meeting?"

Nordenholt's voice remained unchanged.

"No, I did not expect *you* to have worked out the details of this scheme. I will confine myself to principles if you wish it. I see that in the fourth clause you anticipate the purchase of foreign grain, though at an enhanced price. May I ask where you propose to secure it? It is common knowledge that it cannot be obtained within the Empire, so presumably you have some other granary in your minds. Possibly you have already taken steps."

The face of the Colonial Secretary lit up with a flash of malice.

"You are quite correct in both conjectures. Australia and Canada have suffered so severely from the Blight that we can expect nothing from them, and I am afraid that Russia is in the same condition. But we have actually issued instructions to agents in America to purchase all the wheat which they can obtain, and advices have arrived showing that we control already a very large supply."

"Excellent forethought. I fear, however, that it has been wasted through no fault of yours. At ten o'clock this morning, the Government of the United States prohibited the export of food-stuffs of any description. You will not get your supplies."

"But that is contrary to their Constitution! How can they do that?" The Prime Minister was evidently startled. "And how do you come to know of it while we have had no advice?"

"A censorship was established over the American cables and wireless just before this decision was made public. They do not wish it to be known here until they have had time to make their arrangements. My information came through my private wireless, which was seized immediately after transmitting it."

"But . . . but . . ." stammered the Home Secretary, "this complicates our arrangements in a most unforeseen manner. It is a most serious piece of news. Biles, we never took that into account."

"Sufficient unto the day, Saxenham. This Government has been in difficult places before; but we always succeeded in turning the corner successfully. Don't let us yield to panic now. If we think over the matter for a while, I do not doubt that we shall see daylight through it in the end."

Nordenholt listened to this interchange of views in scornful silence.

"One of the details which have still to be thought out, I suppose, Biles," he continued. "Don't let it delay us at present. There is another point upon which I wish some information."

The meeting was a curious study by this time. Almost without seeming to notice it, Nordenholt had driven the three Cabinet Ministers into a corner; and he now seemed to dominate them as though they were clerks who had been detected in scamping their work. Personality was telling in the contest, for contest it had now become.

"This news which I have given you implies that the twelve-weeks' supply of food in the country is all that we have at our command anywhere. What do you propose to do?"

"We shall have to take stock and begin the issue of ration tickets as soon as possible."

"Twelve-weeks' supply; how long will that last the country under your arrangements?"

The Colonial Secretary made a rapid calculation on a sheet of paper.

"As we shall need to carry on till the next harvest, I suppose it means that the daily ration will have to be reduced to less than a quarter of the full amount—three-thirteenths, to be exact."

"And you are satisfied with that calculation?"

The Colonial Secretary glanced over his figures.

"Yes, I see no reason to alter it. Naturally it will mean great privation; and the working class will be difficult to keep in hand; but I see no objection to carrying on till next year when the harvest will be due. The potato crop will come in early and help us."

Nordenholt looked at him for a moment and then laughed contemptuously. Suddenly his almost pedantic phraseology dropped away.

"Simpson, you beat the band. I never heard anything like it."

Then his manner changed abruptly.

"Do you mean to say," he asked roughly, "that you haven't realised yet that there will be *no* next harvest? Don't you understand that things have changed, once and for all? The soil is done for. There will be no crops again until every inch of it is revivified in some way. 'The potato crop will come in early and help us!' I've consulted some men who know; and they tell me that within a year it will be impossible to raise more than a small fraction even of the worst crop we ever saw in this country."

The Premier was the only one of the three who stood fast under this blow.

"That is certainly a serious matter, Nordenholt," he said; "but there is nothing to be gained from hard words. Let us think over the case, and I feel sure that some way out of this apparent *impasse* can be found. Surely some of these scientific experts could suggest something which might get us out of the difficulty. I don't despair. Past experience has always shown that with care one can avoid most awkward embarrassments."

"The 'awkward embarrassment,' as you call it, amounts to this. How are you going to feed fifty millions of people for an indefinite time when your supplies are only capable of feeding them normally for twelve weeks? Put them on 'three-thirteenth rations' as Simpson suggests; and when the next harvest comes in you will find you have a good deal less than 'three-thirteenth rations' per head for them. What's your solution, Biles? You will have to produce it quick; for every hour you sit thinking means a bigger inroad into the available supplies. Remember, this is something new in your experience. You aren't up against a majority you can wheedle into taking your advice. This time you are up against plain facts of Nature; and arguments are out of court. Now I ask a plain question; and I'm going to get a straight answer from you for once: What are your plans?"

The Premier pondered the matter in silence for a couple of minutes; then, apparently, the instinct of the old Parliamentary hand came uppermost in his mind. The habits of thought which have lasted through a generation cannot be broken instantaneously. With a striving after dignity, which was only half successful he said:

"Parliament is about to meet. I shall go there and lay this matter before the Great Inquest of the nation and let them decide."

"Three days wasted; and probably two days of talk at least before anything is settled; then two days more before you can bring anything into gear: one week's supplies eaten up and nothing to show for it. Is that your solution?"

"Yes."

"You are determined on that? No wavering?"

"No."

"Very good, Biles. I give you the fairest warning. On the day that you meet the House of Commons, I shall place upon the paper a series of questions which will expose the very root of the Mazanderan scandal, and I shall supply full information on the subject to the Opposition Press. I have had every document in my possession for the last year. I can prove that you yourself were in it up to the neck; I have notes of all the transactions with Rimanez and Co. And I know all about the Party Funds also. If that once gets into print, Biles, you are done for—thumbs down!"

He imitated the old death sign of the Roman arena. The Premier sat as if frozen in his chair. His face had gone a dirty grey. Nordenholt towered over him with contempt on his features. Suddenly the Colonial Secretary sprang to his feet.

"This is blackmail, Nordenholt," he cried furiously. "Do you think you can do that sort of thing and not be touched? You may think you are safe behind your millions; but if you carried out your threat there isn't a decent man who would speak to you again. You daren't do it!"

"If you speak to me like that again, Simpson, I'll take care that no decent man speaks to you either," Nordenholt said, calmly. "There's another set of notes besides those on Mazanderan. I have the whole dossier of the house in Carshalton Terrace in my desk. I'll publish them too, unless you come to heel. It will be worse than Mazanderan, Simpson. It will be prison."

In his turn, the Colonial Secretary collapsed into his chair. Whatever the threat had been, it had evidently brought him face to face with ruin; and guilt was written across his face.

But Saxenham had paid no attention to this interruption. In his slow way he was evidently turning over in his mind what Nordenholt had said to the Prime Minister; and now he spoke almost in a tone of anguish:

"Johnnie, Johnnie," he said. "Deny it! Deny it at once. You can't sit under that foul charge. Our hands were clean, weren't they? You said they were, in the House. There's no truth in what Nordenholt says, is there? Is there, Johnnie?"

But the Premier sat like a statue in his chair, staring in front of him with unseeing eyes. The affairs of the Mazanderan Development Syndicate had been a bad business; and if the connection between it and the Government could be proved, after what had already passed, it was an end of Biles and the total discredit of his Party. Nordenholt, still on his feet, looked down at the silent figure without a gleam of pity in his face. Somehow I understood that he was playing for a great stake, though no flicker of interest crossed his countenance.

The strain was broken by Saxenham getting to his feet. I knew his record, and I could guess what his feelings must have been. He stood there, a pathetic little figure, with shaking hands and dim eyes, a worshipper who had found his god only a broken image. He turned and looked at us in a pitiful way and then faced round to the wrecker.

"Nordenholt," he said, "he doesn't deny it. Is it really true? Can you give me your word?"

Nordenholt's face became very gentle and all the hardness died out of his voice.

"Yes, Saxenham, it is true. I give you my word of honour for its truth. He can't deny it."

"Then I've backed a lie. I believed him. And now I've misled people. I've gone on to platforms and denied the truth of it; pledged my word that it was a malicious falsehood. Oh! I can't face it, Nordenholt. I can't face it. This finishes me with public service. I—I—"

He covered his face with his hands and I could see the tears trickle between his fingers. He had paid his price for being honest.

But the Premier was of sterner stuff. He looked up at Nordenholt at last with a gleam of hatred which he suppressed almost as it came:

"Well, Nordenholt, what's your price?"

"So you've seen reason, Biles? Not like poor Saxenham, eh?" There was an under-current of bitterness in the tone, but it was almost imperceptible. "Well, it's not hard. You take your orders from me now. You cover me with your full responsibility. You understand? You always were good at assuming responsibility. Have it now."

"Do I understand you to mean that you would like to be a Dictator?"

"No, you haven't got it quite correctly. I *mean* to be Dictator."

The Prime Minister had relapsed into his stony attitude. There was no trace of feeling on his face; but I could understand the mental commotion which must lie behind that blank countenance. Under cover of fine phrases, he had always sought the lowest form of Party advantage; his political nostrum had become part and parcel of his individuality, and he had never looked higher than the intricacies of the Parliamentary game. Now, suddenly, he had been brought face to face with reality; and it had broken him. To do him justice, I believe that he might have faced personal discredit with indifference. He had done it before and escaped with his political life. But Nordenholt had struck him on an even more vital spot. If the Mazanderan affair came into the daylight, his Party would be ruined; and he would have been responsible. I give him the credit of supposing that it was upon the larger and not upon the personal issue that he surrendered.

Nordenholt, having gained his object, refrained from going further. He turned away from the upper end of the table and addressed the rest of us.

"Gentlemen, you see the state of affairs. We cannot wait for the slow machinery of politics to revolve through its time-honoured cycles before beginning to act. Something must be done at once. Every moment is now of importance. I wish to lay before you what appears to me the only method whereby we can save something out of the wreck.

"I have been thinking out the problem with the greatest care; and I believe that even now it is not too late, if you will give me your support. This meeting was called at my suggestion; and I supplied a list of your names because all of you will be needed if my scheme is to be carried out. But before I divulge it, I must ask from each of you an absolutely unconditional promise of secrecy. Will you give that, Ross? And you, Arbuthnot? . . ."

He went from individual to individual round the table; and to my astonishment, used my own name with the others. How he knew me, I could not understand.

When he had secured a promise from all present, he continued:

"In the first place, I had better tell you what I have done. Immediately the Blight began to ravage the American wheat-fields, I bought up all the grain which was available from last year's crop and got it shipped as soon as possible. It is on the high seas now; so we have evaded the new prohibition of exports. I need not give you figures; but it amounts to a considerable quantity. This, of course, I carried through at my own expense.

"I have also had printed a series of ration tickets and explanatory leaflets sufficient to last the whole country for three weeks. This also I did at my private charges.

"Further, I have placed orders with the printers and bill-posters for the placarding of certain notices. Some of these, I expect, are already posted up on the hoardings.

"I mention these matters merely in order to show you that I have not been idle and that I am fully convinced of the necessity for speed."

He paused for a few seconds to let this sink in.

"Now we come to the main problem. Saxenham has told you the state of affairs; and I have supplemented it sufficiently to allow of your forming a judgment on the case. We have a population of fifty millions in the country. We have a food supply which will last, with my additions to it, for perhaps fourteen weeks. Beyond that we have nothing in hand. The next supply cannot make its appearance for at least a year. I have omitted the yield of the present crop, as I wish to be on the safe side; and I find that most of the grain is useless. When the new crop comes in, it will be, under present conditions, negligible in quantity owing to the soil-destruction which the *Bacillus diazotans* has wrought. That, I think, is a fair statement of the case as it stands.

"What results can we look for? If we ration the nation, even if we allow only a quarter of the normal supplies per day, our whole stock will be exhausted within the year. There will be a large percentage of deaths owing to underfeeding; but at the end of the year I think we might look forward to having a debilitated population of some thirty millions to feed. Will the new crop give us food for them? I have consulted men who know the subject and they tell me that it is an impossibility. We could not raise food enough, under the present conditions, to support even a reasonable percentage of that population."

He paused again, as though to let this sink in also.

"Gentlemen, this nation stands at the edge of its grave. That is the simple truth."

We had all seen the trend of his reasoning; but this cold statement sent a shiver through the meeting. When he spoke again, it was in an even graver tone.

"You must admit, gentlemen, that we cannot hope to keep alive even half of the population until crops become plentiful once more. There is only a single choice before us. Either we distribute the available food uniformly throughout the country or we take upon ourselves the responsibility of an unequal allotment. If we choose the first course, all of us will die without reprieve. It is not a matter of sentiment; it is the plain logic of figures. No safety lies in that course. What about the second?

"Let us assume that we choose the alternative. We select from the fifty millions of our population those whom we regard as most fitted to survive. We lay aside from our stores sufficient to support this fraction; and we distribute among the remainder of the people the residuum of our food. If they can survive on that scale of rations, well and good. If not, we cannot turn aside the course of Nature."

The Prime Minister looked up. Evidently, behind his impassive mask, he had been following the reasoning.

"If I understand you aright," he said, "you are proposing to murder a large proportion of the population by slow starvation?"

"No. What I am trying to do is to save some millions of them from a certain death. It just depends upon which way you look at it, Biles. But have it your own way if it pleases you.

"Now, gentlemen, the calculation is a simple one. We have enough food to last a population of fifty millions for fourteen weeks. From that we deduct five weeks' supplies for the whole population; which leaves us with four hundred and fifty million weekly rations. We select five million people whom we decide must survive; and these four hundred and fifty million rations will keep them fed for ninety weeks—say a year and nine months. It will really be longer than that; for I anticipate rather heavy ravages of disease on account of the monotony of the diet and the lack of fresh vegetables. That is in the nature of things; and we cannot evade it.

"That, then, is the only alternative. It is, as the Prime Minister has said, a death sentence on by far the greater part of the people in these islands; but I see no way out of the difficulties in which we are involved. It is not we who have passed that sentence. Nature has done it; and all that we can achieve is the rescue of a certain number of the victims. With your help, I propose to undertake that work of rescue."

I doubt if those sitting round the table had more than the vaguest glimpse of what all this meant. When a death-roll reaches high figures, the mind refuses to grasp its implications. Very few people have any concrete idea of what the words "one million" stand for. We only understood that there was impending a human catastrophe on a scale which dwarfed all preceding tragedies. Beyond that, I know that I, for one, could not force my mind.

"We are thus left with five million survivors," Nordenholt continued. "But this does not reach the crux of the matter. The nitrogen of the soil has vanished; and it must be replaced if the earth is ever again to bring forth fruits. That task devolves upon mankind, for Nature works too slowly for our purposes. In order to feed these five million mouths—or what is left of them when the food supply runs out—we have to raise crops next year; and to raise these crops we must supply the soil with the necessary nitrogenous material.

"I have consulted men who know"—this seemed to be his only phrase when he referred to his authorities—"and they tell me that it can be done if we bend our whole energies to the task. All the methods of using the nitrogen of the air have been worked out in detail long ago: the Birkeland-Eyde process, Serpek's method, the Schönherr and the Haber-Le Rossignol processes, as well as nitrolim manufacture and so forth. We have only to set up enough machinery and work hard—very hard—and we shall be able to produce by chemical processes the material which we require. That is what the five million will have to do. There will be no idlers among them. At first it will be work in the dark, for we cannot calculate how much material we require until the agricultural experts have made their experiments upon the soil. But I understand that it is quite within the bounds of possibility that we shall be successful.

"I come now to another point. These five million survivors cannot be scattered up and down the country. They must be brought into a definite area, for two reasons. In the first place, we must have them under our control so that we can make food-distribution simple; and, in the second place, we must be able to protect them from attack. Remember, outside this area there will be millions dying of starvation, and these millions will be desperate. We can take no risks."

He took a roll from behind his chair and unfolded upon the table a large map of the British Isles marked with patches of colour.

"As to the choice of a segregation area, we are limited by various factors. We shall need coal for the basis of our work; therefore it would suit us best to place our colony near one of the coal-fields. We shall need iron for our new machinery; and it would be best to choose some centre in which foundries are already numerous. We shall need to house our five million survivors and we cannot spend time in building new cities for them. And, finally, we need a huge water-supply for that population. On this map, I have had these various factors marked in colour. In some places, as you see, three of the desiderata are co-existent; but there is only one region in which we find all four conditions satisfied—in the Clyde Valley. There you have coal and iron; there are already in existence enormous numbers of foundries and machine-shops; the city of Glasgow alone is capable of accommodating over a million human beings; and the water-supply is ample. This, I think, is sufficient to direct our choice to that spot.

"There are two further reasons why I am in favour of the Clyde Valley. It is a defensible position, for one thing.

North of it you have only a very limited population—some three millions or even less. On the south, it is far removed from the main centres of population in the Midlands and London. This will be an advantage later on. Again, second point, we have to look forward to cultivation next year. Bordering the Clyde Valley, within easy reach, lie the tracts which, before the Blight, used to be the most fertile land in the country. The fields are ready for us to sow, once we have replaced the vanished nitrogen. I think there is no better place which we could select.

"Now, gentlemen, I have put my scheme before you. I have not given you more than the outlines of it. I know that it seems visionary at first; but you must either take it or leave it. We cannot wait for Parliament or for anybody else. The thing must be done now. Will you help?"

A murmur of assent passed round the table. Even the Prime Minister joined in the common approval; and I saw Nordenholt thank him with a glance.

"Very good, gentlemen. I have most of the preliminaries worked out in sufficient detail to let us get ahead. To-morrow we meet again here at nine in the morning, and by that time I hope to have further information for each of you. In the meantime, will you be good enough to think over the points at which this scheme will touch your own special branches of industry? We have an immense amount of improvisation before us; and we must be ready for things as they come. Thank you."

He seated himself; and for the first time I realised what he had done. By sheer force of personality and a clear mind, he had carried us along with him and secured our assent to a scheme which, wild-cat though it might appear, seemed to be the only possible way out of the crisis. He had constituted himself a kind of Dictator, though without any of the trappings of the office; and no one had dared to oppose him. The cold brutality with which he had treated the politicians was apparently justified; for I now saw whither their procrastination would have led us. But I must confess that I was dazed by the rapidity with which his moves had been made. Possibly in my account I have failed to reproduce the exact series of transitions by which he passed from stage to stage. I was too intent at the time to take clear mental notes of what occurred; but I believe that I have at least drawn a picture which comes near to the reality.

The meeting was at its end. Nordenholt went across to speak to the Prime Minister; while the others began to leave the room in groups of two and three. I moved towards the door, when Nordenholt looked up and caught my eye.

"Just wait a minute, Flint, please."

He continued his earnest talk with the Premier for a few minutes, then handed over an envelope containing a bulky mass of papers. At last he came to me and we went out together.

"You might come round to my place for a short time, Flint," he said. "My car is waiting for us. I want you to be one of my right-hand men in this business and there are some things I wish to explain to you now. It may not seem altogether relevant to you; but I think it is necessary if we are to work together well."

VI THE PSYCHOLOGY OF THE BREAKING-STRAIN

With my entry into Nordenholt's house I hoped to gain a clearer insight into certain sides of his character; for the possessions which a man accumulates about him serve as an index to his mind even when his reticence gives no clue to his nature. I had expected something uncommon, from what I had already seen of him; but my forecasts were entirely different from the reality.

The room into which he ushered me was spacious and high-ceilinged; a heavy carpet, into the pile of which my feet sank, covered the floor; a few arm-chairs were scattered here and there; and a closed roll-top desk stood in a corner. One entire side of the room was occupied by bookshelves. Beyond this, there was nothing. It was the simplest furnishing I had ever seen; and in the house of a multi-millionaire it astonished me. I had somehow expected to find lavishness in some form: art in one or other of its interpretations, or at any rate an indication of Nordenholt's tastes. But this room defeated me by its very plainness. There appeared to be no starting-point for an analysis. To me it seemed a place where a man could think without distraction; and then, at the desk, put his thoughts into practical application.

As we entered, Nordenholt excused himself for a moment. He wished to give instructions to his secretary. Some telephoning had to be done at once; and then he would be at my disposal. I heard him go into the next room.

When I am left alone in a strange house with nothing to fill in my time, I gravitate naturally to the bookcases; so that now I mechanically moved over to the serried rows of shelves which lined one side of the room. Here at last I might get some clue to the workings of Nordenholt's mind. Glancing along the backs of the volumes, I found that the first shelf contained only works on metaphysics and psychology. Somewhat puzzled by this selection, I passed from tier to tier, and still no other subject came in view. A rapid examination of the cases from end to end showed me that the entire library dealt with this single theme, the main bulk of the works being psychological.

This discovery overturned in my mind several nebulous conjectures which I had begun to form as to Nordenholt's character. What sort of a man was this, a millionaire, reputed to be one of the shrewdest financiers of the day, who stocked his study entirely with psychological works among which not a single financial book of reference was to be found? Coupled with the stark simplicity of the furniture, this clue seemed unlikely to lead me far.

As I was pondering, the door opened and Nordenholt returned. While it was still ajar, I heard the trill of a telephone bell and a girl's voice giving a number; then the door closed and cut off further sounds. Thus after ten minutes in his house I had gathered only three things about him: he was simple, almost Spartan, in his tastes; he was interested in psychology; and his secretary was a girl and not a man.

He came forward towards me; and again I had the sensation of command in his appearance. His great height and easy movements may have accounted for it in part; but I am taller than the average myself; so that it was not entirely this. Even now I cannot analyse the feeling which he produced, not on myself alone, but upon all those with whom he came in contact. Personal magnetism may satisfy some people as an explanation; but what is personal magnetism but a name? In some inexplicable manner, Nordenholt gave the impression of a vast reservoir of pent-up force, seldom unloosed but ever ready to spring into action if required; and in these unfathomable eyes there seemed to brood an uncanny and yet not entirely unsympathetic perception which chilled me with its aloofness and nevertheless drew me to him in some way which is not clear to me even now. Under that slow and minute inspection, eye to eye, I felt all my human littleness, all my petty weaknesses exposed and weighed; but I felt also that behind this unrelenting scrutiny there was a depth of understanding which struck an even balance and saved me from contempt. I can put it no better than that.

He motioned me to a chair and took another himself. For a few moments he remained silent; and when he spoke I was struck by the change in his tone. At the meeting, he had spoken decisively, almost bitterly at times; but now a ring of sadness entered into that great musical voice.

"I wonder, Flint," he said, "I wonder if you understand what we have taken in hand to-day? I doubt if any of us see where all this is leading us. I see the vague outlines of it before us; but beyond a certain point one cannot go."

He paused, deep in thought for a few seconds; then, as though waking suddenly to life again, offered me a cigar and took one himself. When he spoke again, it was in a different tone.

"Perhaps you wonder why I picked you out—of course it was I who got you invited to that meeting; I wanted to look you over there before making up my mind about you. Well, I have means of knowing about people; and you struck me as the man I needed in this work. I've been watching you for some years, Flint; ever since you made your mark, in fact. You aren't one of my young men—the ones they call 'Nordenholt's gang,' I believe—but you are of my kind; and I knew that I could get you if I wanted you for something big."

In any other man this would have struck me as insolence; but Nordenholt had already established such an influence over me that I felt flattered rather than ruffled by this calm assumption on his part.

"But in some ways it's a disadvantage now that we didn't come together earlier," he continued. "You remember Nelson and his captains—the band of brothers? Nothing can be accomplished on a grand scale without that feeling; and possibly I have left it until too late to get into touch with you. It depends on yourself, Flint. I know you, possibly as well as you know yourself; but you know nothing of me. With my young men," and a tinge of pride came into his voice, "with my young men, that difficulty doesn't arise. They know me as well as anyone can—well enough, at any rate, for us to work together for a common object, no matter how big the stake may be. But you, Flint, represent a foreign mind in the machine. I want you to understand some things; in fact, it's essential that you should see the lines on which I work; for otherwise we shall be at cross-purposes. I wonder how it can be done?"

He leaned back in his chair and smoked silently for a few minutes. I said nothing; for I was quite content to await whatever he had to put into words. I only wondered what form it would take. When he broke the silence, it was on quite unexpected lines. He looked at his watch.

"Three hours yet before we can do anything further. I might as well spend part of it on this; and possibly I can give you an idea of my outlook on things which will help you when we are working together up North.

"When I was quite a child, Flint, I used to take a certain delight in doing things which had an element of risk in them—physical risk, I mean. I liked to climb difficult trees, to work my way out on to dangerous bits of roof, to walk across tree-trunks spanning streams, and so forth. There's that element of risk at the back of all real enjoyment, to my mind. It needn't be physical risk necessarily, though there you have it in perhaps its most acute aspect; but at the root of a gamble of any sort where the stakes are high you find this factor lying, whether it is noticeable or not.

"One of my earliest experiences in that direction took the form of walking along a slippery wall which was high enough to make a fall from it a serious matter. I mastered the art of keeping on the wall to perfection; and then, finding that pall upon me, I endeavoured to complicate it by jumping across the gap made by a gateway. It was an easy distance: I proved that to myself by practising on the ground from a standing take-off. And the nature of the wall offered no particular difficulty, for I tested myself in jumping a similar gap between two slippery tree-trunks laid end to end. Yet when I came to the actual gap in the wall, my muscles simply refused to obey me; and time after time I drew back involuntarily from the spring.

"I was an introspective child; and this puzzled me. I knew that I could accomplish the feat with ease; and yet something prevented my attempting it. I fell to analysing my sensations and tracing down the various factors in the case; and, of course, it was not long until I came to the crucial point. Does this bore you? I am sorry if it does, but you'll see the point of it by-and-by."

While he had been speaking, I had had a most curious impression. His argument, whatever it might be, was evidently addressed to me; and yet all through it I had the feeling that it was not altogether to me that he was talking. In some way I gathered the idea that while he spoke to me his mind was working upon another line, testing and re-testing some chain of reasoning which was illustrated by his anecdote; so that while I looked upon one aspect of it he was scanning the same facts from a totally different point of view and reading into them something which I was not intended to grasp.

"Obviously the crux of the matter was the height of the wall and the fear of hurting myself severely if I missed my leap," he continued. "Once I had discovered that—and of course it took much less time to do so than it takes now to explain the case—I set about another trial. I made up my mind that I would think nothing of the chance of slipping, and that this time I would accomplish the feat with ease. Yet once more I failed to bring my body up to the effort. Something stronger than my consciousness was at work; and it defeated me."

He smiled sardonically at some memory or other.

"I practised jumping along a marked portion of the wall where it was lower; and I found that I could accomplish the distance with ease. Whereupon my childish mind formulated the problem in this way; and I believe that it was correct in doing so. The ultimate factor in the thing was the fear of a damaging fall. Within limits, I was prepared to take the risk; as had been shown by the success on the lower parts of the wall. But at the high place beside the gateway, my resolution had given way under a strain of nervousness. And at once there came into my mind the conception of a breaking-strain. Up to a certain tension, my conscious mind worked perfectly; but, beyond that, there was a complete collapse. Something had snapped under the strain. I may say that I finally accomplished the leap successfully; I simply wouldn't allow myself to be beaten in a thing I knew I could do."

He halted for a moment as though this marked a turning-point in his thoughts.

"This idea of the breaking-strain remained fixed in my child's mind, however; and I used to amuse myself by conjecturing all sorts of hypothetical cases in which it played a part. It finally grew to be a sort of mild obsession with me, and I would ask myself continually: "Why did So-and-so do this rather than that?" and would then set to work to discover the factors at the back of his actions and the tension-snap which had driven him into something which was unexpected from his normal line of conduct.

"You can understand, Flint, how this practice grew upon me. It is the most interesting thing in the world; and the materials for applying it are everywhere about us in our everyday life. I extracted endless amusement from it; and as I grew up into boyhood I found its fascination greater than ever. I took a never-failing interest in probing at the hidden springs of conduct and trying to establish these breaking-strains in the people before me.

"Then, as I grew older I discovered the Law Courts. There you see the philosophy of the breaking-strain brought into touch with real life in a practical form. I used to go and watch some well-known barrister handling a hostile witness; and suddenly I understood that all these men were merely fumbling empirically after the thing that I had studied from my earliest days. What does a barrister want to do with a hostile witness? To break him down, to throw him out of his normal line of thought and then to fish among the dislocated machinery for something which suits his own case. It afforded me endless interest to follow the methods of each different cross-examiner. I learned a great deal in the Courts; and I came away from them convinced that I had found something of more than mere academic interest. This breaking-strain question was one which could be applied to affairs of the greatest practical importance. It was actually so applied in law cases. Why not utilise it in other directions also?"

I found him watching me keenly to see if I followed his line of thought. After a moment, he went on:

"It sounds so obvious now, Flint; but I believe that I alone saw it as a scientific problem. Your blackmailer, your poker-sharp, all those types of mind had been working on the thing in a crude way; but to me it appeared from a different angle. Everyone else had looked on it in the form of special cases, particular men who had to be swayed by particular motives. I began as a youth where they left off. I spent some years on it, Flint, examining it in all its bearings; and finally I evolved a system of classification which enabled me to approach any specific case along general lines. I can't go into that now; but it suddenly gave me an insight into motives and actions such as I doubt if anyone ever had before."

He paused and watched the smoke curling up from his cigar. Again he seemed to be deep in the consideration of some problem connected with and yet alien to what he had been saying. For a time he was lost in thought; and I waited to hear the rest of the story.

"Well, Flint," he went on at last, "it certainly seemed on the face of it to be a very useless accomplishment from the practical point of view; from the standpoint of mere cash, I mean. And yet, it still fascinated me. When I was quite a young man I determined to go to Canada and take up lumber. I was an orphan; there was nothing to keep me in this country, for I had no near relations; and I felt that it might do me good to cut loose from things here and go away into the woods for a time. I had enough capital to start in a small way; so I went. My ideas of the lumber-trade were vague at the time. If I had known what it was, I doubt if I should have touched it.

"At first sight, it looked a hopeless venture. I knew nothing of the trade; I was a youngster then; I'd had no training in financial operations. Failure seemed to be the only outcome; and the men on the spot laughed at me. I simply would not admit that I was beaten at the start; and everything drove me on against my better judgment. And I had one tremendous asset. I knew men.

"I knew men better than anyone else out there. I never made a mistake in my choice. I collected a few good men at the start to help me; and through them I gathered others almost as good. In a year I had made progress; in two years I was a success; and very soon I became somebody to reckon with. And through it all, Flint, I knew practically nothing about the actual trade. That was only a tool in my hands. What I dealt in was men and men's minds. I could gauge a man's capacity to a hair; and I picked my managers and foremen from the very best. They were glad to come to me, somehow. They felt I understood them; and no inefficients were comfortable with me. I never had to discharge them; they simply went of their own accord. I left everything to my staff, for I knew them thoroughly and gauged their capacities to a degree. And because I knew them I found the right place for each man; so that the work went forward with perfect smoothness and efficiency. Before I had been five years there I was on the road to being a rich man."

His tone expressed no satisfaction. It was clear that I was not expected to admire his talents.

"Then, suddenly, came the discovery of platinum on a large scale in the neighbourhood of my district. You know what that meant; but you must remember that in those days it was a very different matter from now. It was like the Yukon gold rush in some of its aspects. The place swarmed with prospectors, mostly men of no education, whose main object was to get as much as they could in a hurry and then go elsewhere to spend the money the platinum brought them. Meanwhile, the platinum market was convulsed, and the price swayed to and fro from day to day. You must remember that in those times the thing was in the hands of a very few men; for the supply was limited. The Canadian mines overthrew the nicely-adjusted balance of the market and everything suffered in consequence; for the uses of platinum directly or indirectly spread over a very large field of human industry."

That part of his history was more or less familiar to me, but I did not interrupt.

"One day it occurred to me that here in Canada we had a case parallel to the state of affairs in the Diamond Fields before the Kimberley amalgamation. Why not repeat Cecil Rhodes' methods? Just as he regulated the price of diamonds, I could regulate the price of platinum if I could get control of the Canadian mines, for they were by far the most important in the world.

"Again, I knew nothing of platinum, just as I had known nothing of lumber; but I was able to pay for the best advice, to pay for secrecy as well; and to judge the experts, I had my knowledge of men to help me. I got the best men, I chose only men whom my insight enabled me to pick out; and I began to buy up claims quietly under their guidance. Here again psychology came in. I could tell at a glance when a man was a "quitter" and when a miner would refuse to sell. I could gauge almost to a sovereign the price that would prove the breaking-strain for any particular owner. I can't tell you how it is done; it is partly inborn, perhaps, partly acquired; but I know that my knowledge is quite incommunicable.

"To make a long story short, I had acquired a very fair percentage of the valuable ground when suddenly I discovered that five other men had been struck with the same idea; and that prices were rising beyond anything I could hope to pay. It was a case for amalgamation; but I did not see my way through it quite so simply. Two of them I knew to be honest. One of them I could not trust, although he had hitherto never shown any signs of crookedness; but I knew his breaking-strain, and I knew also that the temptations to which he would be exposed under any amalgamation scheme would be too great for him. He had to be eliminated. The other two were weak men who could be dealt with easily enough. I needn't give you the details. I approached the two honest men, combined with them, and with the joint capital of the three of us I bought out the third competitor. The other two we dealt with separately, buying out the one and taking the other in along with us. My partners trusted me with the negotiations, again because I knew men and their motives.

"And that was how I made my first million. Remember, I knew nothing about the materials I had handled in the making of it. I never took the slightest interest in the things themselves—and I took very little interest in the money either, for my tastes are simple. What did interest me was the psychology of the thing, the probing among the springs and levers of men's minds, and the working out of all the complex strains and stresses which form the background of our reason and our emotions. The million was a mere by-product of the process.

"But with the million there came another interest. Up to that time I had applied my methods to individual cases; but it struck me, after the strain of the amalgamation negotiations was over, that my generalisations were capable of a wider application. I took up the study of political affairs over here; and I found that my principles enabled me to gauge the psychology of masses even more easily than those of individuals. As a practical test, I stood for Parliament; and got elected without any difficulty. Of course one of the Parties was glad to have me—a millionaire isn't likely to go a-begging at their door for long—but you may remember that I won that election by my own methods. The Party machines tried to copy them, of course, at a later date; but they failed hopelessly because they were merely repeating mechanically some operations which I had designed for a special case.

"I took very little interest in politics, though. I had no sympathy with the usual methods of the politicians; and at times I revolted against them effectually."

He was evidently thinking of the two episodes which had gained him the nickname of the Wrecker.

"When I began, I think I told you that the element of risk enters largely into one's pleasures; and I believe that holds good in politics. The work of a politician, and especially of a Cabinet Minister, is largely in the nature of a gamble. To most of them, politics is an empirical science; for they have little time to study the basis of it. I'll do them the justice to say that I don't think it is a mere matter of clinging to their salaries which keeps them in office; it's mainly that they enjoy the feeling of swaying great events. With an Empire like ours, the stakes are tremendous; and there's a certain sensation to be got out of gambling on that scale. Mind you, I doubt if they realise themselves that this is what they enjoy in the political game; but it is actually what does sway them to a great extent.

"Now so long as it's a mere question of some parochial point, I don't mind their enjoying their sensations. It matters very little in the long run whether one Bill or another passes Parliament; and if they fight over minor questions, I don't care. But twice in my political career I saw that the Party game was threatening trouble on bigger lines. The Anglo-Peruvian agreement and the Malotu Islands question were affairs that cut down to the bed-rock of things; and I couldn't stand aside and see them muddled in the usual way. I had to assert myself there, whether I liked it or not. And when I did intervene, my mental equipment made the result a certainty. *I* knew the country and the country's average opinion in a way that none of them did; and I had only to strike at the vital point. They call me the Wrecker; and I suppose I did bring down two Governments on these questions; but it wasn't so difficult for me.

"But, as I told you, I never had much interest in politics. I like real things; and the political game is more than half make-believe. I still have my seat in the House; but I think they are gladdest when I am not there.

"Well, I am afraid I'm making a long story of it; but I think you will see the drift of it now. Politics failed to give me what I wanted. I had no turn for the routine of it; and I had no wish to be involved in all the petty manoeuvres upon which the nursing of a majority depends. Mind you, I could have done it better than any of them, with that peculiar bent of mine. They consult me whenever a crisis arises; and I can generally pull them through. After all, it's a case of handling men, there as everywhere else.

"However, I wanted something better to amuse me than the squaring of some nonentity with a knighthood or the pacification of some indignant office-seeker who had been passed over. I wanted to feel myself pitted against men who really were experts in their own line. And that was how I came to take up finance in earnest."

He paused again and lighted a fresh cigar. While he was doing so, I watched his face. In any other man, his autobiographic sketch would have seemed egotistical; and possibly I have raised that impression in my reproduction of it; for I can only give the sense of what he said. I cannot put on paper the tones of his voice—the faint tinge of contempt with which he spoke of his triumphs, as though they were child's play. Nor can I do more than indicate here and there that peculiar sensation of duality which his talk took on more and more clearly as he proceeded. It was as though the Nordenholt whom I saw before me were telling his story whilst over behind him stood some greater personality, following the narrative and tracing out in it the clues which were to lead on to some events still in the distant future.

"Finance, Flint," he continued. "That was the field where I came into my own at last. Money in itself is nothing, nothing whatever. But the making of money, the duel of brain against brain with not even the counters on the table, that's the great game. The higher branches of finance are simply a combination of arithmetic and psychology. They're divorced absolutely from any idea of material gain or loss. Railways, steamship lines, coal, oil, wheat, cotton or wool—do you imagine that one thinks of these concrete things while one plays the game? Not at all. They are the merest pawns. The whole affair is compressed into groups of figures and the glimpses of the other man's brain which one gets here and there throughout the operations. And I played a straight game, Flint; no small investor was ever ruined through my manoeuvres. I doubt if any other financier can say as much. I went into the thing as a game, a big, risky game for my own hand; and I refused to gamble in the savings of little men. I took my gains from the big men who opposed me, not from the swarm of innocents."

It was true, I remembered. Nordenholt had played the game of finance in a way never seen before. He had made many men's fortunes—a by-product, as he would have said, no doubt—but no one had ever gone into the arena unwarned by him. When he had laid his plans, carried out his preliminary moves and was ready to strike, a full-page advertisement had appeared in every newspaper in the country. "MR. NORDENHOLT ADVISES THE SMALL INVESTOR TO REFRAIN FROM OPERATING IN WHEAT," or whatever it might be that he proposed to deal in himself. Then, after giving time for this to take effect, he struck his first blow. Wonderful struggles these were, fought out often far in the depths of that strange sea of finance, so that hardly a ripple came to the surface. Often, too, the agitation reached the upper waters and there would be glimpses of the two vast organisations convulsed by their efforts; here a mass of foam only, there some strange tentacle stretching out to reach its prey or to coil itself around a vantage-point which it could use as a fulcrum in further exertions. During this period, the Exchanges of the world would be shaken, there would be failures, hammerings, ruin for those who had ventured into the contest despite the warnings. Then, suddenly, the cascading waves would be stilled. One of the antagonists had gone under.

A fresh advertisement would appear: "MR. NORDEN-HOLT HAS CEASED HIS OPERATIONS." It was a strange requiem over the grave of some king of finance. Norden-holt was always victorious. And with the collapse of his opponent, the small speculators flocked into the markets of the world and completed the downfall.

Finally, after the gains had been counted, he advertised again asking all those who had involuntarily suffered by his contest to submit their claims to him; and every genuine case was paid in full. He could afford it, no doubt; but how many would have done it? I knew from that move of his that he really spoke the truth when he said that money in itself was nothing to him. And it perhaps illustrates as well as anything the impression he produced upon my mind that afternoon. On the one side he was cold, calculating, pitiless to those whom he regarded as his enemies and the enemies of the smaller investor; on the other, he was full of understanding and compassion for those whom he had maimed in the course of his gigantic operations. The Wheat Trust, the Cotton Combine, Consolidated Industries, the Steel Magnates, and the Associated Railways, all had gone down before him; and he had ground their leaders into the very dust. And in every case, he had opened his campaign as soon as they had shown signs of using their power to oppress the common people. It may have been merely a move in his psychological strategy; he may have waited until the man in the street had begun to be uneasy for the future, so that this great intangible mass of opinion was enlisted on his side. But I prefer to think otherwise: and I was associated with Nordenholt in the end as closely as any man. No one ever knew him, no one ever fathomed that personality—of that I am certain. He was always a riddle. But I believe that his cool intelligence, his merciless tactics, all had behind them a depth of understanding and a sympathy with the helpless minority. I know this is almost incredible in face of his record; but I am convinced of its truth.

"At the end of it all," he went on, "I can look back and say that my theories were justified. I knew nothing of finance;

but I chose my advisers well. I knew what my opponents relied upon and what they regarded as points which could be given up without affecting their general position. The rest was simply a matter of psychology. How could I bring the breaking-strain to bear?

"Well, when I left it, the financial world had handed over to me a fortune which, I suppose, has seldom been equalled. There was nothing in it, you know, Flint, nothing whatever. It merely happened that I was trained in a way different from everyone else. They were plotting and scheming with shares and stocks and debentures, skying this one, depressing that one and keeping their attention fixed on the Exchanges. I came to the thing from a different angle. The movements of the markets meant little to me in comparison with the workings of the brains behind those markets. I could foresee the line of their advance; and I knew how to take them in the flank at the right moment. I fought them on ground they could not understand. They knew the mind of the small investor thoroughly, for they had fleeced him again and again. I began by clearing the small speculator off the board; and thus they were deprived of their trump card. They had to fight me instead of ruining him; and they had no idea what I was. It was incredibly simple, when you think of it. That is why you never found anything about my personality in the newspapers. I paid them to leave me alone. No one knew me; and I was able to fight in the dark.

"But when I grew tired of it at last, I had an enormous fortune. What was I to do with it? Money in itself one can do nothing with. If I were put to it, I doubt if I could spend £5,000 a year and honestly say that I had got value for it—I mean direct personal enjoyment. I cast about for some use to which I could turn this enormous mass of wealth. You may smile, Flint, but it is one of the most difficult problems I ever took up. I hate waste; and I wanted to see some direct, practical value for all these accumulated millions. What was I to do?

"I looked back on the work of some of my predecessors. Carnegie used to spend his money on libraries; but do libraries yield one any intimate satisfaction? Can one really say that they would give one a feeling that one's money had been spent to a good purpose? Apparently they did to him; but that sort of thing wouldn't appeal to me. Then there is art. Pierpont Morgan amassed a huge collection; but there again I don't feel on safe ground. Is one's money merely to go in accumulating painted canvas for the elect to pore over? The man in the street cannot appreciate these things even if he could see them. I gave up that idea.

"Then I came across a life of Cecil Rhodes and he seemed to be more akin to me in some ways. Empire building is a big thing and, if you believe in Empires, it's a good thing. There is something satisfactory in knowing that you are preparing the way for future generations, laying the foundations in the desert and awaiting the tramp of those far-off generations which will throng the streets of the unbuilt cities. A great dream, Flint. One needs a prospicience and a fund of hope to deal in things like that. But I want to see results in my own day; I want to be sure that I'm on the right lines and not merely rearing a dream-fabric which will fade out and pass away long before it has its chance of materialisation. I want something which I can see in action now and yet something which will go down from generation to generation.

"I thought long over it, Flint. Time and again I seemed to glimpse what I wanted; and yet it eluded me. Then, suddenly, I realised that I had the very thing at my gates. Youth.

"All over the world there are youngsters growing up who will be stifled in their development by mere financial troubles. They have the brains and the character to make good in time; but at what a cost! All their best energy goes in fulfilling the requirements of our social system, getting a roof over their heads, climbing the ladder step by step, waiting for dead men's shoes. Then, when they come to their own, more often than not their heart's desire has withered. I don't mean that they are failures; but they have used up their powers in overcoming those minor difficulties which beset us all. It was an essay of Huxley's that brought the thing clearly before me. 'If the nation could purchase a potential Watt, or Davy, or Faraday, at the cost of £100,000 down,' he said, 'he would be dirt-cheap at the money.' And with that, in a flash, I saw my way clear. I would go about in search of these potential leaders among our youth. My peculiar insight would suffice to keep me on the right lines there. I would make the way easy for them, but not too easy. I would test and re-test them till I was sure of them. And then I would give them all that they desired and open up the world to them to work out their destinies.

"I did it in time. Even now I'm only at the beginning of the experiment, but already I feel that I have spent my money well. I have given a push to things; and although I can see no further than this generation, I know that I have opened a road for the next. Each of them is a centre for others to congregate around and so the thing spreads like the circles in a pool. I have thrown in the stone; but long after I am gone the waves will be beating outward and breaking upon unknown shores. . . ."

He paused and seemed to fall into a day-dream for a few moments. Then he spoke again.

"That was the origin of my young men, Flint; the Nordenholt gang"—he sneered perceptibly at the words. "Many of them have gone down in the race. One cannot foresee everything, you know, try as one may. But the residuum are a picked lot. They are scattered throughout all the industries and professions of the Empire; and all of them are far up in their own pursuits. I often wondered whether anything would come of it in my day beyond individual successes; but now I see a culmination before me. We shall all go up side by side to Armageddon and my own men will be with me in this struggle against the darkness. Man never put his hand to a bigger task than this in front of us; and I shall need my young men to help me. If we fail, the Earth falls back beyond the Eolithic Age once more and Man has lived in vain."

His voice had risen with pride as he spoke of his helpers; but at the close I heard again the sub-current of sadness come into the deep tones. I had been jarred by his exposition at the meeting, by his apparent callousness in outlook; but now I thought I saw behind the mask.

Again he sat pondering for some moments; but at last he threw off his preoccupation; and when he spoke it was more directly to me than hitherto.

"Possibly you may wonder, Flint, why it is that with all these resources in my hands I have come to you for help; and why I have never approached you before. The fact is, I watched you from your start and stood by to help you if you needed me; but you made good alone, and I never interfere with a man unless it is absolutely necessary. You made good without my assistance; and I thought too well of you to offer any. But I watched you, as I said—I have my own ways of getting information—and I knew that you were just the man I required for a particular section of the work in front of us. Your factory organisation showed me that. There will be an enormous task before you; but I know that you'll be the right man in the right place. I never make a mistake, when it is a case of this kind. You aren't an untried man."

From anyone else, I would have regarded this as clumsy flattery; but so great an influence had Nordenholt acquired over me even in that single afternoon that I never looked at the matter in that light at all. His manner showed no patronage or admiration; it seemed merely that he was stating facts as he knew them, without caring much about my opinion.

"But it seems to me," he went on, "that I've talked enough about personal affairs already. I want to try to give you some views on the main thing in front of us. You and I, Flint, have been born and grown up in the midst of this civilisation; and I expect that you, like most other people, have been oblivious of the changes which have come about; for they have been so gradual that very few of us have noticed them at all.

"When you begin low down in the scale of Creation, you find creatures without any specialised organs. The simplest living things are just spots of protoplasm, mere aggregations of cells, each of which performs functions common to them all. Then, step by step as you rise in the scale, specialisation sets in: the cells become differentiated from one another; and each performs a function of its own. You get the cells of the nerves receiving and transmitting sensation; you get cells engaged in nutrition processes; there are other cells devoted to producing motion. And with this specialisation you get the dawn of something which apparently did not exist before: the structure as a whole acquires a personality of its own, distinct from the individualities of the cells which go to build it up.

"But the inverse process is also possible. When the body as a whole suffers death, you still have a certain period during which the cells have an existence. Hair grows after death, for example.

"Now if you look at the trend of civilisation, you will see that we are passing into a stage of specialisation. In the Middle Ages, a man might be a celebrated artist and yet be in the forefront of the science of his day—like Leonardo da Vinci; but in our time you seldom find a man who is first-class in more than one line. In the national body, each individual citizen is a specialised cell; and if he diverged from his normal functions he would disorganise the machine, just as a cancer cell disorganises the body in which it grows.

"But this civilisation of ours has come to the edge of its grave. It is going to die. There is no help for it. What I fear is that in its death-throe it may destroy even the hope of a newer and perhaps better civilisation in the future. It is going to starve to death; and a starving organism is desperate. So long as it retains its present organised and coherent life, it will be a danger to us; and for our own safety—I mean the safety of the future generations—we must disorganise it as soon as possible. We must throw it back at a step, if we can, to the old unspecialised conditions; for then it will lose its most formidable powers and break up of itself. Did you ever read Hobbes? He thought of the State as a great Leviathan, an artificial man of greater strength and stature than the natural man, for whose protection and defence it was contrived; and the soul of this artificial creature he found in sovereignty. How can we bring about the *débâcle* of this huge organism? That is the problem I have been facing this afternoon.

"The Leviathan's life-blood is the system of communications throughout the country; and I doubt if we can cripple that sufficiently rapidly and effectively to bring about the downfall. It would take too long and excite too much opposition if we did it thoroughly. We must have something subtler, Flint, something which will strike at each individual intelligence and isolate it from its fellows as far as possible. It's my old problem of the breaking-strain again on the very widest scale. We must find some psychological weapon to help us. Nothing else will do."

It seemed as though he were appealing to me for suggestions; but I had nothing to offer. I had never considered such a problem; and at first sight it certainly seemed insoluble. Given that men already had the certainty of death before them, what stronger motive could one bring to bear?

"I must think over it further," he said at last, "I think I see a glimmering of some possibilities. After all, it's my own line."

He dropped the subject and seemed to sink into his own thoughts for a time. When he broke the silence once more, it was on an entirely different subject.

"I wonder if you ever read the Norse mythology, Flint? No? Well, you've missed something. The gods of Greece were a poor lot, a kind of divine collection of Fermiers Généreaux with much the same tastes; but the Scandinavian divinities were in a different class. They were human in a way; but their humanity wasn't of the baser sort. And over them all hung that doom of Ragnarök, their Twilight, when the forces of Evil would be loosed for the final struggle to bring darkness upon the earth. It's the strangest forecast of our present crisis. As Ragnarök drew near, brother was to turn against brother; bloodshed was to sweep the land. Then was to come the Winter, three years long, when all trees were to fail and all fruits to perish, while the race of men died by hunger and cold and violence. And with Ragnarök the very Gods themselves were to pass away in their struggle with all the Forces of Evil and Darkness.

"But they were only half-gods, deified men. Behind them, the All-Father stood; and beyond that time of terror there lay the hope of Gimle, the new age when all would again be young and fair.

"I look beyond these coming horrors to a new Gimle, Flint; a time when Earth will renew her youth and we shall shake free from all the trammels which this dying civilisation has twined about our feet. It will come, I feel sure. But only a few of us leaders will see it. The strain will be too much for us; only the very toughest will survive. But each of us must work to the very last breath to save something upon which we can build anew. There must be no shrinking in either will or emotion. I warn you that it will be terrible. To save mankind from the terror of the giants, Odin gave his eye to Mimir in return for a draught of the Well of Knowledge. Some of us will have to give our lives. . . . A few of us will lose our very souls. . . . It will be worth it!"

I was amazed to find this train of mysticism in that cold mind. Yet, after all, is it surprising? Almost all the great men of history have been mystics of one kind or another. Nordenholt rose; and something which had burned in his eyes died out suddenly. He went to the roll-top desk and took from it a bundle of papers.

"Here are your instructions, Flint. Everything has been foreseen, I think, for the start. Follow them implicitly as far as they go; and after that I trust you to carry out the further steps which you will see are required."

As he was shaking hands with me, another thought seemed to strike him.

"By the way, of course you understand that the whole of this scheme depends for success on our being able to exterminate these bacilli? If we cannot do that, they will simply attack any nitrogenous manure which we use. I am putting my bacteriologists on to the problem at once; but in any case the nitrogen scheme must go ahead. Without it, no success is possible, even if we destroyed *B. diazotans*. So go ahead."

His car awaited me at the door. On the drive home, I saw in the streets crowds gathered around hoarding after hoarding and staring up at enormous placards which had just been posted. The smaller type was invisible to me; but gigantic lettering caught my eye as I passed.

NITROGEN

ONE MILLION MEN WANTED

NORDENHOLT

VII NORDENHOLT'S MILLION

Of all the incidents in that afternoon, I think the sight of these placards brought home to me most forcibly two of the salient characteristics of Nordenholt's many-sided mind: his foresight and his self-reliance. Their appearance in the streets at that moment showed that they formed part of a plan which had been decided upon several days in advance, since time had to be allowed for printing and distributing them; whilst the fact that they were being posted up within two hours of the close of the meeting proved that Nordenholt had never had the slightest doubt of his success in dominating the Ministers.

Later on, I became familiar with these posters. They were not identical by any means; and I learned to expect a difference in their wording according to the district in which they were posted up. The methods of varied personal appeal had long been familiar to the advertising world; but I found that Nordenholt had broken away from tradition and had staked everything upon his knowledge of the human mind. In these advertisements his psychological instinct was developed in an uncanny degree which was clear enough to me, who knew the secret; but I doubt if any man without my knowledge would have seen through the superficial aspect of them quite so readily.

In this first stage of his campaign he had to conceal his hand. The advertisements were merely the first great net which he spread in order to capture every man who would be at all likely to be useful to him, while the meshes had to be left wide enough to allow the undesirable types to slip through. The proclamations—for they really took this form—set forth concisely the exact danger which threatened the food-supply of the country; explained why it was essential that immense masses of nitrogenous material must be manufactured; and called for the immediate enrolment of volunteers from selected trades and professions.

As a primary inducement, the scale of remuneration offered was far above the normal pay in any given line. It was, in fact, so high that I fell at once to calculating the approximate total of wages which would be payable weekly; and the figures took me by surprise when I worked them out. No single private fortune, however gigantic, could have kept the machinery running for even a few months at the uttermost. When I pointed this out to Nordenholt he seemed amused and rather taken aback; but his surprise was at my obtuseness and not at my calculations.

"Well, I'm slightly astonished, Flint. I thought you would have seen deeper into it than that. Hasn't it occurred to you that within six weeks money, as we understand it, will be valueless? If we pay up during the time we are getting things arranged, that will be all that is required. Once the colony is founded, there will be no trade between it and the outside world, naturally; and inside our own group we could arrange any type of currency we choose. But, as a matter of fact, we shall go on just as usual; and Treasury notes sufficient for the purpose are already being printed."

But the cash inducement was not the only one upon which he relied even in his preliminary moves. Patriotism, the spirit of public service, the promise of opportunities for talent and many other driving forces were enlisted in the campaign. These more specialised appeals were mainly sent out in the form of advertisements in the newspapers—great whole-page announcements which appeared in unusual places in the journals. I suppose to a man of enormous wealth most things are possible, especially when the wealth is coupled with a personality like Nordenholt's; but it certainly amazed me to find his advertisements taking the place of the normal "latest news" space in many papers. Nor was this the only way in which his influence made itself felt. The editorial comments, and even the news columns of the journals, dealt at length with his scheme; and he secured the support of papers which were quite above any suspicion of being amenable to outside influence. On the face of it, of course, his plans—so far as they were made public—were obviously sound; but I cannot help feeling that below this almost unanimous chorus of praise in the leading articles there must be some influence at work beyond mere casual approbation. Very probably Nordenholt had seen his way to enlist the sympathy of editors by some more direct methods, possibly by calling the controllers of policy together and utilising his magnetic personality and persuasive powers.

In my own field of work at the first I found some difficulties in my dealings with the Trades Union officials, who were suspicious of our methods. They feared that we contemplated dilution on a huge scale; and they were anxious to know the details of our plans. I consulted Nordenholt on the point and found him prepared.

"Of course that was bound to arise as soon as we began to move on a big scale. Well, you can assure them that we shall act strictly according to the law of the matter. Promise them that as far as working conditions go, we shall begin by letting the men fix their own hours of work; and if any man is dissatisfied with these, we will pay him on the spot a bonus of six months' wages and let him leave instantly if he so desires. "Point out to them that, in the cases of some trades, I may have to enlist the majority of the Unionists in the country; and that I am not going to tie their hands by any previous arrangements: they shall settle the matter for themselves. If that doesn't satisfy them, you may tell them definitely—and put it in writing if they wish—that under no circumstances will I expect my employés to work for longer hours or less pay than any other Trades Unionist in the country."

I jotted the phrase down in my pocket-book.

"I may as well tell you, Flint, that I have given instructions to the recruiting offices. No Trades Union Leader will be engaged by me under any circumstances whatever. It's real working men that I want; and I don't think much of the Union leaders from the point of view of actual work."

He looked at me for a moment and I saw a faint smile on his face.

"It seems to me, Flint, that even yet you haven't managed to see this thing in perspective. You must really get into your mind the fact that there is going to be a clean break between the old system and the new one we are making. Look at the thing in all its bearings. Once we are up North, men shall work for me as I choose and for what I choose. There will be no Factory Acts and Trades Union regulations or any other hindrance to our affairs. They come here and try to put a spoke in my wheel? I don't mind that at all. But I do see that they are trying, whether wilfully or through sheer ignorance, to hamper this work which is essential to the race. Therefore I propose to meet them with fair words. It's not for me to enlighten their ignorance if it has persisted up to now in the face of all this. I make them that promise, and if they can't understand its meaning, that is no affair of mine. *We* know, if they're too dense to see it, that in a few months there won't be a Trades Unionist left in the country, outside the colony! There will be no wages drawn outside our frontier; so even if I paid our men nothing, still I should be keeping my promise to the strict letter."

"I see your point," I said; "all's fair and so forth?"

"Also, we shall have trouble, up there, I have no doubt. Probably there will be a ca' canny party among our recruits. They will have every chance at first. I won't interfere with them. But once the situation clears up a little, I shall deal with them—and I shall do it by the hand of their own fellows. They won't last long. Now get along and promise these officials exactly what I have told you."

I offered no criticisms of his methods. His brain was far better than mine. When I remember that he must have drafted the outlines of his scheme and arranged most of the preliminaries of its execution in less time than it would have taken me to decide upon a new factory-site, I am still lost in amazement at the combination of wide outlook and tremendous concentration of thought which the task involved.

Despite the carefully-planned deterrents which appeared in the proclamations, the recruiting was enormous from the first. "Nordenholt's Million"—as the popular phrase ran—was not really a million at all; but Nordenholt knew the influence of a round figure upon the public imagination and it was near enough for all practical purposes. He had looked on the thing in the broadest possible lines at the start, and had drawn up a rough classification for the use of the recruiting stations. To begin with, he limited the enlistment to men between the ages of twenty-five and thirty-five; though exceptional cases received special consideration. On this basis, he expected to get all the men he required. Three-quarters of a million of these were to be married men with an upper limit of four children, preferably between the ages of six and twelve. In addition to this, he was prepared to accept half a million young unmarried men. Half a million unmarried girls were also selected. The net result of this was that in the end he obtained in round numbers the following classes:

Husbands	. . . .	750,000
Wives	. . . .	750,000
Children	. . . .	2,250,000
Bachelors	. . . .	500,000
Girls	. . . .	500,000
Total	. . . .	4,750,000

That left a margin of a quarter of a million below his original estimate of five millions; and this he kept free for the time being, partly because some of the number would be made up by specialists who did not come under the general recruitment organisation and partly, possibly, for taking in at the last moment any cases which might be specially desirable.

At a later date I had an opportunity of questioning him as to his reasons in laying down this classification: and they struck me as sound.

"In the first place, I want a solid backbone to this enterprise. I get that by selecting the married men. They have got a stake in the thing already in their wives, and especially in their children. I know that the children mean the consumption of a vast quantity of food for which we shall get no direct return in the form of labour; but I believe that the steadying effect introduced by them will be worth the loss. We are going to put this colony under a strain which is about as great as human nature can bear; and I want everything on our side that can be brought there.

"Then again, they will help to form a sort of public opinion. Don't forget that the ultimate aim of this affair is to carry on the race. I could have done that by selecting bachelors and girls in equal numbers and simply going ahead on that basis. But we must have discipline; and unless you have some established order we should simply have ended by a Saturnalia. You couldn't have prevented it, considering the nervous strain we are going to put on these people. I have no use for that sort of thing; so I chose a majority of men with families, whose natural instincts are to keep down the bacchanalian element among the unmarried.

"But in addition to these married men, I needed others who had a free hand and who had only their own lives to risk. In certain lines, the unmarried man can be relied upon where the married man shivers in his shoes to some extent. That accounts for the bachelor element.

"But, since a preponderance of males over females would be bound to lead to trouble, I had to enrol enough girls to bring up the balance. Possibly they may also serve to spur on the younger men to work; and they will be able to help in the actual task before us in a good many ways, like the Munition girls of the War period."

It seemed to me then the only possible solution of the problem; and it worked in practice. We can't tell how things would have fared if any other arrangements had been made, so I must leave it at that. Anyway, I think Nordenholt enlisted two of the strongest instincts of humanity on his side in addition to the fear of hunger: and that was a definite gain.

"Nordenholt's Million" was, of course, a microcosm of the national industries. It would serve no purpose to catalogue the trades which were represented in it. Miners, iron- and steel-workers, electricians and makers of electrical machinery preponderated; but Nordenholt had looked ahead to agriculture and the needs of the population after the danger of famine was past.

In the early stages, the statistical branch—recruited from the great insurance companies—was perhaps the hardest worked of all. The most diverse problems presented themselves for treatment; and they could only be handled in the most rough-and-ready fashion until we were able to bring calculation to bear. Without the help of the actuaries, I believe that there would have been a collapse at various points, in spite of all our foresight.

I have not attempted to do more than indicate in outline the activities which engrossed us at that time. In my memory, it lives as a period of frantic and often very successful improvisation. New problems cropped up at every turn. The decision of one day might entail a recasting of plans in some field which at first sight seemed totally divorced from the question under consideration. Each line of that complex system had to be kept abreast of the rest, so that there was no disjunction, no involuntary halt for one section to come up with the remainder, no clash between two departments of the organisation. And yet, somehow, it seemed to work with more smoothness than we had expected. Behind us all, seated at the nucleus of that complex web of activities, there was Nordenholt, seldom interfering but always ready to give a sharp decision should the need arise. And I think the presence of that cool intelligence behind us had a moral effect upon our minds. He never lessened our initiative, never showed any sign of vexation when things began to go wrong. He treated us all as colleagues, though we knew that he was our master. And under his examination, difficulties seemed to fade away in our hands.

It was not until the meeting of Parliament that the Government connection with Nordenholt's scheme became known to the public; but on the first day of the session the Prime Minister introduced a Bill which subsequently became the Billeting Act; and this brought to light the fact that Nordenholt was not working merely as a private individual. Under the Act, the Government took powers to house the Nitrogen Volunteers, as they were termed, in any locality which might be found necessary. The wording of the Act gave them the fullest power in this matter; but it was so contrived that no one suspected the establishment of only a single Nitrogen Area.

In his speech on the second Reading, the Premier excelled all his previous tactical exercises. He explained very clearly the nature of the peril which threatened the country; and he pointed out that the measure was necessary in order to cope with the danger. The new Nitrogen work would entail great shiftings of labour hither and thither, as the new factories grew up; and it was essential to provide dwellings for the artisans engaged in the industry. Everything must give way to this; and since houses could not be built in the short time available, some sort of arrangement must be made which would, he hoped, be merely temporary. He explained that the Government had empowered Nordenholt to carry out the early arrangements; and he was able to give statistics showing the progress which had already been made during the last few days.

At the same time, he introduced a second Bill, somewhat on the lines of the old Defence of the Realm Act, which enabled the Government to cope with circumstances as they arose without the necessity of prolonged Parliamentary debates.

So ingeniously did he handle the matter that there was practically no opposition to either measure. It must be remembered that the influence of the Press had been exerted almost entirely in favour of Nordenholt's scheme. The previous clamour for action had been succeeded by a chorus of praise; and the bold initiative shown in the Nitrogen plans had been acclaimed throughout the country.

Meanwhile, Nordenholt was making the best of two worlds. Nominally, he was engaged in a private enterprise over which the Government had no control; actually, he had the whole State machinery at his back to assist him in his operations. This dual nature of the matter enabled him to carry out his work with a minimum of interference from red taped officials, while at the same time he was able to command the resources of State Departments in any line wherein they could be of service to him. After the passing of the two Acts, the Government adjourned Parliament, to avoid the putting of awkward questions; so that during the ensuing weeks the Nitrogen undertaking could progress without any fear of interference or undue publicity.

Transport was the first problem which occupied Nordenholt's attention. It was in this connection that I caught my first glimpse of the "Nordenholt Gang" at work. The executive staffs of the railways were left intact, but one day there descended upon them a quiet little man in spectacles with full authority in his pocket. Grogan had apparently never been connected with railways in his life, as far as I knew, but he took control of the whole system in the country without showing the faintest sign of hesitation. How he acquired his knowledge, I never learned; but I gathered that he had originally made his mark by his investigations of the effect of trade-routes upon commerce.

His work was to indicate the broad outlines of the scheme, and the railway officials then filled in the details. Yet I was told that he seemed to know to a truck the demands which his projects would entail upon the railways; and he never put forward anything which led to a breakdown. I think he had that type of mind which sees straight through the details to the core of an undertaking and which yet retains in due perspective the minutiae of the machinery.

And it was not only the railways which he had in his charge. All the motor services were brought under his control as well. It was a bewilderingly complex affair; and he had to act as a kind of liaison centre between the two departments, clearing up any troubles which arose and co-ordinating the twin methods of transport. I think he had the power of mental visualisation developed to an abnormal extent; and his memory must have been quite out of the common. To assist him, he had the largest railway map I have ever seen—it covered a whole floor—and on it were placed blocks of metal showing the exact situation of every truck, carriage and locomotive in the kingdom. These were moved from time to time by his assistants in accordance with telegraphic information; and if he doubted his recollections at any moment he could go and study the groupings upon it.

I remember seeing him once when things had got slightly out of gear, his hands full of telegraph forms, his feet encased in felt slippers to avoid marking the surface of the map, studying a point in the Welsh system where a number of trucks had been stranded in sidings. With the briefest consideration he seemed to come to a decision, for he gave his orders to an assistant:

"Locomotive, Newport to Crumlin, *via* Tredegar Junction. (It can't go through Abercarne, because the 3.46 is on the line now and I don't want to waste time shunting.) Then on to Cwm—C-w-m—to pick up twenty-seven trucks in the siding. All right. After that, back to Aberbeeg—b-double-e-g—since the line is blocked at Victoria by No. 702. Then Blaina—B-l-a-i-n-a—and Abergavenny. All right. . . . Stop a moment. Map-measure, please. Motor Fleet 37 will be at Abergavenny about then with some stores for the North. Hold train at Abergavenny and wire them to stop No. 37 as it passes. That will fill up ten trucks, I think. All right. Train Hereford, Birmingham, via Leominster. Load twelve trucks Birmingham. Tamworth, pick up five truck-loads—food, that red block there—then North behind No. 605. All right. Then wire Abergavenny to send No. 37 to Monmouth. They'll get their orders there. All right."

So it went on, I am told, hour after hour, throughout the day. Even the details of the diurnal traffic were not sufficient; for as he went along, he planned the night-operations as well. When he retired for the short sleep-time which he took, every point had been regulated for the ensuing five hours.

At first, everything culminated in the word "North"; but almost immediately the whirling traffic on the south going rails had to be considered also, as it grew in volume. How he managed it, I do not know; but he seemed to have some sub-conscious faculty of drawing a balance-sheet of the traffic at any moment; so that he knew if he was sending too much North or too little South. Personally, I imagine that he owed his success to a power akin to that of the professional chess-player who can play a dozen blindfold games at one time. Everybody has the faculty of mental visualisation developed in a greater or less degree; but in Grogan, as far as traffic was concerned, it seems to have attained supernormal proportions. I believe that he actually "saw" in his mind the whole of England covered with his trains and motor fleets and that he had by some means established time-scales which enabled him to calculate the moments at which any train or fleet would pass a series of given points. It was, of course, an immensely more difficult affair than blindfold chess-playing; but I think it clearly depended upon cognate processes.

Congleton, the Shipping Director, had a much easier task. For him there was no trouble of blocked rails or interleaving traffic. His main difficulty arose from berthing accommodation, which was a comparatively simple affair. Most of the food-supplies were transferred North on board ship; and a certain amount of the shifting of population was also done in this way, especially the removal of the Glasgow inhabitants.

I can only give the merest outline of these great operations; for the details are too intricate to be described here. Nordenholt's first step was to commandeer most of the public halls in the country, which were then fitted up with partitions, etc., in order to convert them into temporary dwelling-places for families. Thereafter, he began to move his Nitrogen Volunteers into the Clyde Valley step by step; and simultaneously, under the Billeting Act, he evicted the local population to make room for his men. There was a considerable outcry; and at times the military had to be employed to persuade the reluctant to move out of their homes; but after the first few cases of obstruction had been dealt with firmly, the people recognised that it was useless to protest. Edinburgh was also treated in the same way; for Nordenholt had planned to occupy a belt of country running from coast to coast. He had to find room for a population of five millions; and it was evidently going to be a difficult matter.

Looking back upon it now, it was a wonderful piece of work, carried out without any very serious hitches. To transfer a population of nearly ten millions, and to distribute five millions of that over a wide area of England—for this was the only way in which house-room could be found for them—was a gigantic task. Fabulous sums were expended in finding living-room for the refugees in the houses of residents throughout England; and eventually all of them had roofs over their heads, in private dwellings, in converted halls or in commandeered hotels.

Meanwhile, in Glasgow itself, the ever-growing Nitrogen Area was surrounded with military pickets which prevented the mingling of new-comers and the old population. This precaution of Nordenholt's was mainly directed against the possibility of rioting; for the feeling between the expelled inhabitants and the incomers was extremely bitter: but it served another purpose in that it tended to surround the Nitrogen Area with a certain atmosphere of mystery. This was heightened by the stoppage of all telegraphic and telephonic communication between Glasgow and the South. Soon the only information obtainable in England with regard to affairs in the Clyde Valley came from emigrants; and with the end of the exodus, even the mails ceased and an impenetrable veil fell between the two parts of the island.

A similar screen had fallen between England and Ireland at a slightly earlier date. All postal and telegraphic communication was broken off, and no vessels were permitted to trade with the Irish ports. It was by this means that the knowledge of the great Raid was kept secret. Nordenholt was almost ready to disclose his hand; and the Raid could not be postponed if any cattle were to be obtained alive. By a series of lightning sweeps, the military rounded up all the available live-stock in the island and drove them to the nearest ports, where ships were awaiting them. Bitter guerrilla warfare raged along the tracks of the columns; and the last pages in Irish history were marked with bloodshed. Not that it mattered much, since all were to die in any case before very long.

But I am now coming to the last stages of the exodus. All the required food, all the available machinery and all the Nitrogen Volunteers had been sent up into the Clyde Valley. Without warning, after a secret session, Parliament had resolved to transfer itself to Glasgow. Now came the final moves. On the last day, only pickets of the Military Volunteers—the Labour Defence Force, as Nordenholt had renamed them—were left behind in every important town.

During that night a carefully-planned course of destruction was followed. Every telegraph and telephone exchange was gutted; the remaining artillery was rendered useless; all the printing machinery of newspapers was wrecked; every aeroplane destroyed and practically all aerodromes burned: and as the trains and motors went northward in the night, bridge after bridge on the line or road was blown up. When morning came, there was a complete stoppage of all the normal channels of communication; and up to the Border, the railways had been put out of action for months. It was the second step in Nordenholt's plan.

Hitherto, I have chronicled his successes; but now I must deal with his single failure. He had intended to persuade the King to take refuge in the Clyde Valley, and had even, I believe, found a residence for him near Glasgow. Here, however, he met with a rebuff. I never learned the details of the interview; but it appears that the King refused to save himself. He felt it his duty to share the fate of his people. Nordenholt pleaded that if the King himself would not come, at least the Prince of Wales might be sent; but here also he failed to carry his point. The Prince point-blank rejected the suggestion. Knowing Nordenholt, I could hardly conceive that his persuasive proposals could fail to take effect; but it was evident that he met with no success.

"He understood perfectly," Nordenholt said to me later. "Both of them thoroughly understood what it meant. I think they felt that a Crown rescued at that price wouldn't be worth wearing. At any rate, they refused to come North."

VIII   THE CLYDE VALLEY

Hitherto my narrative has had a certain unity; for I have
been describing a chain of events, each of which followed
naturally from its fore-runners; but now comes a bifur-
cation. I have explained how the Clyde Valley had been
isolated, step by step, from the rest of the country; and
when the last food-stores and troops had been brought
into the Nitrogen Area, communications between the
two districts ceased. From that moment, the two regions
had different histories; and I cannot deal with them in
an intertwined chronological sequence. I shall therefore
continue my account of the Clyde Valley experiment now;
and shall deal later with the collapse of civilisation in
England.

When planning his colony, Nordenholt decided to occupy a belt of country between the Forth and Clyde which
contained all the required materials in the form of coal
and iron. Other things, such as copper, he brought into
the region in quantities which he believed would suffice
for months.

The frontier included something like a thousand square
miles of territory; and within the boundary lay the whole
industrial tract of mid-Scotland with its countless pits,
mines, foundries, factories, ship-building yards and other
resources.

Under Congleton's arrangements, as many ships as possible had been brought into the Clyde and Forth at the last moment; and thereafter the Navy blocked the entrances with mine-fields upon an enormous scale. Nothing, either surface craft or submarine, could have penetrated either estuary.

Aerial defence was a secondary matter. No invasion in force would come by that road; and the destruction of the aerodromes had disposed of any early attempts at mere malicious damage. Defences were established, however, around the central area; and to accommodate the aeroplanes and airships which had been brought North, immense flying-grounds were laid out on the level reaches of the lower Clyde.

The storage of the food-supplies cost much thought; but by utilising every spare corner, including railway and tramway depots, it had been possible to get them all under cover and under guard. A strict rationing system was put in force, though the allowance was quite up to normal quantities. The main trouble was, as Nordenholt had anticipated, a shortage of vegetables; and there was also a considerable deficit in the meat-supply. However, after a complete census had been taken, it seemed likely that we should be able to hold out without much difficulty.

These material factors had given little trouble in our arrangements; but when the human counters came into the question, the resulting complications were much greater than appeared at first sight. Taking the problem at its simplest, we had coal at the one end and manufactured nitrogenous products at the other; and the quantity of the latter depended roughly on the amount of the former, since coal represented our source of energy and also part of our raw material in certain of the processes employed. But, in addition, we needed coal for lighting, either by gas or electricity, and also for heating; so that our actual coal output had to be larger than that required for the mere fixation of nitrogen. Then the number of miners had to be adjusted in proportion to those of the remaining workmen in each stage of the process; for it was wasteful to feed men who were employed in producing a superfluity which could not be utilised. Again, the problem was complicated by the fact that the coal could not immediately be used as it was hewn. Time had to be allowed for the construction and erection of the machinery whereby the atmospheric nitrogen was to be fixed; and this introduced further complications into the calculations. Finally, to omit intermediate details, the number of labourers required for spreading the nitrogenous manure upon the soil was governed by the quantities of this material which could be prepared.

But even when calculations had been made which covered all this ground, a further factor entered into the problem. In dealing with a million workers, death, disease and accidents have to be taken into account, since in their effects they touch large numbers of individuals. The incidence of these factors is not uniform in all trades; and hence corrections had to be introduced to bring the various groups into proportion.

The whole of these calculations had, of course, been made during the period of enrolment; and the reason I lay stress upon them at this stage is to show how accurately each section of the machine was dovetailed into the neighbouring parts. It was impossible to foresee everything: in fact what happened showed that some factors are beyond calculation. But when the Nitrogen Area started as a going concern, everything possible had been provided for, as far as could be seen. It was no fault of Nordenholt's that things went as they did in the end.

With the segregation of the Nitrogen Area from the rest of the Kingdom, and the transference of Parliament to Glasgow, a problem arose which required instant settlement. A dual control in the district might have been fraught with all manner of evil possibilities; and it was essential, once for all, to decide where the ultimate power lay. Nordenholt allowed no time to be wasted in the matter. At the first meeting of the House of Commons after the Area was definitely closed, he took his seat as a Member and moved the adjournment of the House on a matter of urgent public importance. His speech, as reported officially, was very short.

"Mr. Speaker—Sir, I have watched the proceedings in this House closely during the last weeks; and I have noted that a certain number of members seem animated by a spirit of factious opposition to the Government measures. I call the attention of the House to the state of grave peril in which we all stand; and I ask them if this conduct has their support. I have no wish to complicate matters. We have all of us more responsibility on our shoulders than we can bear; and I have no sympathy with these methods.

Those who think with me in this matter will vote with me in the lobby. I move that this House do now adjourn."

The motion was seconded and the question put without further debate. About forty members went into the lobby against Nordenholt. While they were still there, he drew a whistle from his pocket and blew three shrill blasts. A picket of the Labour Defence Force entered the House in response to the signal and arrested the malcontent members, whom they removed in custody. When the remainder of the Members returned to the Chamber, Nordenholt took his stand before the Mace.

"Gentlemen"—he dropped the usual ceremonial form of address—"I wished to allow these members who do not agree with me to select themselves; and I adopted the simplest and most convincing method of doing so, though I could have laid my hand on every one of them without this demonstration. These gentlemen, it appears, are not satisfied with the manner in which things are being done here. I would point out to you that the creation of the Nitrogen Area has been mine from the start; and that the machinery of it is controlled by me now. There is no room for dual control in an enterprise of this magnitude. I offer you all positions in which you can help the remnant of the nation in saving itself; but there are no such positions in this House. Do you agree?"

For a moment there was silence, then an angry murmur ran from bench to bench. Nordenholt continued:

"Those members who were removed from the House will to-night be embarked on airships; and by this time to-morrow I trust that they will all be safely landed, each in the constituency which he represents. Since they do not wish to aid us in the Nitrogen Area, it is fitting that they should go back to their constituents and assist them in the troubles which are about to break upon them. Are you content?"

Again there was a murmur, but this time less defiant.

"Finally, gentlemen, as I hear some whispers of constitutionalism, I have here a Proclamation by the King. He has dissolved Parliament. You are no longer clothed with even the semblance of authority."

The assembly was thunderstruck; for there seemed to be no reply to this.

"I may say," continued Nordenholt, "that some of you are of no personal value in this enterprise. These gentlemen also will be returned to their proper residences immediately. The remainder, whom I can trust, will be so good as to apply at my offices to-morrow, when their work will be explained to them. There is only one ultimate authority here now—myself."

It was a sadly diminished assembly that appeared on the morrow. Neither the Prime Minister nor the Colonial Secretary was found among its numbers.

With the working men who formed the majority of the Nitrogen Volunteers, Nordenholt's methods were entirely different. Here he had in the first stages to conciliate those with whom he dealt and to educate them gradually into an understanding of the task before them. In the beginning, no man worked more than eight hours per day or five days a week; and the general run of the workmen had a thirty-five hour week. Nordenholt's object in this was two-fold. In the first place, he instilled into the men that he was an easy task-master; and secondly, he was able, by keeping check of the output, to place his finger upon those men who even under those easy conditions were not doing their full share. These workers he proposed to eliminate at a later period; but he wished to allow them to condemn themselves.

Next he set going various newspapers. The contents of these, of course, dealt entirely with doings within the Nitrogen Area; but their readers soon grew accustomed to this: and as the main object of the journals was propaganda, the less actual news there was in them, the more likely it became that the propaganda would be read for want of something better.

Through these papers, he began to explain very clearly the necessity for the work upon which they were engaged, handling the subject in all manner of ways and making it seem almost new each time by the fresh treatment which it received from day to day. During this period no hint of the underlying purpose of the Nitrogen Area was given, beyond the suggestion that it was a convenient spot, in view of its natural resources.

In order to alleviate any grievances which they might feel, he devised a system of workmen's committees, one for each trade; and the members of these bodies were elected separately by the married and unmarried men in proportion to their numbers. In this way he secured a majority of the more responsible men upon each committee, although no fault could be found with the method of election. Whatever grievances were ventilated by these committees were met immediately or the reasons against compliance with the demands were clearly and courteously explained.

In fact, throughout this stage of the Nitrogen Area history, Nordenholt's main object was to show himself in the light of a comrade rather than a task-master. He was building up a fund of popularity, even at considerable cost, in order that he might draw upon it later. It was a difficult game to play; for he could not afford to drive with an altogether loose rein in view of the necessity for haste; but, as he himself said, he understood men; and he was perhaps able to gain their confidence at a cheaper rate than most people in his position could have done. Like myself, he believed that fundamentally the working man is a sound man, provided that he is dealt with openly and is not made suspicious.

Within a fortnight, in one way and another, practically every man in the Area understood the importance of his work. I question whether this was not the greatest of Nordenholt's triumphs, though perhaps in perspective it may seem a small affair in comparison with other events. But the generation of enthusiasm is a difficult matter, much more difficult than feats which produce immediate effects.

In one respect Nordenholt gauged the psychology of the masses accurately. He did not make himself cheap. Except at a few mass meetings which he addressed, none of the rank and file ever saw him at all. He knew the value of aloofness and a touch of mystery.

But he did not confine himself to moves made openly upon the board. Behind the scenes he had collected an Intelligence Division, the existence of which was known only to a few; and by means of it he was able to put his finger on a weak spot or a centre of disaffection with extraordinary promptitude. Grievances were often remedied long before the appropriate committee had been able to cast their statement of them into a definite form. Nor, as I shall have to tell later, did this Intelligence Division confine its operations to the Nitrogen Area itself; for its network spread over the whole Kingdom.

As soon as the machinery of the Area was working satisfactorily, Nordenholt took a step in advance. The Workmen's Committees were supplied with the actual statistics of production and it was explained to them that speeding-up must begin. The ultimate object was still concealed; but sufficient information was laid before them to show that at their present rate of output the nitrogenous materials prepared by the end of the twelve months would be totally insufficient to yield food enough for even the population of the Area itself, without taking the outer regions into account. They were then asked to suggest means by which output might be raised; and time was given them to think the matter out in all its bearings. Without hesitation they agreed that there must be an increase in productivity.

To raise the output and also to check the points where any loss was occurring, Nordenholt introduced a series of statistical charts and at the same time divided the workmen in each trade into gangs of a definite number.

At the end of each week, these charts were submitted to the Trade Committee and the gangs which were failing to do their share were indicated. By pointing out that a fixed quantity of material must be obtained per week unless disaster were to ensue, Nordenholt was able to make it clear to the Committees that slackness in one gang entailed extra exertions on the rest. There was no question of an employer trying to force up the standard of work: it was simply a question whether they wished to starve or live.

The effect of this was striking; and certainly it was a novelty in working conditions. Every man became a policeman for his neighbours, since he knew that slackness on their part would demand greater exertions upon his own. The Committees instituted a system of inspectors, nominated by themselves, to see that work was properly carried out; and these inspectors reported both to the Committees and to Nordenholt himself, through special officials. Before long, both the Committees and Nordenholt had an extensive black list of inefficient workers; and the stage was being set for another drastic lesson.

For three days the Area newspapers contained full accounts of the state into which things had drifted; and it was made obvious even to the most ignorant what the inevitable result would be if the output were not raised. Then, having thus prepared his ground, Nordenholt summoned a meeting of workmen delegates. It was the first time that most of those present had seen him; and I think he counted upon making his personality tell. He had no chairman or any of the usual machinery of a meeting;

everything was concentrated upon the tall dark figure, alone upon the platform.

It was a short speech which he made; but he delivered it very slowly, making every point tell as he went along and leaving time for each statement to sink well home into the minds of his audience. He began by a clear account of the objects for which they were working—and he had the gift of lucid exposition. He handled the statistical side of the matter in detail, and yet so simply that even the dullest could understand him. When he had completed his survey, every man present saw the state of affairs in all its bearings.

Then, for the first time, he explained to them that those in the Nitrogen Area were all that could be saved; and that their salvation could be accomplished only at the cost of labour far in excess of anything they had anticipated.

"Now, men," he continued, "remember that I am not your task-master. I am merely striving, like yourselves, to avert this calamity; and I think I have already shown you that I have spent my best efforts in our common cause. I have no wish to dictate to you. I leave the decision in your own hands. Those of you who wish to starve may do so. It is your own decision; even though it involves your wives and families, I will not interfere. I ask no man to work harder than he thinks necessary.

"But I put this point before you. Is it right that a man who will not strain himself in the common service should reap where he has not sown? Is it right that any man should batten upon the labour of you all while refusing to do his utmost? Will you permit wilful inefficiency to rob you and your children of their proper share in the means of safety? Or do you believe that this community should rid itself of parasites?

"I leave myself entirely in your hands in the matter. I take no decision without your consent. If you choose to toil in order that they may take bread from your children's mouths, it is no affair of mine. I will do my best for you all, in any case. But I would be neglecting my duty did I not warn you that there is no bread to spare. Every mouthful has been counted; and even at the best we shall just struggle through.

"These are the facts. Do you wish to retain these inefficients among you? Without your consent, I can make no move. I ask you here and now for your decision."

He held the meeting in the hollow of his hand. Cries of "No. Away with them. No spongers," and the like were heard on all sides. Nordenholt held up his hand, and silence came at once. The meeting hung on his words.

"Those in favour of allowing this inefficiency to continue, stand up."

No one rose.

"Very good, men. I will carry out your decision. This meeting is at an end."

The morning papers contained a full report of his speech; but before they were in the hands of the populace, Nordenholt had acted. All the ca' canny workmen had been arrested during the night, along with their families, and removed to the southern boundary, where they were placed on trains and motors ready for transport to the Border. The thing was done with absolute silence and with such efficiency that it seemed more like kidnapping than an ordinary process of arrest. Nordenholt knew the advantage of mystery; and he proposed to make these disappearances strike home on the public mind. The inefficients vanished without leaving a clue behind.

At the Border, each of them was supplied with provisions exactly equivalent to the rations remaining in the outer world; and they were then abandoned as they stood. Nothing was ever known of their fate. When the works opened again in the morning, their fellows missed them from the gangs and time enough was allowed for their disappearance to sink in; after which a redistribution took place which closed up the gaps. But the very mystery served to heighten the effect of the lesson. For the first time, Fear in more than one form had entered the Nitrogen Area.

I remembered what Nordenholt had said to me some weeks earlier: "I shall deal with them—and I shall do it by the hand of their own fellows."

So you can understand the roaring tide of industry which mounted day by day in the Area. This sudden stroke had done more than anything else to convince the people of the seriousness of the situation. Ten thousand men had been condemned and had vanished on an instant—Nordenholt made no secret of the number; and the remainder realised that things must indeed be grave when a step of this kind had been necessary. He had given no time for amendment: condemnation had been followed by the execution of the sentence: and it was they themselves who had pronounced the decree.

They could not lay it upon his shoulders. And the veil of mystery which enwrapped the fate of the convicted ones had its value in more than one direction. Had Nordenholt caused them to be shot, public sympathy would have been aroused. But this impenetrable secrecy baffled speculation and prevented men from forming any concrete picture which might arouse compassion.

Choosing his moment, Nordenholt announced that, in future, the factories would be run continuously, shift after shift, throughout the twenty-four hours. For a time he called a halt to the newspaper campaign for increased output. He would need this form of publicity later; and he did not wish it to become staled by constant repetition.

For the present he was satisfied. Everything was now in train and he was into his stride all along the line. At last statistics were accumulating which would enable him to gauge exactly how the machinery was running; and he held his hand until a balance-sheet could be drawn with accuracy.

At this point in my narrative I am trying to produce a conspectus of the Nitrogen Area as it was during that period in its career. I leave to the imagination of my readers the task of picturing that gigantic concentration of human effort: the eternal smoke-cloud from a thousand chimney-stalks lying ever between us and the sun; the murky twilight of the streets at noon; the whir of dynamos and the roar of the great electric arcs; the unintermittent thunder of trains pouring coal into the city; and, above all, the half-naked figures in the factories, toiling, toiling, shift after shift in one incessant strain through the four-and-twenty hours. No one can ever depict the details of that panorama.

But alongside this vast outpouring of physical energy there lay another world, calm, orderly and almost silent, yet equally important to the end in view: the world of the scientific experts in their laboratories and research stations. To pass from one region to the other was like a transition from pandemonium to a cloister.

Nordenholt had grouped his experts into three main classes, though of course these groups by no means included all the investigators he controlled. It was here that the Nordenholt Gang were strongest, for the path of the scientific man is one which offered the greatest chances to Nordenholt's scheme for the furthering of youth.

In the first place came the group of chemists and electricians who were engaged upon the improvement of nitrogen fixation methods; and between this section and the factories there was a constant *liaison*; so that each new plant which was erected might contain the very latest improvements devised by the experts.

The second group contained the bacteriologists, whose task it was to investigate the habits of *B. diazotans*, to determine whether it could be exterminated in any practical manner and to discover what methods could be employed to prevent its ravaging the new crops when they were obtainable.

Finally, the experts in agriculture overlapped with the chemical group, since many of the questions before them were concerned with the chemistry of the soil. I have already mentioned how the action of *B. diazotans* disintegrated the upper strata of the land and reduced the soil to a friable material. This formed one of the most troublesome features in the cultivation problem, since the porosity of the ground allowed water to sink through, and thus plants sown in the affected fields were left without any liquid upon which they could draw for sustenance. It was J. F. Hope, I believe, who finally suggested a solution of the matter. His process consisted in mixing colloid minerals such as clays with the soil and thus forming less permeable beds; and the agricultural experts were able to establish the minimum percentages of clay which were required in order to make crops grow.

I have mentioned these points in order to show how much we in the Area depended upon the pure scientists for help. But it must not be supposed that only those lines of scientific investigation capable of immediate application were kept in view by Nordenholt. I learned later, as I shall tell in its proper place, that he had cast further afield than that.

I cannot give details of the work on the scientific side, because I have no intimate acquaintance with them; but I met the results on every hand in the course of my own department's affairs. From day to day a new machine would be passed for service and put into operation, some fresh catalyst would be sent down for trial on a large scale after having been tested in the laboratory, or there might be a slight variation in the relative quantities of the ingredients in some of our factory processes. There was a constant touch between research and large-scale operations.

In the course of this I used often to have to visit the Research Section; and in some ways I found it a mental anodyne in my perplexities. These long, airy laboratories, with their spotless cleanliness and delicate apparatus, formed a pleasant contrast to the grimy factories and gigantic machines among which part of my days were passed. And I found that the popular conception of the scientific man as a dry-as-dust creature was strangely wide of the mark. It may be that Nordenholt's picked men differed from others of their class; but I found in them a directness in speech and a sense of humour which I had not anticipated. After the hurry and confusion of the improvisation which marked the opening of the Nitrogen Area, the quiet certainty of the work in the Research Section seemed like a glimpse of another world. I do not mean that they talked like super-men or that the investigations were always successful; but over it all there was an atmosphere of clockwork precision which somehow gave one confidence. These men, it struck me for the first time, had always been contending with Nature in their struggle to wrest her secrets from her; while we in the other world had been sparring against our fellows with Nature standing above us in the conflict, so great and so remote that we had never understood even that she was there. Now, under the new conditions, all was changed for us; while to these scientific experts it was merely the opening of a fresh field in their long-drawn-out contest.

During the inception of Nordenholt's scheme, my own work had dealt with varied lines of activity which brought me into contact with diverse departments of the machine; but when the transfer to the Clyde Valley took place, I settled down into more definite duties. Nordenholt had picked me out, I believe, on the strength of my knowledge of factory organisation; and my first post in the North dealt with this branch. Thus in the earlier days, my work took me into the machine-shops and yards where the heavy machinery was being built or remodelled; and so I came into direct contact with the human element.

But as time went on, the range of my control increased; and as my work extended I had to delegate this section more and more to my subordinates. I became, through a gradual series of transitions, the checker of efficiency over most of the Area activities.

The under-current of all my memories of that time is a series of curves. Graphs of coal-supply from each pit, so that the fluctuation of output might be controlled and investigated; graphs of furnace-production from day to day, whereby all might be kept up to concert-pitch; graphs comparing one process with another in terms of power and efficiency; graphs of workmen's ages and effectiveness; graphs of total power-consumption; graphs of remaining food-supplies extrapolated to show probable consumption under various scales; graphs of population changes; graphs of health-statistics: all these passed through my hands in their final form until I began to lose touch with the real world about me and to look upon disasters costing many lives merely as something which produced a point of inflexion in my curves.

Nordenholt had established his central offices in the University and had cleared the benches from all the classrooms to make room for his staff. It was probably the best choice he could have made; since it provided within a limited area sufficient office-room to house everyone whom he might wish to call into consultation at a moment's notice at any time; and it had the further advantage that all the scientific experts had been given the University laboratories to work in, so that they also were within easy call. He himself had chosen as his private office the old Senate Room. The Randolph Hall had been fitted up as a kind of card-index library wherein were stored all the facts of which he might be in need at any time; and the Court Room was converted into his secretary's office and connected with the Senate Room by a door driven through the wall.

In Nordenholt's office a huge graph extended right across the wall over the fireplace. It was an enormous diagram, covering the period from the starting of the Nitrogen Area and extending, as far as its numbered abscissae were concerned, beyond the harvest-time in the next year. Each morning, before Nordenholt came to his office, the new daily points were inserted on it and joined up with the preceding curves. One line, in red, expressed the amount of food remaining; another, in green, showed the quantity of nitrogenous material synthesised up to date; whilst the third curve, in purple, indicated approximately the crop which might be expected from the nitrogenous manure in hand. Of all the sights in the Nitrogen Area,

I think that series of curves made the deepest impression upon me. It was so impersonal, a cold record of our position and our prospects, untinged by any human factor. The slow rise of the green curve; the steady fall of the red line—our whole future was locked up in these relative trends.

I remember one morning in Nordenholt's office, where I had gone to consult him on some point or other. We had discussed the matter in hand; and I was about to leave him when he called me back.

"I haven't seen much of you lately, Flint," he said. "Sit down for a few minutes, will you? I want a rest from all this for a short time; and I think it would do you good to get clear of things for a while also. What do you do with yourself at nights?"

I told him that I usually worked rather late.

"That won't do as a steady thing. I know the work has to be done; and I know you have to work till midnight, and after it often, to keep abreast of things. But if you do it without a break now and again you'll simply get stale and lose grip. You may keep on working long hours; but what you do in the end won't be so efficient. Take to-night off. Come to dinner with me and we'll try to shake loose from Nitrogen for a while. I've asked Henley-Davenport also."

I accepted eagerly enough, though with a somewhat rueful feeling that it meant harder work on the following day if I was to overtake arrears. But I wanted to meet Henley-Davenport. As I mentioned at the beginning of this narrative, before the irruption of *B. diazotans* into the world, he had been engaged upon radioactivity investigations; and I was anxious to hear what he was doing. I knew that Nordenholt set great store by his work—he was one of the Nordenholt young men—and I was interested. But my main reason for accepting was, of course, Nordenholt himself. As time went on, he fascinated me more and more; and I grasped at every opportunity of studying his complex personality. I doubt if I have been able to throw light upon it in these pages. I have given vignettes here and there to the best of my ability; but I know that I have failed to set down clearly the feeling which he always gave me, the distinction between the surface personality and the greater forces moving behind that screen. The superficial part is easy to describe; but the noumenon of Nordenholt is a thing beyond me. I only felt it; I never saw it: and I doubt if any man ever saw it fully revealed.

Just then the door of the secretary's room opened and someone came in. Curiously enough, I had never seen Nordenholt's secretary before. She seemed to be about twenty-four, fair-haired and slim, dressed like any other business girl; but it was her face which struck me most. She looked fragile and at the corners of the sensitive mouth I thought I saw evidences of strain. Somehow she seemed out of place amid all this grimness: her world should have been one of ease and happiness.

"These are the figures you wanted with regard to A. 323, Uncle Stanley," she said, as she handed over a card.

"Thanks, Elsa. By the way, this is Mr. Flint. You've heard me speak of him often. My ward, Miss Huntingtower, Flint. She acts as my secretary."

We exchanged the commonplaces usual to the situation. I noticed that Nordenholt's voice changed as he spoke to her: a ring of cheerfulness came into it which was not usually there. In a few minutes he dismissed her and we sat down again.

"Now, Flint, there's another example of the effect of too hard work. We're all running things rather fine, nowadays. As for myself, it doesn't matter. So long as I can see this year through, it's immaterial to me what the ultimate effect may be. I can afford to run things to their end. But you younger people have most of your lives before you. I'm not hinting that you can spare yourselves; but you must try to leave something for the future. When it's all over, we shall still need directors; and you must manage to combine hard work now with enough reserve force to prevent a collapse in the moment of success.

"That's why I planned amusement for the workers as well as a time schedule for the factories. We aren't dealing with machines which can be run continuously and not suffer. We have to give the men a change of interest. I suppose some of you thought I was wrong in cumbering ourselves with all these football players, actors and actresses, music-hall artistes and so on, who produce nothing directly towards our object? For all I know you may jib at the sight of the thousands who go down to the Celtic Park every Saturday afternoon to watch a gang of professionals playing Soccer. I don't. I know that these thousands are getting fresh air and exercising their lungs in yelling applause. I couldn't get them to do it any other way; and I want them to do it. Then the halls and theatres occupy them in the evenings when they aren't working; and that keeps them from brooding over their troubles. I don't want men to accumulate here and there and grouse over the strain I put on them. That's why I picked out the best of the whole Stage and brought them here. The Labour section is getting better value for its amusement money than it ever got in its life before; and I'm getting what I want too.

"That's why I cornered tobacco and liquor also. We must remove every scrap of restraint on pleasure, Flint, or we should have trouble at once. They must have their smoke and they must have drink in moderation. You can't run this kind of colony on narrow lines.

"And there's another thing, perhaps the most important of all under the conditions we are in: religion. I'm not talking about creeds or anything of that kind. I've studied most of them from the point of view of psychology; and they're empty things; life left them long ago. But behind all that mass of outworn lumber there's a real feeling which can't be neglected if we are to get the best out of things. That's why I brought all these ministers of the various denominations into the Area. We must have them; and as far as I could, I picked the best of them. But I'll have no idlers here. They have to do their day's work with the rest of us and do their teaching afterwards. Every man ought to be able to *do* something. After all, Christ was a carpenter before He took up His work. That's what has been wrong with ninety per cent of parsons since the Churches started. They don't know anything practical and they mistake talk for work. What was the average sermon except expanding a text, with illustrations—diluting the Bible with talk, just as a dishonest milkman waters his milk.

"Well, I've picked the best I could get; and I've given them a free hand. But I wish I were sure where it is all going to lead. It's the most difficult problem I ever tackled, I know. Our conditions aren't parallel, but I am half-afraid of reproducing the story of the Anabaptists in Münster. You can't get heavy physical and mental tension in an unprepared population without seeing some strange things. I introduced these ministers as a brake on that line of development.

"And what a chance they have! It's when men are most helpless that they turn to religion; and here we are going to have a field in which much might be sown. If only they are equal to the times! But it's no affair of mine. They must work out their own salvation and perhaps the salvation of their people if they can.

"As for us, Flint, we've got enough work of our own in this world. Take my advice and clear every idea of humanity out of your mind: stick to your curves and graphs and don't think beyond them. If once you let your imagination stray over the real meaning of them—in toil and pain and death—you'll never be able to carry on. I can't help seeing it all; and that's why I pin myself to the Curve there. I don't want to look beyond it. I want to keep myself detached from all that as far as possible; for I can't afford to be biased. It's difficult; and in a few weeks more it will be still harder, when these unheard cries of agony go up in the South. But what can one do? I must shut my ears as best I can and go forward; or everything will fall to pieces and we shall save nothing out of the wreck. What a prospect, eh?

"Now, Flint,"—he sprang up—"off to work again, both of us. We can't afford to waste time if we are to have an evening free from worry. I'll see you at dinner."

As I reached the door, he called me back and spoke low:

"By the way, Miss Huntingtower doesn't know all our plans. Keep off the subject of the South. She hasn't been told anything about that; and I want to keep it from her as long as I can. You understand?"

"Yes, if you wish it. But surely she must have some knowledge of the state of affairs. You can't have managed to keep her in the dark about the whole thing?"

"It wasn't difficult. She looks after certain special branches of my correspondence and so on; and nothing except actual Area business passes through her hands, so she has seen nothing beyond that. And once she finishes her work for the day I've made it a rule for her that she takes no further interest in the situation. I told her she must get her mind clear of it at night, or she would get stale and be no use to me. That was quite enough. She doesn't even read the newspapers."

"But what's the use of keeping her in the dark? She is bound to know all about it soon enough."

"There's a great difference, Flint, between learning of a thing after it is irrevocable and hearing of it while there is time to protest against it. Once a catastrophe is over, it *is* over; and the shock is lighter than if one feels it coming and struggles against it. I don't wish Miss Huntingtower to hear anything about the South until the whole thing is at an end down there. She'll accept it then, since there is nothing else for it. I don't wish her to be put in the position of feeling that she ought to do all she can to prevent its coming about. You understand?"

IX INTERMEZZO

In order to understand the impression which that evening left upon me, it is necessary to bear in mind the conditions under which I had been living for the last few weeks. In the earlier stages I had been oscillating between my office, with its ever-accumulating mass of papers, on the one hand; and the grime and clangour of the factories and furnaces upon the other. Then, gradually, I saw less and less of the concrete machinery of our safety and slipped almost wholly into the work of control from a distance. Lists, sheets of figures, graphs, letters dictated or read, telephonic communications, reports from factory managers, all surged up before me in a daily deluge. My meals were eaten hurriedly at a side-table in my office; and my lights burned far into the morning in the attempt to cope with the torrent which I had to control. Often as the dawn was coming up through the smoke-clouds of the city I walked home with a wearied mind through which endless columns of figures chased each other; and my eyes had broken down under the strain to the extent that I had to use pilocarpine almost constantly. I was beginning to look back on the old life in London, with its theatre parties and dinners, as if it were another existence which I should never re-enter. I seemed shut off from it by some nebulous yet impenetrable curtain; and when I thought of it at times, I felt that it had passed away beyond recall. All the softer side of civilisation, it seemed, must go down, once for all, in this cataclysm; and from our efforts a harder, harsher world would be born. Ease and luxury had vanished, leaving us stripped to our necessities.

And suddenly I found myself in the old surroundings once more. I was ushered into a room which, though its simplicity recalled Nordenholt's other environments, still betrayed a woman's hand at every point. There was no litter of meaningless nicknacks; every touch went to build up a harmonious whole: and it was unmistakably a feminine mind which had designed it. As I glanced down the room, I saw Miss Huntingtower standing by the fireplace; and it flashed across me that, whether by accident or design, the room formed a framework for her.

As she came forward to meet me, her smile effaced the strained expression which I had noticed in the morning. In these surroundings she seemed different, somehow. The artistry of the room fitted her own beauty so that each appeared to find its complement in the other. It seemed to me that she was designed by destiny for this environment, and not for the harder work of the world. And yet, she gave no suggestion of triviality; there was no hint of a feminine desire to attract. It must have been that she harmonised so well with the frame in which I saw her. And the personality which gazed from her eyes seemed in some way to blend with this world of shaded lights, graceful outlines and innate simplicity.

Nordenholt came into the room almost at once with a grave apology to Miss Huntingtower for being late.

"Convenient having a house in the University Square," he said to me. "If we hadn't taken over some of these professors' residences, it would have meant such a waste of time getting to and fro between one's home and the office. That was one reason why I selected the University as a centre. We had the whole thing ready-made for us."

Henley-Davenport arrived almost at once; and we went down to dinner. I had begun to re-acclimatise myself in these surroundings; but I still recall that evening in every detail. The shaded candles on the table, which soothed my straining eyes, the glitter of silver and crystal on the snowy cloth, Nordenholt's lean visage half in shadow except when he leaned forward into the soft illumination, Henley-Davenport's sharp voice driving home a point, and Miss Huntingtower's eager face as she glanced from speaker to speaker or put a question to one of us: with it all, I seemed back again in my lost world and the Nitrogen Area appeared to belong to another region of my life.

But even here it penetrated, though faintly. The usual topics of conversation were gone: theatres, books, all our old interests had been uprooted and cast aside, so that we could only take them up in the form of reminiscence. And, as a matter of fact, we talked very little about them. I tried one or two tentative efforts; but Henley-Davenport, who had known Nordenholt and his ward longer than I, made very little attempt to follow me: and I soon gathered that Miss Huntingtower was better pleased with other subjects.

What appeared to interest her most was the general situation; and I was rather flattered to find that she seemed anxious to hear my own views.

She seemed to be one of those people who are gifted with the faculty of drawing one out. I don't mean that she sat silent and merely listened; but she had the knack of stimulating one to talk and of keeping one to the main line by occasional questions, which showed that she had not only followed what had been said but had silently commented upon it as one went along. Yet she never appeared to lose her charm by aping masculinity. Her outlook was a feminine one in its essentials, even if her mind was acute. And she had the gift of naturalness. There was no artificiality either in look or speech. She made me feel almost at once as though I had known her for years.

One thing I did notice about her. Whenever Nordenholt spoke she seemed to hang on his words and to weigh them mentally. The two seemed to be joined by some intimate bond of understanding; and I could see that Nordenholt was proud of her in his way.

Dinner drew to an end, and Nordenholt began to question Henley-Davenport about his researches. Miss Huntingtower interrupted at the beginning with a request for simple language.

"If you begin talking about uranium-X_1 and mesothorium-2, then I won't understand you, and I want to know what it is all about."

"Well, Miss Huntingtower, I think I can make it plain without using uranium-X_1 or even eka-tantalum; but it's hard that I should be forbidden to use all these fine-sounding words, eh? Isn't it? I submit under protest. It takes away half the pleasure of telling things when one has to put them in mere vulgar English.

"Well"—he had an extraordinary habit of interjecting "well" and by inflecting it in various ways, making it serve as a kind of prelude to his sentences, a sort of keynote, as it were—"Well, I take it that you know what radioactivity is. Some of the atoms are spontaneously breaking down into simpler materials, and in that breakdown they liberate an amount of energy which is immeasurably greater than anything we can obtain by the ordinary chemical reactions which occur when coal is burned or when gas is lighted.

"Well, if we could tap that store of energy which evidently lies within the atom we should have Nature at our feet. She would be done for, beaten, out of the struggle: and we should simply have to walk over the remains and take what we wanted. Until the thing is actually done, none of us can grasp what it will mean; for no one has ever seen unlimited energy under control in this world. We have always had to fight hard for every unit of it that we used.

"Well, there is no doubt that atoms *can* be broken down. All the radioactive elements split up spontaneously without any help from us. But the quantities of them which we can gather together are so extremely minute that as a source of energy they are feebler than an ordinary wax vesta, for all practical purposes.

"So far, so good. We know the thing can be done; but we haven't hit on the way of doing it. Is that clear?"

"Quite clear, thanks," said Miss Huntingtower, with a smile. "Radium without tears, Part I. Now the second lesson, please."

"Well, don't be too optimistic. There may be tears in the second part. It's a little stiffer. The majority of the elements are perfectly stable; they undergo no radioactive decompositions; so that they give off no energy. But all the same, if our views are right, they contain a store of pent-up energy quite as great as that of the radioactive set. It's like two clocks, both wound up. One of them, the radioactive clock, is going all the time and the mainspring is running down. You know it is going because it gives out a tick; and we recognise radioactivity by certain tests of a somewhat similar type, only we 'listen' for electrical effects instead of the sound-waves you detect when the clock ticks. Now the second clock, the one that is wound up but hasn't been started, is like the ordinary element. If you could give it a shake, it would start off ticking.

"Well, what we want to do is to start the non-radioactive elements ticking. We are looking for the right kind of shake to give them in order to start them off. If we can find that, then we shall get all the energy we need, because we can utilise enormous quantities of material where now we have only the traces of radioactive stuff."

"A risky business," said Nordenholt. "Your first successful experiment will be rather catastrophic, won't it?"

"Probably. But I've left full notes of everything I've done, so someone else will be able to continue if anything happens to me.

"Well, the real trouble is that it takes a lot to shake up the internal machinery of an atom. Rutherford did it long ago by using a stream of alpha-particles from radium to smash up the nitrogen atom. That was in 1920 or thereabouts. You see, we have no ordinary force intense enough to break up atoms of the stable elements; we have to go to the radioactive materials to get energy sufficiently concentrated to make a beginning.

"Now, what I have been following out is this. Perhaps I can show you it best by an experiment. Can you get me some safety match-boxes?"

A dozen of these were brought, and he stood them each on its end in a line.

"Now," he continued, "it requires a certain force in a blow from my finger to knock down one of these boxes; and if I take the ten boxes separately, it would need ten times that force to throw them all flat. But if I arrange them so that as each one falls it strikes its neighbour, then I can knock the whole lot down with a single touch. The first one collides with the second, and the second in falling upsets the third, and so on to the end of the line.

"Well, that is what I have been following out amongst the atoms. I know that the alpha-rays of radium will upset the equilibrium of other atoms; and what is wanted is to get the second set of atoms to upset a third and so forth. Hitherto I have not been able to hit upon the proper train of atoms to use. Somehow it seems to sputter out half-way, just as a train of powder fails to catch fire all along its line if one part of it isn't thick enough to carry the flame on. But I have got far enough to show that it can be done.

It's rather pretty to follow, if one has enough imagination to read behind the measurements. You really must come and see it, Nordenholt."

"Do you think it will come out soon?" asked Miss Huntingtower.

"Sooner or later, is all one can say. But it might come any day."

Nordenholt rose from the table.

"I'll come across now, if you can let me see that experiment," he said. "I'm more interested than I can tell you; and I want to discuss some points with you. I'm taking the evening off anyway, and I may as well make myself useful. How long will it take—an hour? All right. Flint, will you amuse Miss Huntingtower till I get back?"

He and Henley-Davenport went out, leaving us to return upstairs.

For a time we talked of one thing and another till at last, by what transitions I cannot now remember, we touched upon her secretaryship, and I asked her how she came to occupy the post.

"Do you really want to know?" she asked. "I warn you it will be rather a long story if I tell you it; and it will probably seem rather dull to you."

"Don't be afraid. I am sure I shall not find it dull."

"Well, let's pretend we are characters in a novel and the distressed heroine will proceed to relate the story of her life. 'I was born of poor but honest parents. . . .' Will that do to start?"

"Must you begin at the beginning? I usually skip first chapters myself."

"I'm sorry, but I have to begin fairly early if you are to understand. Mr. Nordenholt isn't my uncle, really, you know. My father was a distant relation of his. When Father and Mother died I was quite a tiny child; I only remember them vaguely now: and Uncle Stanley was the only relation I had in the world. I believe, too, that I was the only relative he had, certainly I was the only one I ever heard him speak of, except Father and Mother. It was just after he had made his fortune in Canada, and he must have been about thirty then. It appears that Father had written to him much earlier, asking him to look after me if anything happened to him and Mother; and when they were drowned—it was a boating accident—he came home to this country and took me to live with him.

"I was only about eight then, and I missed Father and Mother so. I cried and cried; and he spent hours with me, trying to comfort me. Somehow he did me good. I don't know how he did it; but he seemed to understand so well."

Again I had come across a new side in Nordenholt's character. I could hardly picture that grim figure—for even at thirty Nordenholt must have been grim—comforting that tiny scrap of humanity in distress. And yet she was right: he did understand.

"And with it all, he didn't spoil me. He knew, of course, that when I grew up I would have more money than I knew what to do with; and he determined that I should get the full pleasure out of it by coming to it unspoilt and with unjaded feelings. He brought me up in the simplest way you can imagine. I had no expensive toys, but I liked the ones I had all the better for that. It gave more scope for the imagination, you see: and I had even more than the child's ordinary imaginative power. When we played fairy tales together he used to be the Ogre or the Prince Charming, and I could see him so well either way. He laughs now when I remind him that he used to make a good Prince Charming.

"Well, so it went on, year after year; and we grew up with more in common than either father and daughter or brother and sister. Somehow I picked up his ways of looking at things; and I caught from him something of his understanding of people. He never put any ideals before me; but I think he himself gave me something to carve out an ideal from. Oh, there's nobody like Uncle Stanley! I don't know anybody who comes up to his shoulder."

"I've only known him for a few weeks, Miss Huntingtower," I said, "but I've seen enough to agree with you in that."

"Have you? I'm so glad. It shows that we're the same sort of person, doesn't it? For I know some people hate him—and I hate them for it!"

She clenched her teeth with an air that was half-play, half-earnest.

"I'm going to skip a few years and come to the fairy-tale part of my story: the Three Wishes. When I grew up, Uncle Stanley told me that he had settled an immense sum on me and that I could do exactly as I wished. I think I failed him at that point. He expected me to go and have a good time; and—I didn't. I didn't want to have a good time. I had been thinking over all he had done for me; and I wanted something else entirely. I wanted to give him something in return for all his kindness to me when I was a tiny little thing; and I was afraid that he wouldn't let me. I went to him one day and asked him to give me three wishes. Now even with me, Uncle Stanley is careful; and he wanted to know what the wishes were before he would promise.

"'I don't know myself yet,' I said, 'but I want to feel that I have three things in reserve that I can ask you to do.' 'I promise no impossibilities,' he told me, 'but if the things are really possible, you can have them.' 'Very well,' said I, 'the first of them is that I want to be trained as a secretary.'

"He laughed at me, of course; and when I persisted, he pointed out to me that I was my own mistress and that I needn't have asked his permission to get trained. 'You've wasted one of your wishes, Elsa,' he said, 'and I'm going to hold you to your bargain.' 'Well, I wanted your consent to it anyway,' I told him.

"I went and took a secretary's training, the most complete I could get. You don't know how I enjoyed it. I hated the work, of course; but I felt all the time that I was getting ready to be of use to Uncle Stanley; and even the dullest parts of the thing seemed to be lightened by that.

"When I was fully trained, I went to him again. 'I want my second wish now: I want you to take me as your private secretary.' I don't know that he was altogether pleased then. I think he imagined that I would be a nuisance or inefficient or something. But he kept his promise and took me to work with him.

"You can't guess what I felt about it. I worked hard; I did everything correctly; and I knew him better than anyone else, so that I could help him just when he needed it. Of course, I'm not his only secretary; but I know I suit him better than any of the others. I've begun to pay off my debt to him bit by bit; and yet I always seem just as deep in as ever. He's always been so good to me, you know. But still, I *am* useful to him; and I'm not merely there on sufferance now. I know he appreciates my work."

"I doubt if you would be there long if he didn't," I said. "From what I have seen of him he isn't likely to employ amateurs even as a favour. I think he would have let you see you were useless unless you had made good."

"Oh, if he had been the least dissatisfied with me I would have gone at once as soon as I saw it. I want to be a help and not a hindrance. But now I have answered your question, although it has taken rather a long time to do it."

Some inane compliment came to my lips but I bit it back without speaking it. She didn't seem to be the sort of girl who wanted flattery.

"I think you are helping more than Mr. Nordenholt with your work just now," I said at length. "You seem to have found your way into the centre of the biggest thing this country has ever seen."

Her face clouded for a moment.

"Yes, it's a great thing, isn't it? But do you ever think what failure might mean, Mr. Flint? Think of all these poor people starving and of us unable to help them. It would be terrible. Sometimes I think of it and it makes me feel that we bear a fearful responsibility. I don't mean that I personally have any real responsibility. I don't take myself so seriously as all that. But the men at the head, Uncle Stanley and the rest of you—it's a fearful burden to take on your shoulders. I'm only a cog in the machine and could be replaced to-morrow; but you people, the experts, couldn't be replaced. Fifty millions of people! I can't even begin to understand what fifty million deaths would mean. I do hope, oh, I do so hope that we shall be successful. If anyone but Uncle Stanley were at the head of it I should doubt; but I feel almost quite safe with him at the helm. He never failed yet, you know."

"No," I said, "he never failed yet."

What would she think when the full plans of Nordenholt—who "never failed yet"—were revealed to her? I wondered how this fragile girl would take it. She wouldn't simply weep and forget, I was sure. She seemed to have high ideals and she evidently idolised Nordenholt. It would be a terrible catastrophe for her. I dreaded the next steps in the conversation, for I did not want to lie to her; and I saw no other way out of it if she turned the talk into the wrong channel.

Nordenholt's hour was up and I began to feel that the old life was slipping away from me again. For a few minutes we sat silent; for she did not speak and I was afraid to reopen the conversation lest she should continue her line of thought. I watched her as she sat: the tiny shoe, the sweep of the black gown without a sparkle of jewellery to relieve it, the clean curves of her white throat, and over all the lustre of her hair. Would there be any place for all this in the new world? I wondered. Things would be too hard for her fragility, perhaps.

As ten o'clock struck Nordenholt came in. He looked more cheerful than when he had left us, though as he dropped into a chair I noticed that he seemed to be physically tired.

"Henley-Davenport asked me to make his excuses to you, Elsa. He wants to work out something which struck him when we were over at his laboratory; so I left him there."

He smoked for a while in silence, as though ruminating over what he had seen.

"That's a brave man if you want to see one," he said at last. "From what he told me, there will be a terrible explosion the first time he manages to jar up his atomic powder-magazine; and yet he goes into the thing as coolly as though he were lighting a cigarette. I hope he pulls it off. More hangs on that than one can well estimate just now. It may be the last shot in our locker for all we know."

"But surely, Uncle Stanley, you have foreseen everything?"

"I'm not omniscient, Elsa, though perhaps you have illusions on the point. I do what I can, but one must allow a good deal of latitude for the unpredictable which always exists. And in this affair, I am afraid the unpredictable will not be on the helping side. But don't worry your head over that; we can't help it. What's wrong with you to-night. You look more worried than usual. Tired?"

"Not specially."

"Would you sing to us a little?"

"Only something very short, then." She moved to the piano. "What do you want?"

"Oh, let's see. . . . I'd like . . . No, you wouldn't care for it. Let's think again."

"No, no, Uncle Stanley; I'll sing anything you wish," she said, but when he asked for the second Song in Cymbeline, her brows contracted.

"Must you have that one? Won't the first song do instead?"

"I'd rather have the other. Only the last two verses, for I see you are tired."

She sat down at the piano and played the preliminary chords. I had never heard the air, possibly it was an unusual setting.

> Fear no more the lightning flash,
> Nor the all-dreaded thunder-stone;
> Fear not slander, censure rash;
> Thou hast finished joy and moan;
> All lovers young, all lovers must,
> Consign to thee, and come to dust.

It was a wonderful piece of singing. In the first lines her voice rose clear and confident, reassuring against the mere physical perils. Then with the faintest change of tone, just sufficient to mark the shift in the form of menace, she sang the third line; and let a tinge of melancholy creep into the next. With the last couplet something new came into the music, possibly a drop into the minor; and her voice seemed to fill with an echo of all lost hopes and spent delights. Then it rose again, full and strong in the mandatory lines of the final verse, set to a different air, till at last it died away once more with infinite tenderness:

Quiet consummation have;
And renownèd be thy grave.

I sat spellbound after she had ended. It was wonderful art. She closed the piano and rose from her seat.

"I can't imagine why you dislike that air," said Nordenholt.

"Oh, it's so gloomy, Uncle Stanley. I don't care to think about things like that."

"Gloomy? You misread it, I'm sure. I wish I could be sure of Fidele's luck.

Fear not slander, censure rash.

Which of us can feel sure of being free from these? Not I. And what better could one wish for in the end?

And renownèd be thy grave.

How many ghosts could boast of that after a hundred years?"

"Well, none of us will know about that part of it," she said lightly. "But I don't think you need trouble about the 'censure rash.' None of your own people will blame you; and I know you care nothing for the rest. Even if they all turned against you, you would always have me, you know."

"Is that a promise, Elsa?" he asked gravely; and something in his tone made her glance at him. "Would you really stand by me no matter what happened? Don't say yes, unless you really mean it."

She stood in front of him, eye to eye, for a moment without speaking.

"I don't understand," she said at last. "You never doubted me before. It hurts. Of course I promise you.

No matter what happens I won't leave you. But you must promise never to send me away until I want to go."

"Very good, Elsa, I promise."

The strain seemed to relax in a moment. I don't think they realised how strange it all seemed to me. They were living in their own world, and I was outside, I felt, rather bitterly. And of course, none of us was quite normal at that time.

Miss Huntingtower came to me and held out her hand.

"Thanks so much for coming, Mr. Flint. Somehow I feel as if I had known you for years instead of only a few hours. Now I'll say good-night and leave you with Uncle Stanley."

"Wait a minute, Elsa," said Nordenholt. "It seems to me that all three of us have been cooped up indoors too much lately. Our nerves are getting on edge. Don't deny it, Flint, in your case. You haven't a leg to stand on. I heard you differing from one of your clerks to-day. We'd all be the better for fresh air now and again. One afternoon a week, after this, we'll take a car out into the country. I can do my thinking there just as well as anywhere else; and Mr. Flint can drive to keep his mind off business. That's settled. I told you before that amusement of some sort has to come into our routine, Flint; so you must just make up your mind to it. I can't replace you if you collapse; so I can't allow you to go on like this. You don't look half the man you were six weeks ago."

I required no pressing, partly because I knew that Nordenholt was right in what he said.

X THE DEATH OF THE LEVIATHAN

In this narrative I must give some account of the happenings in the outer world; for, without this, the picture which I am attempting to draw would be distorted in its perspective. At this point, then, I shall begin to interleave the description of the Northern experiment with sketches of the state of affairs elsewhere; and later I shall return to the more connected form of my narrative.

It may reasonably be asked how it comes about that I am able to give any account at all of occurrences in England immediately after the closing of the Nitrogen Area, since I have taken pains to show the complete severance of land-communications between the two sections of the country. I have already hinted that all connection between these regions was not abolished.

Nordenholt feared an invasion of the Clyde Valley by some, at least, of the multitudes in the South as soon as they became famine-stricken. It was hardly to be expected that, with the knowledge of the food in the North which they had, they would remain quiescent when the pinch came; and it was essential to have warning of any hostile movements ere they actually gained strength enough to become dangerous. For this purpose, he had organised his Intelligence Department outside as well as within the Area.

There was no difficulty in introducing his agents into any district. Night landings by parachute from airships, or even the daylight descents of an aeroplane on a misty day, were simple enough to arrange; and his spies could be picked up again at preconcerted times and places when their return was desired.

In this way, there flowed into the Nitrogen Area a constant stream of information which enabled him to piece together a connected picture of the affairs outside our frontier.

I have had access to the summaries of these documents; and it is upon this basis that I have built the next stage of my narrative. These reports, of course, were not published at the time.

As to the rest of the world, I have had to depend upon the wireless messages which were received by the huge installation Nordenholt had set up; and also upon the various accounts which have been published in more recent times.

I have already mentioned that the last stage of the exodus involved the destruction, as complete as was practicable, of roads, railways and telegraphic communications; and I have mentioned also the breaking-up of newspaper printing machinery. Following his usual course, Nordenholt had determined on utilising to the full the psychological factors in the problem; and it was upon the moral rather than on the mere physical effect of this disorganisation that he relied in his planning.

The immediate effect upon the Southern population seems to have been all that he had hoped. On the morning after the last night of the exodus, England was still unperturbed. The absence of the usual newspapers was accepted without marked astonishment; for no one had any idea that it was more than a temporary interruption. Each city and town assumed simply that something had gone wrong in their particular area. No one seems to have imagined that anything but a local mishap had occurred. The failure of the telegraphs was also discounted to some extent.

The local railway services continued to run without exciting comment by their intermittent character; for already Grogan's operations had disorganised them to such an extent that ordinary time-tables were useless.

The food-supply was still in full swing under the rationing system which Nordenholt had introduced; and no shortage had suggested itself to anyone, even among the staffs of the local control centres.

Thus for at least a couple of days England remained almost normal, with the exception of the disorganisation of the communications between district and district. There was no panic. The population simply went along its old paths with the feeling that by the end of the week these temporary difficulties would be overcome and things would clear up.

The next stage was marked by the increasing difficulty of communications. Owing to the withdrawal of Grogan and his staff, simultaneously with the disappearance of the greater part of the available locomotives into the Nitrogen Area, the train services fell more and more into disorganisation. Within a very short time, travel from one part of the country to another could only be accomplished by the aid of motors.

The newspapers had been restarted; but they were no longer the organs to which people had been accustomed. Printed from presses usually employed for books, they could not be produced in anything approaching the old quantities; and the break-up of communications had shattered their organisation for the collection of information. They were mere fly-sheets, consisting of two or three leaves of quarto size at the largest and containing very little general news of any description. Not only were they printed in small numbers, but the difficulties of circulating the available copies were considerable; so that within a very short time the greater part of the population had to depend upon information passing orally from one to another.

This was the state into which Nordenholt had planned to bring them. His agents, proceeding upon a carefully considered plan, formed centres for the spread of rumours which grew more and more incredible as they were magnified by repetition. Hostile invasions, the capture of London, the assassination of the Premier, anarchist plots, earthquakes which had interrupted the normal services of the country, all sorts of catastrophes were invoked to account for the breakdown of the system under which men had dwelt so long. But the period of rumours exhausted the belief of the people. Very soon no one paid any attention to the stories which, nevertheless, sped across the country in the form of idle gossip.

Having thus manoeuvred the inhabitants of England into a state of total disbelief in rumour, Nordenholt made his next move. Hundreds of aeroplanes ranged over the country, firing guns to attract attention and then dropping showers of leaflets which were eagerly collected and read. In these messages from the sky, a complete account was given of the efforts which were being made in the North to save the situation. Short articles upon the Nitrogen Area and its vital importance to the food-supply were scattered broadcast; and by their clear language and definite figures of production they carried conviction to the minds of the readers. Here, at last, was reliable news.

No hint, of course, was given in these aerial bulletins of the real purpose underlying the Nitrogen Area. Their whole tone was optimistic; for Nordenholt wished to make his final blow the heavier by raising hopes at first. Once his agents had assured him that the people believed implicitly in his aeroplane news-service, he struck hard.

In my account of his explanation of his breaking-strain theory, I have indicated roughly the general lines upon which his attack was based. He had accomplished the breakdown of the social organism into its component parts by the interruption of communications throughout the land; but the final stage of the process was to be the isolation of each individual from his fellows as far as that was possible.

Suddenly, the news leaflets became charged with a fresh type of intelligence. At first there was a single item describing the detection of two cases of a new form of disease in the Nitrogen Area. Then, in succeeding issues, the spread of the epidemic was chronicled without comment.

PLAGUE SPREADING

TWENTY CASES TO-DAY

The next bulletins contained detailed accounts of the symptoms of the disease, laying stress upon the painful character of the ailment. It was said in some ways to resemble hydrophobia, though its course was more prolonged and the sufferings entailed by it were more severe.

Then further accounts of the extension of the scourge were rained down from the sky:

PLAGUE TOTAL: 10,000 CASES

NO RECOVERIES

Hitherto the news had confined the Plague to the Nitrogen Area; and people had not thought it would spread beyond these limits; but in the next stage of the propaganda this hope was taken from them. The messages to Southern England described how the disease had made its appearance in Newcastle and in Hull; those leaflets intended for the western districts also gave the same information. In the North of England, the intelligence took the form of accounts of the discovery of the plague in London. In every case, care was taken that there was no direct communication between the "affected centre" and the spots where the news was dropped.

The penultimate series of publications was in the form of lists of precautions to be taken to avoid the disease. It was described as contagious and not infectious; and people were advised to avoid mingling with their neighbours as far as possible. Complete isolation would ensure safety, since it had been established that the plague was not airborne. Horrible details of the sufferings of patients were also published.

Finally, the last group of leaflets represented a steady crescendo.

ENORMOUS SPREAD OF PLAGUE IN NITROGEN AREA

100,000 CASES

SPREAD OF PLAGUE THROUGH ENGLAND

ONLY A FEW DISTRICTS FREE

NITROGEN AREA DECIMATED

POPULATION DYING IN THE STREETS

DOOM IN THE CLYDE VALLEY

TOTAL FAILURE OF NITROGEN SCHEME

DEATH OF NORDENHOLT

The ultimate message was hurriedly printed with blotched type:

THE NITROGEN AREA IS ALMOST UNINHABITED, THE REMAINDER OF THE POPULATION HAVING FLED IN PANIC. THE PLAGUE IS SPREADING BROADCAST OVER ENGLAND AND SCOTLAND. ISOLATE YOURSELVES, OTHERWISE SAFETY IS IMPOSSIBLE.

After this had been dropped from the air, the skies remained empty. No aeroplanes appeared.

Thus, with a stunning suddenness, the population of the kingdom learned that their hopes were shattered. It is true that there were still channels of communication open here and there through which the news might have spread to contradict the stories from the sky. But Nordenholt had done his work with demonic certainty. By the very form of his attack he closed these few remaining routes along which the truth might have percolated. Strangers were forbidden to enter any district for fear that they might bring the Plague with them; and thus each community remained closed to the outer world. With the increase in the terror, even neighbouring villages ceased to have any connection with one another. The Leviathan was dead.

With this closing of the avenues of communication, the problem of food-supply became acute. The rations remaining in each centre were distributed hurriedly and inefficiently among the population; and then the end was in sight.

I have no wish to dwell upon that side of the story. I saw glimpses of it, as I shall tell in due course, but all I need do here is to indicate certain results which flowed naturally from the condition of things.

When the coal- and food-shortage became acute, the population divided itself naturally into two classes. On the one hand were those who, moved either by timidity of new conditions or a fear of the Plague, fortified themselves in their dwellings and ceased to stir beyond their doors until the end overtook them; whilst, on the other, a second section of the population driven either by despair or adventurousness, quitted the districts in which it knew there was no hope of survival and went forth into the unknown to seek better conditions.

Thus in the ultimate stages of the *débâcle*, the country resembled a group of armed camps through which wandered a floating population of many thousand souls, growing more and more desperate as they journeyed onward in search of an unattainable goal. In the movements of this migratory horde, two main streams could be perceived. Those who had set forth from the cities knew that no food remained in the large aggregations of population; and they therefore wandered ever outward from their starting-point; the country legions, knowing that the land was barren, fixed their eyes upon the great centres in the hope that there the stores of food would still be unexhausted. Both were doomed to disappointment, but despair drove them on from point to point.

Of all the centres of attraction, London formed the greatest magnet to draw to itself these floating and isolated particles of humanity. Like fragments of flotsam in a whirlpool, they were attracted into its confines; and once within that labyrinth, they emerged no more. Lost in its unfamiliar mazes, they wandered here and there, unable to escape even if they had wished to do so; and no Ariadne waited on them with her clue. Perhaps I overrate the strangeness of the spectacle and lay more stress upon it than it deserves. It may be that in the depths of the country even weirder things were done. But London I saw with my own eyes in the last stages of its career; and I cannot shake myself free from the impression made upon me by that uncanny shadow-show beneath the moon.

Gradually but surely the tide of human existence ebbed in Britain outside the Nitrogen Area. Here and there in the central districts there might be isolated patches whereon some living creatures remained by accident with food sufficient to prolong their vitality for a little longer; but after a few months even these were obliterated and the last survivors of the race of men were to be found clinging to the coasts of the island where food was still to be procured from the sea. Some of them struggled through the Famine period under these conditions; but most of them perished eventually from starvation; for even in the marine areas conditions were changing and the old abundant harvest of sea-creatures had passed away. The herring and other edible fish were driven to new feeding-grounds. The supply brought in by the fishing-boats diminished steadily, until at last men ceased to go out upon the waters and gave up the struggle. The winter was an exceptionally bitter one—possibly the change in the surface conditions produced by *B. diazotans* affected the world-climate, though that is still a moot point—and the cold completed the work. Long before the spring came, Britain was a mere Raft of the *Medusa* lying upon the waters and peopled by a handful of survivors out of what had once been a mighty company.

XI FATA MORGANA

To explain how I came to witness the spectacle of London in its extremity, I must go back to the evening at Nordenholt's which I have already described. He persisted in his project of forcing us into the fresh air, often twice or thrice a week if the weather was favourable; and to tell the truth, I was nothing loath. Over a hundred hours of my week were spent in concentrated mental activity under conditions which removed me more and more from direct contact with human affairs as time went on; and I looked forward with pleasure to these brief interludes during which I could take up once more the threads of my old life and its interests.

Nordenholt himself contributed but little to the conversation on these excursions. Sometimes he brought with him one of his numerous experts and spent the time in technical discussions; but usually he occupied the back seat of the car alone, lost in his thoughts and plans, while I drove and Miss Huntingtower sat beside me.

As our time was limited, and we wished to avoid the city as much as possible, our routes were mainly those to the west, by the Kilpatrick Hills or the Campsies. We never pushed farther afield, as Nordenholt had forbidden me to go outside the boundaries of the Nitrogen Area. I think he was afraid of what she might see by the roadside if we passed the frontier.

Even during these few short afternoons, I came to know her better. Somehow I had got the impression that she was graver than her years justified; but I found that in this estimate I was mistaken. She was sobered by the responsibility of her work, but underneath this she seemed to have a natural craving for the enjoyment of life, and a capacity for making the best of things which was suited to my own mood. She was quite unaffected; I never found her posing in any way. Whether she chattered nonsense—and I believe both of us did that at times—or was discussing the future, she gave me the impression of being perfectly natural.

We used to make all sorts of plans for the future of the world, once the danger was past; half-trivial, half-serious schemes which somehow took on an air of fairy-tale reality. "When I am Queen, I will set such and such a grievance right"; "In the first year of my Presidency, I will publish an edict forbidding so and so." Between us, on these drives, we planned a fairy kingdom in the future, a new Garden of the Hesperides, a dream-built Thelema of sunlit walls and towers and pleasure-grounds wherein might dwell the coming generations of men. The future! Somehow that was always with us. Less and less did we go backward into the past. That world was over, never to return; but the years still to come gave us full scope for our fancies and to them we turned with eager eyes.

The diversion grew upon us as time went on. It was always spontaneous, for our work gave neither of us an opportunity for thinking out details; and each afternoon brought its fresh store of improvisations. Through it all, she was the dreamer of dreams; it was my part to throw her visions into a practically attainable form: and gradually, out of it all, there arose a fabric of phantasy which yet had its foundations in the solid earth.

It took form; we could walk its streets in reverie and pace its lawns. And gradually that land of Faerie came to be peopled with inhabitants, mere phantasms at first, but growing ever more real as we talked of them between ourselves. Half in jest and half in earnest we created them, and soon they twined themselves about our hearts. Children of our brain, they were; dearer than any earthly offspring, for from them we need fear no disappointments.

Fata Morgana we christened our City, after the mirage in the Straits of Messina; for it had that mixture of clear outline and unsubstantiality which seemed to fit the name.

So we planned the future together out of such stuff as dreams are made on. And behind us, grim and silent, sat Nordenholt, the real architect of the coming time.

He never interrupted our talks; and I had no idea that he had even overheard them until one day he called me into his office. He seemed unusually grave.

"Sit down, Jack," he said, and I started slightly to hear him use the name, since hitherto I had always been simply "Flint" to him. "I've got something serious to discuss with you; and it won't keep much longer."

He looked up at the great Nitrogen Curve above the mantelpiece and seemed to brood over the inclinations of the red and green lines upon it. They were closing upon one another now, though some distance still separated them.

"Did it ever occur to you that I can't go on for ever?"

"Well, I suppose that none of us can go on for ever; but I don't think I would worry too much over that, Nordenholt. Of course you're doing thrice the work that I am; but I don't see much sign of it affecting you yet."

"Have a good look."

He swung round to the light so that I could see his face clearly; and it dawned upon me that it was very different from the face I had seen first at the meeting in London. The old masterfulness was there, increased if anything; but the leanness was accentuated over the cheek-bones and there was a weary look in the eyes which was new to me. I had never noticed the change, even though I saw him daily—possibly because of that very fact. The alteration had been so gradual that it was only by comparing him with what I remembered that I could trace its full extent.

"Satisfied, eh?"

"Well, there is a change, certainly; but I don't think it amounts to much."

"The inside is worse than the surface, I'm afraid. But don't worry about that. I'll last the distance, I believe. It's what will happen after the finish that is perplexing me now."

I muttered something which I meant to be encouraging.

"Well, have it your own way, if you like," he replied; "but I *know*. I have enough energy to see me through this stage of the thing; but this is only a beginning. After it, comes reconstruction; and I shall be exhausted by that time. I can carry on under this strain long enough to see safety in sight; but someone else must take up the burden then. I won't risk doing it myself. I must have a fresh mind on the thing. So I have to cast about me now for my successor."

It was a great shock to hear him speak in this tone. Somehow I had become so accustomed to look up to Nordenholt as a tower of strength that it was hard to realise that there might some day be a change of masters. And yet, like all his views, this was accurate. When we reached the other bank, he would have strained himself to the utmost and would have very few reserves left.

"I've been watching you, Jack," he went on. "I've got fairly sharp ears; and your talks in the car interested me."

I was aghast at this; for I had believed that these dreams and plannings were things entirely between Miss Huntingtower and myself. They certainly were not meant for anyone else.

"At first," he went on, "I thought it was only talk to pass the time; but by-and-by I saw how it attracted you both. After all, there are worse ways of passing an afternoon than in building castles in the air. But what I liked about your castles was that they had their roots in the earth. You have a knack of solid building, Jack, even in your dreams. It's a rare gift, very rare. I felt more friendly to you when I followed all that."

There was no patronage in his tone. As usual, he seemed to be stating what appeared to him an obvious conclusion.

"The upshot is," he went on, "that I'm going to dismiss you from your present post and put you in charge of a new

Department dealing with Reconstruction. There will be one condition—or rather two conditions—attached to it; but they aren't hard ones. Will you take it?"

Of course I was taken completely aback. I had never dreamed of such a thing; and I hardly knew what to say. I stammered some sort of an acceptance as soon as I could find my voice.

"Very good. You cut loose from your present affairs from this moment. Anglesey will take over. You can give him all the pointers he asks for to-day; and after that he must fend for himself. I'll have no two minds on that line of work.

"Now as to the new thing. It will make you my successor, of course; and I want to start with a word of warning. Unlimited power is bad for any man. You have only to look at the example of the Caesars to see that: Caligula, Tiberius, Nero, you'll find the whole sordid business in Suetonius. And I can tell you the same thing at first hand myself. I've got unlimited power here nowadays; and it isn't doing me any good. I feel that I am going downhill under it daily. You'll probably see it yourself before long, although I've fought to keep it in check. So much for the warning.

"Now as to the conditions. I admired your dream-cities, Jack. I wish you could build them all in stone. But even if you were to do that, they would still have to be peopled; and I doubt if you will find the men and women whom you want for them among the present population. Mind you, I believe you have good material there; but it has a basis in the brute which none of your dream-people had.

You don't realise that factor; you couldn't understand its strength unless you saw it actually before you: and my first condition is meant to let you see the frailty with which you will have to contend and which you will have to eliminate before you can see that visionary race pacing the gardens in your Fata Morgana. It's all in full blast within five hundred miles of here. London is thronged with people just the same as those down there in the factories; and I want you to see what it amounts to when you take off the leash. So the first condition is that you go down to London and see it with your own eyes. I could prepare you for it from the reports I have; but I think it will be better if you see it for yourself and don't trust to any other person. I'll make all the arrangements; and you can leave in a couple of days."

I am no enthusiast for digging into the baser side of human nature, and the prospect which he held out was not an inviting one to me. But I could see that he laid stress upon it, so I merely nodded my consent.

"Now the second condition. I daresay that you alone could plan a very good scheme of reconstruction; but it would be a pure male scheme. You can't put yourself in any woman's place and see things with her eyes, try as you will. But this Fata Morgana of yours, when it rises, has to be inhabited by both men and women; and you have to make it as fit for the women as for the men. That's where you would collapse."

"I suppose you're right. I don't know much about a woman's point of view. I never had even a sister to enlighten me."

"Quite so. I judged as much from some things. Well, my second condition is that you take over Elsa as a colleague. It was hearing the two of you talk that gave me the idea of using you, Jack; so it is only fair that she should have a share in the thing also."

"But would Miss Huntingtower leave you?"

"I'll try to persuade her. Anyway, leave it to me. But remember, Jack, not a word to her about London or the South. She knows nothing of that yet. I've kept her work confined entirely to Area affairs. I want to spare her as long as I can; for she'll take it hard when it comes. She'll take it very hard, I'm afraid. Until you're back from London I shall say nothing to her about your being away, lest she asks where you have gone."

I was still dazzled by the promotion he had promised me; and I thanked him for it, again and again. When I left him, my mind was still full of it all. I don't know that I felt the responsibility at first; it was rather the chance of bringing things nearer to that dream-city which we had built upon the clouds, that I felt most strongly. I had no doubt that I could lay the foundations securely; and upon them Elsa could build those fragile upper courses in which she delighted. It would be our own Fata Morgana, but reared by human hands.

So I dreamed. . . .

XII NUIT BLANCHE

The aeroplane which carried me southward alighted on the Hendon flying-ground when dusk was falling. As we crossed Hertfordshire I had seen in front of me, to the south-east, a great pall of cloud which seemed to hang above the city; and as the daylight faded, this curtain became lit up with a red glow like the sky above a blast-furnace.

When we landed, I found that all arrangements had already been made by Nordenholt; for after I had removed my flying kit an untidy-looking, unshaven man made his appearance, who introduced himself as my guide for the night. He advised me to have a meal and try to snatch a little sleep before we started. We dined together in one of the buildings—for Nordenholt had spared the Hendon aerodrome in the general destruction of the exodus, though he had burned all the aeroplanes which were there at the time—and during the meal my guide gave me hints as to my behaviour while I was under his charge, so that I might not attract attention under the new conditions. Above all, he warned me not to show any surprise at anything I might see.

After I had dozed for a time, he reappeared and insisted on rubbing some burnt cork well into my skin under the eyes and on my cheeks, and also giving my hands and the rest of my face a lighter treatment with the same medium.

"You look far too well-fed and clean to pass muster here. There's very little soap left now; and most of us don't shave. Must make you look the part."

He handed me two .45 Colt pistols and a couple of loaded spare magazines.

"Shove these extra cartridges into a handy pocket as well. The Colts are loaded and there's an extra cartridge in the breech of each. That gives you eighteen shots without reloading; and sixteen more when you snick in the fresh magazines. You know how to do it? Pull down the safety catches. If you have to shoot, shoot at once; and shoot in any case of doubt. Don't stop to argue."

A motor-car was waiting for us with two men in the front seats. The glass of the wind-screen bore a small square of paper with a red cross printed on the white ground; and I saw that one of the side-light glasses had been painted a peculiar colour. My guide and I climbed into the back seats and the car moved off. When we passed out of the aerodrome I observed that the entrance was defended by machine-guns; and a large flag of some coloured bunting was flown on a short staff. As it waved in the air, I caught the letters "P L A G U E" on it. "To keep off visitors," said my guide. "By the way, my name's Glendyne. Oh, by Jove, I've forgotten something important." He took out of the door-pocket a couple of armlets with the Red Cross on them and fastened one on my left arm, putting the other one on himself. I gathered that they formed part of his disguise. It was night now. The sky was clear except for some clouds on the horizon and the full moon was up, so that we hardly needed the head-lights to see our way. Again I noticed the peculiar red glow which I had seen from the aeroplane; but now, being nearer, I saw flickerings in it. There were no artificial lights, either of gas or electricity, in the streets through which we passed. Very occasionally I saw human forms moving in the distance; but they were too far off for me to distinguish what sort of person was abroad. In the main, the figures which I espied were reclining on the ground, some singly, others in groups; and for a time I did not realise that these were corpses.

We soon diverged from the main road and drove through a series of by-streets in which I lost my sense of direction until at last I discovered that we were passing the old Cavalry Barracks in Albany Street.

"Halt!"

The car drew up suddenly and in the glare of our head-lights I saw a group of men carrying rifles and fixed bayonets; bandoliers were slung across their shoulders, but otherwise there was no sign of uniform.

"Where's your permit? . . . Doctor's car, is it? We've been taken in by that once before. Never again, thank you. Out with that permit if you have it, or it will be the worse for you."

The armed group covered us with their rifles while Glendyne searched in his pocket. At last he produced a paper which the leader of the patrol examined.

"Oh, it's you, Glendyne? Sorry to trouble you, but we can't help it. A medical car came through the other night and played Old Harry with a patrol at Park Square; so we have to be careful, you see. I think it was some of Johansen's little lot who had stolen a Red Cross car. Stephen got them with a bomb at Hanover Gate later in the evening and there wasn't enough left to be sure who they were. Why they can't leave this district alone beats me. They have most of London left to rollic in; and yet they must come here where no one wants them. By the way, where are you going?"

"Leaving the car at Wood's Garage. Going down to the Circus on foot after that, I think; probably via Euston, though."

"All right. I'll telephone down. Sanderson's patrol is out there in Portland Place and he might shoot you by accident. I'll get him to look out for you on your way back."

"Thanks. Very good of you, I'm sure."

Our car ran forward again to the foot of Albany Street, where we turned in to a large public garage.

"What was that patrol?" I asked Glendyne.

"Local Vigilance Committee. Some districts have them. Trying to keep out the scum and looters."

"But what about this being a medical car?"

"I *am* a medical. Was an asylum doctor before Nordenholt picked me out for this job. Medical cars can go anywhere even now; but we can do better on foot for the particular work you want to-night."

He seemed to be a man of few words; but I had been struck by the empty state of the garage and wished to know where the usual multitude of cars had gone.

"Most owners took their machines away in the rush out of London. Any cars left were looted long ago. Have to leave a guard now on any car, otherwise we'd have the petrol stolen before we were back. You'll see later."

There were no lights burning in the Euston Road, either in the streets or at house-windows. Coming in the car, I had given little heed to the lack of passers-by; but here, in a district which swarmed with population in the old days, I could not help being struck by the change of atmosphere. All inhabitants seemed to have vanished, leaving not a trace. I asked Glendyne if this region was entirely deserted; but he explained to me that in all probability there were still a number of survivors.

"No one shows a light after dark in a house if they can help it," he said. "It simply invites looters."

"The full moon stood well above the house-tops, lighting up the streets far ahead of us. Wheeled traffic seemed non-existent; nor could I see a single human being. Just beyond the Tube Station, however, I observed what I took to be a bundle of clothes lying by the roadside. Closer inspection proved it to be a complete skeleton dressed in a shabby suit of serge. While I was puzzling over this, Glendyne, seeing my perplexity, gave me the explanation."

"Looking for the flesh, I suppose? Gone long ago. *B. diazotans* takes care of that, or we should have had a real Plague instead of a fake one, considering the number of deaths there have been. As soon as life goes out, all flesh is attacked by bacteria, but *B. diazotans* beats the putrefying bacteria in quick action. You'll find no decaying corpses about. Quite a clean affair."

Leaving the skeleton behind us, we continued our way. I suppose if I had been a novelist's hero I should have examined the pockets of the man and discovered some document of priceless value in them. I must confess the idea of searching the clothes never occurred to me till long afterwards; and I doubt if there was anything useful in them anyway.

As we walked eastwards towards Euston I noticed that the red glow before us was shot now and again with a tongue of flame. We passed several isolated corpses, or rather skeletons, and suddenly I came upon a group of them which covered most of the roadway. I noticed that all the heads pointed in one direction and that the greater number of the dead had accumulated on the steps of a looted public-house. Noticing my astonishment, Glendyne condescended to explain.

"Crawled there at the last gasp looking for alcohol to brace them up for another day, I expect. See the attitudes? All making for the door. Hopeless, anyway. The stuff must have been looted long before they got near it. Curious how one finds them like that, all clustered together, either at the door of a pub or the porch of a church. A Martian would think that drink and religion were the only things which attracted humanity in the end."

It was near Whitfield Street that I saw a relic of the exodus from London. Two cars, a limousine and a big five-seater, had collided at high speed; for both of them were badly wrecked, and the touring-car had been driven right across the pavement and through a shop-front. To judge from the skeletons in the limousine, its passengers had been killed by the shock.

Leaving this scene of disaster, we walked eastward again. I glanced up each side-street as I passed, but there were no signs of living beings. In the stillness, our footsteps rang upon the pavements; but the noise attracted no one to our neighbourhood. It was not until we reached the corner of Tottenham Court Road that I was again reminded of my fellow-men. A sound of distant singing reached my ears: fifty or a hundred voices rising and falling in some simple air which had a strangely familiar ring, though I could not recall exactly what it reminded me of at the time. The singers were far off, however; for when we halted at the street-corner I could see no one in Tottenham Court Road; and we went on our way once more.

The notice-boards at the gate of Euston Station were covered with recently-posted bills; and seeing the word PLAGUE in large letters upon some of them I halted for a moment to read the inscriptions. They were all of a kind: quack advertisements of nostrums to prevent the infection or to cure the disease. I was somewhat grimly amused to find that there was still a market for such trash even amid the final convulsion of humanity. The only difference between them and their fore-runners was that instead of money the vendors demanded food in exchange for their cures. Flour, bread, or oatmeal seemed to be the currency in vogue.

The station itself was dark; but here and there in the Hotel windows glowed with lamp or candle-light. "Probably some select orgy or other," was Glendyne's explanation; and he refused to investigate further. "No use thrusting oneself in where one isn't wanted. In these times the light alone is a danger signal when you know your way about."

It was in Endsleigh Gardens that we came across another living creature. Half-way along, I caught sight of a figure crouching in a doorway. At first I took it for a skeleton; but as we drew near it rose to its feet and I found that it was a man, indescribably filthy and with a matted beard. When he spoke to us, I detected a Semitic tinge in his speech.

"Give me some food, kind gentlemen! Jahveh will reward you. A sparrow, or even some biscuit crumbs? Be merciful, kind gentlemen."

"Got none to spare," said Glendyne roughly.

"Ah, kind gentlemen, kind gentlemen, surely you have food for a starving man? See, I will pay you for it. A sovereign for a sparrow? *Two* sovereigns for a sparrow? Listen, kind gentlemen, five pounds for a rat—eight pounds if it is a fat one. I could make soup with a rat."

"There's no food here for you."

"But, gentlemen, you don't understand; you don't understand. I can make you rich. Gold, much fine gold, for a miserable sparrow—or a rat! You think I am too poor to have gold? You despise me because I am clothed in rags? What are rags to me, who am richer than Solomon? I can pay; I can pay."

He kept pace with us, shuffling along in the gutter; and I noticed that the sole of one of his boots flapped loose at each step he took. After glancing around suspiciously as though afraid of being overheard, he continued in a lower tone:

"Jahveh has laid a great task upon me. I can *make* gold! Give me food, even the smallest scrap, and you shall be richer than Solomon. All that your hearts desire shall be yours, kind gentlemen. Apes, ivory, peacocks and the riches of the East shall come to you. I will give you gold for your palaces and you shall deck them with beryl and chrysoberyl, sapphire, chrysolite and sardonyx. Diamonds shall be yours, and the stones of Sardis. . . . These do not tempt you? I curse you by the bones of Isaac! May all the burden of Gerizim and Ebal fall upon you!"

He broke off, almost inarticulate with rage; then, mastering himself, he continued in a calmer tone.

"A few crumbs of bread, kind gentlemen; even the scrapings of your pocket-linings. Or a sparrow? Think what can be bought with my gold. Slaves to your desire, concubines of the fairest, brought from all the parts of the world, whose love is more than wine . . ."

It enraged me to hear this filthy object profaning all the material splendours of the world; and I thrust him aside roughly. My movement seemed to bring his suppressed anger to its climax.

"You doubt me? You will not hear the word of Jahveh's messenger? See, I will make gold before you; and then you shall fall down and offer me all the food you have—for I know you have food. Look well, O fools; I will make gold for you this moment."

He stooped down as though lifting something invisible in handfuls and then made the motion of throwing.

"See! My gold! I throw it abroad. Look how it glitters in the light of the moon. Hear how it tinkles as it falls upon the pavement. There"—he pointed suddenly—"see how the coins spin and run upon the ground. Gold! Much fine gold! Is it not enough? Then here is more."

He repeated his motion of lifting something, this time with both hands as though he were delving in loose sand.

"See! Gold dust! I throw it; and it falls in showers. I scatter it; and there is a golden cloud about us. I give it all to you, kind gentlemen. Surely all this is worth a rat, a fat one; a rat to make soup?"

He looked at us expectantly, holding out his empty hands as though they contained something which he wished us to examine.

"Still you are not convinced? Not so much as a sparrow for all this gold? I have fallen amid a generation of vipers. Ha! You would rob me of my gold; you would take it all and give me not so much as a rat? But I shall escape you. Even now I go to prepare the streets of the new Jerusalem. Jahveh has commanded me that I make them ready with my finest gold. He has prepared the smelting-furnace here in this city; it burns with fire; and I have but to lay my gold in its streets so that they shall all be covered. I go! Gold! Gold!"

He ran from us; and we heard his voice in Gordon Street crying "Gold! Gold!" as he went.

After he had left us, we came by Upper Woburn Place into Tavistock Square; and it was here that I met the first *petroleuse*. Some houses were burning in Burton Crescent. Suddenly at the corner of the entry I saw a figure appear, an oldish woman in rags, carrying a petrol tin and a dipper. She hobbled along, throwing liquid from her tin at every house-door as she passed. Sometimes she broke a window and threw petrol into the room beyond. I lost sight of her when she turned into Burton Street; but she soon reappeared, having evidently exhausted her stores. She now carried an improvised torch in her hand with which she set fire to the petrol spilled about the doors on her previous passage. Soon each doorway was a mass of flames; and she retired into Burton Crescent, with a final glance to see that her work had been well done.

"That sort of thing is going on all over the East End now," said Glendyne, "and you see that it is spreading westward too. It began by the East Enders running out of coal. Then they took to lighting bonfires in the streets with wood from the houses, to keep themselves warm. And finally houses caught fire and they got the taste for destruction. You're seeing the last of London. There are no fire-brigades now. It's only a question of time before the whole city is ablaze."

Russell Square was dark like all the rest of the streets; but the moon lit it up sufficiently for us to see what was going on in Southampton Row, where a band of men were engaged in breaking into a druggist's shop.

"What do they expect to find there?" I asked. "It doesn't seem very promising from the looter's point of view."

"Cocaine and morphia, of course," Glendyne replied, "or ether to get drunk on, if they aren't very sophisticated. They'll do anything to keep down hunger pangs nowadays, you know."

We crossed the south side of Russell Square, making for Montague Street, when my attention was attracted by the sound of singing which I had previously heard in Tottenham Court Road. The voices were nearer this time; and I was able to make out one line of the song:

Here we go dancing, under the Moon . . .

"What's that?" I asked Glendyne.

"What? Oh, that? Some of the Dancers, I expect. We'll come across them later on, no doubt. Nothing to be alarmed about. Come along!"

Just as we were moving on, however, at the turning into Montague Street there came a soft whirring behind us; a great limousine car drew up at the kerb; and from its interior descended a tall figure which approached us. As he drew near, I saw in the moonlight that it was a thin and white-haired man, showing no signs of the usual grime. He seemed a gentle old man, out of place in this city of nightmare; but as I looked more closely into his face I could see something abnormal in his eyes.

"You will excuse me for interrupting you, gentlemen; but I wish to put an important question to you. What is Truth?"

Glendyne gave an impatient snarl in reply. Probably he was completely *blasé* by this time; and took little interest in the vagaries of the human mind. As for myself, I was so taken aback by this latest comer that I could only stare without answering.

The old man looked at us eagerly for a moment; then disappointment clouded his face and he turned back to his car. We watched him without speaking as he stepped into it. The chauffeur drove on, leaving us as silently as he had come.

When we reached the great gates of the British Museum, I was somewhat surprised to find them standing wide. I suppose that even amid the abnormalities of this new London my memory was working upon its old lines, and it seemed strange to see this entrance open at that time of night. To my astonishment, Glendyne turned into the court.

"I just want to show you a curious survival in the Reading Room here."

Inside the building, all was dark; but by the light of an electric torch we found our way to the back of the premises. The Reading Room was dotted here and there with tiny lights like stars in the gloom; and within each nimbus I saw a face bent in the study of a volume.

"Still reading, you see," said Glendyne. "Even in the last crash some of them are eager for knowledge. How they find the books they want passes my comprehension; for, of course, there is no one left to give them out. But they seem able to pick out what they need from the shelves."

He threw his flashlight here and there in the gloom, lighting up figure after figure. Some of them turned and gazed toward us with dazzled eyes; but others continued their reading without paying us any attention. It reminded me of a glimpse into the City of Dreadful Night; but it seemed better than the things we had met in our wanderings outside. After all, there was something almost heroic in this vain acquirement of learning at a moment when human things seemed doomed to destruction.

As we emerged from the Museum, it seemed to me that the glare of the flames in the sky was brighter; but this may have been due merely to the increased sensitiveness of my retina after the darkness within the building. We turned to the right and followed Great Russell Street westwards.

We crossed Oxford Street and turned down Charing Cross Road. At the lower end of the street, houses were burning furiously, and I could hear the sound of the fires and the crash of falling girders. Beyond Cambridge Circus the road was impassable. Sutton Street seemed to be the only way left to us. As we came into it, I noticed that the dead were much more numerous here and that many of them held clasped in their skeleton hands a crucifix or a rosary.

"Making their way to St. Patrick's when they died," Glendyne explained to me. As we came closer to the church, we found living mingled with the dead. Some of them were so feeble that they could crawl no further; but others were still making efforts to drag themselves nearer to the door. Organ music came from the porch, and I halted amid the dead and dying to listen to the voices of the choir:

Dies irae, dies illa
Solvet saeclum in favilla . . .

It was weirdly apposite, there in the centre of that burning city. Then the choir continued:

Tuba mirum spargens sonum
Per sepulchra regionum
Coget omnes ante thronum.

Hardly had the thunder of the great vowels died away when from the crowd around us came a bitter cry, the sound of some soul in its agony. It startled me; and as I turned round, there ran a movement through that multitude of dead and dying, as though in very truth the trumpets had called the dead to life and judgment. The cry had been heard within the church; for a priest came to the porch and blessed them. It seemed to bring comfort to those alive.

"Let's get out of this," I said to Glendyne. "We can't help; and it's needless to stay here. I can't stand it."

"All right," he said philosophically. "Personally, I don't mind this so much as some of the other things one sees. These people, you know, by their way of it, have put themselves under the protection of the Church. Their path is clear. There's only Death now for them, and, after all, each of us comes to that in his own time. *They* will go out with easy minds."

As we came into Soho Square, I was reminded of the fact that even in this city of the dying, human passions still remained. From Greek Street came the sound of revolver shots: three in rapid succession, evidently a duel, and then a gasping cry, followed by a final shot. Then silence for a moment; and at last the noise of heavy footfalls dying away in the direction of Old Compton Street.

"What's that?"

"How should I know?" Glendyne retorted. "Probably some of the foreign scum settling a difference among themselves. We never bother about this district. Too dangerous to poke one's nose into. If I were to go and try to help, I'd most probably get shot for my pains. One gets to know one's way about, after a time. A few weeks ago I tried the Good Samaritan on one of these foreigners and he almost succeeded in knifing me for my pains. I suppose he thought I was one of his friends come to finish the job. He was shot through the lung anyway, so I don't suppose I could have helped much, even if I had persisted."

Soho Square was deserted. The mingled red and silver light from the burning houses and the moon lay across it; but nothing moved. We turned northward into Soho Street. It also was empty when we entered it; but while we walked up it a figure entered it from the Oxford Street end. As it approached, Glendyne made a gesture of recognition, and when the two met it was evident that they were well acquainted with one another.

"That you, Glendyne? Glad to see you again. It's a week since we met, I think."

It was a tall, thin clergyman with a clear-cut ascetic face, clean-shaven in spite of the prevailing lack of soap. For the first time that night I saw that the city had thrown up a man who was definitely sane. His keen glance, his air of competence and his matter-of-fact mode of speech were in strong contrast to what I had become accustomed to expect from the inhabitants of this Inferno. Glendyne introduced me with some perfunctory words which left my presence unexplained; and the clergyman seemed to accept me without comment.

"Things are going from bad to worse, Glendyne," he said. "I'm sometimes tempted to take advantage of your offer and clear out some of these places with a bomb or two."

"What's wrong now?" Glendyne inquired, without much apparent interest.

"Well, I can stand a good deal—have had to, you know. But when it comes to open idolatry in the West End, I must say I begin to draw the line."

"Remember two can play at that game, if you *do* begin. If you interfere with them, they will interfere with you."

"Of course, you're quite right. So far we have had no persecution; I'll say that for them. But sometimes temptation is as bad as persecution, or even worse. Persecution couldn't last long now anyway; and it would only knit us together: but temptation is a different matter. I've lost two girls in the last three days—enticed away by the Dancers. Sickening business, for one knows how that always ends. One of them was taken from my side as we were walking along the street together; and I was jammed in the crowd and could do nothing. She just cracked up, got hysterical and darted off. I lost sight of her almost at once. Of course she never came back. Damn them!" he ended with extraordinary bitterness.

"Well, it can't be helped. You do all that a man can do to keep them sane; and if you fail, it's no fault of yours."

"What has that to do with it?" cried the clergyman vehemently. "Do you think I care one way or another for that? It's the sight of these souls going down to damnation that I care about. In a few days we must all meet our Judge, and these poor things go before Him soiled in body and soul! *That's* what hurts, Glendyne. Six months ago we were all living a normal life; I was preaching the Gospel and doing my best to bring light into these people's lives. I doubt I was slack in some ways, knowing what I do now. I didn't realise the gulfs in the darkness through which we walked in this world. I knew very little of the horrors lurking under the surface. And now comes this outpouring of Hell! I used to think one should cover up all the worst in life, keep it from one's eyes. Perhaps if I had known more, I might have been of more use now. But at first I didn't know. I didn't recognise the forms under which temptation could come. Half my flock had fallen before I had opened my eyes to what was happening. Think of that! My sheer ignorance of life, look what it has cost!"

"Well, well," said Glendyne. "No use crying over spilt milk, is there? You did your best according to your lights. You weren't trained as a mental specialist, you know."

"Thanks so much, Bildad Redivivus, but I'm afraid your argument helps no more nowadays than it did a few thousand years ago in the Land of Uz. I *ought* to have known better; but I shut my eyes. I thought these things unclean and despised them; and now they have ruined my work because I did not take the trouble to understand them.

"You can't guess what it is like now, Glendyne. They are celebrating the Black Mass in Hyde Park and holding Witches' Sabbaths. All the old evil things which we thought had died out of the race have reappeared, all the foulest practices and superstitions have come to life. It's terrible."

"The old gods were never dead, although you pretended they were. Now they have come again, you have got to make the best of it. It's not for long, anyway. Another week or two and the last food will be gone."

"I pray for that day, Glendyne. I never thought to see it; but I go on my knees many times daily and pray that it may come soon. Some of my people I know will be stedfast; but the contagion attacks the younger ones with an awful swiftness."

"Collective hysteria. I know. Keep them indoors as much as possible, especially the girls. You can do nothing more."

"I suppose not. Anyway, I'll do what I can, if only I can hold out till the end myself. And to think that once I used to imagine that a minister's life circled round through sermons, prayer-meetings and visiting the sick! Why, I didn't know the beginnings of it!"

"Don't worry about the past. I'm speaking as a medico now. Get on with your work and leave the thinking till you have time for it. Eternity's pretty long, you know."

"Well, if I take your advice I must be getting back to my work. Good-night, both of you. I'll see you next week again, perhaps, Glendyne."

He walked on, leaving us to continue our exploration. Glendyne was silent for some minutes. When at last he spoke, it was in a graver tone than I had heard him use before.

"That's a splendid chap," he said, looking back over his shoulder at the tall figure behind us. "I don't envy him, though. His awakening has been a rude one in this affair. Six months ago he knew absolutely nothing of life. He was earnest and all that; but a perfect child in things of the world. The result was that when the blow came he was absolutely helpless. He fought for a time with the old platitudes—and he fought well, I can tell you, for he has a tremendous personality. But he was out of court from the first. I've seen things done under his very eyes without his even noticing what was happening. At last I gave him a few pointers from my own experience; and now he has some vague ideas what the temptations really are and how he can best counter them. And he works like a Trojan. A splendid chap. What a chance he has, if he had only had the knowledge; and how he regrets it now, poor beggar. You know, at the very first, he simply led his people down the slope without knowing it. Worked up their religious emotion, you see, until they were simply gunpowder for the flame. What a mess! And all with the best intentions too."

It was an extraordinarily long speech from Glendyne; and it gave me some measure of his liking for the clergyman. I gathered that they often met in the course of their work.

By this time we had emerged into Oxford Street. Glendyne was about to cross the road, when suddenly he caught sight of a train of figures, about a hundred and fifty in all, I should say, who were advancing up the middle of the street. Each had his hands on the shoulders of the person in front of him and the procession advanced towards us slowly, whilst I heard again the air with which I had become familiar.

"The Dancers!" muttered Glendyne. "Keep a grip on yourself, now, Flint. No hysteria, if you please."

I was angry at being treated in this way, for I am not an hysterical subject either outwardly or inwardly; but as the procession drew nearer I realised that he was right to give me a sharp warning. They advanced slowly, as I said, keeping time to the air which they sang and which I now recognised as being something like one of the old nursery lullabies I heard when I was a child. It had the knack of penetrating far into one's subconsciousness and bringing up into the light all sorts of forgotten childish fancies which had long slipped from my waking thoughts. There was no regularity in the dancing, except that the whole procession kept time to the air: each individual danced as he chose, provided that he kept his hands upon the shoulders before him so that the line remained intact. Men and women were intermingled without any order in the company. Their faces were rapt, as though in some ecstasy; and a strange, compelling magnetism seemed to emanate from the whole scene.

> Here we go . . . dancing . . . under the . . . Moon,
> Lifting our . . . feet to the . . . time of the . . . tune.
> Come, brother, . . . Come, sister, . . . join in our . . . line;
> Join with us . . . now in this . . . dancing divine.

So they came up toward us, while that strange magnetic attraction grew ever stronger upon me. For some reason which I could not fathom, I felt a profound desire to join in the procession. A kind of hallucinatory craving came over me, though I fought it down. At last Glendyne's voice broke the spell.

"Fine example of choreomania, isn't it? Perfectly well-recognised type. The old Dancing Mania of the fourteenth century. Bound to arise under conditions like the present."

The phrases fell on my ear and by their matter-of-factness seemed to come between me and the fascination which the lullaby and the rhythmical motion had begun to exercise upon my mind. Almost without any feeling whatever, I watched the Dancers approaching.

> Here we go . . . dancing . . . under the . . . Moon.
> Join in our . . . chain, it will . . . break all too . . . soon.
> When this verse . . . ends, then . . . scatter like . . . rain;
> And each dance a . . . lone till we . . . form it a . . . gain.

At the last word of the verse, the procession dissolved into a whirling crowd of figures, dancing, springing, spinning in their aimless evolutions. We were caught up in the mob; and only Glendyne's grip on my arm prevented my being jostled from his side. A knot of the Dancers came about us and strove to excite us into their revels. Women with tossing hair besought us breathlessly to join them; men dragged at us, striving to bring us out among them. All the faces wore the same look of ardency, the same expression about the lips. Some were weary; but still the excitement bore them up in their convulsions. The temptation to join them became almost irresistible; and I felt myself being drawn into their ranks when suddenly the singing broke out once more.

Here we go . . . dancing . . . under the . . . Moon . . .

The procession reformed in haste, gathering length as it went; and the Dancers began again to move eastward along Oxford Street. I watched them go, still feeling the attraction long after they were past; and only some minutes later I realised that Glendyne was still gripping my arm.

"Perhaps you understand now the way in which those two girls were lost," he said. "A slight weakening of control, eh? Not so bad for a man; but when a girl gives in to it! . . . Let's go up Rathbone Place, now. I expect we may meet something interesting in that direction."

Interesting! I had had enough of interest these last few minutes. I was still quivering with the rhythm of that doggerel song. However, I followed him across Oxford Street, into Rathbone Place. Here the clothed skeletons lay more thickly about our path. Between Oxford Street and Black Horse Yard I counted thirty-seven. Many of them lay in the road; but the majority were huddled in corners and doorways, as though the poor wretches had sought a quiet place in which to die. In the distance I heard wild shouting and the sound of something like a tom-tom being beaten intermittently; whilst in the silences between these outbursts, the roar of the flames somewhere in the neighbourhood came to me over the roofs.

At the corner of Gresse Street, a gaunt creature sidled up to us furtively; looked us up and down for a moment; and whispered to me: "Are *you* one of us?" Then, catching sight of the Red Cross on my arm, he fled into the darkness of the side-street without waiting for an answer.

In Percy Street, the *petroleuses* were at work, methodically drenching houses with oil and setting them alight. One side of the street was already ablaze; and the light wind was blowing clouds of sparks broadcast over the neighbouring roofs. London was clearly doomed. Nothing could save it now, even had anyone wished to do so. As we stood at the street-corner, one of the hags passed us and snarled as she went by:

"We'll roast you out of the West End soon, you—burjwaw! There'll be lights enough for you and yer women to dance by when Molly comes with her pail. You've trod us down and starved us long enough. It's our turn now. It's our turn now, d'yer hear? I could burn ye as ye stand"—she drew back her bucket as though to drench us with petrol—"but I want ye to dance with the rest to make it complete. We'll fix ye before long, we will."

At the southern end of Charlotte Street a rough cross had been erected in the middle of the road and to it clung the remains of a skeleton. Most of the bones had fallen to the ground, but enough remained to show that a body—dead or alive—had been crucified there at one time. Over the head of the cross was nailed a placard with the inscription:

ACHTUNG!

EINGANG VERBOTEN.

WIR SIND HIER ZU HAUSE

STÖREN UNS NICHT.

Glendyne was evidently acquainted with the placard, for he did not come forward to read it. He turned to the left and led me into Upper Rathbone Place.

"Mostly Germans in Charlotte Street now," he said. "A branch of the East End colony, and just about as bad as their friends. I pity anyone who falls into their hands. Ugh!"

He spat on the ground as though he had a bad taste in his mouth.

"Thank goodness, this is only a small colony, for that sort of thing is apt to contaminate everything in its neighbourhood. Down East it's on a bigger scale. Hark to that!"

Across the house-roofs between us and Charlotte Street there came a long quivering cry as of someone in the extremity of physical and mental agony; then it was drowned in a burst of laughter. Glendyne gritted his teeth.

"To-morrow night, if the moonlight holds, I'll have an aeroplane down here and give them a taste. They're all of a kind, in there; so it's easy enough to be sure we get the right ones. Loathsome swine!"

We cut across into Newman Street. At the door of St. Andrew's Hall a weird figure was standing—a man dressed as a faun, evidently in a costume which had been looted from some theatrical wardrobe. When he caught sight of us, he ran in our direction, leaping and bounding in an ungainly fashion along the pavement and halting occasionally to blow shrilly upon a reed pipe.

"Pan is not dead!" he cried. "I bring the good tidings! All the world awakes again after its long sleep; and the fauns in the forests are pursuing the hamadryads and following the light feet of the oreads once more upon the hills of Arcady. Io! Io! Evohé! Swift be the hunting!

"The Old Gods slumbered; but Echo, watching by rock and pool, ever answered our calling through the years. Awake! Awake! O Gods! Hear again the pipes of Pan!"

He blew a melancholy air upon his instrument, prancing grotesquely the while.

"Syrinx, reed-maiden, men have not forgotten thee! Again they hear the wailings of thy soul in the pipes of Pan."

He danced again, looking up at the moon.

"Diana! Long hast thou watched us from thy throne in the skies, but now the nights of thy hunting are come once more. Prepare the bow, gird on thy quiver and come with us again as in the days of old. Dost thou remember the white goat? Join us, O Huntress!"

Again he made music with his pipes.

"Syrinx, Syrinx! I come to seek thee in the reeds by the river. Awake! The world begins anew."

And crying "Syrinx, O Syrinx!" he ran from us and disappeared into Mortimer Street.

Glendyne turned into Castle Street East. I could not see any reason for these continual turnings and windings in our wanderings, but I suppose that he had some definite itinerary in his mind, some route which would give him the best opportunity of exhibiting to me the varied aspects of London at this time. Here again the skeletons lay scattered, though there appeared to be no aggregations of them in any particular localities. Behind us, the Tottenham Court Road district seemed ablaze; and flames leaped above the house-roofs to the east.

Suddenly, after we had passed Berners Street, I heard a confused sound of shouting, yells, running feet and the notes of a horn. Glendyne started violently and dragged me rapidly into the shelter of a house-door near the corner of Wells Street.

"This is a case where the Red Cross is no protection," he said hurriedly. "It's Herne and his pack. Keep as much under cover as you can. We shall probably not be noticed," he added. "They seem to be in full cry. There!"

As he spoke, a single man rushed into view at the corner. He was running with his head down, looking neither to right nor left, but I caught a glimpse of his face as he passed and I have never seen terror marked so deeply on any countenance. He was evidently exhausted, yet he seemed to be driven on by a frantic fear which kept him on his feet even though he staggered and slipped as he went by.

"The quarry," said Glendyne. "Now comes the pack."

Almost on the heels of the fugitive, a horde of pursuers swept into sight: about forty or fifty men and women
running with long, easy strides. Some of them shouted
as they ran, others passed in silence; but all had a dreadful air of intentness. It was more like the final stage of
a fox-hunt than anything else that I can recall. Leading
the crew was a huge negro, running with an open razor
in his hand; and I saw flecks of foam on his mouth as he
passed. Next to him was a chestnut-haired girl wearing an
evening dress which had once been magnificent. She had
kilted up the skirt for ease in running. A silver horn was
in her hand; and on it she blew from time to time, whilst
the pack yelled in reply. The whole thing passed in a flash;
and we heard them retreating into the distance towards
Oxford Street.

"What's that ghastly business?" I asked Glendyne. I had
pulled out my pistol almost unconsciously when the pack
swept into sight; but he had laid a grip on my wrist and
prevented me from firing.

"The nigger in front was Herne—Herne the Hunter,
they call him. They hunt in a pack, you see, and run down
any isolated individual they happen to come across in
their prowlings. I wish we could get hold of them; but
they seldom come near any of the picketed areas. They
can get all the sport they need without that. Once the
hunt is up, they recognise nothing. That's why I told you
the Red Cross wouldn't save you. If they chase, they kill;
and they seem able to run anyone down. I never heard of
a victim escaping them."

"What do they do it for?"

"Pleasure, fun, anything you like. It gives them a peculiar delight to hunt and kill. You see, Flint, in these times the instincts which are normally under control have all broken loose upon us; and the hunting instinct is one of the very oldest we have. In ordinary times, it comes out in fox-hunting or grouse-shooting or some wild form like that. But nowadays there is no restraint and the instinct can glut itself to the full. Man-hunting is the final touch of pleasure for these creatures."

"Who was the girl at the head of them?"

"Oh, that? She was Lady Angela." He gave a sneering laugh. "What an incongruity there is in some names! Satanita was what she ought to have been christened if everyone had their rights. And yet, in the old days, one could never have suspected this in her. I knew her, you know, and I more than liked her. She used to sing me old French songs; and one of them was rather a horrible production. It ought to have put me on my guard; but I suppose every man is a fool where women are concerned."

He broke off and hummed to himself a snatch of an old air:

Pour passer ces nuits blanches,
Gallery, mes enfants,
Chassait tous les dimanches
Et battais les paysans.
Entendez-vous la sarabande? . . .

"And so now she's running a kind of Chasse-Gallery on her own account along with that human devil, Herne. It shows how little one knows."

Just as we approached Oxford Mansions, I heard the sound of a pistol-shot, and when we came up to the spot we found a still warm body with a Colt automatic clasped in its hand. "Suicide," said Glendyne briefly, after examining the body. "The short way out."

There was nothing to be done, so we turned away. As we did so a black shadow dropped out of the sky and I saw a huge crow alighting by the side of the corpse. I think that this incident made as great an effect upon me as any. Times had changed indeed when crows became nightbirds. Glendyne watched me drive the brute away from the corpse without attempting to help.

"What's the use? It will be back as soon as we go; and I don't suppose you want to stay here all night? Birds are desperate for food nowadays, and that fellow may give you more than you expect if you don't leave him alone. The old fear of man has left them, you know, nowadays."

Before we had gone many steps, we encountered another inhabitant, a cadaverous young man with an acid stain on his sleeve. He stopped and wished us "Good-evening," being apparently glad to meet someone to whom he could talk. It was a relief to find that he appeared to be perfectly sane. I had become so accustomed to abnormality by this time that I think his sanity came almost as an unexpected thing. I asked him what he did to pass the time.

"I was working at some alkaloid constitutions when the Plague came, and I just went on with that. I've got one definitely settled except for the position of a single methyl radicle, now; and I think I shall get that fixed in a day or two. But probably you aren't a chemist?"

"No. Not my line."

"Rather a pity—for me, I mean. One does like to explain what one has done; and there's no chance of that now."

It seemed to me a pity that this enthusiast should be lost. Probably Nordenholt could find some use for him.

"I think I could put you in touch with some other chemists if you like; but you would need to trust me in the matter. Is there anyone depending on you, any relatives?"

"No, they're all gone by now."

"Well, I think I might manage it. I believe I could put you in the way of being some use; and it might be the saving of your life, too, for I suppose your food is almost out."

A famished look came into his face and I realised what food meant to him.

"Could you? I'd be awfully grateful. I'm down to the laboratory stores of glycerine and fatty acids now for nourishment, and it's pretty thin, I can tell you. Could you really do something?"

In his excitement, he clutched my arm: and at that he recoiled with a look of horror on his face.

"You damned cannibal!" he cried. "Did you think you would take me in? I suppose your friend was standing by with the sandbag, eh?"

He retreated a few steps and cursed me with almost hysterical violence.

"If I had a pistol I would finish you," he cried. "You don't deserve to live. And to think you nearly took me in. I suppose you would have enticed me to your den with that fairy-tale of yours."

And with an indescribable sound of disgust he turned and ran up Margaret Court, cursing as he went.

"What's all that about?" I asked Glendyne. "It's more than Greek to me."

"Of course you wouldn't understand. I forgot that you people up in the North don't know there's a famine on. Don't you see that when he gripped your sleeve he found a normal arm inside instead of a starved one; and he drew the natural conclusion."

"What natural conclusion?"

"Really, Flint, you are a bit obtuse. You know that food here is almost unprocurable except by those who have rationed themselves carefully from the start and have still some stores to go on with. How do you think the rest of them live? Of course the poor beggar found you in normal condition and he jumped to the conclusion that you were a cannibal like a large number of the survivors. What else could he think? He imagined that we were holding him in talk until we could sandbag him or knock him out somehow for the sake of his valuable carcase. See now?"

This seemed to be the last straw. Curiously enough, I had never given a thought to the food problem. I had simply assumed that these people in the streets were living on hoarded stores. Cannibalism! I had never dreamed of such a thing in London, even this London.

Glendyne laughed sarcastically at the expression on my face. "Why, you are nearly as innocent as my poor clerical friend," he said at last. "Can't you understand that *nothing* counts nowadays. There isn't any law, or order, or public opinion or anything else that might restrain brutes. You've got the final argument of civilisation in your pocket—a brace of them, besides the loose cartridges— and that's the King and the Law Courts nowadays. The only thing left is the strong hand; everything else has gone long ago. For the most of the survivors there isn't any morality or ethics or public spirit. They simply want to live and enjoy themselves; and they don't care how they do it. Get that well into your head, Flint."

Over the next part of our exploration I may draw a veil. We traversed the stretch from Oxford Circus to Regent Circus, which was the centre of the remaining life of London in those days. One cannot describe the details of saturnalia; and I leave the matter at that. It surpassed my wildest anticipations. At Piccadilly Circus I found a gigantic negro acting as priest in some Voodoo mysteries. The court of Burlington House had been turned into a temple of Khama. I was glad indeed when we were able to make our way into the less frequented squares to the north. Even the quiet skeletons seemed more akin to me than these wretches whom I saw exulting in their devilry. Glendyne had under-estimated the thing when he said that there was no public opinion left to control men and women. There was a new public opinion based on the principle of "Eat, Drink, for to-morrow we die"; and the collective spirit of these crowds urged humanity on to excesses which no single individual would have dared.

We came to the Langham by Cavendish Square and Chandos Street. As we stood at the hotel door, I could see the lights of the bonfires and hear the yells and shrieks of the revellers at the Circus; but Langham Place was comparatively quiet. Eastward, the sky was ruddy with the flames of the burning city; southward, the bonfires shone crimson against the pale moonlight; to the north, up Portland Place, the streets were half in shadow and half lit up by the brilliancy of the moon.

We walked northward, taking the unshadowed side of the road. Glendyne had shown me the worst now, and only the return to our car remained before us. I drew a breath of relief as we turned the bend of Langham Place and the bulk of the Langham Hotel cut us off from the sight of these lights behind us. Here, under the moon, things seemed purer and more peaceful.

We came to the corner of Duchess Street without seeing anyone; but just as we reached the crossing, a familiar figure stepped out. It was Lady Angela. This time I could see her plainly in the moonlight; a tall, chestnut-haired girl, beautiful certainly, but with the beauty of an animal type, tigress-like. Her dress was torn and a splash of fresh blood lay across her breast. In her hand was the silver horn which I had noticed before. She started as she recognised Glendyne.

"Well, Geoffrey," she said; "we haven't met for some time. You're looking thinner than when I saw you last."

It was just as if she were greeting a friend whom she had lost sight of for a few weeks. She did not seem to see the incongruity of things. For all that her tone showed, they might have met casually in a drawing-room.

"It's no use, Angela, I saw you in Berners Street to-night, you and your beasts. I knew all about you long ago. You needn't pretend with me."

She flushed, not with shame I could guess, but with anger.

"So you disapprove, do you, little man? You're one of the kind that can't understand a girl enjoying herself, are you? But if I were to whistle, you would come to heel quick enough. You were keen enough on me in the old days and I could make you keen again if I wished."

She drew herself up and, despite her tattered dress and disordered hair, she made a splendid figure. Her voice became coaxing.

"Geoffrey, don't you think you could take me away from all this? It isn't my real self that does these things; it's something that masters me and forces me to do them against my will. If you would help me, I could pull up. You used to be fond of me. Take me now."

Glendyne did not hesitate.

"It's no good, Angela. You're corrupt to the core, and you can't conceal it. I've no use for you. You couldn't be straight if you tried. Do you think I want the associate of a nigger? And what a nigger at that!"

She began to answer him, but her voice choked with fury. She raised the silver horn to her lips; blew shrilly for a moment and then cried: "Herne! Herne! Here's sport for you! Here's sport!"

"I might have known that brute wouldn't be far off if you were here," said Glendyne bitterly. "Flint, use your shots in groups of three. It's a signal to the patrol. We may pull out yet. Here they come, the whole pack!"

There was a trampling of feet in Duchess Street and I heard quite close at hand the hunting-cries of the band of ruffians. Glendyne fired nine times into the darkness of the street and we turned to run. Lady Angela watched us at first without moving, brooding on her revenge. By the time we had gone fifty yards, the whole pack was in full cry after us up Portland Place.

"We may run across Sanderson's car before they get us," Glendyne panted as he ran beside me. "The triple shots may bring him. Run for all you're worth."

He had removed the empty magazine as he ran and now turned for a moment and fired thrice in rapid succession at our pursuers. I did the same. But there was no check in the chase. We still maintained our distance ahead of them, but we gained nothing. All at once I began to find that I was falling behind. I was hopelessly out of training; and my side ached, while my feet seemed leaden. I ran staggeringly, just as I had seen the other quarry run in the earlier part of the night; and I gasped for breath as I ran.

I shall never forget that nightmare chase. Once I turned round and fired to gain time if possible. I heard Glendyne's pistol also, more than once. But nothing seemed to check the pursuit. I felt it gaining on me; and the silver horn sounded always nearer each time it blew. It was no distance that we ran, but the pace was killing. I was afraid that we might be cut off by a fresh party emerging from Cavendish Street or Weymouth Street; but we passed these in safety. I learned afterwards that Herne's band hunted like hounds, in a body, never separating into sections. Their pleasure was in the chase as much as anything; and they employed no strategy to trap their victims.

Just south of Devonshire Street I stumbled and fell. Glendyne wheeled round at once and tried to keep off the pack with his pistols; but as I rose to my feet again I saw them still coming on. The moon showed up their brutal faces hardly twenty yards away. I had given myself up for lost, when Glendyne shouted: "Lie down!" and rolled me over with his hand on my shoulder while he flung himself face downwards on the road. A dazzling glare shone in my eyes and passed; and then I saw a motor swinging in the road and the squat shape of a Lewis gun projected over its side.

I turned over and saw the pack almost upon us. Then came the roll of the Lewis gun and the maniacs stopped as though they had struck some invisible barrier. Herne crashed to the ground. Lady Angela staggered, stood for a moment fumbling with her horn, and then fell face downward. The remainder of the band turned and fled into Weymouth Street.

Glendyne picked himself up and went across to Lady Angela's body. She was quite dead, at which he seemed relieved. I understood better when I saw one of the men in the patrol car going round amongst the wounded and finishing them with his revolver.

Sanderson, the patrol leader, spoke a few words to Glendyne; and then the car swung off into Park Crescent and disappeared. The whole thing had taken only a few seconds; and we were left alone with the dead.

"It's all right now, Flint," said Glendyne. "They won't dare to come back. Besides, the leaders are gone"—he kicked the negro's body—"and they were the worst. I'll take this as a souvenir, I think."

He picked up the little silver horn; and I wondered what it would remind him of in later days.

It was in Park Crescent that I got my last glimpse of the new London. On the pavement, half-way round to Copeland Road Station, I saw something moving; and on examining it closely I found that it was a dying man. All about him were rats which were attacking him, while he feebly tried to keep them at bay. He was too weak to defend himself and already he had been badly bitten. There was nothing to be done; but Glendyne and I stood beside him till he died, while the rats huddled in a circle about him, waiting their chance. Glendyne kept them back by flashing his electric torch on them when they became too venturesome.

That was my last sight of London in these days; and looking back upon it, I cannot help feeling that this squalid tragedy was symbolical of greater things. The old civilisation went its way, healthy on the surface, full of life and vigour, apparently unshakable in its power. Yet all the while, at the back of it there lurked in odd corners the brutal instincts, darting into view at times for a moment and then returning into the darkness which was their home. Suddenly came the Famine: and civilisation shook, grew weaker and lost its power over men. With that, all the evil passions were unleashed and free to run abroad. Bolder and bolder they grew, till at last civilisation went down before them, feebly attempting to ward them off and failing more and more to protect itself. It was the dying man and the rats on a gigantic scale.

I came back to the Clyde Valley a very different being. Now I knew what had to be fought if our Fata Morgana was to rise on solid foundations; and the task appalled me.

XIII RECONSTRUCTION

When I saw Nordenholt again after my return, I found that I had no need to describe my experiences. He seemed to know exactly where I had been and what had happened to me. I suspect that Glendyne must have furnished him with a full report of the night's doings.

"Well, Jack," he greeted me; "what do you think of things now?"

"I'm down in the depths," I confessed frankly. "If that's what lies at the roots of humanity, I see no chance of building much upon such foundations. The trail of the brute's over everything."

"Of course it is! The whole of our machine is constructed on a brute basis. Did you need to go to London to see that? Why, man, every time you walk you swing your left hand and your right foot in time with each other; and that's only a legacy of some four-footed ancestor which ran with the near fore-leg and off hind-leg acting in unison. Of course the brute is the basis. A wolf-pack will give you a microcosm of a nation: family life, struggles between wolf and wolf for a living, co-operation against an external enemy or prey. But don't forget that humanity has refined things a little. Give it credit for that at least. People laugh at the calf-love of a boy; but in many cases that has no sexual feeling in it; it has touched a less brutal spring somewhere in the machine. There's altruism, too; it isn't so uncommon as you think. And patriotism isn't necessarily confined to a mere tooth-and-claw grapple with a hated opponent; it might still exist even if wars were abolished. I know you're still under the cloud, Jack; but don't think that the sun has gone down for good simply because it's hidden. All I wanted you to see was that you must be on your guard in your reconstruction. You and Elsa were planning for an ideal humanity. I want you to make things bearable for the flesh-and-blood units with which you have to work. Don't strain them too high."

"I wish I could find my way through it all," I said. "But anyway I see your point. What you wanted was to let me know which was sand and which was rock to build on, wasn't it? You were afraid I was mistaking it all for solid ground?"

"That's about it. Remember, with decent luck you ought to have a clean slate to start with. Most of our old troubles have solved themselves, or will solve themselves in the course of the next few months. There's no idle class in the Nitrogen Area; money's only a convenient fiction and now they know it by experience; there's no Parliament, no gabble about Democracy, no laws that a man can't understand. I've made a clean sweep of most of the old system; and the rest will go down before we're done."

"I know that, but to tell the truth I don't know where to begin building. It seems an impossible business; the more I look at it the less confidence I have in myself."

"Don't worry so much about that. You'll see that it will solve itself step by step. It's not so much cut-and-dried plans you need as a flexible mind combined with general principles. It's the principles that will worry you."

"I suppose you are right," I said.

"It's obvious if you look at it. Your first stages will be the getting of these five million people into two sets: one on the land to cultivate it; the other still working on nitrogen. That's evident. The whole of that part of the thing is a matter of statistics and calculation; there's nothing in it, so far as thinking goes. After that, you have to arrange to get the best out of the people mentally and morally; and I think Elsa will be a help to you there. By the way, she refuses to leave me."

"Then how am I going to get her help?"

"Oh, I've arranged that she is to have lighter work and she'll have the evenings free; so you and she can consult then, if you will."

This seemed to be enough to go on with.

"There's another thing, Jack," he continued, "I've got good news for you. It appears from the work that the bacteriologists are doing that *B. diazotans* is a short-lived creature. According to their results, the whole lot will die out in less than three months from now, as far as this part of the country is concerned. Apparently it combined tremendous reproductive power with a very short existence; and it's now reaching the end of its tether. So in three months we ought to be able to get the nitrogenous stuff on to the fields without any fear of having it decomposed. That was what always frightened me; for if *B. diazotans* had been a permanent thing, the whole scheme would have collapsed. I foresaw that, but we just had to take the chance; and I always hoped that if the worst came to the worst we might hit on some anti-agent which would destroy the brutes. You know that in some places it hasn't produced any effect at all; the local conditions seem against it, somehow."

Reconstruction! I remember those early days when I sat in my office for hours together, making notes of schemes which I tore up next day with an ever-increasing irritation at my own sterility. Given a clean slate to start with, it seems at first sight the easiest thing in the world to draw the plans of a Utopia, or at any rate to rough in the outlines when one is not hampered by details. Try it yourself! You may have better luck or a greater imagination than I had; and possibly you may succeed in satisfying yourself: but remember that I had real responsibility upon me; mine was not the easy dreaming of a literary man dealing with puppets drawn from his ink-pot, malleable to his will; it was a flesh-and-blood humanity with all its weaknesses, its failings, its meannesses that I had to deal with in my schemes.

I cannot tell how many sketches I made and discarded in turn. Most of them I had not even courage to put upon the files; so that I cannot now trace the evolution of my ideas. I can recall that, as time went on, my projects became more and more modest in their scope; and I think that they seem to fall into four main divisions.

At the start, I began by imagining an ideal humanity, something like the dwellers in our Fata Morgana; and from this picture I deducted bit by bit all that seemed unrealisable with humanity as it was. I cut away a custom here, a tradition there, until I had reduced the whole sketch to a framework. And when I put this framework together upon paper and saw what it contained, I found it to be an invertebrate mass of disconnected shreds and tatters with no life in it and no hope of existence. I remember even now the disappointment which that discovery gave me. I began to understand the gulf between comfortable theories and hard facts.

In the next stage of my development, I leaned mainly upon the future. I was still under the sting of my disillusion; and I discarded the idea that existing humanity could ever enter the courts of Fata Morgana. I tried to plan foundations upon which the newer generations could rise to the heights. Education! Had we ever in the old days understood the meaning of the word? Had we ever consciously tried to draw out all that was best in the human mind? Or had we merely stuffed the human intellect with disconnected scraps of knowledge, the mere bones from which all the flesh had wasted away? We had a clean slate—how often my mind recurred to that simile in those days—could we not write something better upon it than had been written in the past? A chasm separated us from the older days; we need be hampered by no traditions. Could we not start a fresh line?

I pondered this for days on end. It seemed to be feasible in some ways; but in other directions I saw the difficulties to the full. The clean slate was not a real thing at all. Environment counts for so much; and all the adult minds in the community had been bred in the atmosphere of the past. Their influence would always be there to hamper us, bearing down upon the younger generations and cramping them in the old ideas. There could be no clean severance between present and future, only a gradual change of outlook through the years.

My third stage of evolution led on from this conclusion. I accepted the present as it was and then tried to discover ways in which improvements might be made in the future. Again I spent days in picking out faults and making additions to the fabric of society; and at the end of it all I found, as I had done before, that the result was a patchwork, something which had no organic life of its own.

At this point, I think, I began to despair entirely; and I fell back upon pure materialism. I considered the matter solely from the standpoint of the practical needs of the time; for there I felt myself upon sure ground. Whatever happened, I must have ready a concrete scheme which would tide us over our early stages in the future.

I secured statistics showing the proportions of the population which would be required in all the different branches of labour during the coming year; and in doing this I had to divide them into groups according as they were to work on the land or were required for keeping up the supply of fixed nitrogen from the factories. My charts showed me the areas which we expected to have under cultivation at given dates in the future. I was back again in the unreal world of graphs and curves; and I think that in some ways it was an advantage to me to eliminate the human factor. It kept me from brooding too much over my recollections of humanity in its decline.

On this materialistic basis, the whole thing resolved itself into a problem of labour economy: the devising of a method whereby the greatest yield of food could be obtained with the smallest expenditure of power. Here I was on familiar ground; for it was my factory problem over again, though the actual conditions were different. There were only two main sides to the question: on the one hand I had to ensure the greatest amount of food possible and on the other I had to look to the ease of distribution of that food when it was produced. The idea of huge tractor-ploughed areas followed as a matter of course; and from this developed the conception of humanity gathered into a number of moderately-sized aggregations rather than spread in cottages here and there throughout the country-side. Each of these centres of population would contain within itself all the essentials of existence and would thus be a single unit capable of almost independent existence.

Having in this way roughed out my scheme, other factors forced themselves on my attention. I had no wish to utilise the old villages which still remained dotted here and there about the country-side. Their sizes and positions had been dictated by conditions which had now passed away; and it seemed better to make a clean sweep of them and start afresh. From the purely practical standpoint, the erection of huge phalansteries at fixed points would no doubt have been the simplest solution of the problem; but I rejected this conception. I wanted something better than barracks for my people to live in. I wanted variety, not a depressing uniformity. And I wanted beauty also.

Step by step I began to see my way clearer before me. And now that I look back upon it, I was simply following in the track of Nature herself. To make sure of the material things, to preserve the race first of all; then to increase comfort, to make some spot of the Earth's surface different from the rest for each of us, to create a "home"; lastly, when the material side had been buttressed securely, to turn to the mind and open it to beauty: that seems to me to be the normal progress of humanity in the past, from the Stone Age onwards.

It was at this period that Elsa Huntingtower came more into my life. While I was laying down the broad outlines of the material side of the coming reconstruction, I had preferred to work alone; for in dealing with problems of this nature, it seems to me best to have a single mind upon the work. It was largely a matter of dry statistics, calculations, graphs, estimates, cartography and so forth; and since it seemed to me to be governed almost entirely by practical factors, I did not think that much could be gained by calling for her help. I waited till I had the outlines of the project completed before applying to Nordenholt in the matter. When I spoke to him, he agreed with what I had done.

"I don't want to see your plans, Jack. It's your show; and if I were to see them I would probably want to make suggestions and shake your trust in your own judgment. Much better not."

"What about Miss Huntingtower's help? Am I not to get that?"

"That's a different matter entirely. She ought to give you the feminine point of view, which I couldn't do. Let's see. She can consult with you in the evenings. Will that do?"

I agreed; and it was arranged that thereafter I was to spend the evenings at Nordenholt's house, where she and I could discuss things in peace. Nordenholt left us almost entirely to ourselves, though occasionally he would come into the room where we worked: but he refused to take any interest in our affairs.

"One thing at a time for me, nowadays," he used to say, when she appealed to him. "My affair is to bring things up to the point where you two can take over. Your business is to be ready to pull the starting-lever when I give you the word. I won't look beyond my limits."

And, indeed, he had enough to do at that time. Things were not always smooth in the Nitrogen Area; and I could see signs that they might even become more difficult. Since I had left my own department, I had gained more information about the general state of affairs; and I could comprehend the possibilities of wreckage which menaced us as the months went by.

I have said before that it is almost impossible for me to retrace in detail the evolution of my reconstruction plans; and in the part where Elsa Huntingtower and I collaborated, my recollections are even more confused than they are with regard to the work I did alone. So much of it was developed by discussions between us that in the end it was hard to say who was really responsible for the final form of the schemes which we laid down in common. She brought a totally new atmosphere into the problem, details mostly, but details which meant the remodelling of much that I had planned.

One example will be sufficient to show what I mean. I had, as I have mentioned, planned a series of semi-isolated communities scattered over the cultivable area; and I had gone the length of getting my architects to design houses which I thought would be the best possible compromise: something that would please the average taste without offending people who happened to be particular in details. I showed some of these drawings to her, expecting approval. She examined them carefully for a long time, without saying anything.

"Well, Mr. Flint," she said at last, "I know you will think I am very hard to please; but personally I wouldn't live in one of these things if you paid me to do it."

"What's wrong with them? That one was drawn by Atkinson, and I believe he's supposed to be a rather good architect."

"Of course he is. That's just what condemns him in my mind. Don't you know that for generations the 'best architects' have been imposing on people, giving them something that no one wants; and carrying it off just because they are the 'best architects' and are supposed to know what is the right thing. And not one of them ever seems to have taken the trouble to find out what a woman wants, in a house. Not one.

"Don't you see the awful sameness in these designs, for one thing? You men seem to think that if you get four walls and a roof, everything is all right. Can't you understand that one woman wants something different from another one?"

There certainly was a monotony about the designs, now I came to look at them.

"Now here's a suggestion," she went on. "It may not be practical, but it's your business to make it practicable, and not simply to accept what another man tells you is possible or impossible. You say that your trouble is that you want to standardise, so as to make production on a large scale easy. So you've simply set out to standardise your finished product; and you want to build so many houses of one type and so many of another type and let your people choose between the two types. Now my idea is quite different. Suppose that you were to standardise your *material* so that it is capable of adaptation? You see what I mean?"

"I'm afraid I don't," I said.

"Like Meccano. You get a dozen strips of metal and some screws and wheels; and out of that you can build fifty different models, using the same pieces in each model. Well, why not try to design your girders and beams and doors and so forth, in such a way that out of the same set you could erect a whole series of different houses. It doesn't seem to me an impossibility if you get someone with brains to do it."

"It sounds all right in theory; but I'm not so sure about the practical side."

"Of course if you put some old fogey on to it he won't be able to do it; but try a young man who believes in the idea and you'll get it done, I'm sure. It may mean making each part a little more complicated than it would normally be; but that doesn't matter much in mass-production, does it?"

"It's not an insuperable difficulty."

"Well, another thing. Get your architect to draw up sketches of all the possible combinations he can get out of his standardised material; and then when people want a house, they can look at the different designs and among them all they are almost sure to find something that suits their taste. It is much better than your idea of three or four standard house-patterns, anyway."

"I'll see what can be done."

"Oh, the thing will be easy enough if you mean to have it. A child can build endless castles with a single box of bricks; and surely a man's brain ought to be able to do with beams and joists what a child does with bricks."

I give this as an example of her suggestions. Some of her improvements seemed trivial to me; but I took it that it was just these trivial things that made all the difference to a feminine mind; so I followed her more or less blindly.

Our collaboration was an ideal one, notwithstanding some hard-fought debatable points. More and more, as time went on, I began to understand the wisdom Nordenholt had shown in demanding that I should take her into partnership. Our minds worked on totally different lines;

but for that very reason we completed each other, one seeing what the other missed. I found that she was open to conviction if one could actually put a finger on any weak point in her schemes.

And, behind the details of our plans, I began to see more and more clearly the outlines of her character. I suppose that most men, thrown into daily contact with any girl above the average in looks and brains, will drift into some sort of admiration which is hardly platonic; but in these affairs propinquity usually completes what it has begun by showing up weak points in character or little mannerisms which end by repelling instead of attracting. In a drawing-room, people are always on their guard to some extent; but in the midst of absorbing work, real character comes out. One sees gaps in intelligence; failures to follow out a line of thought become apparent; any inharmony in character soon makes itself felt. One seldom sees teachers marrying their girl-students. But in Elsa Huntingtower I found a brain as good as my own, though working along different lines. I expect that her association with Nordenholt had given her chances which few girls ever have; but she had natural abilities which had been sharpened by that contact. She puzzled me, I must admit. My mind works very much in the concrete; I like to see every step along the road, to test each foothold before trusting my weight upon it. To me, her mental processes seemed to depend more upon some intuition than did mine; but I believe now that her reasoning was as rigid as my own and that it seemed disjointed merely because her steps were different from mine. My brain worked in arithmetical progression, if I may put it so, whilst hers followed a geometrical progression. Often it was a dead heat between the hare and the tortoise; for my steady advance attained the goal just when her mysterious leaps of intelligence had brought her to the same point by a different path.

It was not until we had cleared the ground of the main practical difficulties that we allowed ourselves to think of the future. At first, everything was subordinated to the necessity of getting something coherent planned which would be ready for the ensuing stage after the Nitrogen Area had done its work. But once we had convinced ourselves that we had roughed out things on the material side, we turned our minds in other directions as a kind of relaxation. Of course we held divergent opinions upon many questions.

"What you want, Mr. Flint, is to build a kind of human rabbit hutch, designed on the best hygienic lines. I can see that at the back of your mind all the time. You think material things ought to come first, don't you?"

"I certainly want to see the people well housed and well cared for before going any further."

"And then?"

"Oh, after that, I want other things as well, naturally."

"Well, I'll tell you what I want. I want to see them *happy*."

I can still remember that evening. The table between us was covered with papers; and a shaded lamp threw a soothing light upon them. All the rest of the room was in shadow; and I saw her face against the setting of the darkness behind her. In the next room I could feel the slow steps of Nordenholt in his study, pacing up and down as he revolved some problem in his mind.

"When I think about it," she went on, after a pause, "you men amaze me. In the mass, I mean, of course; I'm not talking about individuals. There seem to be three classes of you. The biggest class is simply looking for what it calls 'a good time.' It wants to enjoy itself; it looks on the world just as a playground; and it never seems to get beyond the stage of a child crying for amusement in a nursery. At the end of things, that type leaves the world just where the world was before. It achieves nothing; and often it merely bores itself. It doesn't even know how to look for happiness. I don't see much chance for that type in the future, now that things have changed.

"Then there's a second class which is a shade better. They want to make money; and they're generally successful in that, for they are single-minded. But in concentrating on money, it seems to me, they lose everything else. In the end, they can do nothing with their money except turn it into more. They can't spend it profitably; they haven't had the education for that. They just gather money in, and gather it in, and become more and more slaves to their acquisitive instincts. To a certain extent they are better than the first type of men, for they do incidentally achieve something in the world. You can't begin to make money without doing *something*. You need to manufacture or to transport goods or develop resources or organise in some way; so mankind as a whole profits incidentally.

"Then you come to the last of the types: the men who want to *do* something. Activity is their form of happiness.

All the inventors and discoverers and explorers belong to that class, all the artists and engineers and builders of things, great or small. Their happiness is in creation, bringing something new into the world, whether it's new knowledge or new methods or new beauty. But they are the smallest class of all."

"What amazes you in that?"

"The difference in the proportions of men in the different classes, of course. You know what the third type get out of life: you're one of them yourself. Wouldn't things be better if everyone got these things? Don't you think the pleasure of creation is the greatest of all?"

"Of course I do; but that's because I'm built that way. I can't help it."

"Well, I think that a good many of the rest of us have the instinct too; but it gets stifled very early. It seems to me that our education in the past has been all wrong. It has never been education at all, in the proper sense of the term. It's been a case of putting things into minds instead of drawing out what the mind contains already."

I was struck by the similarity between her thoughts and my own upon this matter; but after all, there was nothing surprising in that; it was what everyone thought who had speculated at all on the problem. She was silent for a time; then she continued:

"It's just like the thing we were speaking of to-night. A child's mind is like a box of bricks; and each child has a different box with bricks unlike those of any other child. Our educational system has been arranged to force each child to build a standard pattern of house from its bricks, whether the bricks were suitable or not. The whole training has been drawn up to suit what they call 'the average child'—a thing that never existed. So you get each child's mind cramped in all sorts of directions, capacities stifled, a rooted distaste for knowledge engendered—a pretty result to aim at!"

"I don't think you realise the difficulties of the thing," I said. "The younger generation isn't a handful; it's a largish mass to tackle: and one must cut one's coat according to one's cloth. The number of possible instructors is limited by the labour market."

"Hearken to the voice of the 'practical man.'" She laughed, but not unkindly. "You don't seem to realise, Mr. Flint, that things *can* be done if one is determined to do them—physical impossibilities apart, of course. When a conjurer devises a trick, do you think that he sets out by considering his available machinery? Not at all. He first thinks of the illusion he wants to produce; and he fits his machinery to that. What we need to do is to fix on our aim and then invent machinery for it. You seem to me always to put the cart before the horse and to work on the lines: 'What can we do with the machinery we have?' That's all wrong, you know. We're on the edge of a new time now; and we can do as we please. The old system is gone; and we can set up anything we choose. What we have to be sure is that the end we work toward is the right one."

We discussed education from various points of view, I remember; but what struck me most in her ideas was the emphasis which she laid on the faculty of wonder. One of her fears was that, in the stress of the new time, life would become machine-made and that the human race might degenerate into a mere set of engine-tenders to whom the whole world of imagination was closed.

"I would begin with the tiny children," she said, "and feed their minds on fairy tales. Only they would be new kinds of fairy tales—something to bring the wonder of Fairyland into their daily life. The old fairy tales were always about things 'once upon a time' and in some dim far-off country which no child ever reached. I want to bring Fairyland to their very doors and keep some of the mystery in life. I wouldn't mind if they grew superstitious and believed in gnomes and elves and sprites and such things, so long as they felt the world was wonderful. We mustn't let them become mere slaves to machinery. Life needs a tinge of unreality if one is to get the most out of it, so long as it is the right kind of unreality. Did you ever read Hudson's *Crystal Age*?"

"No, I never came across it."

"Do you mind if I show you something in it?"

She rose and took down a book from its shelf; then, coming back into the lamplight, searched for a passage and began to read:

"'Thus . . . we come to the wilderness of Coradine . . . There a stony soil brings forth only thorns, and thistles, and sere tufts of grass; and blustering winds rush over the unsheltered reaches, where the rough-haired goats huddle for warmth; and there is no melody save the many-toned voices of the wind and the plover's wild cry. There dwell the children of Coradine, on the threshold of the wind-vexed wilderness, where the stupendous columns of green glass uphold the roof of the House of Coradine; the ocean's voice is in their rooms, and the inland-blowing wind brings to them the salt spray and yellow sand swept at low tide from the desolate floors of the sea, and the white-winged bird flying from the black tempest screams aloud in their shadowy halls. There, from the high terraces, when the moon is at its full, we see the children of Coradine gathered together, arrayed like no others, in shining garments of gossamer threads, when, like thistledown chased by eddying winds, now whirling in a cloud, now scattering far apart, they dance their moonlight dances on the wide alabaster floors; and coming and going they pass away, and seem to melt into the moonlight, yet ever to return again with changeful melody and new measures. And, seeing this, all those things in which we ourselves excel seem poor in comparison, becoming pale in our memories. For the winds and waves, and the whiteness and grace, have been ever with them; and the winged seed of the thistle, and the flight of the gull, and the storm-vexed sea, flowering in foam, and the light of the moon on sea and barren land, have taught them this art, and a swiftness and grace which they alone possess.'"

The moonbeam-haunted vision which the words called up seemed to touch something in my mind; a long-closed gate of Faery swung softly ajar; and once more I seemed to hear the faint and far-off horns of Elfland as I had heard them when I was a child. Wearied with toil in my ruthless world of the present, I paused, unconscious for a moment, before this gateway of the Unreal. I felt the call of the seas that wash the dim coasts of Ultima Thule and of the strange birds crying to each other in the trees of Hy-Brasil.

Miss Huntingtower sat silent; and when I came out of these few seconds of reverie, I found that she had been watching my expression keenly:

"You 'wake from day-dreams to this real Night,' apparently, Mr. Flint. I could see you had gone a-wandering, even if it was only for an instant or two. I'm glad; for it shows you understand."

I have given an account of some of these apparently aimless and inconclusive discussions between us in order to show clearly the manner in which we went to work. At first, we oscillated between the practical side of things, the planning of houses, the laying out of towns, the applications of electricity and so forth, on the one hand, and the most abstract considerations of the mental side of the problem on the other. I remember that one evening we began with the desirability of uniforms for the population while at work. I was in favour of it on the grounds that it would facilitate mass-production and would also mark the worker's trade and possibly thus develop a greater *esprit de corps*. She conceded these points, but insisted that women should be allowed to dress as they chose, once their work was done. This brought us to the question of luxury trades, and so led by degrees to the consideration of the cultivation of artistic taste and finally to the problems of Art in general under the new conditions. Looking back, I see that our earlier advances were mainly gropings towards something which we had not clearly conceived ourselves. We did not know exactly what we wanted; and we threshed out many matters more for the sake of clarifying our ideas than with any real intention of applying our conclusions in practice.

Gradually, however, things grew more definite as we proceeded. We had certain ideas in common, general principles which we both accepted: and as time went on, this skeleton began to clothe itself in flesh and become a living organism. She converted me to her idea that happiness meant more than anything, provided it was gained in the right way. Altruism was her ideal, I found, because to her it appeared to be the most general mode of reaching contentment. At the back of all her ideas, this ideal seemed to lie. She wanted the new world to be a happy world; and each of her suggestions and all of her criticism took this as a basis.

It seems hardly necessary to enter into an account of the final form which we gave to our plans. It was not Fata Morgana that we built; but I think that at least we laid the foundation-stone upon which our dream-city may yet arise. These far-flung communities which you know to-day, these groves and pleasure-grounds, these lakes and pleasances, bright streets and velvet lawns, all sprang from our brain: and the children who throng them, happier and more intelligent than their fathers in their day, are also in part our work, taught and trained in the ideals which inspired us. If anything, we were too timid in our planning, for we had no clue to what the future held in store for us. Had we known in time, we might have ventured to launch into the air the high towers of Fata

Morgana itself to catch the rising sun. On the material side, we could have done it; but I believe we were wise in our timidity. Dream-cities are not to be trodden by the human foot. The refining of mankind will be a longer process than the building of cities; and only a pure race could live in happiness in that Theleme which we planned.

Looking backward, I think that during all these hours of designing and peering into the future I caught something of her spirit and she something of mine. By imperceptible stages we came together, mind reaching out to mind. Unnoticed by ourselves, our collaboration grew more efficient; our divergences less and less.

I can still recall these long lamp-lit evenings, the rustle of her skirts as she moved about the room, the cadences of her voice, the eagerness and earnestness of her face under its crown of fair hair. Often, as we moulded the future in that quiet room with its shaded lights, we must have seemed like children with an ever-new plaything which changed continually beneath our hands. Meanwhile, over us and between us stood the shadow of Nordenholt, ever grimmer as the days went by, carrying his projects to their ruthless termination like some great machine which pursues its appointed course uninfluenced by human failings or human desires. To me, at that time, he seemed to loom above us like some labouring Titan, aloof, mysterious, inscrutable.

XIV WINTER IN THE OUTER WORLD

My narrative has hitherto been confined to affairs in the British Isles; but to give a complete picture of the time I must now deal, even though very briefly, with the effects of *B. diazotans* in other parts of the globe. My account will, of necessity, be incomplete: because our knowledge of that period is at best a scanty one.

I have already indicated the part which the great airways played in distribution of *B. diazotans* over the world; but once it had been planted in the new centres to which the aeroplanes carried it, other factors came into action. From South-western Europe, the North-East Trade Winds bore the bacilli across the Atlantic and spread them upon the seaboard of South America, especially around the mouths of the Amazon. The winds on the coast of North America caught up the germs and drove them eventually to Scandinavia and even further east. New Guinea, Borneo, Sumatra and the other islands of the chain were devastated from the Australian centres. Madagascar was contaminated also, though the point of origin in this case is not definitely known. Probably the ocean currents played their part, as they certainly did in the destruction of Polynesian vegetation.

Climate had a considerable influence upon the development of the bacilli, once they were scattered. In the Tropics, they multiplied with even greater rapidity than they had done in the North Temperate Zone. On the Congo and in the Amazonian forests they seem to have undergone a process of reproduction almost inconceivably swift. Those which drifted up into the frigid regions of the North and South, however, appear to have perished almost without a struggle: either on account of the low temperature or the lack of nitrogenous material, they produced very little effect in either of these districts. The sea-plants seem to have been unaffected by them there; and one of the strangest results of this inactivity was the complete change in habits of various fishes, which now sought in the freezing North the feeding and breeding-grounds which suited them best. The herring left the North Sea and the cod quitted the Banks in search of purer water. On the other hand, the great masses of weed in the Sargasso Sea were almost completely destroyed, along with the other accumulations south-east of New Zealand and in the North Pacific.

It must not be assumed, however, that wherever the colonies of *B. diazotans* alighted, devastation followed as a matter of course. For some reason, which has never been made clear, certain areas proved themselves immune from attack; so that they remained like oases of cultivable land amid the surrounding deserts. The areas thus preserved from sterility were not of any great size; usually they amounted only to a few hundred acres in extent, though in isolated cases larger tracts were found unaffected here and there.

With the recognition of the world-wide influence of *B. diazotans*, the land became divided into two sections:

the food-producing districts and the consuming but non-productive areas. Nowhere was there sufficient grain to make safety a certainty. In America, most of the available food-stuffs were still in or near their places of origin when the panic began to grow.

In the matter of meat, things were much in the same state. Those countries which produced great supplies of cattle prohibited exports; and the beasts were hurriedly slaughtered and the carcases salted to preserve them, as soon as the failure of the grass made it impossible to conserve live-stock.

Each country offered features of its own in the *débâcle*; but I can only deal with one or two outstanding cases here.

The European conditions were so similar to those which I have already depicted in the case of Britain that I need not describe them at all. Southern Russia fared better than her neighbours; for after the Famine there were still some remnants of her population left alive; and it seems probable that the lower density of the Russian population retarded the extinction of humanity in this region long after the worst period had been reached in the western area.

In Africa and India, the course of the devastation was marked by risings in which all Europeans seem to have perished. Thus we have no descriptions of the later stages of the disaster in either case.

In China, the inhabitants of the densely-populated rice-growing districts of Eastern China were the first to have the true position of affairs forced upon their notice; and, leaving their useless fields, they began to move westwards. At first the stirrings were merely sporadic; but gradually these isolated movements reinforced one another until some millions of Chinese were drifting into Western China and setting up reactions among the populations which they encountered on their way. From Manchuria, great masses of them forced their way up the Amur Valley into Transbaikalia. Others, sweeping over Pekin on the road, emerged upon the banks of the Hoang Ho. The inhabitants of the Honan Province moved westward, increasing in numbers as they recruited from the local populations *en route*. A massacre of foreigners took place all over China.

In its general character, this huge wandering of the Mongol races recalls the movements which led eventually to the downfall of the Roman Empire; but the parallel is illusory. In the days of Gengis Khan, the Eastern hordes could always find food to support them on their line of march, either in the form of local supplies which they captured, or in the herds which they drove with them as they advanced. But in this new tumultuous outbreak, food was unprocurable; and the irruption melted away almost before the confines of China had been reached. Some immense bands descended from Yunnan into Burmah; but they appear to have perished among the rotting vegetation. Another series of smaller bodies penetrated into Thibet, where they died among the snows. The furthest stirrings of the wave appear to have been felt in Chinese Turkestan; and apparently Kashgar and Yarkand were centres from which other waves might have spread: but it seems probable that these westernmost movements were checked by the tangle of the Pamirs and Karakorams. Nothing appears to have reached Samarkand. But here, again, it is difficult to discover what actually did occur. Any survivors who have been interrogated are of the illiterate class, who had no definite conception of the route which they followed in their wanderings.

The history of Japan under the influence of *B. diazotans* is of especial interest, since it presents the closest parallel to our own experiences. At the outbreak of the Famine, the practical minds of the Japanese statesmen seem to have acted with the promptitude which Nordenholt had shown. They had not his psychological insight, it is true; but they had a simpler problem before them, since they could ignore public opinion entirely. Fairly complete accounts of their operations are in existence, so far as the outer manifestations of their policy are concerned, though we know little as yet of the inner history of the events.

Kiyotome Zada appears to have been the Japanese Nordenholt. Under his direction, two great expeditions raided Manchuria and Eastern China with the object of capturing the largest possible quantity of food-stuffs. It is probable that these two invasions, with the consequent loss of food-supplies, led to the great stirrings among the population of China. A Nitrogen Area was set up in the South Island, the Kobe shipyards being its nucleus. Thereafter the history follows very closely upon that of the Clyde Valley experiment, except in its last stages.

Among the other Pacific communities the Famine proved almost completely destructive. I have already told of the spreading of *B. diazotans* through the chain of islands between Australia and Burmah. In Australia itself no attempt was made to found a nitrogen-producing plant on a sufficiently large scale.

One curious episode deserves mention. In the earlier days of the Famine, news reached the Australian ports that certain of the Polynesian islands were still free from the scourge; and a frenzied emigration followed. But each ship carried with it the freight of *B. diazotans*, so that this exodus merely served to spread the bacilli into spots which otherwise they might not have reached. Before very long the whole of Polynesia was involved in the disaster. Some diaries have been discovered on board deserted vessels; and in every case the history is the same: the long search through devastated islands, the discovery at last of some untouched spot in the ocean wilderness, the rejoicings, the landing, and then, a few days later, the realisation that here also the bacillus had made its appearance. What seems most curious is the fact that in many cases it was weeks before the ship's company grasped the apparently obvious truth that their own appearance coincided with the arrival of the fatal germs. It never seems to have occurred to any of them that they bore with them the very thing which they were trying to escape. So they went from island to island, seeking refuge from a plague which stood ever at their elbow, until at last their stores failed.

On the West Coast of South America a new phenomenon appeared. The huge deposits of nitrates in Bolivia and South Peru formed the best breeding-ground for *B.*

diazotans which had yet been detected, with the result that nitrogen poured into the atmosphere in unheard-of volumes. In most places the winds were sufficient to disperse these invisible clouds of gas; but in some spots the arrival of the bacilli coincided with a dead calm, so that the nitrogen remained in the neighbourhood in which it was generated. The great salt swamp in the Potosi district furnished the best example of this phenomenon. The whole surface frothed and boiled for days together; and the atmosphere in the neighbourhood became so heavily charged with nitrous fumes that the air was almost unbreatheable. All the inhabitants of the district fled before this, to them, inexplicable danger; and the effects extended as far as Llica and the railway junction at Uyuni. In this "caliche" district, the destruction of combined nitrogen probably attained its maximum; and the propagation of *B. diazotans* never reached such a level in any other part of the world.

But with this enormous multiplication of the bacilli, other events followed. Carried north and east by winds, these huge quantities of the germs found their way into the headwaters of the Amazon and its tributaries, and were thus carried eastward into the very heart of the tropical forests, where they continued to breed with almost inconceivable rapidity. Soon the whole of the vegetation in this region was in a decline; and the Amazon valley degenerated into a swamp choked with dead and dying plants. Humanity was driven out long before the end came. Animal life could not persist in the midst of this noisome wilderness.

The same phenomena appeared, though in a different form, over the southern part of South America. Here also the great rivers formed the main distributing agencies for the bacilli; and the whole cattle-raising district was devastated. The stock was slaughtered on a huge scale as soon as it became clear that vegetation had perished; but owing to mismanagement and transport difficulties the preservatives necessary to make the best of the meat thus obtained were not procurable in sufficient quantities. Nevertheless, by converting as much as possible into biltong, more than sufficient was preserved to keep a very large part of the population alive during the Famine; and in later days, by trading their surplus dried meat for cereals and nitrogenous compounds, they succeeded in rescuing a greater proportion of lives than might have been anticipated.

To complete this survey of the world at that period, the effect of *B. diazotans* upon North America still remains to be told. I have already given some information with regard to the spread of the Blight across the Middle West; but I must mention that it was in this part of the world especially that these curious isolated immune areas were observed, wherein the bacillus seemed to make no headway. Thousands of acres in all were found to be untouched by the denitrifying organisms.

At the time of the Famine the civilisation of North America was in a curious condition, mainly owing to the influx of a foreign element which had taken place to a greater and greater extent after the War. The immigrants had come in such numbers that assimilation of them was impossible, and in this way the stability of the central Government was weakened. To a great extent the Southern States had fallen into the hands of the negroes, but similar segregations were to be found in other parts of the country. Germans accumulated in one State, Italians in another, East Europeans and Slavs in yet other areas. Thus Congress became subject to the group system of government, with all the weaknesses which such a system brings in its train.

When *B. diazotans* first made its appearance in the Continent the Government in power was composed of feeble men, without character and unfitted for bold decisions. The prohibition of cereal exports was a measure arising from panic rather than foresight; and once this had been put in operation, the Government rested on its oars and awaited the turn of events.

Thus at this period the United States presented the spectacle of a series of unsympathetic communities united by the slender bonds of a weak central Government, and divided amongst themselves by the very deepest cleavages. The grain-growing districts regarded the cities as parasites upon the food-supply which had been raised; while the city population, having only secured a certain amount of the available food-stuffs, looked upon the Middle Westerners as an anti-social group of hoarders. But even within these two large groups, minor cleavages had come to light. The poorer classes, appalled at the rise in prices, had begun to cry out against the rich. Hasty and ill-considered legislation was passed which, instead of curing the troubles, merely served to augment them;

and soon the whole country was seething with undercurrents of hatred for government of any kind.

With so much inflammable material, an outbreak was only a question of time; and soon something almost akin to anarchy prevailed. Food at any price became the cry. Those who controlled great stores of grain had to defend them; those who lacked sustenance had no reason to wait in patience. Civil war of the most bitter type broke out almost simultaneously throughout the country.

Hostilities took a form which had never been imagined in any previous fighting. In the old days one of the main objectives in the siege of an area was the shutting out of supplies from the besieged garrison. In this American war, however, the exact opposite held good. A starving population encircled the areas in which food was stored and endeavoured to force its way in; while the defenders were well supplied with rations. Nor was this all. It was well recognised among the besiegers that the supplies within the besieged area were insufficient to meet the demands which would be made upon them if the attacking force as a whole broke through the line of the defence; and therefore each individual attacker felt that his comrades were also his competitors, whom he had no great desire to see survive. Again, in the previous history of warfare, any loss on the part of the garrison was irreparable, since no reinforcements could penetrate the encircling lines of enemies; but in this new form of combat any member of the attacking force was willing to secede to the garrison if they would allow him to do so, since by this means he could secure food. Thus the casualties of the garrison could be made good simply by admitting besiegers to take the place of those who had been killed.

In the main, these sieges took place at points where the harvested grain, such as it was, had been accumulated for transport; but even the areas which had proved immune from the attacks of *B. diazotans* were attacked by far-sighted men who looked beyond the immediate future and who wished to control these remaining fertile areas in view of next year's supplies.

I have before me the diary of a combatant in one of these operations; and it appears to me that I can best give an idea of the prevailing conditions by summarising his narrative.

At the time of the outbreak he resided in Omaha; and the earlier pages of his journal are occupied by a description of some rioting which occurred in that city, ending with its destruction by fire. During the upheaval he became possessed, in some way which he does not describe, of a rifle, a considerable amount of ammunition, a certain store of food. Thus equipped, and accompanied by four friends similarly provided, young Hinkinson was able to get away in a Ford car from Omaha in advance of the main body of citizens who were now left houseless. Rumours of food-supplies led them towards Cedar Falls; but at Ackley they discovered the error of their information and were for a time at fault. Turning southward, they followed various indications and finally located a fertile area in the triangle Mexico-Moberly-Hannibal. At Palmyra, their motor broke down permanently; and they were forced to abandon it. Collecting as much of their equipment as they could carry, they tramped along the railway line and eventually reached Monroe City, which was very close to the outer edge of the contest raging around the fertile area.

From indications in the diary, it seems clear that Hinkinson and his companions expected to find at Monroe City some sort of headquarters of the attacking forces; but as they were unable to discover anything of the kind, they continued their march, being joined by a small band of other armed men who had arrived at Monroe City about the same time as themselves.

Almost before they were aware of it, they blundered into the firing-line. Apparently they had already been much surprised to find no signs of a controlling spirit in charge of the operations; but their actual coming under fire seems to have astounded them. They had expected to find a vast system of trench-warfare in existence; and had been keenly on the look-out for signs of digging which would indicate to them that they had reached the rear positions of the attacking force. What they actually found, as bullets began to whistle around them, was a thin line of civilians with rifles and bandoliers who were lying flat on the grass and firing, apparently aimlessly into the distance. At times, some of the riflemen would get up, run a few yards and then lie down again; but there seemed to be no discipline or ordered activity traceable in their methods. It appeared to be a purely individualistic form of warfare.

Hinkinson added himself to the skirmishing line, more from a desire for personal safety than with any understanding of what was happening. It appears that he lay there most of the afternoon, firing occasionally into the distance from which the bullets came. His four friends were also engaged in his immediate vicinity.

Later in the day his neighbour in the skirmishing line spoke to him and suggested that he might form a sixth in the party. Hinkinson learned from this man that during the night the attackers generally fought among themselves for any food which there might be; and he proposed that the Hinkinson party should stand watch about during the darkness, so as to avoid robbery. They agreed to this; as it seemed the best policy: though Hinkinson himself, in the entry he made at the end of the day, seems to throw doubt upon the likelihood of such proceedings.

Fortunately, they did not entirely trust their new comrade; and one of the five kept awake while pretending to sleep. When the night grew dark they heard movements in the skirmishing line, rifles were still blazing intermittently up and down the front, and here and there they caught the groans of the wounded. But in addition to these sounds, to which they had by this time grown accustomed, they heard scuffles, cries of anger, hard breathing and all the noises of men wrestling with each other. It was a cloudy, moonless night and nothing could be seen. At last, long before dawn, they discovered their friend of the afternoon engaged in rifling one of their food-bags. Finding himself discovered, he fled into the darkness and they never saw him again.

It was not until well on in the next day that Hinkinson made any further discoveries; but fresh surprises were awaiting him. He learned that the firing-line to which he was opposed was not a portion of the defence of the area at all, but was part of the attacking group. This puzzled him for a day or two, to judge from the remarks which he made in his journal; but at length he seems to have understood that his fellow-attackers were almost as much to be feared as the actual defenders.

He gives a sketch on one page of his diary showing the situation as he understood it. In the centre lies the actual fertile area, surrounded by an elaborate system of entrenchments. This zone he terms the Defence Zone. About a mile outside this, but coming much closer in parts, lies what he describes as the Offensive-Defensive Circle. When he reached this section, as we learn from a later part of his journal, he found it very roughly entrenched, the main works being rifle-pits rather than connected trench-lines. This Offensive-Defensive Circle was occupied by part of the attacking force; but the actual fighting in it was upon both front and rear. The holders of this Circle wished to force their way into the Defence Zone; but having gained a start upon the late comers whose firing-line lay still further to the rear, they proposed to retard as far as possible any advance in force from the outermost lines. Thus the combatants of the Circle, as soon as they had forced their way into it, devoted their attention to sniping new-comers who might follow them up; then seizing any opportunity, they made their way forward toward the centre and joined the inner skirmishing line which directed its fire upon the entrenchments of the actual Defence Zone. The outermost region, in which Hinkinson and his friends found themselves, was composed of men who had either arrived late on the field or failed to struggle forward in face of the sniping from the Circle.

In both the outer ring and the Circle the dominating idea was food. There was no commissariat and no central directing body of any kind. When a man joined the outer ring, he knew that he had only the supplies which he carried with him; beyond that, he could count upon nothing except what he could steal from his neighbours. The only chance of life was to fight a way up to the centre as soon as possible and take the chance of being recruited by the garrison.

While the Hinkinson group remained intact, they were able to protect themselves from food-thieves; but on the fourth day in the skirmishing line one of the five was severely wounded; and, knowing how little care was given to wounded men, he shot himself. Two more were killed by snipers on the fifth day. Three days later, Hinkinson managed to establish himself in a rifle-pit of the Circle; and he thus lost sight of his remaining friend.

Life in the Circle was lived under appalling conditions, for it was within range of both the Defence Zone and the outer skirmishing line; and there was very little chance of exercise even at night. Food was scarcer here than in the outer ring; and consequently raids for food were almost incessant during the hours of darkness. Ammunition was also very scarce; and Hinkinson was only able to keep up his supply by searching the bodies which lay in his neighbourhood. After two days in the rifle-pit he seems to have suffered from some form of influenza. The only thing which he notes with satisfaction is the fact that there was no artillery in the whole action. It was a case of rifle-fire from beginning to end.

After his third day in the rifle-pit, he succeeded in making his way into the inner firing-line of the Circle, so that at last he was actually in contact with the Defence Zone. He was astonished to find that the defenders were using up ammunition much faster than the attacking forces; and it is clear that this puzzled him, as he could see no reason for it. He had expected to find them running short.

His entry into the Defence Zone was due, apparently, to a stroke of good luck. On the day which brought him face to face with the defenders, he saw an attack made from the Circle upon the entrenchments before him. It was an utterly haphazard affair: first one man ran forward, then two or three others joined him; and finally the force of suggestion brought the major part of the attackers to their feet and hurled them upon the trenches before them, which at this point were only a few hundred yards away. Despite its random character, it seems to have been successful to some extent. A considerable number went down before a bombing attack made from the trenches; but despite this a fairly large band surmounted the parapet and disappeared beyond. A confused sound of rifle-firing was followed by a short silence; and then a regular volley seemed to have been fired. None of the attacking party reappeared.

According to Hinkinson's reading of the situation, a number of the defenders had been killed in the hand-to-hand struggle in the trenches; and he concluded that this was his best opportunity to endeavour to gain a footing among the defence force, which would now be weakened slightly and possibly anxious for recruits.

At this point, his diary is illegible and I can throw no light upon the subjects included in the hiatus. When it becomes readable again, I find him a member of the defending group.

Apparently on this side of the debatable land discipline was as marked as it was absent from the other side. The death penalty was inflicted for the slightest error. Once or twice Hinkinson seems to have run considerable risks in this direction through no great fault of his own.

He found that the defence problem was in some ways a complex one, whilst in other directions it was simplified considerably by the unique conditions of the new warfare. Owing to the enormous perimeter which had to be defended, the garrison was almost wholly used up in forming a very thin firing-line which was liable to be rushed at any point by strong bodies of the attacking force, as, indeed, he had already seen himself. Given sufficient spontaneous co-operation for a raid, the trenches could be entered without any real difficulty by the survivors of a charge. But once within the defended lines, the attackers were accepted as part of the defence force, provided that their numbers were not in excess of the casualties produced by their onset. Thus the *personnel* of the trench-lines changed from day to day, dead defenders being replaced by successful raiders whose main interest had changed sides. Under such conditions, the maintenance of discipline was a matter which required the sternest measures. The garrison was always up to full strength; but its members were not a military body in the usual sense, since they changed from time to time as new recruits took the places of the killed. Of *esprit de corps* in the usual meaning of the words there was not a trace; but its place was taken by the instinct of self-preservation, which seems to have made not a bad substitute.

As to the question of ammunition-supply, which had puzzled Hinkinson so much during his experiences in the outer zones, it became simple when once he was inside the trench-lines. There appears to have been a regular traffic by aeroplane between the food-area and the outer world, munitions being imported by air in exchange for food which the air-craft took back on their return trips.

Readers can now picture for themselves the state of the world after the Famine had done its worst. The great cities which marked the culmination of civilisation had all shared the fate of London; and most of the towns had gone the same road. All the vast and complex machinery which mankind had so laboriously gathered together in these teeming areas had been destroyed by fire.

Here and there—in Scotland, in Japan, and in a couple of American centres—Nitrogen Areas were in full activity; and the traditions of pre-Famine times were being kept alive, though with profound modifications; but outside the boundaries of these regions the only human beings left in the world were a mere handful, scattered up and down the globe and existing hazardously upon chance discoveries of food-stuffs here and there. The Esquimaux had a better prospect of survival than most of these relics of civilisation.

But the trifling changes involved in the downfall of humanity were overshadowed by the effects of *B. diazotans* upon the face of the earth. All that had once been arable land became a desert strewn with the bones of men. The vast virgin forests of America, Northern Europe and tropical Africa became mere heaps of rotting vegetation: pestilential swamps into which no man could penetrate and survive. Apart from these regions, the land-surface was sandy, except where boulder-clay deposits kept it together. Water ebbed away in these thirsty deserts; and with its disappearance the climate changed over vast areas of the world.

Those who went out in the early aeroplane exploring expeditions across these stricken and barren lands came to understand, as they had never done before, the meaning of the abomination of desolation.

XV DOCUMENT B. 53. X. 15

I think I have made it clear that when I took over the Reconstruction at Nordenholt's request I did so in a disinterested spirit, by which I mean that no personal aims of my own were concerned. I began the work solely in the hope that my plans would ensure the welfare of some millions of people, hardly any of whom I knew as individuals. It is true that I put my whole heart into the task and that I strove with all my might to bring its conclusion within the scope of possibility. I could do no less, in view of the immense responsibility which I had undertaken. Possibly my narrative has minimised the labour which the effort involved; if so, I cannot help it.

Even my early stages of collaboration with Elsa Huntingtower failed to alter this attitude of my mind. I still saw the problem as one in which great masses of people were involved; and although I appreciated the fact that these masses were composed of individuals each with his or her separate destiny to work out for good or ill, yet it never occurred to me to regard myself as one of them.

I think that the vision of Fata Morgana, growing ever clearer in my mental vision, forced my thoughts into a fresh channel. In my mind's eye I saw that happy city, thronged with its joyous people; and gradually I began to picture myself treading those lawns and wandering amid its gardens. Alone? No, I wanted some kindred spirit, someone who could share the victory with me; and Elsa Huntingtower was the only one who had part and lot in it. She and I had built its dreaming spires together by our common labour; and it was with her that I would stray in fancy through its courts. Of all humanity, we two alone had rightful seizin in its soil.

It was late before I recognised where all this was leading me; but when at last I awakened, it drove me with ten-fold force. I wanted no dim future through which I might rove as a shadow among shadows; they had served their turn in the scheme of things and brought me face to face with reality. If Paradise lay before me, Eve must be there, else it would be a mockery: if I had to face failure, I needed a comforter. I wanted Elsa.

I mistrust all novelists' descriptions of the psychology of a man in love. To me, that passion seems an integration of selfishness and selflessness each developed to its highest pitch and so intimately mingled that one cannot tell where the dividing line between them lies. Luckily, analysis of this kind is beyond the scope of my narrative. The affairs of Elsa Huntingtower and me, so far as they concerned ourselves alone, have no place upon my canvas; but since in their reactions they impinged upon a greater engine, I cannot pass them over in silence without omitting a factor which must have had its influence upon events.

I suppose, from what I see around me, that the average man falls in love by degrees. He seems to be subjected to two forces which alternately act upon him in opposite directions, so that his advance to his goal is intermittent and sometimes slow. In my case, there was nothing of this wavering. Somehow, as soon as I realised what my feelings were, I could not delay an hour longer than was necessary. The real fact was, I suspect, that I did not suddenly fall in love, though I seemed, even to myself, to have done so. In all probability I had been falling in love for weeks without knowing it; and when the illumination came, the long sub-conscious travail had prepared me for instant action.

As it happened, it was one of the days on which we usually motored into the country. At two o'clock I was in the Square with the car; and almost at once the door opened and Elsa appeared. My dreams had far outrun reality; and as the slim fur-clad figure came down the steps I felt my pulse leap. It lasted only for a moment, but I think she read my face like an open book. Behind her came Nordenholt, looking very tired. I could not help seeing the change which the last months had made in him. The deep lines on his face were deeper still; his eyes seemed to be different in some way, though as piercing as ever; and his step had lost the lightness it had when I saw him first in London. He looked me over, as he usually did, but said nothing as he stepped into the back of the car. Elsa took her customary place beside me; and it gave me a novel thrill as I arranged the rug about her. It seemed as though something had fallen from my eyes so that I saw her in a new and wonderful aspect.

As we drove westward and over the Canal, I noticed that she seemed disinclined to talk; and as I myself was busy with my dreams, I did not try to force the conversation. We had passed Bearsden and were in the open country before she had spoken three sentences; and even these were wilfully commonplace. Reflecting on this, and being myself surcharged with emotion, I was vain enough to guess that she was thinking of me and of what I had to tell her; for I had a curious feeling that she must know what was in my mind. So the milestones swept by, and still the three of us remained silent.

It was a dreary landscape through which we drove; but all landscapes in those days were bleak and sinister. In the little wood beyond Bearsden, the trees were uprooted and slanting here and there, owing to the new soil giving them no support. Some, which had threatened to fall across the road, had been cut down. Further on, the Kilpatrick Hills loomed over us, dark from the lack of vegetation; while across the Blane valley, once so green, the smooth folds of the Campsies lay black under the wintry sky. Only here and there, where snow covered the ground, did things remind one of the old days.

Past the Half Way House, along Stockiemuir with its blasted heather under its snow, up the hill at the foot of Finnick Glen the great car ran; and yet none of us spoke a word. Once, after that, Nordenholt gave me a direction; and we turned off toward Loch Lomond.

When we reached the lochside, beyond Balloch, he made me stop the car.

"I'm going to get out here and walk up towards Luss," he said. "You take the car on to the head of the loch and pick me up on the way back. Don't hurry. I want some exercise."

The door slammed; and we moved off. I looked back and saw him standing by the water-side; and it struck me that his attitude was that of an old man. He stood with his hands in the pockets of his motor-coat; and his position seemed to exaggerate the stoop of his shoulders. He looked so very, very tired. I realised, all at once, that he was ageing long before his time, worn out by his colossal task. An emotion which was as much dismay as pity swept over me in an instant. Then, as I watched, he pulled himself up and stood erect again, gazing over the water to the desolate islets. The car swung round a corner; and when I looked back once more, he was out of sight.

But that picture haunted me as I drove up the loch. I guessed at last what this struggle was costing him. Somehow I had never realised it before. I had come to regard Nordenholt as almost akin to the natural forces, the embodiment of some great store of energy which worked upon human destiny calmly and ever certainly. I had looked up to his strength and leaned upon it unconsciously, knowing only that it was there. And now, in that brief vision, I had seen that my support was itself weakening, even though for an instant. There had been a recovery, the old dominating attitude reappeared as he pulled himself together again. But before this I had never seen effort in that attitude; and I saw it now. Even in my exalted condition, the sight of that weary figure struck down into my memory.

Elsa had not looked back. She sat beside me, her clean-cut profile emerging from her dark furs, gazing straight before her at the road ahead. We ran through Luss without a word to each other. My heart was throbbing with excitement; and yet I hesitated to break the silence. Some miles further up the road, before we reached Tarbet, she asked me to stop the car and suggested that we should go down to the water's edge.

It was there that I at last found speech and, having found it, poured out what I had to say in a torrent of words none of which I can remember now. I had rehearsed that scene many a time in my mind, and yet it all came unexpectedly. I had never anticipated this opportunity. I had thought that some time, when we talked of the future we were planning, I would tell her what I needed to make it complete. And I had thought of how she would take my pleading: I had forecast how she would look and what she would reply. But in none of my visions had I foreseen the reality.

She listened to me coldly, almost as if her mind were occupied with other things. I grew more passionate, I think, striving to make her understand my emotion; and yet she seemed almost indifferent to what I said. At last I stopped, chilled by this aloofness which I did not understand. In my wildest imaginings I had never thought of this *dénouement* of the situation. I think I must have grown cold myself: for though I can recall nothing of my previous words, the rest of the scene is graven on my mind. For some moments after I had ceased, she remained silent; then at length she spoke, with an accent in her voice which I had never heard before. I remember that she had taken off one glove and stood twisting it in her hands while she talked.

"I got you to stop the car here because I have something to ask you, something of tremendous importance to me. Forgive me if I put it first and don't answer you immediately. I'm . . . I'm very grateful for all you have said. But this thing comes before everything; and you must let me ask you about it before we come to . . . to our own affairs."

A pang of apprehension shot through me. What could she be driving at which was of greater importance than our future?

"As I was going over my papers to-day," she went on, "I came across one which seemed to have been missorted. It didn't belong to my section. I glanced at it casually; and then I read it. Have you any idea what it referred to?"

"No."

"It said things I could hardly grasp. Even now I think it must be a mistake. I can't believe it was a real document. It must have been a hoax or something like that. And yet, it had the usual serial numbers on it: B. 53. X. 15."

My throat was dry, but I managed to pull myself together and make a sound like "Well?" She came close to me and looked me straight in the eyes—so like Nordenholt's gaze in some ways—and I tried to bring my features into a mask.

"Is it true that everyone outside the Area has been left to die? Is it true that there has been a deliberate plot to starve all the men, all the women, even the little children in the country? Tell me that, and tell me at once. Don't wait to wrap it up in fine phrases. Tell me the truth *now*."

I stood before her, silent.

"So it *is* true; and you knew it! You acquiesced in it. You even helped in it; I can see it in your face. You cur!"

Still I could not find my voice. This was a different scene from that I had thought of only ten short minutes before. It was not that I felt anything myself, except a sort of dull comprehension that my dreams were shattered; but the sight of the pain in her face moved me more than I could express in words. I wanted to help her. I wanted to justify the plan Nordenholt had made. And yet something kept me tongue-tied. I could find no phrase to open my explanations. The outpouring of speech which I had found so easy only a few seconds earlier now seemed dried up. I merely watched her, saying nothing. For a time she struggled with herself, trying to master her feelings. All this time her face had been set; not a tear had come to her eyelashes.

"I have a right to know who planned this," she continued, after a pause. "Do you know what I thought at first? I suspected Uncle Stanley. I even suspected *him*. But I don't, now. I know him too well. I didn't even question him about it. I didn't want to worry him until I had found out whether it was true or not. But it *is* true. Who planned it? Answer me!"

There was no concealment possible. Once she had the clue, she would discover everything almost immediately. Not even delay was to be gained by a lie. And with her clear eyes upon me, I could not have lied even had I wished to do so. She might never be mine; but I was hers to do as she wished. For a moment I hesitated, turning over in my mind the idea of referring her to Nordenholt himself; but I abandoned that almost instantaneously. The shock would be greater if it came from him; better let me bear the brunt.

"Your uncle planned it. I helped him."

"Uncle Stanley! You don't expect me to believe that? It shows how little you know of us both if you think . . ."

Her voice became tinged with doubt, and tears, too, came into it. The evidence was too clear. Only Nordenholt could have carried out such a gigantic scheme. And possibly she read the truth in my face as well. For a moment she seemed frozen, a rigid and silent statue. All the flush had left her cheeks and above the softness of her furs her features seemed as though carved in marble. When she spoke again, she seemed to be trying to convince herself.

"Did Uncle Stanley suggest it? I can't believe it. It's impossible. He couldn't do a thing like that. You don't know him. He couldn't. He couldn't. I know he couldn't."

Even in that moment of tension, I could not help reflecting how little a woman can know of a man's mind. Half our mental processes are shut off from them, as probably half of theirs are closed books to us. The great barrier of sex divides us; and our outlook upon the world can never be the same. This girl had been in close communion with Nordenholt through most of her life; and yet she failed to recognise at once as his handiwork the greatest achievement to which he had put his powers.

She wavered on her feet. I stepped forward to catch her but she struck aside my hand. Then she seated herself on a bank. I looked away; and when I saw her again she was sitting, her face buried in her hands, while her fragile figure shook with suppressed sobbing.

"Elsa," I said, "you don't understand. It's come upon you suddenly; and you've been swept off your feet by it. But it was all for the best. It had to be done."

She looked up. On her face, still wet with tears, I saw only contempt and bitterness.

"It had to be done?" she echoed. "Do you mean that forty millions of people *had* to be robbed of their food and left to starve? Can't you see what it means, or are you made of stone? Think of men seeing their mothers dying; think of lovers watching their sweethearts starve; and the children in their mothers' arms. And you, *you* say calmly that 'It had to be done.' You aren't a machine. You had the right to choose. And you chose *that*!"

"You don't understand," I repeated wearily. Somehow the strain of the situation seemed to have robbed me of my forces.

"No, I don't understand. How can I, when it means that the men I thought most of in the world turn out to be nothing but murderers on a gigantic scale? I can't believe it, even yet. Is it . . . is it all a mistake? Oh! I want to wake up out of this nightmare; I want to wake up. Tell me it's a nightmare and not real."

Her voice sounded almost like that of a terrified child in the dark.

"It's no nightmare," I said. "Try to see what it meant. There wasn't enough food for us all. Somebody had to die if the rest were to be saved."

"And so you elected to be one of the rest? I congratulate you. A most laudable decision, I am sure," she said contemptuously. "It would indeed have been a pity if you had gone short of food in order to save the lives of a mere score of children; tiny, helpless little things that can't do more than cry as they starve."

"You don't understand," I repeated. "There was no chance of saving them in any case. They were doomed from the start. All we did was to ensure that *somebody* would survive. If the food had been evenly distributed, we should all have died; but your uncle laid his plans to save millions of people. Surely you can see that?"

She thought for a moment; and then attacked in a fresh direction.

"Who gave you the right to choose among them? You seem to think you are a demi-god with the power of life and death in your hands. How could *you* take the responsibility of the choice? And how could you bear to save yourself when you knew other men, and perhaps better men, had to die? I can't understand you. You're so different from what I thought you were. Somehow all my ideals seem to be breaking. You and Uncle Stanley were the two finest men I had met. I never dreamed for a moment that you would turn out to have feet of clay. And now . . ."

I tried hard to put our case before her. I explained the state of things at the outbreak of the Famine. I gave her figures to prove that Nordenholt had only worked to save what he could from the disaster. It was all of no avail. I think that the picture of the starving children filled her mind to the exclusion of almost everything else; and that she hardly listened to what I said. Once she whispered to herself, "Poor little mites," just when I thought I had caught her attention at last. I gave it up in the end. She looked away across the loch, where the first stars were lighting up behind the hills; and we stood in silence, so close in space, so remote from each other in our thoughts. At last she spoke again.

"Still I don't understand it all. I see your view; but I can't share it. It seems so cold-blooded, so horrible. But I can't understand you, just when I thought I knew you through and through. Tell me, how could you talk of Fata Morgana and all our dreams when you *knew* that this terrible thing was happening? That's what I don't grasp."

"I can't explain it to you. Probably I keep my mind in compartments. But never mind about me, Elsa; I'm done for now. I don't matter. But you mustn't condemn your uncle along with me. He never led you on to dream dreams, so you haven't that against him. I want you to believe me that he has been a saviour and not a destroyer, as you seem to think. Don't lose your faith in him until you understand. Don't prejudge things till you know everything. Speak to him yourself before you come to a conclusion. He depends on you, more than you think, perhaps. And he's worked himself to the bone to save those few millions that are left to us. Don't judge him till you know everything."

She looked at me more kindly than she had done since the beginning.

"That's just what I should have expected from what I knew of you, Mr. Flint. You think of him first and don't bother about yourself. You aren't selfish. I can't understand you, somehow. You seem such a mixture; and until to-day I had no idea you were a mixture at all. It's all so difficult."

She ended with a choke in her voice and turned towards the car. I followed her and switched on the head-lights, ready to start. She climbed into her seat; and I put the rug around her knees. Just as I was on the point of starting, she spoke again.

"You've told me all I need to know; but I must hear it from Uncle Stanley himself. I'll go on being his secretary. I'll do all I can to help. But I hate you both. Yes, if this is true, I hate him too. What else do you expect? You look on yourselves as saviours, it seems. You may be that, but you certainly are murderers. You can't even see why I abhor you both. That shows you the gulf between us. Oh, I hate you, I hate you, with this cold calculation of yours: so much food, so many lives. Is that the way to handle human destinies? Drive on."

A little further down the road, she spoke again in a quivering voice which she strove to keep level and cold:

"This ends any work together. I couldn't bear it in your case. With Uncle Stanley it's different. I will go back to my old place with him. But I never want to see *you* again, Mr. Flint. I've lost two illusions to-day; and I don't wish to be reminded of them more than I need be. I promised him that I would always help him; and I'm going to keep my promise, cost what it may. But I never promised *you* anything."

For a few minutes I drove on in silence. The whole world seemed to have fallen around me. All that I had longed for, all my future, seemed to have collapsed in that short afternoon. I was not angry; I don't think I was even completely conscious of what it all meant. I felt stunned by an unexpected blow. At last I roused myself.

"Elsa," I said, "do you remember the first evening we met?"

She never moved.

"You sang that dirge from Cymbeline, you remember? When you're calmer, I want you to think over it. I don't want you to have any regrets. Mr. Nordenholt can't last for ever under this strain. Think carefully."

She made no sign that she had heard me speak. The car whirred through the dusk, while we sat silent and aloof from each other. It was a return very different from that which I had hoped for when I set out. I was almost glad when, further down the loch, the beams of the headlights showed us the figure of Nordenholt in the road. I pulled up the car beside him; and Elsa leaned forward in her seat.

"Uncle Stanley, Mr. Flint has told me everything. I saw a document this morning, B. 53. X. 15; and I forced Mr. Flint to explain what it meant. Did you really plan this awful thing?"

I could not see Nordenholt's face in the shadow; but his voice was as steady as ever in his reply. Afterwards I realised that he must have foreseen such a situation as this long before.

"It is perfectly true, Elsa. Anything that Mr. Flint has told you is probably correct, though his connection with the matter is very slight."

"But he says that you planned it all and that he helped you. I can't . . . I can't quite understand it all. It's a mistake, isn't it? It's not your real plan, surely. You're going to save all these people in the South, aren't you?"

"Every soul that can be saved by me will be saved, Elsa. You can count on that."

"But you will give them all a chance of life, won't you? You won't take away all the food from them?"

"There's no food to spare."

For a few moments there was silence. Elsa made a sudden movement, and I guessed that she had recoiled from Nordenholt's touch. At last she spoke again, in a way I had not anticipated.

"Do you remember my three wishes, Uncle Stanley? You gave me two of them and now I want the third. You promised me the whole three; and you never broke your word yet. I want you to save these people in the South. That's my third wish."

I think it was that which made me realise the gulf that yawned between us, more than anything that had gone before. How could she imagine that Nordenholt's vast machine could be deflected on account of some childish promise? And yet her voice had taken on a new tone of confidence; everything, she thought, was going to be set right. It seems she must have believed, even then, that the treatment of the South was only one of a number of alternative schemes; and that she could force the adoption of some other, not so good, perhaps, but still possible, as a solution. Her very belief in Nordenholt's powers led her to assume that he must have several plans ready pigeon-holed, and that the rejection of one merely entailed the substitution of some other which was already cut and dried.

"When that promise was made, Elsa, there was one condition: your wish was not to be an impossible one. This *is* impossible."

"Oh!" There was such an agony in her voice that I felt it rasp my already over-tried nerves.

"That is final, Elsa. There is nothing more to be said."

For almost a minute she made no reply. In the silence I could feel her struggling for control of her voice. When at last she spoke, she seemed to have fought down her emotion, for her tone was almost indifferent:

"Very well, Uncle Stanley. You refuse to help these people; but I am not so easy in my mind. I will go into the South myself and do my best to help them; and if I cannot help, I can at least take the same risks as they do. *I* can't stay here, well fed and well cared for when they are suffering."

"You will not do that, Elsa. No, I don't mean to prevent you going if you wish, though you have no idea what you would be going to. But I haven't brought you up to be a shirker; and you're needed here. You have the whole of your work at your finger-ends and if you go it will dislocate that department temporarily; and we can't afford to have even a temporary upset at this stage. You promised you would stay, no matter what happened; and I ask you to keep your promise now. I also tell you that I need you, and your work here is helping to save lives in the Area, more lives than you could ever save outside. Now do you wish to go?"

She thought for a time, evidently weighing one thing and another. While she was still silent, I broke in, wisely or unwisely I did not know.

"If Elsa goes into the South, Nordenholt, I go with her to look after her. You must find someone else to take my place. I can't let her go alone."

Nordenholt's voice was as calm as ever.

"You understand, Elsa? If you go, you take away Mr. Flint; and although I can replace you in your department, I doubt if I can get anyone as good as he is in his line. Go South and you cripple one of the essential parts of the Area. Stay here, and you help us all towards safety—and we are not near the safety-line yet. Which is it to be? I put no pressure on you. I only point out what I think is your duty."

I had expected some angry reply, some hurried decision which might bring disaster in its train; but luckily things took a different turn. I believe that the strain had been too great for her. Now came the collapse; and before I knew what had happened, she had broken into tears. Nordenholt leaned over her, trying to comfort her; but it was useless; and he let her work out her fit of emotion to the end. At last she pulled herself together.

"If you are sure you need me, I will stay. But I hate you both. I hate the work. I hate the Area and everything in it.

I'll keep my promise to you; but things will never be the same again . . . And, oh, this morning I was so happy."

Nordenholt climbed aboard the car without another word, and I drove on into the dark. Now and again I heard a half-suppressed sob from the girl at my side; but that was all. At the door of Nordenholt's house I stopped. Elsa left me without uttering even "Good-night." I watched her tall, slim figure go up the steps and disappear; and something blinded me. I found Nordenholt standing at the side of the car.

"Poor chap," he said, with an immense pity in his voice. "So you're involved too? I wish it had been otherwise. Well, well; I couldn't hope to keep it from her much longer at the best. But I'm very, very sorry. She'll take it so hard. Her type never looks at these things the way we do."

He paused and looked at me keenly in the light of the terrace lamps. When he spoke once more, his voice sounded very weary.

"Stand by me, Jack. Get your part ready in time. Don't flinch because of this. I'm nearly at the end of my tether."

I could not trust myself to speak. We shook hands in silence, and he went up the steps into the house.

XVI IN THE NITROGEN AREA

I have no wish to dwell overmuch upon my own affairs in this narrative; for they formed a mere ripple on the surface of the torrent of events which was bearing all of us along in its course. Yet to exclude them entirely would be to omit something which is of importance; for they must have influenced my outlook upon the situation as a whole and possibly made me view it through eyes different from those which I had used before.

My dreams and desires had come to the ground almost ere they were in being; and what made it more bitter to me was that I felt they had been crushed, not on their merits, but merely as subsidiaries which had shared in the collapse of a more central matter. I guessed that Elsa had, to some extent, at any rate, shared my feelings; and it was this which made the downfall of my hopes all the harder to bear.

Try as I would, I could find no reason behind her attitude; and even now, looking back upon that time, I cannot appreciate her motives. In the whole affair of the Nitrogen Area I had been guided by purely intellectual considerations. Nordenholt himself had advised me to keep a tight rein upon any feelings which might divert me from this course. And I was thus, perhaps, less able to appreciate her standpoint then than I would have been a few months earlier.

On her side emotion, and not intellect, was the guiding star. The picture of starving millions which had broken upon her without warning had overpowered her normally clear brain. Thus there lay between us a gulf which nothing seemed capable of filling. I thought, and still believe, that emotion is a will-o'-the-wisp by which alone no man can steer a course; but it is useless to deny its power when once it has laid its influence upon a mind. Even had she given me a chance, I doubt if I would have tried to reason with her; and she gave me no chance. I never saw her alone; and when she met me perforce or by accident, she treated me practically as a stranger. All the long evenings of planning and dreaming had gone out of our lives.

As soon as I could make an opportunity, I questioned Nordenholt as to the state of affairs. He answered me perfectly frankly.

"Elsa has never said a word to me about the South. I think she shrinks from the idea even in her own mind; and she shrinks from me because of it, as I can see. But she sticks to her work, even if she loathes coming into contact with me daily; and I keep her as hard at it as I can. The less time she has to think, the better for her; and I don't mean to leave her any time to brood over the affair. Poor girl, you mustn't feel hard about her, Jack. I can understand what it means to her; and to you also: and her part is the saddest. She simply hates me now; I can feel it. And neither of us can help her, that's the worst of it."

To Nordenholt himself the situation must have been a terrible one; for Elsa was closer to him than any other human being could ever be: and the position now was worse even than if he had lost her entirely. I am sure that he had never felt anything more than affection for her; but she had become more to him, perhaps, just for that reason. I often used to think that they formed natural complements for one another: he with his great build and powerful personality, she with her slender grace and her character, strong as his own, perhaps, but in a far different sphere.

It was about this period *B. diazotans* began to die out from the face of the world which it had wrecked. I have already told how Nordenholt had given me the news when it was still a possibility of the future. From their studies upon isolated colonies of the microbe, the bacteriologists had predicted its end. They had found a rapid falling-off in its power of multiplication; and the segregation of a number of the pests soon led to their perishing.

When it became clear that *B. diazotans* was doomed, Nordenholt began to send out scouting aeroplanes to collect samples of soil from various districts and bring them back to the laboratories of the Nitrogen Area where they could be examined. All told the same tale of extinction. Gradually, the aeroplanes were sent further and further on their journeys into the stricken lands; and at last it became clear that as far as a large part of Europe was concerned, the terror was at an end. The soil, of course, was completely ruined; but there was little to fear in the way of a recrudescence of the blight.

It seems, nowadays, very strange that we had not already foreseen this result; for the cause of it lay upon the surface of things. Once the denitrifying bacteria had destroyed all the nitrogen compounds in the soil, there was nothing left for them to live upon; and they perished of starvation in their turn, following in the track of all the larger organisms which their depredations had ruined.

As soon as Nordenholt had established the definite decease of *B. diazotans* in the accessible parts of the European continent, he sent out the news to the whole remaining world with which he was in touch through his wireless installation; and after some time had been spent in various centres in which the remnants of humanity were gathered together, word came back from the most widely-separated areas that all over the world *B. diazotans* had ceased to exist. In many places it had even left no traces of any kind behind it; for as some of the bacteria died their bodies, being nitrogenous, had served as food for those still living; until at last the merest trace of their organisms was all that could be found in the soil.

So this plague passed from the world as swiftly as it came; and its passing left the future more certain than seemed possible in the early stages of its career.

But if our gravest danger was thus removed, we in the Nitrogen Area had other troubles which were nearer to us at that time. In his very earliest calculations, Nordenholt, as I have told, had foreseen that disease would be prevalent owing to the monotony of the diet which was entailed by our conditions. The lack of fresh vegetables and the use of salted meat gave rise to scurvy, which we endeavoured to ward off by manufacturing a kind of synthetic lime juice for the population. The success of this was not complete, however, and the disease caused a very marked falling-off in the productive power of our labour. For a time it seemed as though we were actually losing ground in our factories, just at the moment when the destruction of the denitrifying bacteria had raised our hopes to a high degree.

Nor was scurvy our only trouble. The debilitated health of the people laid them open to all sorts of minor diseases, with their concomitant decline in physical energy. Of these, the most serious was a new type of influenza which ravaged the Nitrogen Area and caused thousands of deaths. Here again, a fall in output coincided with the growth and spread of the disease; but since the death-roll was a heavy one, the number of mouths diminished markedly as well; so that it almost appeared as though the two factors might balance each other. If there were less food in the future, there would be fewer people to consume it.

I think the period of the influenza epidemic was one of the most trying of all in the Nitrogen Area. As the reported cases increased in number, individual medical attention became impossible; for many doctors died of the scourge, and we could not risk the total annihilation of the medical profession. Treatment of the disease was standardised as far as possible and committed to the care of rapidly-trained laymen. Possibly this led to many deaths which might have been avoided with more efficient methods; but it was the only means which would leave us with a supply of trained medical men who would be required in the future.

On the heels of the influenza epidemic, and possibly produced by it, came a period of labour unrest in the Area. It was only what I had always anticipated; for the strain which we were putting upon the workers had now increased almost to the breaking point. There was no way out of the difficulty, however; for unless the work was done, the safety of the whole community would be imperilled. None the less, I could not help finding excuses in my mind for those toiling millions. To them, the connection between the factories and the food-supply must have been difficult to trace; for they could hardly follow all the ramifications in the lines between the coal in the pits and the next harvest which was not even sown.

Nordenholt succeeded in stifling most of the disaffection by means of a fresh newspaper campaign of propaganda. He had given his journals a long period of rest in this direction, purposely, I believe, in order that he might utilise them more effectively when this new emergency arose. But though he certainly produced a marked effect by his efforts, there remained among the workers an under-current of discontent which could not be exorcised. It was not a case of open disaffection which could have been dealt with by drastic methods; the Intelligence section were unable to fasten upon any clear cases of what in the old days would have been called sedition. It was rather a change for the worse in the general attitude and outlook of the labouring part of the community: an affair of atmosphere which left nothing solid for Nordenholt to grasp firmly. Though I was out of direct touch with affairs at the time, even I could not help the feeling that things were out of joint. The demeanour of the workers in the streets was somehow different from what it had been in the earlier days. There was a sullenness and a tinge of aggressiveness in the air.

And in Nordenholt himself I noticed a corresponding change. He seemed to me by degrees to be losing his impersonal standpoint. The new situation appeared to be making him more and more dictatorial as time went by. He had always acted as a Dictator; but in his personal contact with men he had preserved an attitude of aloofness and certainty which had taken the edge off the Dictatorship. Now, I noticed, his methods were becoming more direct; and he was making certain test-points into trials of strength, open and avowed, between himself and those who opposed him. He always won, of course; but it was a different state of things from that which had marked the inception of the Nitrogen Area. There was more of the master and less of the comrade about him now.

Yet, looking back upon it all, I cannot but admit that his methods were justified. The disaffection was noticeable; and only a strong hand could put it down. Nordenholt's tactics were probably the best under the circumstances; but nevertheless they brought him into a fresh orientation with regard to the workers. Instead of leading them, he began more and more openly to drive them along the road which he wished them to take.

I see that I have omitted to mention the attempted invasion of the Nitrogen Area from the coasts of Europe which took place just before this. To tell the truth, it was so complete a fiasco that it had almost passed from my mind; but a few words may be devoted to it here.

When the Famine had done its work in Germany there still remained for a time a number of inhabitants who had seized the food in the country by force and who were thus enabled to prolong their existence while their fellows died out. They belonged mainly to the old military class. When they in turn ran short of supplies, their natural thought was to plunder someone weaker than themselves; and learning of the existence of the Clyde Valley colony, they determined that it furnished the most probable source of loot. Apparently they imagined that the Fleet in the Firth of Forth was deserted; for in order to excite no suspicion they had kept their airships at long-range in the reconnaissances which they undoubtedly made in advance of their actual onset; and it seems most probable that they imagined they had nothing to fear beyond the risks incident to the invasion of an unprotected country. At least, so it appears to me; and there were no survivors of the expedition from whom the truth might have been discovered.

Under cover of night, they seem to have put most of their men on board merchant ships and sailed for the British coast at a time which would have brought them off the land in the early hours of the morning when, no doubt, they expected to get ashore without attracting attention, since they must have supposed all the coastal inhabitants had perished. Actually, however, their manoeuvres had been followed by the seaplane patrol which cruised in the North Sea; and as soon as they left port, the Fleet was got into a state of preparedness. The two forces met somewhere on the high seas; the German squadron, utterly defenceless, was sunk without any resistance worthy of the name.

This was the only actual attempt at invasion which the Nitrogen Area had to repel; for Nordenholt's aeroplane propaganda had checked any desire on the part of the survivors of the Famine in this country to approach the Clyde Valley under any conditions.

Though Nordenholt succeeded in suppressing the outward manifestations of labour unrest at this period, I think it is fairly clear that he was unable to reach down to the sources of the trouble. At the root of things lay a vague dissatisfaction with general conditions, which it was impossible to exorcise; and this peculiar spirit manifested itself in all sorts of sporadic forms which gave a good deal of trouble before they could be got under control.

For example, at about this time, there was an outbreak of something akin to the dancing mania which I had seen in London. It began by a rapid extension of normal dancing in the halls of the city; but from this it soon passed into revelry in the public squares at night; and finally took the form of corybantic displays in the streets. As soon as it began to demoralise the people, Nordenholt applied the drastic treatment of a fire-hose to the groups of dancers;

and, between this method and ridicule, he succeeded in stamping out the disease before it had attained dangerous proportions.

But this was only one of the symptoms of the grave troubles which were menacing the success of Nordenholt's plans. I do not doubt that he had foreseen the condition into which affairs had drifted; but it seems to me that he recognised the impossibility of eradicating the roots of the discontent. Its origin lay in the actual material and moral states of affairs; and without abandoning his whole scheme it was impossible to change these things.

I know that during these months he stiffened the discipline of the Labour Defence Force considerably in view of eventualities; and he had frequent conferences with the officers in command of its various units. I guessed, from what I saw, that in future he intended to drive the population into safety if he could hot lead them there; and I confess that at times I took a very gloomy view of our chances of success.

It was during this trying period, I think, that Nordenholt's young men were his greatest source of strength. He was always in touch with them; and in some way he seemed to draw encouragement from them while spurring them on to further efforts. They seemed to lean on him and yet to support him in his work; and often I felt that without some comradeship as this our whole plans would have been doomed to failure. The Nordenholt Gang practically occupied all the posts of any responsibility in the

Nitrogen Area; and this, I expect, rendered the working of the machine much smoother than it would otherwise have been.

Since my new work brought me into touch with many fresh departments, my acquaintance with Nordenholt's men increased; and I was amazed to find the ramifications of his system and the super-excellence of the human material in which he had dealt. They were all young, hardly any were over thirty-five and most were younger; yet they seemed to have a fund of moral courage and self-reliance which struck me especially in those dark times. They never seemed to doubt that in the end things would come right. It was not that they blindly trusted in Nordenholt to the exclusion of common sense: for they all seemed to face the facts quite squarely. But behind their even weighings of the situation I detected an unspoken yet whole-hearted belief that Nordenholt would bring us through without a hitch. Hero-worship has its uses, when it is soundly based; and all of them, it was easy to see, had made Nordenholt their hero. When I thought over the many-sided nature of their activities and the differences of personality among them, I could not help finding my view of Nordenholt himself expanding. They were all picked men, far above the average; their minds worked on different lines; their interests were as divergent as the Poles: and yet, one and all, they recognised Nordenholt as their master. I do not mean that he excelled them in their own special lines: for I doubt, in many cases, whether he had even a grip of the elements of the subjects which they had made their own. But he had been able to impress upon all these various intellects the feeling that he was in a class by himself; and that effect implied immense personality in him.

Despite their widely different fields of activity, there was a very strong *esprit de corps* among them all; and it was not for some time that I felt myself to be received on equal terms with the rest. I think they felt that I was outside their particular circle, at first. But the real passport into it was efficiency; and when I had had time to show my power of organisation, they accepted me at once as one of themselves.

Of them all, I think Henley-Davenport interested me most, though I can hardly put into words the reasons which led to this attraction. I never learned how Nordenholt had discovered him originally; but I found that when Henley-Davenport began to open up the subject of induced radioactivity, Nordenholt had stepped in and bought up for him a huge supply of various radioactive materials which he required in his work and which he had despaired of acquiring on account of their enormous cost.

What struck me most about him was his fearlessness. Once he gave me, incidentally in the course of a talk upon something else, a suggestion of the risks which his work entailed. It seemed to me that I would have faced half a dozen other kinds of death rather than that one. Purely as a matter of physiological interest, he told me that the effect of radioactive materials on a large scale upon the human body would exceed the worst inventions of mediaeval torturers.

"The radiations, you know," he said, drawing at his cigarette. "The radiations have a knack of destroying tissue; but they don't produce immediate effects. The skin remains quite healthy, to all appearances, for days after the damage is done. Then you get festering sores appearing on the affected parts.

"Well, on a large scale, the affected parts will be the whole surface of the body; so that in itself will be pretty bad, as you can see. Poor old Job will have to take a back seat after this.

"Then, again, I expect enormous quantities of radioactive gas will be evolved; and probably one will breathe some of it into one's lungs. The result of that will be rather worse than the external injuries, of course. I doubt if a man will last half an hour under that treatment; but that half-hour will be the limit in pain."

"Can't you use a mask or some lead protection?" I asked. "Or could you not fix up the whole thing in a bomb-proof case which would keep the rays from things outside?"

"Well, that's the first thing one thinks of, naturally; but to tell the truth it's impracticable for various reasons. Some of them are implicit in the nature of the processes I'm using; but even apart from that, look at the state of affairs when the thing does go off with a bang. It will be one of the biggest explosions, considering the amounts I have to use; and if I'm going to be flung about like a child's toy, I prefer to fly light and not have a sheet of lead mail to go along with me and crush me when I strike anything. As to a mask, nothing would stick on. You would simply be asking to have your face driven in, if you wore anything of the kind.

"No, I've been lucky so far. I've only lost three fingers in a minor burst-up. And I'm going to stake on my luck rather than risk certain damage. But if I can only pull it off, Flint . . . Nordenholt thinks a lot of it; and I don't want to disappoint him if I can help it. If I do go to glory, I'll at least leave something behind me which will make it more than worth while."

Nordenholt, I learned later, *did* "think a lot of it." I spoke to him on the subject one day; and I was astonished to find how much stress he laid on the Henley-Davenport work.

"You don't realise it, Jack; but it's just on the cards that our whole future turns on Henley-Davenport. I see things coming. They're banking up on the horizon already; and if the storm bursts, nothing but Henley-Davenport can save us. And the worst of it is that he doesn't seem to be getting ahead much at present. It's no fault of his. No one could work harder; and the other two—Struthers and Anderson—are just as keen. But it doesn't come out, somehow. And the tantalising thing is that he has proved it *can* be done; only at present it isn't economical. He gets energy liberated, all right; but where we need a ton of gunpowder, he can only give us a percussion cap, so to speak. If only he can hit on it in time . . ."

For my own part, that period was depressing. All the joy had gone out of my work. Only after I had lost her did I realise how great a part Elsa had played in my planning of the future. Her disappearance cast a shade over all my schemes; and soon I gave up entirely the side of the recon-struction in which we had collaborated. I could not bear to think over again the lines along which we had worked so intimately in common. I simply put them out of my mind and concentrated my attention exclusively upon the material aspects of the problem.

I have said this quite freely; though possibly the reader may look upon me as a weak man for allowing such fac-tors to enter into so vast a matter. Had I been superhu-man, no doubt, I could have shut my mind to the past; and gone forward without flinching. But I never imagined that I was a super-man; and at this time especially I felt anything but superhuman. I was wounded to the quick; and all I desired was to avoid the whole subject of Elsa in my thoughts. And when I come to think of it, it seems quite probable that I did my best work in this way. If I had continued to dream of Fata Morgana and all its wonders, I should simply have drugged myself with a mental opiate and my work would have suffered on other sides.

Elsa's whole attitude to Nordenholt and myself had been a puzzle. I could not understand why she should have been so bitter against us; for try as I could, I failed to see anything discreditable in our doings. The logic of events had thrust us into the position we occupied, it seemed to me; and I could not appreciate her view of the situation.

Nordenholt kept silence on the subject for some days after our trip up Loch Lomond; but he finally gave me his views in reply to urgent questioning.

"I think it's something like this, Jack: from what I know of Elsa in the past, she's got a vivid imagination, very vivid; and it happens to be the pictorial imagination. Give her a line of description, and she has the power of calling up the scene in her mind, filling in missing details and producing something which impresses her profoundly."

"Well, I don't see what that's got to do with calling me a brute," I said. "It doesn't seem to help me much."

"It's quite clear to me. The few details she got from that confounded missorted form were enough to start her imagination. She instinctively called up a vision of starving people, suffering children and all the rest of the affairs in the South. And you know, Jack, these visions of hers are wonderfully clear and sharp. It wasn't you who built Fata Morgana on these afternoons; it was her imagination that did it and you followed in her track."

"Yes, you're quite right, Nordenholt. I don't think I would have so much as thought of dream-cities if she hadn't led the way. And she certainly had the knack of making them seem concrete."

"Very well; assume she had this vision of starving humanity. You know her type of mind—everything for others? What sort of effect would that picture produce upon her? A tremendous revulsion of feeling, eh? Her whole emotional side would be up in arms; and she has strong emotions, though she doesn't betray them. Her intellectual side didn't get a chance against the combination of that picture and her ideals. It was simply swept out at once.

"But in spite of all her emotions, she's level-headed. Sooner or later she'll begin to think more calmly. And she's very just, too. That ought to help, I think. Oh, I don't despair about her; or rather, I wouldn't despair about her if it weren't for some things that are coming yet. I'm not going to buoy you up with any hopes, Jack, for I believe in dealing straight. I can't let you hope for much; we've both lost enormously in her eyes. But I've seen cases in which her imagination misled her before and her reason came out in the end. It may be so this time. But don't expect anything, Jack; and don't try to gain anything. She's a very straight girl, and if she finds she has been wrong she won't hesitate to come and admit it to you without any encouragement on your part. But it has been a horrible affair for her; and you must remember that, if you think hardly of her at times."

"*I* think hardly of her! You don't know me, Nordenholt, or you wouldn't say that."

"Well, for both our sakes, I hope her intellect will get control of her feelings. I hate to see her going about her work and know that she has lost all faith in me now. She was the one creature in the world that loved me, you know, Jack; and it's hard."

Then he laughed contemptuously, as though at his own weakness.

"It's quite evident I'm not the man I was, Jack. But somehow, in this affair we're both in the same boat to some extent; and I let that slip out. You see that Elsa hasn't the monopoly of an emotional temperament!"

All great undertakings with uncertain ends appear to run the same course. First there is the period of inception, a time of high hopes and eager toil and self-sacrifice; then, as the novelty wears away, there follows a stage in which the first enthusiasm has died down and an almost automatic persistence takes the place of the great emotional driving-force of the early days; later still, when enthusiasm has vanished, there comes a time when the meaner side of human nature reasserts itself. My narrative has reached the point of junction between these last two divisions; and the pages which I have yet to write must perforce deal mainly with the troubles which beset us in the period of lassitude and nerve-strain which followed naturally upon the other phases of the situation.

I have thrown this chapter into a series of isolated sections; for I believe that such a treatment best suggests the state of things at the time. We had lost the habit of connected thought, as far as the greater events were concerned. Our daily round absorbed our attention; and it was only occasionally that we were jarred out of our grooves by some event of salient importance.

The whole atmosphere which surrounded us was depressing; and it slowly and surely made its impression upon our minds and formed the background upon which our thoughts moved. The gloom of the smoke-filled sky had its reaction upon our psychology. The old sunlight seemed to have vanished from our lives. And at this time we were all beginning to pay the price for the feverish activity of the earlier days in the Area. Our work, whether mental or physical, wearied us sooner than before; and its monotony irritated our nerves. Such recreations as we had—and they were few enough at this time—failed to relieve the tension. Among the labouring classes, in particular, this condition of lassitude showed itself in a marked degree.

Nordenholt, with his finger on the pulse of things, grew more and more anxious as time went on. On the surface, he still appeared optimistic; but from chance phrases here and there I deduced that his uneasiness was increasing; and that he anticipated something which I myself could not foresee. Knowing what I do now, it seems to me that in those days I must have been blind indeed not to understand what was before us; but I frankly confess that I missed the many signs which lay in our path from day to day. When the disaster came upon us, it took me almost completely by surprise.

XVII   PER ITER TENEBRICOSUM

After Elsa had rejected any further collaboration with me, I was forced at times to consult Nordenholt upon certain points in my schemes which seemed to me to require the criticism of a fresh mind; and I thus fell into the habit of seeing him in his office at intervals.

"Things are in a bad way, Jack," he said to me at the end of one of these interviews. "You don't see everything that's going on, of course; so you couldn't be expected to be on the alert for it; but it's only right to warn you that we're coming up against the biggest trouble we've had yet in the Area."

"Of course things are anything but satisfactory, I know," I replied. "The output's going down and there seems to be no way of screwing the men up to increase it. But is it really fatal, do you think? We seem even now to have the thing well in hand."

I glanced up at the great Nitrogen Curve above the fireplace. The red and green lines upon it appeared to me to show a state of affairs which, if not all that we could wish, was at least satisfactory as compared with what might have been. Nordenholt followed my glance.

"That practical trend of mind which you have, Jack, sometimes keeps you from seeing realities. What lies at the root of the trouble just now isn't output or slackness or anything like that. These are only symptoms of the real disease. It's not in the concrete things that I see the danger, except indirectly. The true peril comes from the intangibles; ideas, states of mind, sub-conscious reflections. I've told you often that the material world is only the outward show which hardly matters: the real things are the minds of the men who live in it. It's their movements you need to look at if you want to gauge affairs."

"I stick to what I know, Nordenholt, as I've often told you. I'm no psychologist; and I have to look on the material side because I'm out of my depth in the other. But let's hear what you have in your mind about the state of affairs."

"Well, you've been busy enough with your own work; so probably you haven't had time to observe how things are going; but I can put the thing in a nutshell. We've weathered a good many difficulties; but now we're up against the biggest of them all. I see all the signs of a revival in the near future—and it isn't going to be a Christian revival. It spells trouble of the worst description."

Now that my attention had been drawn to the point, a score of incidents flashed across my mind in confirmation of what he said. I had noticed an increased attendance at the meetings of street-preachers; and also a growth in the number of the preachers themselves. As I went about the city in the evenings I had seen in many places knots of people assembled round some speaker who, with emotion-contorted visage, was striving to move them by his eloquence.

Once I had even stopped for a few minutes to listen to a sermon being preached outside the Central Station by the Reverend John P. Wester; and I still remembered the effect which it had produced upon me. He was a tall man with a flowing red beard and a voice which enabled him to make himself heard to huge audiences in the open air. He repelled me by the cloudiness of his utterances—I hate loose thinking—and also by the touch of fanaticism which clung to his discourses; for I instinctively detest a fanatic. Yet in spite of this I felt strangely attracted by him. He had the gift of gripping his hearers; and I could see how he played upon them as a great musician plays upon a favourite instrument. Remotely he reminded me of Nordenholt in the way in which he seemed to know by instinct the points to which his rhetorical attacks should be directed; but the resemblance between the two men ended at this. It was always reason to which Nordenholt appealed in the end; whilst emotional chords were the ones which the Reverend John fingered with success.

"Now you've told me, I believe you're right," I said. "I *have* seen signs of something like a revival. The crowds seem to be taking a greater interest in religion."

"I wish they would," Nordenholt returned, abruptly. "They won't get it from the Reverend John. He's out for something quite different. It's just what I feared would happen, sooner or later. It always crops up under conditions like those we are in just now. We've strained the human machine to its utmost in all this work; and we're on the edge of possibilities in the way of collective hysteria.

"Now that man Wester is at the root of half the trouble we are having just now. I don't mean that he is creating it; nothing of that sort: but his personality forms a centre round which the thing collects. The thing itself is there anyway: but if it weren't for him and some others, it would remain fluid; it wouldn't become really dangerous. But Wester is a fanatic and with his oratorical powers he carries the weaker people off their feet, especially the women. He's got a following. What worries me is, where he's going to lead them. He's got a kink in him. Still, I'm trusting that we may be able to weather the thing without using force even now. But if he goes too far, I'll break him like *that*."

He tapped a stick of sealing wax on his desk and broke it in two. Again I reflected how unlike this was to the Nordenholt I had known at first, the man who could unfold huge plans without so much as a gesture to help out his meaning. He must have read the thought in my eyes, for he laughed, half at himself, I think.

"Quite right, Jack. These theatrical touches seem to be growing on me, of late. I must really try to cure myself. But, all the same, I mean to keep my eye on the Reverend John. If he sets up as a prophet—and I expect he will do that one of these days—I'll take the risk and put him down. But it's a tricky business, I can tell you. Until he actually becomes dangerous, I shall let him go on."

It was only natural, after that, for me to take more interest in the career of the Reverend John. I even attended one of his open-air meetings from start to finish; and I was still more impressed by his command over his hearers. The material of his sermons seemed to me commonplace in the extreme: it was not by the novelty of his subjects but by his personal force that he impressed his audiences and raised them to a state of exaltation. Zion, the River, the Tree of Life, Eden, the loosing of burdens, rest and joy eternal: all the old phrases were utilised. From what I heard of his preaching, it seemed to me innocuous. A brief time of suffering and sorrow upon earth and then the heavens would open and the Elect would enter into their endless happiness: these appeared to be the elements of the creed which he expounded; and I could see little reason for Nordenholt's anxiety.

At last, however, I began to notice something novel in the sermons. The change came so gradually that I could hardly be sure when it began. Probably he had opened up his fresh line so tentatively that I had not observed it at the time; and it was only after he had already been changing step by step in his subject that I became clearly conscious of his new tone.

With the greatest skill he contrived to use the old expressions while inflecting them with a fresh intention. At last, however, there could be no doubt as to his meaning. It was no longer Christianity that he preached, but a kind of bastard Buddhism. Up to that point in his career he had spoken of earthly affairs as a trial through which we must pass in order to attain to bliss in the Hereafter; but in his newer phase the things of the material world became entirely secondary.

Eternal rest, eternal joy, eternal peace: these were his main themes; and to the exhausted and nerve-racked population they had an attraction of the most subtle kind. The Reverend John was a psychologist like Nordenholt, though he worked in a narrower groove; and he well knew how to utilise the levers of the human consciousness. Eternal rest! What more attractive prospect could be held out to that toil-worn race?

Slowly, with the most gradual of transitions, he began to assume the mantle of a prophet; and with that phase new names began to emerge in his discourses. The Four Truths, the Middle Path, the Five Hindrances, Arahatship, Karma: these cropped up from time to time in sermons which were daily becoming wilder in their phraseology.

I have no wish to be unfair to the Reverend John. He was a fanatic; and no fanatic is entirely sane. I am sure, also, that in the earlier stages of his campaign he strove merely for the spiritual good of the people as he understood it. But it is necessary to say also that I believe he became crazed in the end; and that the ultimate effect of his preaching led us to the very edge of disaster. It is not for me to weigh or judge him; he preferred his visions to material safety; whilst my own mind is concerned more with the things of this earth than with what may come later.

His preaching now passed into a stage where even I could appreciate its dangerous character. More and more, his sermons took the form of belittlings of the material world; while the joys of eternal life were held up in comparison. It was not long until he was openly questioning whether our human existence was worth prolonging at all. Would it not be better, he asked, to throw off these shackles of the Flesh at once rather than live for a few years longer amid the sorrows and temptations of this world? Why not discard this earthly mantle and enter at once into Nirvana?

This appeared to me a mere preaching of suicide; but if his followers chose to adopt his suggestions, it seemed to me a matter for themselves. I had always regarded suicide as the back-door out of life; though I had never underestimated the courage of those who turn its handle. Yet it seemed to me evidence of a certain want of toughness of fibre, a lack of fitness to survive; and, personally, I had no desire to retain in the world anyone who seemed unable to bear its strains.

His next phase of development, however, opened my eyes. By this time he had become a great power among the people. Many a king has been treated with less reverence than his followers showed to him. Crowds flocked to his meetings, standing thickly even when they stretched far beyond the reach of that magnificent voice. In the streets he was saluted as though he were a superhuman agent. There were attempts made to get him to touch the sick in the hope that he might heal them.

From afar, Nordenholt watched all this rising surge of emotion. In some ways, the two men resembled each other; but their motives were wide apart as the Poles. Both had their ideals, higher than the normal; but these ideals were in deadly antagonism to each other. Both, it is possible, were right; but the clash of right with right is the highest form of tragedy; and collision between them was inevitable.

"The Reverend John has been a great disappointment to me, Jack," Nordenholt admitted to me one day. "That man has the makings of a great demagogue or a great saint in him; and it seems to me that the spin of the coin has gone against me, for I thought the saint would come uppermost. He isn't as big as I thought he was. His head has been turned by all this adulation; and unless I am mistaken again we shall find him becoming a public danger before very long. He thinks he has his own work to do, preparing for the Kingdom of Heaven; and in doing that he seems to sweep aside all earthly affairs as trifles. He despises them. I don't. To me, he seems to be like a child in a game who won't abide by the rules. His heaven may be all right; but if it is to be attained by shirking one's work on earth—not *striving* to live—it seems to me a poor business. I think life is important, or it wouldn't exist; and I'm working to keep it in existence. He seems to believe it is of no value, if he really means what he says. We can't agree, that's evident."

It was not long before the Reverend John's campaign filled even my mind with apprehension. His style of preaching changed and grew more incoherent; his phraseology became wilder; and a minatory tone crept into his sermons. And the tremendous personality of the speaker, coupled with all the art of the orator, made even these obscure ravings powerful to influence the minds of his hearers.

He began to speak of curses from heaven upon a generation which had forgotten the right path. The Famine was a sign that all life was to be swept from the earth's face. And thence he passed to the proposition that any struggling against the Famine was a hindrance to the workings of the universe.

I think that it was about this time that he discarded ordinary clothes and began to go about clad in a curious garment manufactured from the skin of some animal. Except for his fiery beard, he recalled the sandal-shod John the Baptist represented in old illustrated Bibles. Nor was he alone in this fashion: some of his more prominent adherents also adopted it, though in their cases the results were not so imposing.

And now things moved rapidly towards their end.

The Reverend John preached daily in the streets, predicting a universal entry into Nirvana. His curses against those who worked for the physical salvation of the people to the detriment of their Karma became louder and more frequent; and it was not long until he spent most of his energies in comminations. From cursings, he passed to threats; and his attacks upon Nordenholt grew in vehemence day by day. And still Nordenholt, to my growing wonder, held his hand and forbore to strike.

By this time the religious mania was spreading rapidly throughout the population of the Area. The skin-clad followers of the Reverend John ran nightly through the streets crying that the Great Day was at hand and calling upon the people to repent of their sins and turn to righteousness. Strange scenes were witnessed; and stranger doctrines preached. It was a weird time.

Meanwhile, the preaching of the revivalist was becoming more and more exalted. He named himself a Prophet, the last and the greatest. He began to be more definite in his predictions; events which he foreshadowed were foretold as coming to pass at stated dates. At last he gave out that three days later he and his followers would publicly ascend to heaven in a cloud of glory; and that the world of earthly things would pass away as he did so.

And still Nordenholt held his hand. I could not understand it; for by this time I had seen where the teaching of the Reverend John was leading us. Work was slowing down in the factories; crowds of all classes were spending their whole time following their Prophet; and the mere numbers of them were becoming a serious menace to the safety of the Area. At last I became so anxious on the subject that I went to consult Nordenholt on the matter. I had begun to doubt if he appreciated the gravity of the situation.

I found him sitting before the fire in his office, smoking and gazing before him as though wrapped in his reflections.

"Look here, Nordenholt," I said. "I suppose you grasp the seriousness of affairs nowadays? Isn't it about time something was done? It seems to me that you'll need to grasp this nettle before long anyway. Why let it grow any bigger?"

"Afraid I'm losing my grip, eh? Not yet, Jack, not yet awhile. But I will *grasp* it before long. I'm only waiting the proper moment. I've waited for weeks; and now I think it's nearly due at last."

"But the man's insane, Nordenholt. You see that, don't you? Why wait any longer. Grab him now and be done with it—at least that's what I should do if I were in charge."

"No, I'm going to give him three days more. If I interfered now, it would spoil everything. Wait till he has seen his prophecy fail, and then we can tackle him."

"I don't see any use waiting; but I suppose you know best."

"I do know best, Jack, believe me. Come back here in three days, at half-past eleven, and you'll see my methods. I'm going to teach these people a lesson this time."

He leaned back in his chair and fixed his eyes on the old stone image of the Pope's head which, under its glass bell, forms part of the mantelpiece.

"What differences there are in the way religion works on a man, Jack. There was an old chap in the dark ages, that Pope; and he believed in spreading the light by education. He founded the University here. And then you have this fanatic to-day whose one idea seems to be to reduce everything to chaos again. What a difference! And yet each of them thinks that he is inspired to do the right thing in his day."

He threw away the end of his cigar and rose.

"Come back in three days, Jack. You'll see it all then. I needn't explain it now."

The events of the following two days filled me with uneasiness; and I began to fear that for once Nordenholt had erred in his calculations. The tumult and agitation centring around the figure of the revivalist increased; his preaching became more and more menacing; and it seemed to me that he had been allowed too much rope. By this time he was quite frankly attacking the whole scheme of the Nitrogen Area as an act of impiety which would call down the wrath of the Divinity in the immediate future. And mingled with these cursings he poured forth his prophecies, which grew hourly more detailed. He and his Elect would ascend into the sky at noon, he declared; and that all men might see this come about, he proposed to take his stand by the Roberts' statue in Kelvingrove Park, from which eminence he would be visible to the assembled crowds.

Rumours ran through the Area, growing wilder and yet more wild as they passed from lip to lip. Even the most unimaginative of the population felt the strange electric power which seemed to flow out from the revivalist; and the tales of his doings were magnified and distorted out of all semblance of reality. Just as Nordenholt had predicted, all the formless unrest of the Area crystallised round the personality of the preacher and took shape and substance. Work was abandoned by the greater part of the Area labour; and the factories, usually thronged by shift after shift, remained almost untenanted during those two days in which the populace awaited the promised miracle.

Meanwhile the followers of the revivalist redoubled their efforts and their conduct grew less and less restrained. The labourers who remained at work were assaulted by bands of these fanatics, and driven from the doors of the factories. Order seemed to have vanished from the Area; for I found that Nordenholt had withdrawn the Labour Defence Force entirely from the streets, allowing the madmen to do their will. It seemed as though the Area were being permitted to relapse into chaos.

The uninterrupted preaching of the revivalist had wrought the whole population into a state of strained expectation. Even those who scoffed at his claims were affected by the atmosphere of the time; and there was in most minds an uneasy questioning: "Suppose that it should all be true?"

At half-past eleven, I went to Nordenholt's office as I had promised. He was alone, seated at his huge desk. The usual mass of papers had been cleared away and I noticed that their place had been taken by a small piece of apparatus like a telephone in some respects and an ordinary electric bell-push on a wooden stand. Temporary wires ran from these to the window.

"Come in, Jack. You're just in time for the curtain."

"It seems to me, Nordenholt, that the curtain ought to have been rung down on this thing long ago. You've waited far too long, if you ask me."

"I don't think I've miscalculated. And to tell you the truth, Jack, this is the biggest thing I've had to think out so far. It's make or break with us this time; and we've never been as near disaster before. But I've thought it out; and I believe I'm right. Have a cigar."

He pushed a box across to me and I cut and lit one mechanically.

"This thing here," he tapped the instrument, "is a dicta-phone. The transmitter's fixed up in the statue over there."

He nodded in the direction of the Park below our windows. I got up and looked out. As far as my view reached, the ground was concealed by a closely-packed crowd of people, all standing motionless and intent upon the group on the open space around the statue. There had been some singing of hymns earlier in the morning; but now the vast concourse had fallen silent as their expectation rose to fever-heat and the hour of the miracle drew near.

"I'm going to give him every chance," said Nordenholt's voice behind me. "Let him pull off his miracle if he can. If he can't, then I expect trouble; and at the first word of danger I hear, I'll settle with him at last. I don't mind his preaching suicide; but if he starts to threaten the work of the Area, it will be on his own head."

The three-quarters had struck from the great bells above our heads; and, a few minutes later, Nordenholt switched on the dictaphone. Suddenly the clarion voice of the revivalist seemed to fill the room in which we stood.

"My brothers! In a few brief moments I shall leave you, ascending in glory to the skies. While I am yet with you, heed my words. Turn from this idle show which blinds your eyes. Turn from this heavy labour and unceasing toil. Turn from this valley of sin and sorrow. Turn from the lusts of the flesh and the lures of material things. Long and weary has been the way; life after life have we suffered, but when we pass into Nirvana there is rest for you, rest for each of you, eternal rest! O my brothers, all that are worn with the bearing of burdens, all that are taxed beyond your powers, all that are a-faint and borne down, follow after me into Nirvana, where none shall be a-weary and where all shall rest. There shall be no more toil, no more fatigue, no more striving and no more labour. There shall be rest, everlasting rest, a long sweet slumber under the trees, while the river flows by your feet and its murmur lulls you in your eternal rest."

Even in the harsh reproduction of the dictaphone I could feel the magic of the cadences of that splendid voice, soothing, comforting, promising the multitude the prize which to them must have seemed the most desirable of all. And through it all the steady repetition of "Rest" ran with an almost hypnotic effect. Incoherent though it was, the appeal struck at the very centre of each over-driven being in that throng.

"Rest, rest for all. Surcease of toil. Do you not feel it already, my brothers? Languor creeps over you; you faint as you stand. And I promise rest to you all. Follow me and you shall rest in those fields; there where you may dream away the long, long days among the flowers, lying at ease. There where the songs of birds shall but stir you faintly in your dreams, and all the tumult of the world shall be stilled within your ears."

He paused; and the silence seemed almost like a continuation of his speech. The multitude seemed frozen into stone. Then came an isolated phrase:

"Into Nirvana; Nirvana where there is rest . . ."

The voice died away in a soothing murmur which yet had its compelling power. Nordenholt looked at his watch.

"Two minutes yet. So far, he hasn't been actively objectionable; but I can guess what is coming."

Again the dictaphone sounded.

"But a few moments now, my brothers, then I and my Elect shall ascend into the skies. Look well, O my brothers. Mark our passage to our rest."

His voice ceased. There was a dead silence. Then, suddenly, with a preliminary vibration of machinery, the clock above us struck. Four double chimes for the quarters and then the heavy note of the hour-strokes. Nordenholt listened grimly until all twelve had been rung. Then I heard his voice, even as ever, without the faintest tinge of irony:

"The passing bell!"

With the twelfth stroke there came through the windows a great wave of indescribable sound, the loosing of breath among the thousands who were gathered far below us in the Kelvin valley. Then again there was silence. Nordenholt suddenly leaned forward to his desk and placed his finger on the ivory button.

"Now's the danger-point, Jack. He'll try to divert attention from his failure. But I'm ready for him."

I began mechanically to count seconds, with no particular reason, but simply because I felt I must do something. Two minutes passed; and then through the windows came a long groaning note, the voice of the multitude smitten with disillusion at the failure of the miracle which they had expected. It rolled in a huge volume of sound across the Park and then died away.

Suddenly the dictaphone poured out a torrent of words. The voice was no longer calm; all the quiet strength had gone out of it, and, instead, the tones were those of an infuriated man seeking some object upon which to wreak his anger. But with all his rage the Reverend John had a ready mind. In a moment he seems to have seen a possible loophole of escape.

"No!" he cried, "I will not ascend for yet awhile. Work remains to be done here, in this godless city; and I will renounce my rest until it has been brought to its end. Life must cease ere I can seek my rest. I bid you follow me that we may accomplish the task which has been laid upon me. Over yonder"—he evidently pointed towards us—"over yonder sits the Arch-Enemy; he who strives to chain pure spirits in this web of flesh. His hand is on all this city, so that the smoke of her burning goes up to the skies. Break asunder the chains which he is forging. Destroy the evil works which he has planned. Wreck the engines which he has designed. Come, my brothers; the doom is pronounced against all the works of his hand. Come, follow me and end it all. Destroy! Destroy! so that this world of sorrow and of sin may pass away like an evil vision and life may be no more. Destroy! Destroy!"

Nordenholt, listening intently, pressed his finger upon the ivory stud. There was a moment's pause, and then from the eastern end of the building came a sound of machine-guns. It lasted only for a few seconds and then died out.

"They couldn't miss at that range," said Nordenholt. "That's the end of the Reverend John personally. But I doubt if we are finished with him altogether even now."

XVIII   THE ELEVENTH HOUR

I have set down all my doubts as to the wisdom of Nordenholt's treatment of the Reverend John; and it is only right to place on the other side the fact that events proved he had gauged matters better than I had done. He had foreseen the trend of the revivalist's thoughts and had deduced their climax, probably long before Wester himself had understood the road he had placed his feet upon. Nordenholt had allowed the excitement to grow without check, even to its highest point, without interfering in the least; because he calculated that the supreme disillusion would produce a revulsion of feeling which could be attained in no other way. And his calculation proved to be correct. Morally shaken by the failure of the miracle which they had been led to expect, and which many of them had counted upon with certainty, the populace allowed itself to be driven back into the factories and mines without a word of protest. Their dreams were shattered and they fell back into reality without the strength to resist any dominant will. It seemed as though the last difficulties were disappearing before us; and that the path now led straight onward to our goal. So I thought, at least, but Nordenholt doubted. And, as it turned out, he again saw more clearly than I. We might be done with the Reverend John; but the Reverend John had not finished with us, dead as he was.

The next ten days saw the institution of a merciless system in the works and mines of the Area. During the period of the revivalist's activity there had been an accelerated fall in the output; and Nordenholt determined that this must be made good as soon as possible. Possibly also he believed that a spell of intense physical exertion would exhaust the workers and leave them no time to indulge in recollections and reflections which might be dangerous. Whatever his motives may have been, his methods were drastic in the extreme. The minimum necessary output was trebled; and the members of any group who failed to attain it were promptly deported into the desert of the South. Surely entrenched behind the loyalty of the Labour Defence Force, Nordenholt threw aside any concealment and ruled the whole Area as a despot. The end in view was all that he now seemed to see; and he broke men and threw them aside without the slightest hesitation. More than ever, it seemed to me at this time, he was like a machine, rolling forward along its appointed path, careless of all the human lives and the human interests which he ground to powder under his irresistible wheels. I began to think of him at times in the likeness of Jagannatha, the Lord of the World, under whose car believers cast themselves to death. But none of Nordenholt's victims were willing ones.

Unlimited power, as Nordenholt himself had pointed out to me, is a perilous gift to any man. The human mind is not fitted for strains of this magnitude; and even Nordenholt's colossal personality suffered, I believe, from the stress of his despotic rule. But where a smaller man would have frittered away his energies in petty oppression or aimless regulation, Nordenholt never lost sight of his main objective: and I believe that his harshness in the end arose merely from his ever-growing determination to bring his enterprise to success. Concentrating his mind entirely upon this, he may have suffered from a loss of perspective which made him ruthless in his demands upon the labouring masses of the Area. If this were so, I cannot find it in me to blame him, in view of the responsibility which he bore. But I have a suspicion that he feared a coming disaster, and that he was determined to take time by the forelock by forcing up production ere the catastrophe overtook us.

After the death of the revivalist, his followers disappeared. The meetings at street corners no longer took place; the wild skin-clad figures ran no more through the city. I believe that Nordenholt took steps to arrest those of the inner circle who escaped the machine-guns in the Park; but many of them seem to have slipped through his fingers in spite of the efficiency of his Secret Service. Probably they were kept in concealment by sympathisers, of whom there were still a number in spite of the general disillusionment. On the surface, the whole movement appeared to have been arrested completely; but, as we were to learn, it was not blotted out.

I can still remember the first news of the disaster. A trill on my telephone bell, and then the voice of Nordenholt speaking:

"Hullo! . . . That you, Jack? . . . Come over here, will you? . . . At my office. I may need you . . . It's a bad affair . . . What? . . . Two of the pit-shafts have been destroyed. No way of reaching the crowd underground. I'm afraid it's a bad business."

When I reached his office he was still at the telephone, evidently speaking to the scene of the catastrophe.

"Yes? . . . Shaft closed completely? . . . How long do you think it will take to reopen it? . . . Permanent? Mean to say you can't reopen it? . . . Months? . . . How many men below just now? . . . Six hundred, you think? . . . That's taking the number of lamps missing, I suppose . . . Well, find out exactly as soon as you can."

He rang off and was just about to call up another number, the second pit, I suppose, when the telephone bell sounded an inward call.

"Yes? . . . What's that? Numbers what? . . . Three, seven, eight, ten, thirteen, fourteen . . . Ring off! I'll speak to you again."

He rang furiously for the exchange.

"Put me through to the Coal Control. Quick, now . . . Hullo! Is that you, Sinclair? . . . Nordenholt . . . Send out a general call. Bring every man to the surface at once . . . Yes, every pit in the Area. Hurry! It's life or death . . . Report when you get news."

Without leaving the instrument he called up another number.

"Go on. No. 14 was the last . . . Take down these numbers, Jack . . . 3, 7, 8, 10, 13, 14, 17, 18, 19 . . . That all? . . . Good. Get me the figures of losses as soon as you can. Also a note of the damage. Good-bye."

Behind this disjointed sequence of phrases I had caught hints of the magnitude of the calamity; and I was to some extent prepared for what I heard when he had time to turn to me at last.

"Eleven pits have been destroyed almost simultaneously, Jack. No. 23 and No. 27 went first; and then that list I gave you just now. There are no details yet; but it's quite evidently malicious. Dynamite, I think, to judge from the few facts I've got. The shafts are completely blocked, as far as we know; and every man underground is done for."

"How many does that amount to?"

"There are no figures yet; but it will run into more than three figures anyway."

Again the shrill call of the telephone bell sounded. He took up the receiver.

"Yes? . . . What's that? No. 31 and No. 33? . . . Complete block? No hope? . . . Do your best."

He turned to me.

"Two more gone, before we could get the men up. It's a very widespread affair. I told you we hadn't done with the Reverend John."

"What's he got to do with it?" I asked, astonished.

"Some of his friends carrying out the work he left unfinished. They mean to smash the Area; and they've hit us on our weakest point, there's no doubt. No coal, no work in the factories, no nitrogen. This is serious, Jack."

Another call on the telephone brought the news that three more pits had been destroyed. Nordenholt rang up the Coal Control once more and urged them to even greater haste in their efforts to get the men to the surface. Then he turned back to me.

"Do you realise what it all means, Jack? As far as I can see, it's the beginning of the end for us. We can't pull through on this basis; and I doubt if we have heard the full extent of the disaster even now."

I have endeavoured to convey the impression made upon my mind by the first news of the catastrophe; but little purpose would be served by continuing the story in detail. All that morning we stood by the telephone, gathering in the tale of disaster bit by bit in disjointed fragments as it came over the wire. Here and there, items of better news filtered through: reports that in some pits the whole of the underground workers had been brought safely to the surface, accounts of the immunity of certain shafts. But as a whole it was a black record which we gathered in. The work had been planned with skill; and the execution had not fallen below the level of the plan. In one or two cases the miscreants had been detected in the act and captured before they had time to do any damage; but these discoveries were very few. As far as most of the pits were concerned, we never were able to establish how the work had been done; for all traces were buried under the debris in the wrecked shafts, which have been left unopened ever since the catastrophe. One thing was certain, the whole of the workers actually in the galleries at the time of the explosions were lost for good and all. They were far beyond the reach of any human help.

It is no part of my plan to do more than indicate the horror of this calamity. I draw no pen-pictures of the crowds around the pit-heads, the crying of the women, the ever-recurring demands for the names of the lost. These were features common to all mining accidents in the old days; and this one differed from the rest only in its magnitude and not in its form.

Owing to the colossal scale of the casualty list it was impossible to minimise the matter in any way. Nordenholt decided to tell the truth in full as soon as the total losses were definitely established. He gave his newspapers a free hand; and by the late afternoon the placards were in the streets.

TERRIBLE DISASTERS IN COAL DISTRICT

MANY SHAFTS BLOCKED

ALL UNDERGROUND WORKERS ENTOMBED

11,000 DEAD

To most of those who read the accounts of the catastrophe, it seemed a terrible blow of Fate; but we at the centre of things knew that the immediate loss was as nothing in comparison with the ultimate results which it would bring in its train. All the largest pits were out of action. The coal output, even at the best, could not possibly keep pace with the demands of the future; and with the failure of fuel, the whole activities of the Area must come to a standstill. Just on the edge of success, it seemed all our efforts were to be in vain. From beyond the grave the dead fanatic had struck his blow at the material world which he hated; and we shuddered under the shock.

Throughout that day I was with Nordenholt. I think that he felt the need of someone beside him, some audience which would force him to keep an outwardly unshaken front. But to me it was a nightmare. The *débâcle* in itself had broken my nerve, coming thus without warning; but Nordenholt's prevision of the ultimate results which it would exercise seemed to take away the last ray of hope.

"It's no use whining, Jack; we've just got to take it as well as we can. First of all, the coal output will cease entirely for a long time. Not a man will go into even the 'safe' pits after this until everything has been examined thoroughly; and that will take days and days. It's no use blinking that side of it."

"Why not force them in?" I asked. "Turn out the Defence Force and drive them to the pits. We *must* have coal."

"No good. I know what they're thinking now; and even if you shot half of them the rest wouldn't go down. It's no use thinking of it. I know."

"Why didn't the Intelligence Section get wind of it?"

"Don't blame them; they couldn't have done more than they did. Don't you realise that if a man is prepared to sacrifice his life—and these fanatics who did the damage were the first victims themselves—there's nothing that can stop him? The Intelligence people had nothing to go on. The whole of this thing was organised and carried through by a handful of men, some of whom were evidently employed in the pits themselves. It was so rapidly planned and executed that no secret service could have got at it in time. Remember, we're making explosives on a big scale, so that thefts are easy."

"And if you're right, what is to happen?"

"Go on as long as we can; then see how we stand; and after that, if necessary, decimate the population of the

Area so as to bring our numbers down to what we can feed in future. There's nothing else for it."

"I hope it won't come to that, Nordenholt."

"It's no choice of mine; but if it's forced on me, I'll do it. I'm going to see this thing through, Jack, at *any* cost now. Millions have been swept out of existence already by the Famine; and I'm not going to stick at the loss of a few more hundred thousands so long as we pull through in the end."

In the main, Nordenholt's forecast of the attitude which the miners would adopt proved to be correct. A certain number of workers, braver or less imaginative than the rest, returned to work in the "safe" pits in the course of a day or two; but the main bulk of the labour remained sullenly aloof. Nothing would induce them to set foot in the galleries. Work above-ground they would do, wherever it was necessary to preserve the pits from deterioration; but they had no intention of descending into the subterranean world again. Better to starve in the light of day than run the risk of hungering in some prison in the bowels of the earth. Neither threats nor cajolings served to move them from this decision.

Nordenholt, as a last resource, sent exploring parties into the South to examine the deserted coal-fields of England in the hope that some of them might be workable; but the various missions returned with reports that nothing could be done. During the period since the mining population had died out, the pits had become unsafe, some by the infiltration of water, others by the destruction of the machinery and yet more by the disrepair of the galleries. Here and there a mine was discovered which could still be operated; and parties were drafted South to work it; but in most cases so much labour was required to put the shafts and galleries in repair that we were unable to look forward to anything like the previous coal-supply even at the best.

Meanwhile Nordenholt, day by day, grew more and more grim. While there was any hope of utilising the mining population, he clung to it tenaciously; but as time passed it became clearer that the Area had received its death-blow. He began to draft his ex-miners into other branches of industry bit by bit; but with the fall in the coal-supply there was little use for them there, since very soon all the activities of the Area would have to cease.

I watched him closely during that period; and I could see the effect which the strain was producing upon him. The disaster had struck us just when we seemed to have reached the turning-point in the Area's history, at the very time when all seemed to be sure in front of us. It was a blow which would have prostrated a weaker man; but Nordenholt had a tenacity far above the ordinary. He meant, I know, to carry out his decision to decimate the Area if necessary; but he held his hand until it was absolutely certain that all was lost. I think he must have had at the back of his mind a hope that everything would come right in the end; though I doubt if his grounds for that belief were any but the most slender.

For my own part, I went through that period like an automaton. The suddenness of the catastrophe seemed, in some way, to have deadened my imagination; and I carried on my work mechanically without thinking of where it was all leading us. With this new holocaust looming over the Area, Elsa seemed further away than ever. If she had revolted at the story of the South, it seemed to me that this fresh sacrifice of lives in the Area itself would deepen her hatred for the men who planned it.

It seemed the very irony of Fate that Nordenholt should choose this juncture to tell me his views on her feelings.

"Elsa seems to be coming round a little at last, Jack," he said to me one day, "I think her emotional side has worked itself out in the contemplation of the Famine; and her reason's getting a chance again."

"What makes you think that?" I asked. "I haven't seen anything to make me hopeful about it."

"You wouldn't notice anything. You don't know her well enough—Oh, don't get vexed. Even if you are in love with her, you've only known her for a very short time, whereas I've studied her since she was a child. I know the symptoms. She's coming round a little."

"Much good that will do now! If you decimate the Area it will be worse than ever. I hate to think of my own affairs in the middle of this catastrophe; but I simply can't help it. If your plan goes through, it's the end of my romance."

He played with the cord of his desk telephone for a moment before replying. I could see that he had some doubt as to whether he ought to speak or not. At last he made up his mind.

"If you're brooding over things as much as all that, Jack, I suppose I must say something; but I'm very much afraid of raising false hopes. You wonder, probably, why I don't go straight ahead and weed out the useless mouths now and be done with it? Well, the fact is I'm staking it all on the next couple of days. Henley-Davenport seems, by his way of it, to be just on the edge of something definite at last. If he pulls it off, then all's well. If not . . ."

"What do you mean?"

"If Henley-Davenport gets his results, we won't need coal; because we shall have all the energy we require from his process. I've stretched things to the limit in the hope that he will give us the ace of trumps and not the two. If he succeeds, we don't need to weed out the Area; we can go on as we are; and we shall be absolutely certain to pull through with every soul alive. But I shouldn't have told you this, perhaps; it may be only a false hope and will just depress you more by the reaction. But you look so miserable that I thought I had better take the risk."

"When do you expect to know definitely?"

"He promised me that within two days he would be able to tell me, one way or the other. Of course, even if he fails now, he may pull it off later; but I can only wait two days more before beginning the elimination of all the useless mouths in the Area. Everything is ready to put into operation in that direction. But I hope we may not need these plans. It's just a chance, Jack; so don't build too much on it."

It was advice easy enough to give; but I found it very hard to follow. All that day my hopes were rising; things seemed brighter at last: and it was only now and again that I stopped to remind myself that the whole thing was a gamble with colossal stakes. Even Nordenholt himself was afraid to count too much upon Henley-Davenport, though I knew that he believed implicitly in his capacity. But even as I said this to myself I felt my spirits rising. After the certainty of disaster which had confronted us, even this hazard was a relief. For the first time in many weeks I began to build castles in the air once more. I was half-afraid to do so; but I could not help myself. And as the hours passed by bringing no news of success or failure, I think my nerves must have become more and more tense. A whole day went by without news of any kind.

The morning of the following day seemed interminable to me. I knew that within another twenty-four hours Nordenholt would have given up all hope of Henley-Davenport's success and would be setting in motion the machinery which he had devised for reducing the population of the Area; and as hour after hour passed without bringing any news, I became more and more restless. I tried to work and to ease my mind by concentrating it upon details; but I soon found that this was useless. Strive as I might, I could not banish the thought of the tragedy which hung over us.

At 3.27 p.m.—I know the exact minute, because my watch was stopped then and I read the time from it afterwards—I was standing beside my desk, consulting some papers on a file. Suddenly I heard a high detonation, a sound so sharp that I can liken it to nothing familiar. The air seemed full of flying splinters of glass; and simultaneously I was wrenched from my foothold and flung with tremendous violence against my desk. Then, it seemed, a dead silence fell.

I found that my right hand was streaming with blood from various cuts made by the razor-edges of the broken glass of the window. More blood was pouring from a gash on my forehead; but my eyes had escaped injury. When I moved, I found I suffered acute pain; though no bones seemed to be broken. The concussion had completely deafened me; and, as I found afterwards, my left ear-drum had been perforated, so that even to this day I can hear nothing on that side.

All about me the office was in confusion. Every pane of glass had been blown inward from the windows and the place looked as though a whirlwind had swept through it, scattering furniture and papers in its track. The shock had dazed me; and for several minutes I stood gazing stupidly at the havoc around me. It was, I am sure, at least five minutes before I grasped what had happened. As soon as I did so, I made my way, still in intense pain, down the stairs and into the quadrangle.

The pavements were littered with fragments of broken glass which had fallen outward in the breaking of the windows; but there was not so much of this as I had expected, since most of the panes had been driven inward by the explosion. Quite a crowd of people were running out of the building and making in the direction of the new Chemistry Department in University Avenue. I followed them, noticing as I passed the Square that all the chimney-pots of the houses seemed to have been swept off, though I could see no traces of them on the ground.

Later on, I found that they had been blown down on the further side of the terrace.

When I came in sight of the Chemistry building I was amazed, even though I was prepared for a catastrophe. One whole wing had been reduced to a heap of ruins, a mere pile of building-stone and joists flung together in utter confusion. Here and there among the debris, jets of steam and dust were spouting up; and from time to time came an eruption of small stones from the wreckage. The remainder of the edifice still stood almost intact save for its broken windows and shattered doors.

What astonished me at the time was that the whole scene recalled a cinema picture—violent motion without a sound to accompany it. I saw spouts of dust, falling masses of masonry, people running and gesticulating in the most excited manner; yet no whisper of sound reached me. It was only when someone came up and spoke directly to me that I discovered that I was temporarily stone deaf; for I could see his lips moving but could hear nothing whatever.

Like everyone else, I began to remove the debris. I think that we understood even then that it was hopeless to think of saving anyone from this wreckage, but we were all moved to do something which might at least give us the illusion that we were helping. As I pulled and tugged with the others, I began to appreciate the enormous power of the explosive which had been at work. In an ordinary concussion, iron can be bent out of shape; but here I came across steel rafters which were cut clean through as though by a knife. I remember thinking vaguely that the explosive must have acted, as dynamite does, against the solid materials around it instead of spending its force upwards; for otherwise the whole place would have suffered a bombardment from flying blocks of stone.

For some time I toiled with the others. I saw Nordenholt's figure close at hand. Then the sky seemed to take on a tinge of violet which deepened suddenly. I saw a black spot before my eyes; and apparently I fainted from loss of blood.

Even now, the causes of the Chemistry Department disaster are unknown. Henley-Davenport and his two assistants perished instantaneously in the explosion—in fact Henley-Davenport's body was never recovered from the wreckage at all. A third assistant, who had been in the next room at the time, lived long enough to tell us the exact stage at which the catastrophe occurred; but even he could throw no direct light upon its origin.

From Henley-Davenport's notes, which we found in his house, it seems clear that his efforts had been directed towards producing the disintegration of iron; and that on the morning of the accident he had completed his chain of radioactive materials which furnished the accelerated evolution of energy required to break up the iron atoms. As we know now, he succeeded in his experiment and his iron yielded the short-period isotopes of chromium, titanium and calcium until the end-product of the series—argon—was produced. The four successive alpha-ray changes, following each other at intervals of a few seconds, liberated a tremendous store of intra-atomic energy; but, knowing the extremely minute quantities with which Henley-Davenport worked, it seems difficult to believe that the explosion which destroyed his laboratory was produced by this trace of material. To me it seems much more probable that his apparatus was shattered at the moment of the first disintegration of iron and that thus some of the short-period products were scattered abroad throughout the room, setting up radioactive change in certain of the metallic objects which they touched. No other explanation appears to fit the facts. We shall never learn the truth of the matter now; but knowing Henley-Davenport's care and foresight, I cannot see any other way of accounting for the violence of the explosion.

Luckily for us, no radioactive gas is produced by the disintegration of iron; for had there been any such material among the decay products it is probable that most of those who had run to the scene of the disaster would have perished.

When I recovered consciousness again I found myself lying on a couch. A doctor was bandaging my hand. Nordenholt, looking very white and shaken, was sitting in a chair by the fire. At first I was too weak to do more than look round me; but after a few minutes I felt better and was able to speak to Nordenholt.

"What has happened? Did they get Henley-Davenport out of the wreck?"

"No, there's no hope of that, Jack. He's dead; and the best thing one can say is that he must have been killed instantaneously. But he's done the trick for us, if we can only follow his track. He evidently tapped atomic energy of some kind or other. Did you notice the sharpness of the explosion before you were knocked out? There's never been anything like it."

"What's going to happen now?" I was still unable to think clearly.

"I've sent Mitchell down to Henley-Davenport's house to look at his last notes—he kept them there and he promised me to indicate each day what he proposed to do next, so that we'd have something to go on if anything like this happened. Mitchell will ring up as soon as he has found them."

I heard afterwards that among the ruins of the laboratory Nordenholt had been struck by a falling beam and had just escaped with his life; but his voice gave no hint of it. I think that his complete concentration upon the main problem prevented him from realising that he might be badly hurt.

The telephone bell rang suddenly and Nordenholt went to the receiver.

"Yes, Mitchell . . . You've got the notes? . . . Good . . . You can repeat what he was doing? . . . No doubt about it? . . . All right. Start at once. We must have it immediately, cost what it may . . . Come round here before you begin; but get going at once. There isn't a minute to spare."

Nordenholt replaced the receiver.

"I thought I could trust Henley-Davenport," he said. "He's left everything in order, notes written up to lunch-time complete and a full draft of his last experiment, which will allow Mitchell to carry on."

A few minutes later, Mitchell himself appeared and gave us some further details. In his jottings, Henley-Davenport had suggested some possible modifications of the experiment which had ended so disastrously; and Mitchell proposed to try the effect of these alterations in the conditions. Before he left us, he sat down at Nordenholt's desk and made a few notes of the process he intended to try, handing the paper to Nordenholt when he had finished. I can still remember his alert expression as he wrote and the almost finical care with which he flicked the ash from the end of the cigarette as he rose from the desk. It was the last time any of us saw him.

"Well, that's all. I'm off."

Nordenholt rose stiffly from his chair and shook hands with Mitchell as he went out. Then he passed to the telephone and rang up a number.

"Is that you, Kingan? Go across to the South Wing of the Chemistry place. Mitchell is there. See all that he does and then clear out before he tries the experiment. We must keep track of things, come what may. If he goes down, you will take on after him. Good-bye."

Just after seven o'clock, there was another tremendous explosion; but this time the concussion seemed less violent than before. Mitchell himself was not killed outright; but he suffered injuries which proved fatal within a few days. Meanwhile the work went on. One after another, the Chemistry section of Nordenholt's young men went into the furnace, some to be killed instantaneously, others to escape alive, but blasted almost out of recognition by the forces which they unchained. Yet none of them faltered. Link by link they built up the chain which was to bring safety to the Area; and each link represented a life lost or a body crippled. Day after day the work went on, interrupted periodically by the rending crash of these fearful explosions, until at last it seemed almost beyond hope that the problem would ever be solved. But ten days later Barclay staggered into Nordenholt's room, smothered in bandages, with one arm useless at his side, and gasped out the news that he had been successful.

Looking back on that moment, I sometimes wonder that we were not almost hysterical with joy; but as a matter of fact, none of us said anything at all. Probably we did not really grasp the thing at the time. I know that I was busy getting a drink ready for Barclay, who had collapsed as soon as he gave his news; and all that I remember of Nordenholt is a picture of him standing looking out of the window with his back to us. Certainly it wasn't the kind of scene one might have imagined.

XIX THE BREAKING-STRAIN

Although Barclay's work furnished us with the means of tapping the stores of energy which lie imprisoned within the atoms of elementary matter, it did not place us immediately in a position to utilise these immense forces for practical purposes. To tell the truth, we were in much the same position as a savage to whom a dynamite cartridge has been given, ready fitted with a detonator. We could liberate the energy, but at first we could not bring it under control.

The next few weeks were spent in planning and building machine after machine. All the best talent of Nordenholt's group of engineers was brought to bear on the problem; but time after time we had to admit failure. Either the engines were too fragile for the power which they employed or there was some radical defect in their construction which could only be detected on trial. Thus the days passed in a series of disappointments, until it seemed almost as though hope of success was fading before our eyes.

During that period, Nordenholt himself grew visibly older. It was the last lap in his great race against Time; and I think that this final strain told on him more than any that had gone before. The mines of the Area were still empty and silent; no fuel was coming forward to fill the gaps in our ever-shrinking reserves; and within a very short period the whole industry of the Area must collapse for want of coal.

His anxiety was marked by a total change in his habits. Hitherto, he had sat in his office, directing from afar all the multitudinous activities of the Area, aloof from direct contact with details. Now, I noticed, he was continually about the machine-shops and factories in which the new atomic engines were being constructed; he had frequent consultations with his engineers and designers; he seemed to be incapable of isolating himself from the progress which was very slowly being made. Possibly he felt that in this last effort he must utilise all the magnetic power of his personality to stimulate his craftsmen in their labours.

Whatever his motives may have been, when I think of him in those last days my memory always calls up a picture of that lean, dark figure against a background of drawing-office or engineering-shop. I see him discussing plans with his inventors, encouraging his workmen, watching the trial of engine after engine. And after every failure I seem to see him a little more weary, with a grimmer set in the lines about his mouth and a heavier stoop in his shoulders, as though the weight of his responsibilities was crushing him by degrees as the days went by.

Yet he never outwardly wavered in his belief in success. He knew—we all knew—that the power was there if we could but find the means of harnessing it. The uncertainty had gone; and all that remained was a problem in chemistry and mechanics. But time was a vital factor to us; and more than once I myself began to doubt whether we should succeed in our efforts before it was too late.

At last came success. One of my most vivid memories of that time is the scene in Beardmore's yard when the Milne-Reid engine was tested for the first time. Nordenholt and I had motored down from the University to see the trial. By this time we were both familiar with the general appearance of atomic engines; but to me, at least, the new machine was a surprise. Its huge, distorted bulk seemed unlike anything which I had seen before: the enormous barrel of the disintegration-chamber overhung the main mass of machinery and gave it in some way a far-off resemblance to a gigantic howitzer on its carriage; and this resemblance was heightened by the absence of fly-wheels or any of the usual fittings of an engine. Although I was an engineer, I could make but little of this complex instrument, designed to utilise a power greater than any I had ever dreamed of; and I listened eagerly to the two inventors as they described its salient characteristics.

Nordenholt, who had seen the plans, seemed to pay little attention to either Milne or Reid. He was evidently impatient for results and cared little for the methods by which they were to be obtained, so long as the machinery did its work.

The last cables were being attached to the engine as we stood beside it; for Nordenholt had insisted on a test being made as soon as the machine was completed. The workmen screwed up the connections, everyone stood back a little, and then a switch was pushed home.

Immediately the whole misshapen bulk seemed to be galvanised into violent activity and with a roar beyond the roof above us the torrent of escaping helium and argon made its way through the exhaust-pipe. The needle of the indicator dial jumped suddenly upward till it registered many thousands of horse-power.

But we had seen all this before and had seen it, too, followed by a collapse; so that we waited eagerly to learn how the engine would stand the strain. For an hour we waited there, while the mechanics poured oil continually into the tanks to keep the racing bearings from heating; and still the machine ran smoothly and the thunder of the escape-pipe roared above us. It was impossible to make oneself heard amid that clangour; and we exchanged congratulations scribbled on odd pieces of paper. After an hour, Milne shut off the disintegrator; and the great engine slowly sank to rest.

All of us were still deafened by the sound of the exhaust; and it was by dumb-show and a handshake that Nordenholt conveyed his thanks to the two designers. I heard a faint cheer from the workmen.

Nordenholt did not stay long. Within a few minutes, he and I were back in the motor, on the way home. As we went, I heard behind us the tremendous blast of the escaping gases; they had restarted the engine; and to my ears it sounded sweeter than any symphony, for it meant safety to us all.

When we reached the University, I noticed that Nordenholt stepped from the car with the air of an invalid. He seemed to have used up all his forces in a last effort; and now he moved slowly and almost with difficulty. At the Randolph Stair, he took my arm and leaned heavily on me as we climbed a step at a time. When we reached the top, he seemed out of breath. At last we reached his office and he dropped into his chair at the desk with visible relief.

"It's my heart, Jack," he said, after a moment or two. "It's been going wrong for months; and I think it's badly strained. I knew it was going; and in ordinary circumstances I would have looked after myself; but it wasn't worth while, as things were. I simply couldn't take things easy. I had to work on until I saw daylight before me or dropped on the way."

He paused, as though pulling his strength together. In the next room I could hear Elsa's typewriter clicking. Nordenholt heard it also; and rose after a few minutes. He went to the door between the two rooms and spoke to her, telling her the news of the engine.

"It's success at last, Elsa. We're through. Everything's safe now."

I heard her voice in reply; and then he closed the door and reseated himself at the desk.

"It's your turn now, Jack. I've done my part. I'm leaving the future in your hands; and I believe you'll make good. I wish I could help you; but I'm done, now. I would only hamper you if I tried to do anything."

I tried to say something reassuring, but the words faltered on my lips. The sight of that drawn face was proof enough. Nordenholt had driven his physical machine as ruthlessly as he had driven his factory workers; and it was clear that he had overstrained his bodily powers. His tremendous will had kept him on his feet until the moment of success; but I could see now what it had cost him. He had drawn on his vital capital; and with the accomplishment of his task a revulsion had set in and the over-tired body was exacting its toll.

As I sat looking at him there, a great feeling of loneliness swept over me. Here, before me, was the man upon whose strength I had leaned for the past months, the mind which had seen so clearly, the will which had held its line so tenaciously; and now, I felt, Nordenholt was leaning on me in his turn. It seemed almost an inversion of the course of Nature; and with the realisation of it, I felt a sense of an enormous loss. In the next stages of the Area's history, there would be no Nordenholt to lean upon: I would have to stand on my own feet, and I doubted my capacity. Almost without my recognising it, I had been working always with Nordenholt in my mind, even in my own department. I had carried out things boldly because I knew that ever in reserve behind me were that brain and that will of his which could see further and drive harder than I could dare; and I had relied unconsciously upon him to steer me through my difficulties if they proved too great for my own powers. And now, by the look on his face and the weariness of his voice, I knew that I stood alone. I had no right to throw my burdens on his shoulders any more.

And with a gulp in the throat, I remembered that he trusted me to go forward. I suppose I ought to have felt some joy in the knowledge that he had left the reconstruction in my hands; but any pride I had in this was swallowed up in that devastating feeling of loss. With the collapse of Nordenholt, something had gone out of my world, never to return. It left me in some way maimed; and I felt as though the main source of my strength had been cut away just when I most needed all my powers.

"You'll do your best, Jack? The Area trusted us. Don't let them down."

I tried to tell him I would do my utmost; but I had difficulty in finding words. I could see that he understood me, however.

"There's one thing I'm sorry about—Elsa. She hasn't come round yet. But she will, in time. She hates me still, I know; and it's a pity, for I need her now, more than I ever did before. I'm a very sick man, Jack. Luckily, this breach between us has let her stand on her own feet. She doesn't need me so much as she did."

He fell silent; and for a time we sat without speaking. When he spoke again, I could see the lines on which his thoughts had been running.

"If anything happens to me, Jack, you'll look after Elsa, won't you? I'd like to know that she was all right. I know it's hard as things are; but you'll do that for me, even though it tantalises you?"

I promised; and then I suggested telephoning for a doctor to look after him.

"Not just now, Jack—I'm tired. I don't want to be bothered answering questions. I'm very tired . . . And I've finished my work at last. We've pulled through. I can take a rest . . . Wake me in a quarter of an hour, will you? I want a sleep badly."

He leaned forward in his chair and rested his face on his arms. In a moment he seemed to fall into slumber. I thought it was probably the best thing for him at the time; and I turned to the fire and to my thoughts.

I fell to thinking of all that had happened since first I met him; and then I cast further back yet to the evening I had spent at Wotherspoon's house. How the disaster had developed step by step, spreading its effects gradually and with slowly-increasing intensity over wider and ever-wider areas. If only Wotherspoon had stuck to chemistry and left bacteriology alone; if only he had chosen some other organisms than the denitrifying bacteria; if only the fire-ball had not come that night; if . . . if . . . if . . . All the might-have-beens rose before me as I gazed at the flickerings in the fire. If only Elsa had followed reason and not emotion . . . if only . . . And so the maddening train of thought went on, minute by minute, while in the next room I could hear the click of her typewriter. Emotion! After all I could not pretend to scorn it, for what were my own feelings but emotion too?

The clock in the tower above me struck a quarter. Nordenholt did not stir and I let him sleep on. It appeared to me that rest was what he needed most.

It seemed curious how divorced I had become from the Past. The old life had been swept away utterly and I found difficulty in recalling much of it to mind. The meeting with Nordenholt, the founding of the Area, my time with Elsa, London in its last days, the Reverend John: these were the things which seemed burned into my memory. All that had gone before was mirage, faint, unsubstantial, part of another existence. Even our Fata Morgana was more real to me than that old life.

And with that I fell back into deeper gloom. I have not tried to paint myself other than I am. I had never reached the height of pure endeavour to which Nordenholt had attained, though sometimes, under his influence, I came near it. And now, at the recollection of our dream-city, I felt a keen pang. Why should I attempt to raise that fabric to the skies, why should I wear myself out in toiling to erect these halls and palaces through which I must wander alone? Why, indeed? What was the population of the Area to me, after all? But even amid my most bitter reflections I knew that I would do my best. Nordenholt had trusted me.

A fresh chime from the great bell overhead roused me from my musings. I went across to Nordenholt, not knowing whether to wake him or not. When I reached his side, something in his attitude struck me. I touched his hand and found it cold.

For a moment, I think I failed to recognise what had happened. Then I shook him gently; and the truth broke upon my mind. That great engine which had wrought so hard and so long would never move again. The brain which had guided the fortunes of the Area up to the last moment had sunk to its eternal rest.

It was some minutes before I was able to pull myself together after the discovery. When I got my feelings under control, I was still badly shaken; for otherwise I would never have done what I did do. I went straight to the door and called Elsa. She was sitting at her desk and she looked up at my voice.

"Well, what is it, Mr. Flint?"

"It's . . . Come here . . . It's Nordenholt; he . . ."

Before I had completed the sentence she had risen and passed me. I think she must have seen something in my face which led her to expect the worst news. She went up to the desk where Nordenholt was still leaning with his face on his arms. Like me, she did not immediately grasp what had happened.

"Uncle Stanley! What's wrong? Aren't you well?"

She rested her hand on his shoulder and shook him gently, just as I had done. In the silence, I heard, far down the Clyde, the roaring of the atomic engine—the great call sweeping across the Area and bearing with it the news of Nordenholt's final triumph. They were varying the running of the machine and the waves of sound rose and fell like the beating of gigantic wings above the city.

Suddenly she turned to me.

"What is it? You don't mean he's *dead*?"

I could only nod in answer; I could not find words. For an instant she stood, leaning over him, and then she slipped down beside his chair and put her arms round him.

"Oh, he's dead. He's dead. He'll never speak to me again! . . . And I hated him, I hated him . . . I made it hard for him . . . And now he can't tell me if he forgives me . . . Oh, what shall I do, Jack? What shall I do? Please help me. He was so good to me; and I hurt him so . . . Oh, please help me, Jack. Tell me he forgave me . . . I've only got *you* now . . ."

XX ASGARD

Immediately after the death of Nordenholt, I took over
the control of the Area and instituted the great reorgan-
isation forced upon us by the new conditions. Almost our
last reserves of coal were used up in the foundries where
we built the new atomic engines; but we succeeded in
manufacturing a number of machines sufficient for our
purposes; and once these were complete, we had no further need of the old-fashioned fuel. The output of nitrogenous materials sprang up by leaps and bounds; and the
danger of starvation was over.

All our miners were sent into the neighbouring areas,
where they were put to work in spreading synthetic
nitrogenous manure upon the fields, after Hope's colloids had been ploughed into the soil to retain water in
the ground. At last came the harvest, poor in most places,
yet sufficient for our needs. The game was won.

It was after this that we began to send aeroplanes over
the world in search of any other remnants of the human
race which had survived. I was too much occupied with
Area affairs to share in these voyages; but the airmen's
reports made clear enough the extent of the catastrophe
which had befallen the planet. As I expected, the site of
London was covered with a mere heap of charred and
shattered ruins cumbering it to an extent that prevented

us from even thinking of rebuilding the city in the new age. It was not worth while clearing away the debris, when other sites were open to us for our new centres of population. The same fate had befallen almost all the great cities, not only in Britain but also across the Continent. Above the ruins of Paris, the gaunt fabric of the Eiffel Tower still stood as a witness to men's achievements in the past; but it was almost alone. Everything capable of destruction by fire had gone down in the frenzy of the last days of the old civilisation.

I have already sketched the effects of the Famine upon the population of the globe. Our explorers found one or two colonies alive in America; and at a slightly later date we got in touch with the Japanese Area. Beyond this, the human race had perished from the face of the earth.

The strangest of all the changes seen by the aerial explorers must have been in Central Africa and the Amazon Valley. There, where vegetable life had seemed undisputed sovereign of vast regions, only a blackened wilderness remained. Fires had raged over great spaces, leaving ashes behind them; but in general there was hardly a trace of the old-time forests and swamps. The Sahara stretched southward to the Equator; and the Kalahari Desert had extended up to the Great Lakes—so quickly had the soil of these regions degenerated into sand. In past ages, man had never tapped these vast store-houses of forest and veldt; and Fate decided that they should go down to destruction still unutilised.

Once the safety-line was passed and we were assured of food sufficient to maintain our people, other troubles faced us; and I am not sure that the next ten years was not really our most dangerous period. Had Nordenholt lived, things would perhaps have been easier for us; but the difficulties besetting us were implicit in the nature of things and I question if he could have exorcised them entirely.

We had, on the one side, a mass of manual labourers whose intelligence unfitted them for anything beyond bodily toil; while on the other hand we had supplies of physical energy from the atomic engines which made the employment of human labour supererogatory. Yet to leave the major part of our population entirely idle was to invite disaster. The development of the atomic engine had at one blow thrown out of gear the nicely-adjusted social machinery devised by Nordenholt; and we had to arrange almost instantly vast alterations in our methods of employment.

It was under the pressure of these conditions that we became builders of great cities. Nineveh and Thebes were our first sketches; then came Atlantis, our main power-station which we built on Islay; after that we erected Lyonnesse and Tara, fairer than the others, for we learned as we wrought. Then, as I began to grope toward my masterpiece, I planned Theleme. And, last of all, the spires and towers of Asgard grew into the sky.

Once the cities had been planned, we employed a further contingent of labour in constructing huge roads between them, gigantic arteries which cut across the country like the Roman ways in earlier centuries, arrow-straight, but broader and better engineered than anything before constructed.

Our building materials were new. The introduction of atomic energy gave us electric furnaces on a scale undreamed of before; and we were able to produce a glassy and resistant substance which can be made in any tint. It is of this that Asgard is constructed; and I believe that no weather conditions alone will wear it down.

As I sit here at my desk, I see outstretched before me the panorama of Asgard, the concrete embodiment of our Fata Morgana, so far as that vision could be made real in stone. It is not the City of our dreams, I admit; yet in its beauty there is a touch of wonder and of mystery that makes it kin to that builded phantom of our minds. None of our cities shall ever bear the name of Fata Morgana, which was the mother of them all. There shall be no profanation of that castle in the air. Instead we have given to our cities titles which link their material splendours to the more ancient glories of myth and tradition; Asgard and Lyonnesse, Tara and Atlantis, Nineveh, Thebes and Theleme.

Rarely, nowadays, do I feel despondent; but when the fit comes over me, I open the box in which I still keep the papers relating to the time when I was planning my garden cities. I finger my documents and turn over my sketches, ever amazed at the gulf which lies between my hopes of that day and our achievements of the present. Here and there, on the margin of some modest ground-plan, I find scribbled notes of caution to myself not to expect such vast projects to be practicable in the near future. And then, after losing myself in this atmosphere of the past, I go to the great windows and look down upon Asgard. For once, at least, in this world, hope has been far outrun by achievement. Splendours of which I never dreamed have come into being and lie before my eyes as I gaze. With all this confronting me, my despondency slips away and I regain sure confidence in the future.

Cities and gardens have I raised in Dreamland. Other cities and other gardens I have seen spring from the ground of this world in answer to my call. But of all these, Asgard is nearest to my heart; for it is the last which I shall create. Other men will surpass me; new wonderlands will rise in the future: but Asgard is my masterpiece and I shall build no more.

Ten years have gone by since the last stone was laid in my city; yet every morning as I come to my windows, I find in it fresh beauties to delight my eyes. Fronting the sea it stands; and its fore-court is a vast stretch of silver sand between the horns of the bay. Behind it the ground rises to a semicircle of low hills set here and there with groves and fretted with silver waterfalls. Through all the changes of the year these slopes are green; for snow never drifts upon them nor do mists gather to hide them from my view. Only the swift cloud-shadows flitting athwart them bring fresh lights and shades into the picture as they pass.

Nor do I weary of this greenery. Slowly vegetation is creeping back upon the face of the world; but still there are vast deserts where no blade grows: and in my own cities I planned masses of verdure so that they might be like oases among the barren spaces of the earth.

Between the hills and the sea, the city stands—a vast space of woods and fields and gardens from among the greenery of which rise here and there high halls and palaces of rose-tinted stone. Here and there amid the green lie broad lakes to catch the sun; and great tree-shadowed pools, like crystal mirrors, stand rippleless among the groves. And throughout the city there is ever the sound of streams and rivulets falling from the hills and making music for us with their murmurings as they pass.

Scattered about this pleasance are the dwellings of my citizens, built of the rose-coloured stone which breaks the monotony of the verdure; but the houses are sparse, for our population is small. Asgard is only for the few who can enjoy its beauties: the many have other cities more suited to their tastes; and they have no wish to come hither. But those who dwell with us have full time to fall under its spell; for Asgard is a city of leisure, though not an idle one. When darkness falls on Asgard, great soft beacons shine out upon the hills, throwing a mellow radiance across the valley; and down in the woods and along the broad ways of the city, the silver lamps are lighted, till all Asgard gleams in outline beside the sea. In the expanses of the parks and under the shadow of the woods are sprays of coloured orbs to guide the passer-by; and from hour to hour these change their tint, so that there is no sameness in them. Often I come to my windows in the night and gaze out upon that far-flung tracery of stars across the valley, rivalling the skies above, as though ten thousand meteors had fallen from the heavens and still blazed where they lay upon the earth. And through my open casement come the faint and perfumed breezes, bringing their subtropical warmth as they blow across the valley; and I hear, faint and afar, the sounds of music mingling with the rustling of the trees. Others may plan; others may build fairer cities in the sun: but I have given my best; and Asgard almost consoles me for the loss of that Fata Morgana which I shall never see.

AFTERWORD: ALFRED WALTER STEWART

Evan Hepler-Smith

Alfred Walter Stewart (1880–1947), the real-life writer behind the pen name "J. J. Connington," was born and raised in Glasgow, the industrial city on the west coast of Scotland that is the setting for the second half of *Nordenholt's Million*.[1] Known as the "Workshop of the Empire" and proud birthplace of James Watt's steam engine, Stewart's hometown cultivated the image that civilization itself—a product exported from Britain to its colonial empire, according to the liberal imperialist ideology dominant among the British scientific and industrial elite—rested on Glasgow's machines, metalwork, and engineers. The city also had a reputation for practical, liberal, affordable education, embodied in the University of Glasgow, where Stewart's father William, a Presbyterian minister, was professor of divinity and biblical criticism.[2] Alfred Stewart began his studies of chemistry at Glasgow, proceeded on to research fellowships at the University of Marburg (Germany) and University College, London, and received his doctorate from Glasgow in 1907. At UCL, he worked closely with J. Norman Collie, an organic chemist with special interest in biological chemical processes and electrochemical experimentation bearing upon theories of the origin of life. Such questions never played a central role in Stewart's chemistry research, but he took them up as a textbook writer and later as a fiction author. "J. J. Connington" dedicated *Nordenholt's Million* to Collie, via the initials *J. N. C.*

Stewart's transition from student to professional researcher was eased by a three-year Carnegie Research Fellowship (it no doubt helped that his father represented Glasgow University on the Carnegie Trust). In his popular writing, Stewart emphasized the crucial importance of such funding for launching scientific careers; it seems plausible that the autocratic industrialist-turned-philanthropist Andrew Carnegie was among the real-life inspirations for the fictional Nordenholt. In 1909, Stewart was appointed as lecturer in organic chemistry at Queen's University in Belfast, a bastion of Presbyterianism in the northwest of Ireland, where descendants of Scottish settlers upheld support for continued British rule against a waxing Irish independence movement. Stewart returned to Glasgow as lecturer in physical chemistry and radioactivity in 1914, a post opened by the departure of the Scottish radiochemist Frederick Soddy, whose research team had made Glasgow a hotbed of research in radiochemistry. In this capacity, Stewart took part in the mobilization of British science for the First World War, conducting research for the British Admiralty. From 1914 to 1918, Stewart was thus immersed in two significant developments in British science and society: the development of nuclear science and speculation about nuclear weapons and energy, and the war-catalyzed rise of businessmen such as the chemical industrialist Alfred Mond and the railroad administrator Eric Geddes into leadership roles in the British government, especially encouraged by British Prime Minister David Lloyd George.[3] British fiction authors, above all the highly influential H. G. Wells, eagerly took up these themes as well, in such works as Wells's *The World Set Free* (1914). In this novel, scientific developments bring about technological dreams and terrors, failures of craven politicians and monarchs lead to disaster, and a technologically-savvy scholarly elite seizes the reins to usher in technocratic utopia. This and similar works of Wells, as well as variations by other contemporary authors, formed a template for Stewart to echo and readers to recognize in *Nordenholt's Million.*[4]

Two years after returning to Glasgow, Alfred Stewart married Lily Coats, member of a prominent family in Paisley, a large town abutting Glasgow, whose members put their thread-manufacturing fortune toward patronage of arts, sciences, and their Scotch Baptist faith. In 1919, Stewart was offered the position of chair of chemistry at Queen's in Belfast, and so Alfred and Lily crossed the Irish Sea once more. Stewart remained in this position through his retirement in 1944. Stewart thus spent the years immediately prior to the writing of *Nordenholt's Million* grappling with new academic and administrative responsibilities, amid a city riven by the urban violence of the 1919–1921 Irish War of Independence. It seems likely that the urban portraits drawn in the second half of *Nordenholt's Million*, contrasting the mission-oriented industrial "Nitrogen Area" of Glasgow with the disordered phantasmagoria of violence in famine-ridden London, were to some degree drawn from Stewart's perspective on these years, with London standing in for Belfast. The Catholic parishioners of St. Patrick's in Connington's London, finding comfort in their Church at the extremity of suffering, would seem to connect to events in Stewart's Belfast in some way or another. One wonders whether the conflicting views and experiences of Jack Flint and Elsa Huntingtower regarding the fictional Londoners—for Jack, cold, utilitarian, humanitarian logic, rigid psychological compartmentalization, unvarnished revulsion mediated by a decidedly racialized, ethnic, gendered way of seeing; for Elsa, deep and abiding empathy, uncompromising principles of justice, refusal to accept the inevitability of lesser evils—might reflect Alfred Stewart's own conflicts over conditions in Belfast with his wife Lily Coats Stewart, or with someone else, or with himself.

Nordenholt's Million was the first of twenty-six novels Stewart published under the name of J. J. Connington, a pseudonym Stewart synthesized from the last name of a Victorian classicist and two easy-to-remember first initials. The second, *Almighty Gold* (1924), focused on financial swashbuckling of the sort hinted at in the Nordenholt backstory in *Nordenholt's Million*. The remainder were mystery stories packed with meticulously reported technical detail. Stewart called them "tec yarns," and they earned him a reputation with contemporary readers as "one of the clearest and cleverest of masters of detective fiction now writing," a master of "exact and mathematical accuracy in the construction of the plot."[5] Connington's orderly plots came with a vision of social order that contemporary readers have found increasingly difficult to stomach. Throughout his corpus, as in *Nordenholt's Million*, Connington's non-white, Jewish, middle- and working-class, and physically disabled characters tend toward foolishness and depravity. So do the novels' depictions of female sexuality. Only pragmatic, well-read, ruthlessly rational men of action seem able to usher events to a happy conclusion and restore stability to a troubled world. As literature scholar Curtis Evans puts it, the "most striking . . . theme in Connington's work is the streak of philosophical Social Darwinist authoritarianism running through it," while Stewart's personal correspondence suggests an unyielding faith in Britain's global empire.[6] Perhaps unintentionally, Connington's novels illustrate how thoroughly entangled scientific research and such social ideologies could be. The 1938 Connington mystery *For Murder Will Speak*, drawing on the cutting-edge biochemistry of steroid hormones, centers on a "glandular disorder" that, according to the novel's physician-scientist, is the physiological basis of both intemperate heterosexuality and homosexuality in women, and that leads a female character in the novel to a tragic end.[7] In his memoirs, Stewart averred that "there is no resemblance between the scientific investigator, working from details towards a solution, and the detective-story writer, starting from his preconceived solution and working back to the details of the plot."[8] Whether this specific theory was an invention of "Connington" or drawn from real-life research, it tends to suggest otherwise: such preconceptions as the patriarchy and colonialism of interwar Britain shaped science and fiction alike.

*

Stewart's career in science spanned the fields of structural organic chemistry, physical chemistry, and radiochemistry. These fields were linked by the methods of spectroscopy—the investigation of chemical substances through analysis of radiation they emitted and absorbed. Upon taking up the chair at Queen's, Stewart made a priority of acquiring new and more powerful instruments for the university's physical laboratory. During the 1920s, his research program involved spectral emissions induced by a high-voltage Tesla transformer, also known as a Tesla coil. Such devices were and are beloved by science museums and steampunk authors for their spectacular, arcing electrical discharges. This was the research that occupied Stewart as he was writing *Nordenholt's Million*, which begins with a similarly dramatic electrical encounter of a different sort.

Stewart's defining contribution to the physical chemistry of radioactivity was a theory of atomic structure, published in 1918.[9] Like numerous other contemporaneous atomic models, Stewart's theory riffed on the "planetary system" conception of the atom proposed by physicist Ernest Rutherford in 1911, with a positively-charged nucleus orbited by negatively-charged electrons. Eschewing the mathematically intensive quantum approach exemplified in the work of Niels Bohr and Arnold Sommerfeld, Stewart's model of the atom was mostly qualitative. And whereas quantum models distinguished nuclear phenomena from chemical interactions mediated by orbiting electrons, Stewart sought a unified explanation for both radioactivity and the valency patterns underlying chemical bonding.

Stewart proposed that the nucleus of an atom consisted of a tightly-bound collection of negative electrons and "positive electrons" in concentric orbits. Some of these nuclear particles might themselves have additional electron "satellites," like a planet and its moons. The mass of the atom was concentrated in this nucleus; additional electrons of negligible mass orbited this nucleus along far-flung elliptical paths, "like those of comets in the solar system."[10] The central nucleus was responsible for the characteristic properties of chemical elements; the "cometary" electrons were responsible for chemical reactions. At more distant points along these orbits, cometary electrons could relatively easily be abstracted or inserted; Stewart proposed this as the mechanism that gave rise to changes in an element's valence, citing the example of divalent iron (which combines with oxygen to form a black pigment) versus trivalent iron (which combines with oxygen to form rust).

The nucleus itself changed only through processes of radioactive decay. But just as comets occasionally approach the sun, so "cometary" electrons occasionally approached the nucleus, Stewart suggested. At this point, they affected the constitutive properties of the element, as if they were part of the nucleus itself. Therefore, changes in valence were changes in elemental identity—at least until a further perturbation restored the original number of electron-comets. Modifications of valency were thus *reversible* changes in an atom's identity, whereas modifications of the nucleus associated with radioactive emissions were *irreversible* changes in an atom's identity. This provided the basis for an analogy between the "normal" chemical phenomenon of change in valence and the radioactive phenomenon known as beta decay. Both changes affected chemical properties without appreciably affecting atomic mass; in Stewart's view, they were parallel changes in element identity. For substances displaying the converse relationship—identical chemical properties, different atomic weights—Frederick Soddy had introduced the term *isotope*, a word coined and suggested to Soddy by the physician and author Margaret Todd. By analogy, Stewart suggested the term *isobar* (meaning "same weight") for fellow members of his equal-mass atomic families. Stewart capped off his theory with an explanation of atomic masses and isotopes involving near-light-speed orbital velocities within his "solar system" atoms and the most famous equation of a scientist eighteen months older than Stewart: Albert Einstein's $E = mc^2$.

Stewart's ruminations on mass-energy relations lived on in the work of his character Henley-Davenport and the atomic climax of *Nordenholt's Million*. Otherwise, his theory of atomic structure went nowhere. Abstracted from this theory, however, the term *isobar* stuck, becoming Stewart's most well-known and enduring contribution to science.

*

By the time "J. J. Connington" published *Nordenholt's Million*, Stewart was already an accomplished author of scientific monographs and books for the science-savvy public. His *Recent Advances in Organic Chemistry* (1908) and *Recent Advances in Physical and Inorganic Chemistry* (1909) were well received by reviewers and student readers. He continually expanded and updated both throughout his career, publishing seven editions of each. The introductions to these books, penned by distinguished colleagues, testify that Stewart was a gifted synthesizer with an eye to the future, talents that would serve him well as a science fiction author.

Fellow Glasgow native and 1904 Nobel laureate William Ramsay penned the introduction for the book on physical and inorganic chemistry. (Stewart likely became acquainted with Ramsay during Stewart's fellowship at University College London, where Ramsay was professor of chemistry.) Describing the ever more massive primary journal literature as "indigestible masses of what is often very crude material," Ramsay wrote that "Dr. Stewart may be likened to a skilful cook, who has trimmed his joint, rejecting all innutritious and redundant excrescences, and has served it up to table in a palatable form. Such essays, I venture to think, will do more to encourage a taste for chemistry than many text-books."[11] In his introduction to the organic chemistry book, Stewart's UCL mentor J. Norman Collie focused on the book's forward-looking orientation: Unlike so many books "covering the same ground, with a fine disregard of the fact that to the pioneers the outlook is constantly changing," Stewart's stood out as one of the few "which are not mere narrations of facts, and which do point out, not only what has been done, but what might be accomplished, and which do make the reader think," marking out "the paths along which the pioneers of the science are likely to go in the immediate future."[12]

Stewart mapped out these paths for a popular audience in his 1914 *Chemistry and Its Borderland*, a well-reviewed work discussing new research in chemistry, its industrial and medical applications, and how best to fund and organize it. Chapter XIII of this book, "Chemical Problems of the Present and Future," takes up chemical aspects of the provision of food and power. Stewart noted that these were questions of the utmost importance: "Given food and power, the mechanical side of our civilization could always exist much as it does at present; but the disappearance of these agents would entail a complete collapse of the whole fabric." Anticipating the eventual exhaustion of coal, Stewart envisioned a future in which tidal engines, windmills, and some yet-unknown method of directly capturing solar radiation would provide the world with power, distributed via improved batteries and perhaps some sort of artificial coal. In addition to these technologies, already known, there was the more distant prospect of harnessing the massive intra-atomic energies that researchers on radioactive elements were just beginning to investigate. Turning to food, "the more fundamental problem," Stewart explained that this boiled down to a question of nitrogen. With the help of a diagram of the nitrogen cycle, he illustrated how "nitrifying bacteria" took nitrogen from the atmosphere, decaying organic matter, and animal wastes and made it available to plants for growth. Complementary "denitrifying bacteria" returned nitrogen back to the atmosphere. However, intensive agriculture had unbalanced this cycle, effecting a massive transfer of nitrogen compounds from soils to waterways and oceans via sewage. Imports of Chile saltpeter had balanced this deficit, but those would soon be exhausted. Fortunately, new power-intensive technologies for fixation of atmospheric nitrogen were beginning to come into use; Stewart predicted that fertilizer-producing "sewage farms" and farming of oceanic kelp would provide supplementary nitrogen sources in the future. After a brief discussion of synthetic foods—synthetic proteins presenting a daunting challenge but one "within the limits of possibility"—Stewart ventured a few closing remarks on the possibility of synthetic life. The accidental discovery of some novel, barely-living organism "might involve us in very serious consequences. Assume that it had great powers of assimilation and reproduction, and we might find it rather a dangerous neighbor. . . . Such speculations, however, take us out of the chemical field entirely, and belong in the meantime to pseudo-science."[13]

There it is: denitrifying bacteria, headlong reproduction, soil exhaustion, looming famine, nitrogen factories, coal scarcity, atomic power. In this 1914 book chapter, Stewart laid out virtually all the scientific and technological ideas he would mobilize as plot points in *Nordenholt's Million*—and, retrospectively, a decent sketch of twenty-first-century renewable energy systems and the non-impossibility of Impossible Burgers.

This brings us back to Stewart's distinction between science and fiction: according to Stewart, science works forward, from details to conclusion, while fiction works backward, from solution to details. A reader working backward from the rise of European fascism and the present science of environmental change will find details in *Nordenholt's Million* that anticipate these developments; working backward from twenty-first-century political and environmental values, they will find many ideas to critique, ideas whose long-term legacies one might wish to grapple with. Conversely, a reader working forward from biographical and historical details may find that the fiction of H. G. Wells, the philanthropy of Andrew Carnegie, the technocratic governance of Alfred Mond, Stewart's nuclear speculations, and life in revolutionary Belfast made a mark on the fictional world of *Nordenholt's Million*. These approaches are not mutually exclusive. They are complementary ways of telling history, just as, notwithstanding Stewart's claims to the contrary, they are complementary ways of writing fiction and doing science.[14] As a chemist, Stewart should have known better. The interplay of making and unmaking, nitrification and denitrification, synthesis and analysis, is what chemistry is all about.

Notes

1. The author gratefully acknowledges the helpful suggestions of three anonymous referees for the MIT Press.

2. On science, engineering, religion, education, and empire in nine-teenth-century Glasgow, see Crosbie Smith and M. Norton Wise, *Energy and Empire: A Biographical Study of Lord Kelvin* (New York: Cambridge University Press, 1989).

3. Keith Grieves, *Sir Eric Geddes: Business and Government in War and Peace* (Manchester: Manchester University Press, 1989).

4. Sarah Cole, *Inventing Tomorrow: H. G. Wells and the Twentieth Century* (New York: Columbia University Press, 2020).

5. Quotations from reviews in *Times Literary Supplement* and *London Daily Mail* for J. J. Connington, *The Two Tickets Puzzle* (1930), quoted in Curtis Evans, *Masters of the "Humdrum" Mystery: Cecil John Charles Street, Freeman Wills Crofts, Alfred Walter Stewart and the British Detective Novel, 1920–1961* (Jefferson, NC: McFarland, 2012), 193–245, on 193–194.

6. Evans, *Masters of the "Humdrum" Mystery*, 194, 236.

7. Evans, *Masters of the "Humdrum" Mystery*, 207–209.

8. Alfred W. Stewart, *Alias J. J. Connington* (London: Hollis & Carter, 1947), x.

9. Alfred W. Stewart, "Atomic Structure from the Physico-Chemical Standpoint," *Philosophical Magazine* 36, no. 214 (1918): 326–336.

10. Stewart, "Atomic Structure," 327.

11. Alfred W. Stewart, *Recent Advances in Physical and Inorganic Chemistry* (London: Longmans, Green, and Company, 1909), xiv.

12. Alfred W. Stewart, *Recent Advances in Organic Chemistry* (London: Longmans, Green, and Company, 1908), xiii, xv.

13. Alfred W. Stewart, *Chemistry and Its Borderland* (London: Longmans, Green, and Company, 1914), 226–247.

14. On the relationship between science fiction and science in modern history, see Amanda Rees and Iwan Rhys Morus, eds., "Presenting Futures Past," *Osiris* 34 (2019) and Peter J. Bowler, *A History of the Future:*

Prophets of Progress from H. G. Wells to Isaac Asimov (Cambridge: Cambridge University Press, 2017).

Bibliography

Bowler, Peter J. *A History of the Future: Prophets of Progress from H. G. Wells to Isaac Asimov*. Cambridge: Cambridge University Press, 2017.

Cole, Sarah. *Inventing Tomorrow: H. G. Wells and the Twentieth Century*. New York: Columbia University Press, 2020.

Evans, Curtis. *Masters of the "Humdrum" Mystery: Cecil John Charles Street, Freeman Wills Crofts, Alfred Walter Stewart and the British Detective Novel, 1920–1961*. Jefferson, NC: McFarland, 2012.

Grieves, Keith. *Sir Eric Geddes: Business and Government in War and Peace*. Manchester: Manchester University Press, 1989.

Kauffman, George B. "Alias J. J. Connington: The Life and Work of Alfred W. Stewart (1880–1947) Chemist and Novelist." *Journal of Chemical Education* 60, no. 1 (January 1983): 38.

Rees, Amanda, and Iwan Rhys Morus, eds. "Presenting Futures Past: Science Fiction and the History of Science." *Osiris* 34 (2019).

Smiles, Samuel. "Obituary Notice: Alfred Walter Stewart, 1880–1947." *Journal of the Chemical Society* (1948): 396–398.

Smith, Crosbie, and M. Norton Wise. *Energy and Empire: A Biographical Study of Lord Kelvin*. New York: Cambridge University Press, 1989.

Stewart, Alfred W. *Recent Advances in Organic Chemistry*. London: Longmans, Green, and Company, 1908.

Stewart, Alfred W. *Recent Advances in Physical and Inorganic Chemistry*. London: Longmans, Green, and Company, 1909.

Stewart, Alfred W. *Chemistry and Its Borderland*. London: Longmans, Green, and Company, 1914.

Stewart, Alfred W. *Alias J. J. Connington*. London: Hollis & Carter, 1947.

Under the pseudonym J. J. Connington, **Alfred Walter Stewart** (1880–1947) wrote seventeen well-received detective novels; *Nordenholt's Million* is his only science fiction novel. Stewart was a distinguished British chemist and author of the popular textbooks *Recent Advances in Organic Chemistry* (1908) and *Recent Advances in Physical and Inorganic Chemistry* (1909). Via a 1918 theory of the physical chemistry of radioactivity, he contributed the term *isobar*—as complementary to the term *isotope*—to science.

Matthew Battles is the author of *Library: An Unquiet History*, *Palimpsest*, and *Tree*, as well as the story collection *The Sovereignties of Invention*. His writing on the cultural dimensions of science, technology, and the natural world have appeared in the *Atlantic*, the *Boston Globe*, and *Orion*. Until recently a director of Harvard's metaLAB, he is now editor of the journal *Arnoldia*, a publication of the Arnold Arboretum.

Evan Hepler-Smith teaches the history of science and technology and environmental history at Duke University. He has a special interest in the history of chemicals and chemistry, information technology, and environmental regulation. His book in progress is entitled *Compound Words: Chemical Information and the Molecular World*. His writing has been published in the *New York Times*, the *Wall Street Journal*, *Public Books*, and Time.com.